Spirit Blade

Book III
of
The Dragon Mage Trilogy

Garey Scheppner

authorHOUSE®

AuthorHouse™
1663 Liberty Drive
Bloomington, IN 47403
www.authorhouse.com
Phone: 1-800-839-8640

Published by AuthorHouse 06/18/2014

ISBN: 978-1-4969-1996-0 (sc)
ISBN: 978-1-4969-1994-6 (hc)
ISBN: 978-1-4969-1991-5 (e)

Library of Congress Control Number: 2014910972

*Any people depicted in stock imagery provided by Thinkstock are models,
and such images are being used for illustrative purposes only.
Certain stock imagery © Thinkstock.*

This book is printed on acid-free paper.

*Because of the dynamic nature of the Internet, any web addresses or
links contained in this book may have changed since publication and
may no longer be valid. The views expressed in this work are solely those
of the author and do not necessarily reflect the views of the publisher,
and the publisher hereby disclaims any responsibility for them.*

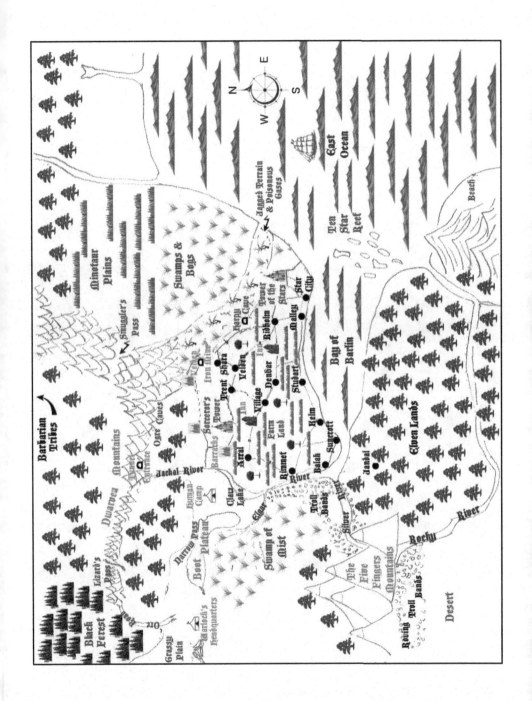

Table of Contents

Part 1

Chapter 1

'The Jackal' grinned maliciously at his opponent, his mace held tightly in his hand. After their first clash, they had both come away with neither one succeeding at landing their blows. Both combatants were better at defensive strategies, preferring to weaken their adversaries by wearing them out, then going on the offensive when the time was right. Thus, the crowd was becoming impatient as the two foes circled one another warily.

Hardig was the smaller of the two, although not by much. He was older, however, and his breathing was somewhat more ragged. What he lacked in youth, he made up for in experience. He was one of the chosen ones, hand-picked to serve in the Emperor's personal guard. That was no small honour. Nevertheless, he had one serious drawback. His right arm was all but useless now. Fortunately, he was left-handed, a distinct advantage against fighters who were used to parrying blows from a right-handed opponent.

The two fighters were closing again when a bright white flash of light suddenly appeared between them. An instant after the light subsided, an old human mage with a long white beard stood between them. The crowd stopped yelling and cheering at this unexpected appearance. Even the emperor himself stood up, stunned.

Hardig started and stepped back. 'The Jackal' was startled too, but regained composure quickly. Snarling in rage at this interference, he stepped forward to pound this intruder into the ground with his mace.

The mage took in his surroundings quickly and spotted the approaching minotaur. With a casual flick of his hand and an inaudible chant, the feral beast was sent flying by an invisible force. The Jackal landed in the dust several feet away with an audible 'whump'. Falling to the ground more lightly at the mage's feet were the spell components the mage had used.

The crowd fell completely silent as the Jackal returned to his feet. The mage looked around at the stands until his eyes rested on the balcony where the emperor stood in shock. Realizing where he was, the mage mumbled, "Oh, dear!" Then he smiled and strode toward the arena entrance. The crowd began to murmur as he went. As he reached the gate, the arena guards barred the way.

"I would like to talk to the emperor," said the mage calmly.

One guard crossed his arms defiantly. "Did he summon you?"

The mage shook his head. "No. But I'm sure he'll want to see me. I'm an old friend."

The other guard laughed. "If you want to see the emperor, you'll have to get past us first."

"Is that all?" asked the mage with a twinkle in his eyes.

The guards looked at one another curiously. Who did this human think he was?

The crowd started getting louder and angrier at this delay. Suddenly, the emperor shouted out. "Bring him to me!" To the combatants, he said, "Resume the fight!"

The crowd roared in anticipation, their attention back on the duo in the center of the arena.

The mage smiled at the guards. "It looks like I've been summoned. We shouldn't keep the emperor waiting."

The guards grumbled and opened the gate. One led the way while the other followed the mage with his sword drawn. The mage didn't seem to mind the weapon at his back as he was led to some inner stairs which led up to the balcony.

The trio soon arrived at the rear of the balcony, out of sight of the stands and arena below. The mage had trouble seeing the emperor with all the security guards in the way. The wall of security was impressive indeed, especially to a mere human.

"Out of the way!" growled the emperor. He pushed roughly between two large guards to examine the newcomer. "What's the meaning of this interruption?" he demanded angrily. "I ought to set you on a spike and let the crows have a hearty feast!" The emperor was not the biggest minotaur in the room, but at nearly nine feet tall, he was an imposing figure. His horns overshadowed everyone else's, being at least a third larger than the next largest of those visible.

The mage chuckled at the angry minotaur. "Your horns have certainly grown since our first meeting, Zylor. They have a tendency to intimidate me every time I see them."

The emperor narrowed his eyes. "You say my name as though we are acquainted. I do not recognize you. Identify yourself or die." His tone was ominous.

The mage nodded. He needed to diffuse the situation quickly. "It is understandable. You knew me when I was much younger in appearance. I am Kazin."

The emperor's eyes widened as recognition dawned on him. "Kazin? The dragon mage? But, you're so -," he paused.

Kazin nodded. "Old. I know. I'm here from the future."

The silence on the balcony was overshadowed by the cheering and yelling of the minotaurs watching the battle in the arena.

Zylor turned to his guards. "Leave us."

"But, Emperor -," objected one guard.

"Enough!" Zylor glared at the others in the room. "He will not harm me. Leave now!"

Grumbling, the guards left the balcony.

When they were alone, Zylor laughed and stepped forward, lifting the hapless mage in a bear hug. Kazin gasped for breath, relieved when the massive beast put him back on his feet.

"You always knew how to make a dramatic entrance," laughed Zylor.

Kazin straightened his rumpled cloak. "It was not on purpose, I assure you. Time travel is tricky at best, even for me."

"It's good to see you again," said Zylor.

"I almost missed you with all those guards around," said Kazin. "Is there some trouble I don't know about?"

Zylor laughed heartily. "It's not my choice. They are very loyal and tend to be over protective. There are times when I feel like a child that needs to be watched carefully. I can hardly do anything for myself anymore." His face darkened. "It's very annoying at times. I wish I could do some fighting and keep in shape, but they won't let me even warm up to the idea." A roar from the crowd drew his attention away. "Come, sit with me. The battle is nearly over."

Kazin decided to indulge the minotaur. This was obviously an important time for the emperor. The quest could wait a little while.

The battle was soon over. Hardig had won, and was standing at attention while Zylor went down to offer him his reward.

"I congratulate you on your victory, Hardig!" said Zylor loudly, so everyone at the arena could hear. He looked at Hardig and his face darkened. This was the part that made every emperor nervous. Hardig was a member of his personal guard, but his victory meant he had the opportunity to challenge for the leadership of all minotaurs.

"Would you like to challenge me for leadership?" asked Zylor in an unemotional tone. "You have earned the right. The prize money is yours regardless!"

Hardig went down on one knee. "Long live Emperor Zylor!" he bellowed.

"Long live Emperor Zylor!" cried the crowd in unison.

Zylor waved at the crowd. His leadership was secure for another four years, until the next election battle. As yet, no one had challenged him since he had come to power, so Zylor assumed he had done a good job - which was true. In truth, he had help of which he wasn't even aware. Each election year, his personal guards drew lots to see which of them would take part in the election battles. Each time, at least two of them would enter the battles, contending for the championship and the chance to become emperor. A pact with the other personal guards ensured they would not make the challenge for leadership. If they did, the pact was broken and the guards would take that individual's life at the earliest opportunity. This was an effective way to ensure Zylor stayed on the throne.

Zylor sometimes wondered why members of his personal guard bothered to fight in the election battles. They were paid well, and had many fringe benefits. But he never considered the true reason behind it. He attributed it to their desire to obtain a higher level of honour - a custom extremely important to the minotaur race in general. Most other minotaurs thought the same thing. Thus, the strategy had paid off. Two of the last three election battles had been won by a member of Zylor's personal guard.

As everyone filed out of the arena, Zylor sat down with his friend in a private room. "So, Kazin, I assume you didn't come back in time just to visit with me."

Kazin nodded. "Indeed. I'm getting set to go on a quest of great importance."

Zylor's eyes lit up. "A quest?" he drawled, intrigued. "Tell me more."

"It's a little complicated," said Kazin, "but it involves going back in time."

Zylor's eyes widened. "Going back in time? Like we did a bunch of years ago?"

In a previous adventure Zylor had accompanied Kazin and his companions into the past to obtain some information pertinent to their quest at the time.

"It will be similar to that, yes," said Kazin.

"Why do you need me?" asked Zylor.

"You are one of the ones who went with me the last time," said Kazin.

"So?"

Kazin hesitated. "It seems our previous exposure to the past may have had something to do with a problem in the distant future."

"I don't follow," said Zylor.

"Like I said," said Kazin. "It's complicated."

"Try me," said Zylor.

Kazin took a deep breath. "In the future things are beginning to disappear."

Zylor sat back but said nothing, waiting to hear more.

"At first, things that aren't obvious or significant vanish, and are forgotten as though they had never existed. Then living things began to vanish, followed by animals, followed in turn by people."

"People vanish?" asked Zylor incredulously. "Have none of them been found?"

"That's the problem," said Kazin. "They vanish as though they had never existed in the first place. As a result, all the things they had done never took place, and those who had known them don't know them because they had never known them in the first place. They are completely forgotten!"

Zylor was aghast. "That's incredible! How can this happen?"

Kazin shook his head. "That's what I aim to find out."

"Wait a minute!" Zylor scratched his chin. "If it's as you say, - these people never existed in the first place - how do you know they did?"

Kazin smiled at his friend's astute observation. "Those of us with stronger levels of magic have taken notice of these events, even though it had taken the disappearance of some of our own kind to react. Even so, there are still many unbelievers among us." Kazin paused. "Our entire future is constantly changing by the disappearances that are happening. If this keeps up, we will have no future left!"

Zylor growled. "That is indeed a problem. But how is that related to our previous trip into the past?"

Kazin shrugged. "Maybe our previous trip had caused a minor change that had become more serious as time had gone on. Do you recall the invisibility ring that Sherman had found?"

Zylor thought a moment, remembering Kazin's human body guard. He nodded. "Yes."

"Well, don't you think it might not have been meant to come with us to the future? Or how about Harran's armour? Harran was a dwarf that was with them during that quest."

Zylor nodded slowly. "I see what you mean. Those things could have changed history as it should have been."

Kazin smiled wanly. "I don't know if it's relevant or not, but Sherman told me on his deathbed that he went on a quest into the past to correct something, but he refused to give me details. He simply told me I would eventually understand. He also told me he couldn't say any more because I told him not to."

Zylor's eyes widened as Kazin spoke. "Sherman's dead?" he whispered hoarsely.

Kazin quickly shook his head. "Not for a while, Zylor. In the distant future, yes, but not in your time here and now."

Zylor exhaled and nodded in sudden understanding. "Of course. I forgot. But why didn't he confide in you? Obviously you were with him when -." He broke off.

Kazin grinned. "Now you see why he couldn't say anything. My future self had to come to the conclusion on my own to go back in time. I've also concluded that my future self -," he pointed to himself, "was to come back to this time to find Sherman and embark on this quest."

"But why at this time?" asked Zylor.

Kazin sat back. "This is the time in my life that I discovered that Sherman had gone on a quest unknown to me. It must be now that my future self -," again he pointed at himself, "has recruited him to go back in time."

"How do I figure in all of this?" asked the minotaur.

"It seems," said Kazin slowly, "that all of us who had gone back in time before were absent while my younger self was dealing with a serious problem at the Tower of Hope." The Tower of Hope was the central gathering point of white-cloaked human clerics who studied and practiced the magic of healing and defense. "I'm sure each of you would have intervened on my behalf if it wasn't for the fact that you were all either absent from this time, or ignorant of my problem, which I doubt."

Zylor raised his fist. "I would never let you down!" he thundered.

"That's what I figured," said Kazin. "I was surprised when the minotaurs and dwarves didn't show up when they were sorely needed. But I didn't exactly have time to go and find out why, either."

"Tell me where and when to send my forces -," began Zylor.

Kazin raised a hand and cut him off. "We cannot change what has been," said the mage seriously, "at least as far as I'm concerned. The problem I speak of will arise in your near future, but you will miss it because I'm hoping you'll be with me."

Zylor sighed and spread his hands. "I'd love to go, but I have a country to run and -."

"I can have you back within a few weeks," interjected Kazin.

"How do you know it won't take longer?" asked Zylor.

"It could take much longer," admitted Kazin, "but I can still bring you back at the same time. That's the beauty of time travel."

"Then why don't we go on this quest and be back in time for dinner today?"

Kazin shook his head. "It's not easy to be that exact. In fact, it's extremely difficult. Coming back so soon could create a paradox where you'll be in two places at once. It's precisely that sort of thing that can cause the sort of disappearances I've been talking about. I can't guarantee the precise time of your return with that much accuracy, so I prefer to leave a leeway of a couple of weeks."

Zylor sat back. "Two weeks is not that long. Even three weeks is acceptable. I have some vacation time coming up. I was planning to go on a boar hunt." He glanced at the door where he knew some of his body guards were stationed. "I'd like to get away from those overprotective guards for a while." He chuckled. "I can just imagine their faces when they find out I'm gone! It would be mass chaos!" He laughed again. "Besides, my battle skills need honing." He looked into Kazin's blue eyes. "Count me in!"

Kazin smiled. "Great! I knew I could count on you!" He rose and hobbled toward the door. "Make your preparations and meet me at the arena entrance in, shall we say, one hour?"

Zylor nodded. "Done." He gestured to Kazin's leg. "What happened to your leg?"

"You mean my limp?"

Zylor nodded.

"I've had it for years. It happened when -," the mage paused. "Funny. I can't seem to remember how I got it." He scratched his head. "I've always limped, Zylor, you know that."

Zylor shook his head. "You walked in here perfectly fine, ever since you showed up in the arena."

Kazin shook his head. "You're mistaken, Zylor. I've always had this limp." A strange expression crossed the mage's face. "See you in one hour." With a few words of magic, the mage disappeared.

Zylor stood facing the spot where the mage had been a moment earlier. He had seen with his own eyes how the old mage had walked moments before with an agile spring to his step. He had always had the limp? Who was he fooling? Then it dawned on the minotaur. This was one of those things that Kazin had been talking about. To the mage, it was as though he had always limped. His history had been rewritten. Zylor clenched his teeth. He knew now that his friend needed his help. Badly. He wouldn't let him down. It was time for action. He grinned his toothy grin. A small taste of bloodlust pumped through his veins and it felt good. It was time to do something exciting again. This was what a minotaur was meant to do! The next problem was how to get away from the guards for a while without raising suspicion.

Chapter 2

"**H**arran!" cried Zylor. He strode swiftly toward a figure clad in chain mail who sat on a log by a small fire. The sun was fading rapidly in the west as the minotaur's long strides moved him quickly toward the small, stout figure. The figure rose and fingered his battle axe nervously at first, but as the minotaur got closer, he relaxed and smiled. Anyone looking at him would never have seen the smile, however, because it was hidden beneath his long, grey-white beard.

"Well, I'll be," said the dwarf dryly as he and Zylor clasped arms in greeting. "You actually came. I wondered if Kazin would be able to convince you to come along on this hair-brained quest of his."

Zylor laughed. "It's good to see you too, Harran." He lowered his hands and peered at the dwarf. "If Kazin hadn't told me where to find you, I wouldn't have known it was you waiting here. Your beard has grown to the point where I don't recognize you!"

Harran self-consciously stroked his beard. "I guess I have changed at that." He looked up at the minotaur's horns. "Your horns are longer than I recollect."

Zylor nodded. "They haven't stopped growing. It's gotten to the point where I can't even go out in public in disguise without someone pointing and identifying me."

"You go out in public in disguise?!" asked the dwarf, bewildered. "Whatever for?"

"Sometimes I just have to get away from the guards," explained Zylor. He shook his head. "It's a long story."

Harran laughed. "I suspect we'll be on a long quest. You can tell me all about it."

Zylor winced. He changed the subject. "Kazin's gone to get Sherman. It will be good to see him again. I'd like to show him some

12

of my new moves." The minotaur made some quick fighting gestures with his arms and fists to show Harran what he meant.

The dwarf stepped back and held up his hands. "Easy, big guy! I don't want to be injured before this quest even begins!"

Zylor stopped and moved closer to the fire to warm his hands. "These high altitudes are rather chilly. I'm not used to it."

Harran sat back down on the log opposite Zylor. "That's why I made the fire. Who knows how long we'll have to wait for Kazin to return with Sherman."

Zylor looked at his stout little friend. He had a deep respect for Harran because of their previous adventures together, and they shared a strong sense of honour. Minotaurs and dwarves were very different races in many respects, but one thing they had in common was their sense of honour. That alone balanced their differences and allowed them to coexist. The border between their two realms had remained virtually unchanged since the dragon wars many generations ago. The dwarves inhabited the mountains and the minotaurs lived in the plains to the east of the mountains.

"I take it Kazin told you about our quest?" asked Harran.

Zylor nodded. "Yes."

"What's your opinion?" asked the dwarf. "From what I could tell, Kazin doesn't seem to know exactly what we are looking for." He patted his chain mail. "He thinks it could be something to do with the artifacts we recovered on our last trip into the past."

"I'm not sure if that's the cause of the trouble," said Zylor, "but I'm certain the trouble originates in the past." He glared at the dwarf as darkness settled over the campsite. As he spoke, the fire light reflected in his eyes. "Kazin has a serious problem to contend with and I, for one, will aid in whatever way I can. I owe him that and more. Honour demands it!"

Harran sat silently for a long moment. When he spoke, Zylor was still glaring at him, the flames in his eyes a malevolent force in its own right. "You're right, Zylor. I was having doubts - not about this quest being legitimate - but whether I might survive this adventure. It sounds dangerous - which doesn't bother me, I might add, - but my people need me. They need a king like your people need an emperor.

But you're right. We wouldn't be in our present positions if it wasn't for Kazin. If he needs our help, honour demands that we aid him." Harran stood and looked across at Zylor's fiery eyes. His own eyes reflected the same thing. "Let it not be said that the king of the dwarves acted without honour!"

Zylor nodded. "I know of no one more honourable than you, dwarf!"

"And I know of no one more honourable than you, Zylor - minotaur!" responded Harran.

After a few moments of glaring at one another, the two companions laughed heartily. With that over, Harran offered the minotaur some dried meat.

Zylor eagerly accepted. As he chewed, he asked the dwarf about something that was bothering him. "Harran, Kazin visited you before he came to get me, correct?"

Harran swallowed a chunk of meat. "That's right."

"Did he have a limp when he visited you?"

Harran shook his head. "No. I would have noticed. We walked a fair bit as I showed him around the royal palace. Why do you ask?"

"He claims he always had a limp," said the minotaur.

The dwarf gave him a strange look.

✗   ✗   ✗   ✗   ✗

Kazin flew north down out of the heights of the Old Dwarven Mountains and relished the warmer air currents the lower he flew. His leathery wings spread out to their maximum width and he barely had to flap them to increase his speed as gravity and wind carried him down. There were few others who could enjoy the freedom he experienced as a dragon mage. Dragons were long gone to parts unknown, and only the rare discovery of a dragon orb made it possible to experience what dragons took for granted. In this new quest, Kazin expected to see others like him, mages who had control of dragons via their orbs or mages who had become dragon mages as a result of controlling the orb of a dragon who had died. The reason for the latter circumstance, of which Kazin was one, was the fact that the orb contained the life force of the dragon during its life. When the dragon died, its life force would fully enter the orb, and whoever had the orb would be able to use that power to become the dragon. Unfortunately, many who tried to control the orb were not mentally strong enough to do so, and wound up controlled by the orb themselves. They became the dragon with all of its vices and desires, with no self-control or concern for others. This usually led to their own destruction, being pursued and killed by humans or their allies, or by the true dragons themselves.

These orbs were a magically created tool the mages of old had originally used to attempt to manipulate dragons to stop attacking settlements. Once successful in trapping a particular dragon's life force, the use progressed into control of the dragons for other purposes. Often a bond was established between mage and dragon. This led to quarrels arising out of jealousy by those who did not have a dragon of their own. Disputes were common, and duels often ended with the death of dragons or mages. If a mage died, the dragon was freed as long as it controlled the orb holding its life force. It would be that dragon's most valuable treasure. Once a bond was created between the dragon and orb, it was permanent and could not be broken. If the orb was destroyed, the dragon would die. If the dragon died, the orb would shatter. There were only extremely rare cases where the orb would remain intact if the dragon died. The effects of finding an undamaged orb were very rare, but would allow the new owner to change into a dragon. Only considerable mental control would allow the owner to maintain control of the orb and its ability. If the orb was damaged but not destroyed, the consequences for handling it were dangerous and unpredictable.

Flying across a riverbed, Kazin noticed a cow lying on its side with crows attacking its carcass. He grunted. And so it begins, he thought grimly. At the time, Kazin thought that this crisis was the worst one he would ever encounter. How wrong he was! It seemed that each crisis was worse than the last. Indeed, the one he had to deal with now made the arising crisis in the present time seem minor in comparison. He flapped his wings to gain speed. The trip into the past had to happen soon, before word spread about the situation below him.

It occurred to the mage that he would need plenty of rest before attempting further time travel. Just coming back to this time to obtain his friends had taxed his magical strength. Glancing below at the fresh green fields opening up beyond the forest borders, he realized there was still time after all. One lone dead cow wasn't enough to spread mass alarm, if it was even discovered.

A small village appeared on the horizon and Kazin circled to land. There was sure to be an inn available in a community of that size. He landed outside the village and transformed himself back into his human form. A few children nearby watched the transformation in amazement and ran to tell their friends what they had witnessed as Kazin took the main road into town. Most of the villagers glanced at the black cloaked stranger in curiosity, but soon continued about their business. Many of them were tall and broad-shouldered, descended from the barbarians who lived along the edges of the mountains. Kazin yearned to warn them of the impending danger, but knew he could not and should not interfere. His goal was to correct something of that very nature - interference. Still, he wondered how many people he saw here would soon die because of his inaction. He shuddered at the thought.

The mage soon found a rustic old inn with a rickety wooden sign bearing a flask of ale beside a fork. It was called 'The Sunset Inn'. Looking at the sky, Kazin realized the day was rapidly coming to a close. The western sky was turning red as blood as the sun made its exit. The red sky would have been beautiful if it hadn't reminded him of the impending disaster. He shuddered and entered the safety of the building.

A fireplace crackled with welcoming warmth at one side of the room and at the other a small group of men sat playing a game of dice. One barbarian banged his mug of ale down on the table as he laughed at the misfortune of one of his comrades. His beer sloshed onto the table but he didn't seem to notice. The others at the table were just as boisterous as he. They were too engrossed in their game to notice the mage or care about his presence.

Kazin chose to sit near the fireplace as the chill of the evening made him uncomfortable. Or maybe it was the continuing fear of what was soon to come to these happy and carefree people.

The mage's thoughts were interrupted by an attractive brown-haired, brown eyed young waitress who was standing over his table. She had crept up on him so silently he flinched in surprise.

The waitress blinked shyly. "Sorry. I didn't mean to startle you. My name is Sara. Would you like to order something to drink?"

Kazin grinned sheepishly. "Yes, please." He gestured over at the table where the others threw dice. "I'll have one of those ales like they're having."

The waitress smiled. "Coming right up. Would you like anything to eat?"

Kazin nodded. "What's your special today?"

"Seasoned chicken with potatoes and mixed greens."

"Sounds good," said Kazin. "I'll have some sweet bread too, if you've got it."

Sara smiled. "Sure thing. I'll be right back."

Kazin watched her retreat to the bar and was stunned by what happened next. The waitress put a mug on the bar under the beer keg and spoke a few inaudible words. The keg started filling the mug while the waitress began wiping down the bar. She watched the mug as she worked and spoke a few words to stop the flow of ale when the mug was nearly full. Then she spoke a few words again and watched the rag as it continued to wipe down the bar. In the meantime, she picked a plate out from under the bar along with a bundle of utensils. Then she turned to the mug, picked it up, and came over to Kazin's table. When she was a few steps away from the bar, the rag stopped moving and went limp as the magic faded. Kazin was about to comment on this unusual use of magic when the waitress chanted again and magically added some fizz to the ale.

"It's our specialty," explained Sara. "I think you'll like it." She turned and walked back to the bar to prepare dinner before Kazin could say anything.

Kazin had only taken a few gulps of the fresh ale when the waitress came back with a tray of food. She deftly set the food before him.

"That was fast!" exclaimed Kazin.

"Magic makes things go so much faster," explained Sara. "How's the ale?"

"Excellent!" said Kazin. "Even a dwarf would be proud to drink it!"

Sara's eyes widened. "You've seen dwarves? We don't have them in these parts."

Kazin suddenly remembered that these people were cut off from the rest of the world by the Old Dwarven Mountains. He nodded. "Yes. But you might get to see them one day soon." If you live long enough, he thought sardonically.

"Really?" she said excitedly.

"One day," he said vaguely. He changed the subject. "I see you use magic for all sorts of menial tasks. Isn't that a bit unusual?"

Sara looked at him quizzically. "How so?"

"Well, where I come from, it's generally frowned upon to use magic for anything other than specific tasks, where magic is often the only way to do something."

"Really? Our queen encourages us to use our magic. She claims grey mages should not be restricted from using magic. Since it's not very strong magic like that of black mages or clerics, we ought to make ourselves useful in every other way that we can. You must not be from these parts. Are you a Southerner?"

Kazin realized she was referring to those who lived south of the Old Dwarven Mountains. "Yes."

"How did you get here? The magical portal between our realms is not open."

Kazin didn't want to tell her he was a dragon mage. It would probably cause a commotion that he didn't need right now. "I used magic."

The waitress narrowed her eyes. "I thought you said using magic for anything other than specific purposes was frowned upon?"

Kazin grinned sheepishly. "My rank entitles me to a few - er - indulgences."

"I see," said the waitress, unimpressed.

"I notice you used some unusual magic for a grey mage," commented Kazin, changing the direction of the conversation.

Sara nodded. "It's a combination of grey and druid magic. Our studies concentrate on living things. The school the queen has built is unique to our realm according to the queen. She trained the teachers, who in turn train us in druid magic. According to the queen, our people are not adept at black or white magic, but those of us who have some inherent magical ability are apparently capable of grey magic and a low level of druid magic. A combination of those magics is quite effective. You should see how some of our farms and crops are prospering!"

Not for long, thought Kazin sadly. "That's interesting," he said instead.

The waitress leaned over and whispered conspiratorially. "There are even rumours that some of the more powerful grey mages can even cause trees to move!"

Kazin thought back to his life in this time period and remembered the importance of treemen at a crucial time during the crisis.

"Fascinating," he said.

Sara suddenly gasped. "Here I am gabbing and your food is getting cold!" She chanted and Kazin's food instantly heated up. A man at the other table called for more ale and Sara winked at the mage before departing. "Enjoy your dinner!"

"Thanks," said Kazin. He ate ravenously and then signed out a room. Once in the warm bed - pre-warmed by Sara's magic - he fell into a deep sleep, thinking about the usefulness of magic in ordinary tasks. The queen had definitely been busy.

The following morning was grey and cool as Kazin left the village. Once beyond sight of the last of the buildings, he did his transformation and climbed into the air. In a few hours he would arrive at Priscilla, the capital city of the queen's realm. The flight was uneventful and Kazin marveled at the reconstruction of the lands below him. Most of that land had been decimated by an evil necromancer over a decade ago, but little evidence of the destruction was still evident. The occasional burned out structure or charred foundation was overshadowed by the newer farm houses and abundant crops.

Priscilla was a large, bustling city. There were many roads and side roads bisecting thousands of houses and shops. Most of the buildings couldn't have been more than a few years old and new constructions were spreading the borders of the city. In the center of the city was a large, beautifully crafted palace. The workmanship surely rivaled the quality of dwarven craftsmen and the architecture of the elves, thought Kazin.

The dragon mage found a location on the ramparts edging the palace and landed. A guard came up to him but hesitated when Kazin did his transformation. The mage pulled his cloak tighter about him as the wind tried to blow it from his shoulders. He turned to the guard and smiled. "Hello there. My name is Arch Mage Kazin and I'd like to speak with Sherman."

The guard regained his composure and nodded. It was obvious to him that the mage was no malicious intruder, and probably had heard mention of his name before. "Right this way, Sir." He led Kazin into a nearby stairwell which led to the palace proper. At the entrance to the inner palace, the guard transferred his charge to the men guarding the entryway. One of them led Kazin to a waiting room and told him to wait while he went to look for Sherman.

Only a few minutes later, the guard returned with a giant of a man following him. The large man was grumbling about the interruption and stopped when he saw the arch mage. "Who are you and what do you want?" he boomed.

Kazin regarded his friend with a yearning brought on by years of his absence. Indeed, it had been decades since Kazin had been at this man's deathbed. It had seemed like a piece of him had been lost then. A long-time friend and protector who had never wavered in his dedication, his humour had been a boost to an otherwise dismal situation. The man was still strong and muscular in appearance, even more so than his barbarian counterparts. His hair was brown and long, just beyond the shoulders, and his arms were bigger than the legs of an ordinary man. He towered around seven feet tall, and his expression at the moment was enough to cause a cowardly man to run and hide.

"Sherman," croaked Kazin. He didn't expect to be so emotional. His eyes were moist.

"That's me," growled Sherman. "I asked who you are. There's a difference, you know."

Kazin smiled and blinked to stop the pending tears from appearing. With great composure, he said in a formal voice, "Arch Mage Kazin, at your service." He gave a modest bow.

Sherman drew a sword and took a menacing step forward. "Don't toy with me!" he almost bellowed. "You are not Kazin!"

Kazin held up a hand and waved his staff in front of him as he cast a spell. Then he bravely stepped forward and looked deep into Sherman's eyes. "Don't be deceived, Sherman. It is I - from the future."

Sherman looked into the eyes beyond the white whiskers. Recognition slowly began to dawn but he didn't make a move. It was not his choice; he was paralyzed.

Kazin squeezed his friend's arm. "It's me, Sherm. I'm older now, that's all." He stepped back a few paces and canceled the spell. The guard who had been watching this seemed relieved. He had been paralyzed too.

Sherman slowly sheathed his sword. He squinted at his old friend. "Is it true? You're Kazin?"

Kazin nodded. He stepped forward slowly and put his arms around the big man, embracing him fiercely. "I've missed you so much," he said in a shaky voice.

Sherman nodded for the guard to leave them and then embraced the feeble old mage uncertainly. "It hasn't been that long," he said awkwardly.

The mage let go of the big warrior and looked up at him. "To me it has been decades. The last time I saw you, you -," his voice broke and he turned away.

The comment about Kazin being from the future finally sank in. If Kazin was as old as he seemed, Sherman himself would surely have been dead. Dragon mages lived long lives just like the dragons they controlled. Ordinary humans lived short lives in comparison. The warrior didn't know what to say. He waited silently for the mage to regain his composure. He could only imagine what Kazin was going through. As Kazin leaned on his staff, any doubts Sherman might have had about the mage were dispelled. The staff was undoubtedly the one his friend carried everywhere with him. It was older and more weathered, but the orb atop the staff was the same vibrant green orb he always remembered. It changed colour for different reasons, but it primarily glowed green as it did now.

The mage suddenly turned back to the big warrior. There was no sadness or tears in his eyes. That was all replaced by a fiercely determined look. "Sherman, I need your help."

✗　　✗　　✗　　✗　　✗

Benny and Lenny exchanged a series of parries and thrusts. They weren't fighting in earnest. They were practicing swordplay. Since they were young, they had both wanted to be like Sherman, the queen's champion. It wasn't uncommon for them to want the same things. They had wanted the same things since they were born. As identical twins, they looked and acted alike in every way. Freckle-faced with short red hair, they endlessly played practical jokes on people, particularly their ward, Sir Wilfred Galado, and to this day no one could truly tell them apart. With hard work, they had made their way into the ranks of the queen's personal guard. At only 20 years of age, it was a remarkable achievement. They were adept with swords and had proven themselves time and again. Nevertheless, they had often broken the rules, but had managed to establish a perfect alibi each time. As a result, Sir Galado couldn't take disciplinary action against them. It annoyed him greatly, but without proof he could do nothing. He had been the brunt of many of Benny and Lenny's practical jokes and he had berated them for it. But he loved them as sons, not having any children of his own. The queen also loved them, and had requested them as sentries for many royal events. She knew they would occasionally leave their posts to flirt with the young ladies, but she also knew their watchful eyes were roving the ballroom for any signs of danger. More than once they had sprung into action, leaving women on the dance floor standing in shock while they removed unwanted guests or troublemakers.

Lenny put his sword up in salute to end his sparring. "I'm beat. How about you?"

Benny lowered his weapon. "Yeah. I've had enough. It's almost time for supper, anyway."

Lenny's stomach growled. "Not a minute too soon, either."

The boys went to the weapons rack and put their weapons away with the others. They paused on their way out of the armoury to stop and gaze admiringly at the massive swords that belonged to Sherman, the queen's personal guard, chief and commander of her armies. The massive battle axe and war hammer were incredible in their quality and craftsmanship. But the weapons that caught their eye were the collection of swords.

Lenny looked around to see if anyone was nearby and then pulled one of the swords from its scabbard. "Wow!" he exclaimed reverently. "It's very lightweight!"

Benny drew another sword and hefted it carefully. He swung it a few times to test its balance. "This one's really well balanced," he remarked. "It must have been made by a dwarf."

"Try this one," said Lenny.

The boys exchanged blades and played with them for a few minutes.

"This one's certainly easy to swing, it's so light!" exclaimed Benny.

"I think this one has a better chance of doing damage," said Lenny. "The blade is very sharp."

"This one's got to be magical," continued Benny. "I'll bet it does more damage than that one."

"Wanna bet?" countered Lenny. There was a tone of challenge in his voice.

"Benny! Lenny!" called a voice from down the corridor. "Come here at once! The math teacher has arrived to give you your studies for today."

Benny and Lenny looked at one another in alarm. They had forgotten their math teacher was coming today. Math was their least favourite subject. Hastily, they sheathed the swords in their scabbards and fled from the armoury.

A moment later, Sir Galado strode into the room. He was of ordinary height, muscular, with dark hair and a dark, finely trimmed mustache. He had a habit of twirling his mustache on the ends and was doing it now as he glanced about the room. Torches in wall sconces lit the room fairly well and there was no way anyone could avoid detection here if they were hiding. "Where have those infernal twins gotten off to this time?" he muttered. He strode from the room via the same exit the twins had used. A hush fell over the armoury with his passing. Everything was in its rightful place except Sherman's two big swords. The twins had inadvertently put them in the opposite scabbards . . .

x   x   x   x   x

Everyone was jubilant as Sherman shook hands with the dwarf and minotaur. The reunion was a welcome change for the trio. When they had last parted, new commitments had prevented any of them from attempting to contact one another. They eagerly related stories of subsequent adventures in their new lives. While they reminisced, Kazin departed to look for the fifth and final companion that he needed for his quest.

When he was far enough away from his friends, he transformed into a dragon and launched himself into the air. He headed west to the shores of North Lake, where he found a sandy beach to land. It was nighttime, but the starry sky gave its reflected light off the primarily calm surface of the lake, and the landing was easy. Kazin came to a running stop and folded his wings back before transforming back into his human form. He stepped toward the lake until the gentle lapping of the waves crested over the edges of his sandals and onto his feet. Here he paused and raised his staff high into the air. The mage began to chant and the staff glowed with a brilliant white light. After a few minutes he stopped chanting and the staff dimmed. He waited for a number of minutes before repeating the procedure. Then, after another pause, he tried again.

At last, a ripple appeared in the surface of the lake and a dark head appeared, blinking in the bright light emanating from the staff.

Kazin quickly dimmed the staff light and spoke to the being who treaded water a short distance from shore. It was natural for this creature to be distrustful of a stranger, particularly one who wielded magic.

"I will not harm you," said the mage in a calm voice, just loud enough for the creature to hear.

"What do you want?" said the creature. Its voice was more like a loud whisper than a voice.

"I'd like you to fetch someone for me," said Kazin, unperturbed by the unusual voice. "His name is Olag. He is a friend of mine."

The creature hissed. "And who calls for him?"

"My name is Kazin."

The creature hissed again. "I know that name. You are a dragon mage."

"That's right," said Kazin.

A short pause ensued. Then the creature spoke. "Prove it."

Kazin sighed. He didn't want to drain his magic like this, but he supposed it was inevitable. "Very well." He stepped back from the water and transformed.

The creature hissed as the transformation took place, suddenly aware that it was much smaller than the giant dragon, and easily within reach of the potentially fiery breath, despite all the water around it. Satisfied with the demonstration, the creature spoke hastily. "I will get him. Where shall he meet?"

"Right here on this shore," rumbled the dragon. "Is sunrise sufficient time to get him here?"

"Sunrise will be fine," hissed the creature, anxiously sliding beneath the waves to carry out the dragon's wishes.

The dragon also departed. He had to bring his friends to this spot and they would camp for the remainder of the night on the beach.

Chapter 3

unrise had not yet materialized when Harran snapped to attention at the sound of a breaking twig. He had the last shift of watch duty and was surprised someone or something had gotten so close without being detected. He winced inwardly at this failure to effectively perform such a simple task. Royal life had made him soft. Undoubtedly he would have to be more alert if he was to be of any help on this quest.

The dwarf peered into the morning mist in the vain attempt to see what may have caused the sound. He didn't have to wait long.

"Don't move!" hissed a voice menacingly.

The voice emanating from the mist was enough to put any dwarf on high alert. Harran thought it was a dreaded lizardman.

"Don't move!" hissed the voice again. "One flinch and your forehead will have a hole in it."

Harran swallowed but said nothing.

"Put your weapon on the ground," continued the voice. "Slowly." The 's' in 'slowly' was drawn out.

Harran obeyed, furious with himself for letting himself get caught like this. When he straightened up, a small figure not much taller than he stood facing him, holding a crossbow aimed at him with steady arms. The face of the creature was froggish in appearance, as opposed to a lizardman's pinched expression. Wide lips spread across a large mouth, and beady eyes protruded from the head, allowing the creature a wide peripheral view. Its webbed fingers ended in sharp claws. Spiked fins ran from the top of its head down its back while narrow red gills ran down the sides of its neck and along the front of its shoulders. It was a cousin of the lizardmen known as a skink warrior.

A shadow suddenly appeared behind the skink warrior and before Harran could acknowledge its existence, the skink warrior was hoisted into the air by a massive brown arm. The skink warrior dropped its weapon and gurgled while struggling vainly against the inhuman grip.

"What have we here?" growled Zylor as he regarded the skink warrior struggling in his grasp.

Harran heaved a sigh of relief. "I believe you're holding onto Olag, if I'm not mistaken."

"Olag?" said Zylor, looking at Harran quizzically. "The skink warrior who helped us win the battle at the Tower of Hope?"

The skink warrior gurgled and Harran nodded. "I think so. It's hard to tell those creatures apart, but I think it's he."

Zylor lowered the skink warrior to the ground and loosened his grip on the creature so it could speak.

The skink warrior regained his breath and spoke in a hoarse whisper. "You can let me go, minotaur. I was merely being cautious. When my counterpart told me Kazin wanted to see me, I was skeptical, as you can imagine. It has been many years since we last spoke."

Zylor released the skink warrior and laughed. "Well I'll be!" he exclaimed. The minotaur slapped Olag on the back with zeal, forcing him to stagger forward into Harran. Olag would have fallen had the dwarf not caught him in mid-step.

Olag hissed and turned angrily on the minotaur, but the sheer size of the hairy beast quelled any further outburst.

Harran further diffused the situation by placing a gentle hand on Olag's shoulder. "It's good to see you, my friend."

Olag sighed and shook his head in resignation. "I should have known I'd run into you guys again."

Zylor was still grinning. "Oh, come on! You like hanging out with us!" His grin vanished. "Not many deserve to have that distinction," he added seriously.

Olag was surprised by the compliment. He fumbled for words and was relieved when a different voice called out from the mist. "Who's making all the racket?"

"We have a visitor, Sherman!" responded Harran.

The warrior appeared and strode into the group. He looked at the skink warrior and smiled. "Olag! You're early!"

Olag shrugged. "I wasn't far away from here when I received the message to come and meet with Kazin. Now I'm wondering whether I should have come at all." He glanced in Zylor's direction as he painfully rubbed the fins on his neck.

"Have you been showing off your latest battle techniques again, Zylor?" chided Sherman.

Zylor chuckled and Olag scowled.

"Let's have breakfast," suggested Harran. He beckoned the skink warrior to follow. "I'll apply some ointment to your bruises, Olag. I'm betting Kazin wants you in perfect condition for our new quest."

Olag had started to follow the dwarf but stopped in mid-stride. "Quest?!"

Zylor laughed behind him. "It looks like we're going to spend some quality time together!"

Olag turned to glare at the minotaur and Zylor laughed even harder. "A glare like that would earn you respect among my kind." He retrieved Olag's weapon and handed it to him. "Sorry about the rough treatment, Olag. Had I known it was you - ." He shrugged.

Olag sighed in resignation and followed Harran to the camp.

When the skink warrior was out of earshot, Sherman said, "I hope you didn't scare him off this quest, Zylor. Kazin insisted he come along since he was with us last time we went back in time."

Zylor shot him a look. "He is honourable. He will come." The minotaur tromped off after the skink warrior.

Sherman followed more slowly, wondering whether skinks - the cousins of lizardmen - could ever be considered honourable. He finally decided that Olag had proven himself in the past. There was no reason to mistrust him now. The human hatred of lizardmen was still a powerful feeling that sometimes got in the way. Minotaurs were also an ancient enemy of humans, yet Sherman wouldn't hesitate to put his life in Zylor's hands. It was no different with Olag. Granted, Sherman hadn't spent as much time with the skink warrior as he had with the minotaur, but Olag had some valuable skills to add to the team, and Kazin trusted him to come along. That was good enough for him.

Kazin was awakened, exhausted from the previous day's exertions. He warmly greeted Olag and repeatedly had to assure him that he was indeed Kazin the dragon mage. Olag wasn't entirely sure about Kazin's older appearance, but the ease with which he got along with the others meant that he must be one and the same as the mage he had known several years back. As the quest and associated conditions were made known, Olag became very nervous. His last experience with going to the past was terrifying enough. What Kazin was suggesting meant he would have to go through all of that all over again.

The others tried to convince him to go along with it, reminding him of his accomplishment in defending the Tower of Hope with his forces of skink warriors. The Tower of Hope, a bastion of the white magic wielders in the human's world who concentrated their magic on the healing of others, was being attacked by enemy forces. An alliance was forged between the white-robed clerics and the skink warriors just prior to this, resulting in an influx of skink defenders at a crucial moment in the battle. The tower held on thanks to the heroics of the skink warriors led by Olag himself.

Olag argued that the quest was not a matter of courage, but wisdom. How could they know that their very idea to go into the past to correct the problem wasn't actually the catalyst?

Kazin had the only convincing answer. The future, as he knew it, needed to be saved. To do nothing was not an option, because the future was literally falling apart.

Olag's last concern was the fact that his race didn't exist in the time they were going back to. If he and his kind did not exist yet, would it be safe for him to go back and make an appearance?

Kazin assured him it was in fact safer to bring him than the others, since, if they didn't know his race, he would be more likely to be trusted by any enemies they encountered. He could potentially obtain information the others couldn't.

Olag was still skeptical, but finally agreed to go along with it. He would be long dead by the time Kazin's uncertain future became an issue anyway.

With that settled, discussion turned to planning the next course of action.

✕   ✕   ✕   ✕   ✕

The mage stepped carefully around and over the bodies, his staff held ready before him. The stench was unbearable, the decay already setting in mere hours after the battle had moved on over the eastern ridge. If it wasn't for his sense-dulling magic, he would have succumbed to the stench long ago.

He looked up as a pair of ravens squabbled over a fresh chunk of flesh nearby. Ravens dotted the landscape, each one poised over its own corpse, pecking ravenously. There were more than enough bodies to go around. This had been one of the fiercest battles of the year, and the quantity of casualties was a testament to that fact. The rising sun was a glaring red in appearance, a sleepless eye overseeing an endless war.

The mage stumbled over an unrecognizable corpse and cursed. What he sought wasn't as readily available as before. He wanted a corpse, human, freshly deceased. Most of what he saw was too far gone to be of any use.

A weak moan sounded nearby and the mage anxiously searched in the direction of the sound. He was beginning to despair when he finally spotted the body. Half buried in gore from some ugly creature lay a soldier in a crumpled heap. Whatever had struck him down had used a blunt instrument to smash his spine. The mage instantly knew this soldier could not live much longer.

The soldier looked pitifully up at the approaching mage as he bent over him. Not knowing what else to do, the mage took the man's hand and held it. The soldier seemed to take comfort from that action and his laboured breathing eased. Moments later, he breathed his last. The mage brushed his hand lightly over the soldier's face to close his eyes. He gently brushed the soldier's dark hair from his face, feeling deeply saddened by the young life that was extinguished so soon in life. Then he stood and pointed his staff at the man's body. He chanted a spell and his body stiffened as he put all of his energy into the effort. A wisp of barely visible steam rose from the body and entered the orb atop his staff. The steam whitened and then faded again as the last of the life essence was absorbed into the staff. When this was completed, the mage stopped chanting and regarded the orb. He spoke a word of magic and it radiated a bright, blinding white light. A nearby raven squawked in irritation and abandoned its corpse in search of one further away. Nodding in satisfaction, the mage canceled the spell and the orb faded. The magical strength was satisfactory. He sighed. This could very well be the last time he could attempt his experiment using the life force from the bodies in this field. After this he would have to go farther afield to obtain the samples he needed. Nevertheless, his staff was now fully loaded and it was time to head back to his cave.

Along the way, he encountered several scavengers poking among the dead for souvenirs. Most of these were goblins who were too cowardly to fight. None of them gave the mage any trouble and most gave him a wide berth. None wanted to tangle with a spell caster. It was just as well. The mage needed the life essence in his staff for his experiments. He had no means of fighting a battle save for the dagger at his side. Only once, a creature came near him, but it backed away when the mage gave a command and his staff lit up with the brilliance of the life force trapped within the orb. The threat of magic was enough to ensure his safe passage.

It took several hours to reach the base of the mountain housing his secret cave. Another half hour of climbing a hidden path brought him to the cave entrance. With a word of magic, the magical warding shielding the cave from unwanted visitors or prying eyes was removed. Before entering, the mage turned to regard the death and destruction below. From his vantage point, the battlefield was a smoking, black ruin. The view, however daunting, was infinitely better than being down there among the stench, death and decay. Way off in the distance, a dragon was visible, undoubtedly headed in the direction where the battle still raged. Shaking his head sadly, the mage turned and entered his domain.

The cave's interior was quite comfortable. It was only a short distance in from outside, but it was spacious. A makeshift forge was set up in one corner and a fissure in the rocks conveniently vented the smoke up to some unknown void within the mountain. A stone workbench was backlit by a couple of torches in sconces on the wall behind it. A comfortable looking black leather chair stood in front of the table and a pile of swords lay in a heap on the floor next to it. Another group of swords lay in a neat row on the floor near the forge.

To the left, on the opposite side of the forge, stood a workbench, containing an anvil and a large hammer. Seated at the table, slumped over fast asleep, was a shaggy looking dwarf in rumpled clothing. Emanating from somewhere within the black beard were loud snores.

The mage shook his head in amusement. How the dwarf could snore with his head hanging down in that position was a mystery.

He walked quietly over to the stone table and put his staff down gently so as not to wake the dwarf. Then he went and picked up a sword from the row in front of the forge. He brought it back to the table and set it down. The mage contemplated the time he had still been back at The Tower of Sorcery, recollecting the studies he undertook under the tutelage of one of the master mages. Apparently, the experimentation of magic at such high levels of complexity was discouraged. He had disagreed, and soon discovered the studies in the tower were hindering his own ambitions with regard to magic. Being much older than the other students didn't help. They were too young and impulsive, and there was no one mature enough to collaborate with. So he left to do experiments on his own. It had taken a few years to find a secluded spot, and another year to set up his workshop to accommodate his experimentation, but it had ultimately worked out well. Over the years he had succeeded in crafting, with the help of the dwarven smith, an extensive array of magical weaponry. But this project would be his ultimate achievement. If he could succeed at this, it would be the most powerful artifact that he, or anyone else, had ever created.

The previous attempts were all failures of varying degrees, as indicated by the pile of swords in disarray beside him. Some of them had varying levels of magic stored within, and others had no magic at all. But none had what he desired. They were all failures as far as he was concerned, but the dwarf convinced him to save them so they could be sold to finance their project. The spirit blade the mage was trying to create would be far more powerful than these specimens. But he hadn't succeeded yet. The mage primarily blamed himself for the failures. The spell was exceptionally complex. He reasoned that it wasn't entirely his fault. The quality of steel in the swords was also an issue. The dwarf had done his best, but imperfections in the steel limited and sometimes even prevented the magic from taking hold.

Closing his eyes, the mage steeled himself for the spell. Then he opened his eyes and picked up his staff. With his other hand, he pulled a number of spell components from his pocket. He pointed the staff at the sword and squeezed the components in his fist. Then he began his spell. At first, only his mouth moved. Then his voice was heard, barely audible. When his incantation was complete, he began again, becoming louder as he chanted. The orb atop his staff began to glow, emanating a milky white iridescence. The mage frowned as he chanted. The spell did not appear to be working. He tried harder, drowning out the sound of the snoring dwarf as his chant rose in volume. Beads of sweat emanated from the pores on his forehead. With all the hard work he had put into this project so far, he was not about to give up. His arm shook with the strain, as did his voice.

Suddenly, ever so slightly, a wisp of the milky light in the staff stretched toward the sword's edge. The mage chanted harder, and the stream of light continued channeling into the sword. Now the sword's blade began to glow with magic as it absorbed the light. The sword's light became brighter as the staff dimmed, its magic transferring to the new object. By now the mage's arm was shaking uncontrollably and his voice trembled with exertion. The spell was nearly complete.

At last, the remaining light in the staff shot into the sword and the connection between staff and sword was broken. The mage stopped chanting and staggered for a moment before falling against the table. He recovered his balance and tried to catch his breath. His chest felt tight and his left arm tingled, but he was too excited to notice. His spell had finally worked!

The mage put down the staff, its energy now fully expended, and picked up the sword. At his touch, the blade gave a momentary flash of white light. The sword had taken the magic! Still gasping, the mage excitedly took the sword out to the cave entrance to examine it in the daylight, as well as to get some fresh air for himself. He held it aloft and regarded it in awe. Still holding it up, he gazed across the plain below where the ravens still feasted.

"This spirit blade is a culmination of the spirits of many of the fallen soldiers and warriors below," murmured the mage in between breaths. "It is the sword of dead heroes."

The mage slowly lowered the sword and gave it one more appraising glance before re-entering the cave.

The dwarf, amazingly, was still asleep. The mage listened and the only sounds in the cave were the crackling of the fire in the forge, the dwarf's snoring, and his own ragged breathing. As he reached the table, the mage was surprised that he still hadn't regained his breath. A weakness he had not known before was engulfing his entire body. At first he thought it was the exertion of the spell, but his chest continued to tighten. His arm lost its strength and the sword fell from his hand to clatter onto the pile of swords that lay at his feet.

The noise finally woke the dwarf with a start. He glanced over at the mage, who stood staring dumbly at the pile of swords at his feet. The grogginess of sleep immediately left the dwarf's mind when he saw the old mage sink to the floor, scattering the pile of swords. Alarmed, he sprang from his chair and bolted to the mage's side. With an expression of triumph mixed with sadness, the mage looked up at the dwarf. He opened his mouth to speak but nothing came out. Trying again, he got his vocal cords to work one last time.

"The spirit blade is ready," he gasped. "It is called The Sword of Dead-," his voice trailed off and his eyes became vacant.

"The Sword of Dead?" murmured the dwarf gruffly. His mind became muddled as the reality of what had just happened set in. "The Sword of Dead?" he repeated dumbly. He looked at the pile of swords nearby. Then he blinked as the implication of what the mage had said dawned in his mind. He frantically scanned the swords with a critical eye but knew it was useless. They were jumbled about and all looked identical, because that was what the mage had instructed him to manufacture.

"Which one is it?" he asked no one in particular.

Chapter 4

ir Wilfred Galado twirled his mustache as he glanced around the armoury. With Sherman gone, it fell to him to take command of the army. He was here to inspect the weaponry available to the soldiers should war break out. It was unlikely to happen, but with rumours of unrest to the south near the mountain, anything was possible. The rumours indicated there was some sort of epidemic causing sickness and death. Mages with healing powers were dispatched to investigate and report back to the queen, but it was too soon to tell what was wrong. Nevertheless, Sir Wilfred Galado took his duty seriously.

Wilfred had been present during Sherman's conversation the previous morning with the queen and was surprised at how adamant he had been about going on an important quest. He said it was to help Kazin, the dragon mage, and that he would be back before very long because time travel was involved.

The queen was not pleased about the idea, but relented at the last minute. Sherman hurriedly left the room, commenting that he needed to get his special magical sword first. Sir Galado knew it must really be important for Sherman to need his magical sword. He never used it unless it was absolutely necessary. Sherman left within the hour, riding on the dragon's scaly back. "You're in charge, Wilf!" he had shouted to Galado upon mounting the fiery beast.

So Sir Galado went ahead with his inspection of the weapons, beginning with the home guard's weapons in the castle. His inspection went well until he got to the place where Sherman's weapons were hung. An empty spot indicated which weapon the big warrior had taken on his mysterious quest. The scabbard to the right of the missing weapon hung askew, no doubt due to Sherman's hasty departure. Wilfred, not patient with disorder, reached out to straighten it. As he let go, it swung back off kilter. He attempted it again, and once again it shifted off kilter. Something was wrong. The soldier grasped the sword's hilt and lifted to see if it was jammed. In so doing, he nearly pulled it free of the scabbard. Shocked at the light weight of the sword, he pulled it out the rest of the way. He swung the sword around deftly and instantly knew it was magical. He regarded the scabbard and noted that it was not exactly the correct match for the sword. Then it dawned on him. This was the sword that Sherman had intended to take with him! The fool had taken the wrong sword and must not have noticed! The hair on the back of his neck stood on end. How important was this sword to the quest? Without waiting to find an answer, Sir Galado hastened to seek out the queen.

The queen was in her chambers and Lenny and Benny stood guard outside her quarters when Sir Galado trudged up to them. "Tell the queen I need to see her at once!" commanded Sir Galado.

The twins looked at one another in alarm. They knew Wilfred was in a state of mind not to be trifled with. They both responded at once and made a move to ring the door chime. Seeing each other make the motion, they both backed off to offer the other the opportunity. Seeing each other back off, they both moved forward again in unison. Both hesitated at the same instant and Sir Galado impatiently pushed them both aside to pull the chime himself.

"I don't have time for your foolish games!" he snapped.

The queen called "enter!" and Sir Galado opened the door and left the twins standing red-faced in the hallway. He closed the door behind him.

"What is it?" asked the queen. She was dressed in her favourite dark-blue velvet robe with silver hems. It was a symbol of her magical experience with druid magic. With fair hair and kind blue eyes, those in her presence rarely felt uncomfortable. But those eyes could turn cold and harsh if she became angered. Many offenders had been fooled into thinking she was naive and weak. But she had a habit of seeing through their lies and deceit. She immediately noticed the look of concern on Sir Galado's face.

Sir Galado explained about the sword to her. "We need to get the sword to Sherman quickly," said Wilfred. "I hope he hasn't gone beyond our reach yet."

"It's likely we're too late already," commented the queen. "Our only chance will be to fly one of the griffins. I can summon one, but who will go?"

"I will," volunteered Sir Galado.

"But I need you here," stated the queen.

"I do not trust anyone else with this task," objected Sir Galado. "This sword is a very powerful artifact. In the wrong hands -." He held out his hand in a helpless gesture.

"That's a good point," admitted the queen. She thought for a moment, then nodded. "Very well. But be back here within the week, whether you find Sherman or not."

Sir Galado bowed. "Thank you, my queen." He left the chamber to make preparations for departure.

Twenty minutes later, he arrived on the castle's ramparts to spot a griffin that waited patiently beside the queen. It was a sight to behold for those who had never seen one before. They had a golden hue to their feathers and were often large enough to carry several people at once. They had four legs and soft fur on the undersides of their bodies. Their wing span was nearly half the diameter of an adult dragon. Few could control them. They had their own way of determining who could approach them or fly on their backs.

"I've given the griffin Sherman's scent," said the queen. "It should be able to track him even if he's riding on the back of a dragon."

Sir Galado nodded. The griffin sensed the importance of the mission and allowed him to climb upon its back. When he was settled, he nodded to the queen.

"Good," said the queen. "It has accepted you. I was concerned it may not allow you near." She pulled some spell components from her pocket. "I will now cast a spell so that you will not be separated from the sword until you find Sherman." She chanted a spell and ended it with 'Sherman'. A shaft of light engulfed Sir Galado and the sword and then dissipated. "There," she said. "It is now a part of you. Good luck, Wilfred." With a wave of her hand, the griffin took to the air. It swung to the south and flew out of sight with its rider.

Lenny and Benny watched the whole thing with interest. They both hoped they could go on exciting missions for the queen someday.

"Back to work, boys," ordered the queen. "The excitement's over for now. While Sir Galado's gone, I expect you to be on your best behaviour."

"Yes, your Majesty," sang the boys in unison. Little did they know how impossible it was to keep that promise.

×　　×　　×　　×　　×

The companions rose early in the morning and Kazin reviewed their plans. He then went through the list of items necessary for their journey. Harran had his ice axe and chain mail. The axe was in his possession the last time he had traveled back in time and the chain mail was given to him before he returned back to his own time, so it was potentially an item that could have altered the future when it should have been left behind.

Sherman patted the sword at his side. "I have the sword you told me to bring."

Kazin nodded. "Good. The rest of the items we need are in here." He pulled a small pouch from his pocket and placed it on the ground in front of him. Then he chanted a quick spell and the pouch grew to many times its normal size.

"Wow!" exclaimed Sherman. "I've never seen that spell before!"

"It's a miniaturizing magic that I've learned somewhere along the way," explained Kazin. "It saves carrying around a giant pack." He untied the string and pried the bag open. Inside, he rummaged around for a moment. "Here it is," he commented, withdrawing a small ring. He presented it to Sherman. "This is the invisibility ring that was accidentally stuck to your boot the last time you came back from the past. It may be key to our quest."

Sherman shuddered as he accepted the artifact. "I had forgotten about that."

Then Kazin withdrew an amulet and handed it to Zylor. "You remember this?" It was an amulet that allowed a spell to be maintained on an individual wearing it, while the spell caster could be free to do other things without draining all their magical energy to maintain the spell.

Zylor's eyes narrowed. "Indeed. I had forgotten where that ended up."

"It took a bit of effort to track it down," said Kazin. He then turned his attention to Olag, who looked somewhat crestfallen.

"I didn't have any magical items in my possession last time," said the skink warrior sadly.

"That's a good thing," said Kazin. "Of all of us, you are the least likely to have caused the disappearing problem we are having. But this time you will have something magical to aid you," said the mage cheerfully. He reached into the sack and withdrew a bow and a quiver full of arrows. "This," he said happily, "is a Quiver of Many Arrows." His smile wavered. "It belonged to my wife, God rest her soul."

"She's dead?!" exclaimed Sherman.

"Not yet," interjected Harran.

It took a moment or two for this to sink in. "Oh, yeah," said Sherman sheepishly. "I forgot. Sorry."

"Won't it interfere with time travel and such?" asked Zylor.

Kazin nodded. "That's a good point, Zylor. But do you remember what happened last time? Olag ran out of arrows and we almost died. I'm not taking that chance this time."

"I'm with you there," said Olag vehemently as he accepted the bow and quiver and slung it over his shoulder. "That's the main reason I'm leery about going on this adventure in the first place."

Kazin chanted again and his sack returned to palm size. He deftly scooped it up and slid it into his pocket. "That's it folks. Let's gather the rest of our gear and be on our way."

The companions did not have much for provisions because Kazin had instructed them to travel light, so they were ready to go within fifteen minutes. Kazin stood apart from the others and transformed from a white-haired old human mage into his dragon form.

"I could never get used to that," commented Olag with a shudder.

"Climb on," ordered Kazin when the transformation was complete.

The companions approached the monstrous beast and Zylor gave the dwarf and skink warrior a boost. He turned to assist the warrior as well, but Sherman was already clambering along the wing to reach the scaly back. The minotaur sprang after him and found a relatively comfortable spot where the wing entered the body.

Kazin turned his head back to peer at them through reptilian eyes. "All set?"

"Yup!" said Sherman. He sounded somewhat nervous but didn't show it. It was uncomfortable for him because he hated heights.

"Let's get on with it," muttered Olag. He didn't like the thought of flying this way either.

Even Harran wasn't happy to leave the ground. "Dwarves were meant to be under the ground, not above it," he had said many times in the past when riding the dragon.

The only one who seemed to be enjoying himself was the minotaur. He grinned as the dragon launched himself high into the air. "I've missed this kind of fun!" he cried as the shoreline slipped past and the open water of North Lake sparkled below.

The sound of the wind rushing past competed only with the sound of leathery wings flapping rhythmically as the mainland disappeared from sight entirely. At this point the dragon banked left to a south westerly direction. The sun gleamed over the horizon behind them, reflecting off the water far below.

"Do we have to fly this high?" asked Sherman anxiously, glancing down at the smooth surface of the lake. "It's really windy so high up."

"Just hold on tight," rumbled the dragon. "The height allows me to see over a wider area, and keeps me from being seen by any ships out on the water."

"We aren't going to go down the whirlpool again, are we?" asked Olag nervously.

"We are," said Kazin.

Olag groaned.

"How will we do it?" asked Harran "I recall the last time we had mermaids to help us breathe under water."

"We won't need them," responded Kazin. "My magic will see to that."

"I hope so," said Zylor.

"Do you even know where the whirlpool is?" asked Sherman. "Last time it was the magical druid ship that brought us there."

Kazin laughed and his belly rumbled beneath them. "I've had plenty of years to find where the whirlpool was located. It can't be found by a regular ship because it magically makes them navigate around it without their knowledge. By flying over it, I can see it and fly toward it. I've also spent a great deal of time studying how to go back in time. I wouldn't risk bringing all of you on this journey if I thought it wasn't achievable with minimal risk. The hardest part will be to cross the swing bridge safely."

Sherman groaned. "Don't remind me."

After that the companions lapsed into silence, their thoughts turned to memories of that adventure years ago. It was an uneventful flight and the companions used the time to catch up on the latest stories since they had last seen one another.

The trip was a long one. The sun passed overhead and then went ahead of them in the west, still reflecting off the vast expanse of water below them. Before long, Kazin began to lower his altitude.

Harran was the first to catch on. "Are we getting close?"

Kazin glanced back at the dwarf who sat forward of the others on his neck. "I can see the whirlpool. It's almost time."

Olag looked down. "You must have exceptional eyesight. I can't see anything."

"What do you want us to do?" asked Sherman.

"Just sit tight," answered Kazin. "When we get close, I'll cast a spell on us to shield us from the water. You won't even get wet."

"Then what?" asked Olag nervously.

"Then I'm going to dive into the whirlpool."

Sherman groaned. "I thought you'd say something like that."

"Just sit back and hold on tight," said Kazin. "It could get rough even with the magic."

"Let's get it over with," stated Zylor firmly. "We've done it before. It can be done again."

The whirlpool was finally visible to the rest of the group as it swirled menacingly below them. The water was frothy white and seemed to spiral at incredible speed, particularly in the middle. It came closer and closer as Kazin dove, picking up more and more speed as he plummeted like an arrow. Everyone held on for dear life.

Soon the whirlpool was the only thing visible, its sheer size making them feel inferior as the edges of the whirlpool rose above them and the center beckoned. At last, Kazin cast a spell and an invisible barrier surrounded them. Just before the companions penetrated the water, Kazin tilted his wings back to reduce the drag as the water churned around them. The spiraling water threatened to spin them around, so Kazin cast another spell that compensated. As the water rose above them, it darkened noticeably. Here was where Kazin had to concentrate. The transition between the whirlpool and the void beyond was still an unknown factor. His curiosity was satisfied moments later when the crushing pressure of the water gave way to black nothingness. At this point, Kazin cast a spell to light his surroundings and was thankful he did. A flat obsidian floor was immediately below him, and he barely had time to change course to avoid crashing into it at high speed. As he flew along the endless floor, he slowed and put his clawed feet down to screech to a halt. When he finally came to a stop, he canceled his shield spell and checked on his passengers.

The companions were still there, but they had been buffeted about from the wild ride. Sherman had tumbled back to Kazin's tail. He looked like he was going to be sick. Harran hung down the side of the dragon's body, held tightly by the strong hairy arm of the minotaur, who's other hand was dug deeply into Kazin's wing with his long claws. Only Olag had not changed position. His scaly hands and feet had kept him secure during the wild flight.

"Are we there?" asked Sherman shakily, looking around at the circle of light given off by Kazin's magical light.

Zylor lowered the dwarf to the ground before releasing his own hold on the dragon. His claws left small marks in the dragon's skin but Kazin gave no indication he felt it. "I suspect we are."

Harran's beard was askew as he sat down on the floor with a gasp. "I sure hope the return trip will go a bit easier."

Olag extracted himself from his position and slid down the dragon's leg to land on his feet. "That went better than I thought," he commented.

"Speak for yourself," grunted Sherman. He carefully crawled down Kazin's wing to the safety of the floor.

With everyone off of his back, Kazin transformed back into his human form. The light he was emitting a moment ago, which seemed to emanate from his reptilian body, now shone with even greater intensity from the orb atop his staff. "I think we should rest," he stated matter-of-factly. No one argued.

They withdrew some food they had brought with them for the journey and had a quick dinner break. Then Kazin rose to his feet and stretched. "It's time to move on. I'd rather not spend the night here if I can help it - not that daytime around here looks any different."

Sherman finished his mug of water and rose. "I'm with you. Lead on."

The others packed up their mugs and stood, looking expectantly at the mage. Kazin chanted a spell and his staff pulled imperceptibly to the left. "This way."

They walked for only about five minutes before a golden door framed in a steel doorway appeared ahead of them. It was only the door and frame. Nothing was around it. It seemed out of place in the vast emptiness of the void they were in.

"It's the same as last time," concluded the dwarf. "The words of warning are above the door."

"Yes," said Sherman. He walked around to the other side of the door. "The saying on this side reads 'The future - to escape the past without fulfilling your destiny will lead to a dead future.'" He turned to Kazin. "Do you suppose someone went through this door and caused a dead future like you were describing?"

"It's certainly possible," said Kazin.

"Then do we go through and bring whoever it was back?" asked Olag.

"No," answered the mage. "I think the better course of action would be to go into the past and prevent them from doing it in the first place - if that's what is causing the problem. We don't know for sure. In addition, I do know the problem originates before your current time, because the 'malfunction', if you will, has already begun."

"Can you control where we end up?" asked Zylor. "You were amazingly accurate in arriving at the arena to find me."

"That's because I had already been there before," said Kazin. "I can use magic to go where I've already been and when, although the 'when' part is difficult. In this case, according to my calculations, the

43

rate of the disappearances tells me we'll have to go back many years, to around the time of the dragon wars."

Sherman whistled. "That was an interesting time in our history."

Kazin nodded. "There were many records, some true, some fictional, about occurrences during that time. Many scholars to this day still debate about what really did or did not happen. I'm hoping we can use that as a smokescreen to do what we have to do, because the more we interfere, the more unstable the future can become."

"So you're saying we should go in, do our thing, and get out with as little fuss as possible."

Kazin nodded. "Yes. But it may not be easy. There are many thieves and brigands during that time. Any one of them could be essential in how our future turns out. We can't just kill them if they stumble upon us. If we have to kill in self-defense, it will have to be as a last resort only."

"That will be difficult," rumbled the minotaur.

Kazin sighed. "I know. But if we don't at least attempt this, the future as we know it will disappear anyway."

"Then let's get on with it," said Harran resolutely.

Kazin nodded. He read the side of the door that led into the past. "The past - Do not disturb the sands of time. To do so will ensure your destruction."

"Then let's ensure our destruction," intoned Zylor.

Kazin cast a spell that he hoped would send them back to the right time in history upon entering the doorway. "Remember to keep as silent as possible so as not to disturb the creatures that linger there," cautioned Kazin. He cautiously turned the brass doorknob but it was stuck. Then he grinned sheepishly. "Oh, yeah. I forgot. This happened last time." He raised his staff and pointed it at the door. With slight concentration, the doorknob turned and the door opened outward. Without looking back, the companions stepped through the opening and the door closed behind them with an audible 'click'.

Chapter 5

The five companions congregated on a small ledge just big enough for them to stand in a tight group. The air was damp and oppressive. The light from Kazin's staff penetrated only so far before being swallowed up by a thick fog. Two posts stood at one end of the ledge and were attached to a swinging crosswalk constructed of wood and rope. It swayed ever so slightly and creaked under the stress of its own weight. Rope railings lined either side of the narrow bridge, whose rungs faded off into the unknown. Turning back was not an option. The door they had entered by had vanished. Peering over the edge of the ledge only confirmed what they already knew from previous experience. The ledge appeared to be free floating. There was nothing but air underneath. The only way they could go was along the crosswalk. It sloped downward toward the middle.

"You lead the way, Zylor," whispered Kazin. "Olag, you follow. Have your bow ready. I'll go in the middle to provide light and magical support. Sherman, you're next. Harran, you take rear guard."

Harran nodded. "Same order as last time."

Kazin nodded. "Any questions?" Everyone shook their heads and drew their weapons.

Zylor tentatively stepped onto the bridge. It creaked but held. He took several slow steps and Olag followed. The others fell into step behind them, an equal distance apart.

With agonizing slowness, they made their way across the bridge, not wanting to awaken the creatures they knew lurked beyond the shadows. All went well for a while, and they reached what they assumed to be the middle of the crosswalk without incident. At this point the bridge began to rise in front of them. The only thing they could hear was the creaking of the crosswalk and their own breathing.

Suddenly, a shriek broke the stillness up ahead, followed by a blood curdling scream. The companions paused and looked at one another in alarm. They had not done anything to alert the creatures of their presence, yet something must have detected them.

More shrieks rent the air ahead followed by several flashes of light. "Get back!" cried a feminine voice. More flashes followed; then more shrieks. The companions soon realized it was not they who had been detected, but someone up ahead.

They didn't have a chance to think about it as Sherman signaled a warning. Something was coming toward them from the rear. Harran braced himself to contend with the approaching creature. It appeared to be some sort of zombie, its decayed flesh and torn clothing an ugly sight to behold.

The bridge vibrated with the approach of many feet. "We have to keep moving!" whispered Kazin as loudly as he dared. More screams were heard ahead of them. Kazin cast a shield above them just as a black bat-like object flew at them, screeching a warning cry to its counterparts. The companions had been detected.

The bat thing didn't get very far as it smashed into Kazin's invisible shield. It fell silently into the blackness below.

Harran sliced off the approaching zombie's head with his ice axe and stepped back as its instantly frozen body fell toward him. Its body, brittle as glass, shattered loudly as it struck the bridge slats. "So much for silence," he grumbled. He turned and headed after the others who were already moving forward rapidly. More shrieks sounded all around them and flashes appeared ahead of them again.

Zylor was moving too fast for Kazin's shield to cover him when a bat thing came screeching toward him. It never reached him as Olag shot two rapidly fired arrows into it. It whooshed past the minotaur harmlessly. The minotaur turned to nod his thanks when two more of those beasts came at him from either side. One fell to Olag's next arrow and the other one would have struck the minotaur had it not been fried by Kazin's lightning bolt. Zylor was merely showered with its ashes. By this time the others caught up to him and he surged ahead once more. But he didn't get far. His right leg broke through one of the wooden slats and he fell awkwardly. Olag ran to assist him in getting disentangled while Kazin did his best to shoot any of the flying creatures that threatened them.

Behind, more zombies appeared and were gaining on them, so Harran and Sherman had to turn to face their attack. Harran chopped mercilessly with the ice axe and Sherman swung his sword above the dwarf's head whenever there was an opening. He had a strange expression on his face as he struck his first enemy in the shoulder. He glanced at his sword in consternation and his face reddened. No one had time to notice the big warrior's hesitation. They all had their hands full. Black bat things rammed ineffectively against Kazin's shield as Zylor was finally freed and the group moved forward again. The pause was good in that a number of zombie bodies were now blocking the path to the rear. Zombies had to throw their counterparts over the side of the bridge to give chase.

Ahead, Zylor saw some zombies, but they were going away from them. He thought it was odd that they appeared to be running away but he didn't care. He sprang into them from behind, his blood lust burning in his veins. He grinned as he felt the sensation, a feeling he had not had in a long time. He hacked into the zombies with a vengeance befitting a minotaur. Zombie body parts flew to either side as he hacked, while Olag and Kazin took care of the winged creatures with arrows and magic.

The winged creatures gave up attacking Kazin's shield and began attacking from the sides where the shield ended to allow the companions to contend with the zombies. The bat things even tried to attack through the slats from underneath. Kazin kept the shield above them and fried the bat things wherever they posed a threat.

Now that they were bogged down again, Harran and Sherman had to deal with the zombies who had once again come from behind. The bridge shook and wobbled dangerously and everyone had to concentrate on keeping their balance as they fought.

Now the female voice could be heard again, louder this time. She was chanting some unknown magic.

A mass of zombies ahead of Zylor appeared to be having difficulty moving. He hacked into them and suddenly he was surprised at how heavy his legs felt. His battle axe felt like it was a hundred times heavier, too. It took tremendous effort to do anything, including breathe. Sheer determination and blood lust kept him moving forward, but the going was very slow.

Kazin noticed Zylor's decrease in speed and his extreme effort in wielding his weapon. He realized something was wrong and used magic to make Zylor stronger. The minotaur moved somewhat easier, but something still slowed him down. It occurred to the mage that Zylor was possibly under some sort of spell intended for the zombies. Flashes of light appeared again, but they seemed weaker than before. A light cry of dismay was heard not far ahead past the throng of zombies. Kazin threw a quick look back to confirm that Harran and Sherman had things under control and directed his attention up front. Zylor was on one knee, weakly swinging his axe at a zombie who fared no better than he. They looked like two warriors who had fought to exhaustion but did not want to give up. Had Kazin's spell been canceled? Even Olag was becoming fatigued. His arrows were flying off target.

Kazin pointed his staff at the milling zombies in front of them and picked them off one at a time, sending them from the bridge with high intensity fireballs. As the crowd of zombies thinned, Kazin could see glimpses of someone in a blue robe who was huddled down on the bridge. The individual was casting some quick spells at the screaming bat things that stunned them with a bright flash of light. Any flying creatures near the flash were immobilized and fell silently into the dark expanse below. Zombies were not only between Kazin's group and the individual, but they were also massed beyond her as well, blocking her escape. All of them were virtually immobile, suffering from the same debilitating condition that was affecting Zylor and Olag. It didn't affect Kazin yet - his magical ability making him more resistant to the magic - but he could feel it in the air around him. Thankfully the dwarf and warrior were still far enough away to be unaffected. Kazin marveled at the cloaked figure's ability to hold off all of the enemies single-handedly.

The blue-cloaked figure cast some more immobilizing spells at the winged creatures. These spells were not as intense as before and the figure moaned in fear. Her magic was weakening.

"Don't worry!" called Kazin. "We'll get you safely away!"

The cloaked figure sprang to her feet, startled. She had been so intent on the bat things she had forgotten about the zombies around her. Only the glint from her eyes could be seen as she stared at the newcomer. One of the bat things chose this opportunity to swoop down on her but Kazin reacted in time. The cloaked figure tensed as Kazin shot a lightning bolt at the creature and blasted a hole right through it. The creature bounced off the cloaked figure and fell to the side to disappear forever.

The cloaked figure flinched at the unexpected contact but stood firm. She now realized this was not another monster but an ally. She threw back her hood to reveal a young, beautiful face with many small freckles and dark blue eyes. Her shoulder length hair was a vibrant red, more vivid than any red hair any of the companions had ever seen. Her eyes were fearful but there was gratitude in her face.

"Who- who are you?" she asked.

Kazin took care of the remaining zombies between them and cast a shield over the woman just as a group of bat things swooped down on her in unison. They smashed into Kazin's shield and flew back, screaming in anger.

"My name is Arch Mage Kazin," said the mage as he checked behind him once more. The barrier of immobile zombie bodies that Harran and Sherman had created prevented any further attack from the rear. The dwarf and warrior were catching their breath and eyed the bat things around them in suspicion. "Can you cancel your spell on my companions?" asked Kazin, indicating Zylor and Olag. He could have done it himself, but he wanted to gain the woman's trust.

The female spell caster wrinkled her nose. "Those creatures are your companions?"

Kazin grinned weakly as he shot a fireball at another bat thing. It shrieked into the depths below. Most of the others were holding their position, waiting for an opening. "Yes, they are, believe it or not. I assure you they won't hurt you."

The female spell caster looked doubtful.

"Look," said Kazin in exasperation, "I could give you all kinds of reasons why I trust them, but this isn't the time or the place. I want to get away from here as much as you do."

The spell caster blinked and nodded. "O.K." She thumbed over her shoulder at the throng of zombies that blocked their path. "Can you get through that?"

Kazin nodded and smiled. "If you release my friends, we'll do just that."

The spell caster nodded. She lifted her hand - she carried no staff - and chanted. Zylor and Olag, who were sitting, weak and exhausted, rose to their feet. Zylor strode forward and the spell caster tensed as the minotaur approached, glaring malevolently. She was prepared to cast a spell on him the instant he made any sudden movement, but he calmly squeezed by her, his weapon lowered. Once past, he growled and raised his battle axe. Then he charged into the throng of zombies. To everyone's astonishment, Zylor took one mere swing and a dozen zombies were thrown into the air. Pieces of them flew so hard and fast they took out a number of the bat things in the process. It was at this point that Kazin realized what had happened. He had assumed that his earlier spell to make Zylor stronger had been canceled, but it was still active because of the pendant the minotaur wore. It ensured that Kazin's spell remained in effect, even after the other spell caster had removed hers.

It took only moments for the minotaur to finish off the zombies. The end of the crosswalk was just beyond. Everyone hurried to the ledge where the golden door awaited. Olag took care of any bat things that ventured near with his arrows while Kazin opened the door. Everyone eagerly stepped through to the other side.

High above the combatants, a large, dark cloud coalesced and writhed in impotent fury as it watched the companions exit the area. For hundreds of years it had accumulated strength from the evil spirits of many of the dead beings in this forsaken place, and it had been poised to finally take control of the first figure to come along in many years. It was very close to succeeding when Kazin and his companions showed up to intervene. Startled by the untimely arrival so shortly after the arrival of the cloaked figure, the cloud had retreated high up and out of sight in the darkness to watch the outcome of the situation, and, seeing the newcomers drive back the zombies with tremendous effort and zeal, it realized too late that it would not escape this place this day. Silently, it vowed not to hesitate the next time. With great anger, it realized it might not see another time traveler for centuries to come, if ever. This only made it more determined to act the next time.

Outside, the bright sunlight was a stark contrast to the damp, dark fogginess of the time travel bridge and forced the companions to blink and squint to get used to it. The door disappeared behind them, so they examined their surroundings. They were at the edge of a mountain looking east at the rising sun. The wind was brisk and cold. The terrain below them was green and lush with pristine forested lands. The southern edge looked slightly more barren as the forest gave way to scrub brush. South, beyond that, was the beginning of a desert.

Harran was the first to speak. "Unless I miss my guess, we're on the eastern face of the Five Fingers Mountains."

"It's not where, but when that I'm more concerned about," said Kazin. "I can only hope my spell was accurate enough to send us back to the right time in our history."

"Why do you want to be in the past?" asked the female spell caster.

The others all turned to the stranger in unison.

"I'm sorry," said Kazin after a moment. "I guess we should introduce ourselves."

The stranger looked around at the companions. "I think I already know who you are - at least I know about you, but not your names."

"How so?" asked Sherman.

The spell caster turned to glance at the big warrior with penetrating blue eyes. "My father wrote about you. You're the 'Guardian'. Am I right?"

Sherman rolled his eyes. "Not that again."

The spell caster turned to Kazin. "And you're the dragon mage." She turned to the dwarf. "And the dwarf is 'the frozen axe'. I saw how your axe shattered the zombies. And the minotaur," she looked up at the towering beast, "is the 'head of horns.'" At last she regarded the skink warrior speculatively. "But you don't fit somehow."

"You said your father wrote about us," interrupted Kazin. "Did he by any chance write the 'Book of Prophesy'?"

The stranger nodded. "Yes. How did you know?"

"We met briefly," said Kazin with a distant look in his eye. "Once."

"Suppose you tell us your name," prodded Harran. "My name is Harran Mapmaker." He decided he liked the young spell caster.

The stranger held out her hand and smiled. "I'm Amelia."

As they shook hands, Harran introduced the others by name. Although nervous about the skink warrior, she shook his hand quickly and then wiped it off on her robe. As Kazin shook her hand, he studied Amelia's eyes and recognized something familiar about her but couldn't place it. He asked her what she was doing on the dangerous swing bridge.

"I asked you first," she said sweetly, her smile catching him off guard.

He decided to take her into his confidence even though Zylor glared at him for doing so. He gave a brief description of his quest and why they were on it, saying only that they hoped to undo what was causing the disappearances in the future.

Amelia's smile faded as he talked. "I see why you need to do something about it," she said when Kazin had finished. "I would try to do the same thing. As for myself, I was just going back to study some gaps in the histories that my father missed. Call it a bit of research, if you like. I know better than to interfere. I just observe from a distance. I've been time traveling for a number of years now."

"How do you know you haven't changed the course of history on one or more of your expeditions?" blurted Sherman. He looked at Kazin for support. "This could be the reason things are going wrong in your time!"

Kazin raised an eyebrow and regarded the spell caster. "That's a legitimate question, Amelia."

Amelia looked indignant. "I wouldn't chance a serious catastrophe like that! I have a magical safeguard to prevent such an occurrence! If anything, it's you who are the cause of the problem you now face!"

Kazin held up a hand to calm the spell caster. "Relax. I'm not trying to point a finger. If you say you're safe guarded against altering the time line, I believe you. We just have to keep our minds open to any possibilities, that's all."

Amelia's temper subsided. "Since you saved my life, and your quest is more important than my research, I'd like to repay you by helping you solve your problem."

Zylor growled. "There will be many dangers to face. We have no time to look after you as well."

Amelia glared at the minotaur. "I can take care of myself!"

"Like you did on the bridge?" leered the minotaur.

Amelia reddened. "I'd have gotten out of there eventually. You'll need me on this quest."

"What have you to offer?" asked Olag.

"I notice you don't have your healer with you," said Amelia. "I have the ability to heal using magic and herbs."

"Are you a cleric?" asked Sherman, referring to the white mages who had that magical ability.

Amelia shook her head. "No, not exactly. I also have some offensive magic."

"Like a grey mage?" asked Harran. Grey mages could do both offensive magic and defensive magic, but their magic was far weaker than either the black or white mages, who concentrated on only offensive or defensive magic respectively.

"Sort of," said Amelia vaguely. "But my magic is stronger."

Zylor sneered. "Likely story."

"I also have the one thing you need to avoid altering history," snapped the spell caster. "I have the orb of seeing." She withdrew a milky white orb from the pocket of her robe, the item barely the size of her palm. "This orb can determine if any object, living or inanimate, will impact the future, and whether interaction with said objects will change the course of history. All I have to do is visualize the object or person within the orb and it will tell me if an action concerning it will cause an imbalance." She looked at the companions defiantly. "And don't try to steal it from me. It works for me and only me!"

"Where did you get such an artifact?" asked Sherman. "Did you find it on one of your expeditions?" He was still suspicious of her.

"Of course not!" spat Amelia. "That would certainly change history! My father made it in conjunction with my mother."

"She was a spell caster too?" asked Harran.

"Yes," said Amelia proudly. "She was the most powerful spell caster in the history of the mermaids!"

"She was a mermaid?!" exclaimed Olag, aghast.

Amelia reddened. She had inadvertently given away a secret she had hidden from everyone else until now. Only she and her father knew. "Yes," she said meekly.

"That artifact, and your abilities, would certainly come in handy, Amelia," said Harran, looking at Kazin for confirmation.

Kazin nodded slowly. "Harran's right. I think our chance encounter was very fortuitous. I would be remiss not to have you along on this quest, Amelia."

Zylor grunted but did not argue. "You'll have to fend for yourself, mage."

Amelia stood her ground. "As long as I don't have to bail you out of trouble all the time."

Zylor laughed. "You have spirit. I'll give you that."

"Come on," said Kazin. "Let's break camp a little way from here where there's less exposure to the wind. We could all use a rest."

"Agreed," said Sherman.

"Follow me," said Harran. "I can see a way down to an area with decent cover." Dwarves were at home in the mountains. They were the most skilled at mountain navigation, both inside and out.

Within an hour they found a level area sheltered from the wind. It was a comfortable spot with plenty of dead brush available to make a fire. Not long after, a pot was boiling with fresh mountain water extracted from a nearby spring. Two rabbits were caught and killed in some nearby thickets thanks to Olag's expert bowmanship. Amelia warned them that to kill too many rabbits in this location could also alter the future but assured them it was safe to shoot a few here according to her orb.

Amelia made herself useful in preparing the meal and spicing it up with some local herbs that none of the others would even have thought of using. Her herbal skills were impressive as they sipped their stew.

"This is incredible!" exclaimed Sherman. "I've never imagined anything could taste so delicious from ordinary vegetation growing right around us like this!"

"I agree," said Harran. "The hill dwarves could learn a lesson from this." Hill dwarves were the ones who lived outside the mountain, while the ordinary dwarves lived inside the mountains.

"It's the least I can do for my rescuers," beamed Amelia. "Thanks again for getting me out of that predicament earlier. Your timing was perfect."

"Think nothing of it," said Kazin. "We would have done the same for anyone in those circumstances."

"Anyone?" asked Amelia, her eyes sharp.

"Yes," nodded Kazin. "Even those we consider enemies. Because if we didn't, they would have had their bodies taken over by spirits - who reside in the bodies of those zombies - and would do their best to rewrite history. They would use that individual's body to go back and save themselves from dying an untimely death and live instead, changing the course of history in the process."

"Good answer," said Amelia. "You understand the real danger on the bridge. The bat things try to knock you off the bridge merely to add souls to their collection. You would then become a zombie like the thousands of others that have had an untimely death. The zombies, on the other hand, try to take a fresh body and use it to go back in time to change the past so they don't die the untimely death in the first place. The bat things don't really care if the zombies succeed, because if the zombies save themselves, they can cause countless others to die untimely deaths because of history being rewritten. This gives the bat things even more spirits to control. The more malevolent the spirit, the more tenacious the zombie, the more deaths that spirit can cause if it prevents its own premature death and goes on killing in the real world."

"How does the zombie take over the new body?" asked Olag.

"Once it gets hold of the new body, the spirit residing within the zombie's body slips into the new host and drives out the living spirit within," answered Amelia. "Usually there is a battle for the host body, but the attacking spirit is powerful due to desperation, and the original spirit is unprepared for such an attack. It gets ejected and fed to the bat things, who give it a zombie body to inhabit for eternity, because it has received an untimely death."

Sherman shuddered. "That's not a fate I would want to endure."

"Me neither," said Harran.

"That's the price you could pay for wanting to go back in time," said Amelia. "You take a great chance if you want to alter things in the past."

After they had eaten, Kazin suggested they rest for a while as he needed to regain his strength before carrying on. He explained that traveling in the late evening was best since they would be less noticeable as he flew around in dragon form.

Amelia agreed, pointing out that if they were in the right time in history, dragons were known to be seen frequently and many villages had sentries watch for them in order to alert their archers and mages to spring to the defense of the city should one be spotted. Once near a city, they would be wise to land before being spotted, and then walk the rest of the way like ordinary travelers so as not to attract more attention.

Kazin agreed and found a comfortable spot to lie down. In minutes he was asleep.

Harran agreed to take the first watch and made his way a short distance back up the mountain so as to have a better vantage point. He chose a location where he could oversee the camp and any access points should an intruder come along.

Amelia volunteered to clear up the dishes and then climbed up to join the dwarf. She found him to be more amicable than the others and wanted to get to know him better. She sat down beside him on a moss-covered log and sat silently for a while. Then she broke the stillness - the wind had died down somewhat - and asked him about his name. "Harran, is your last name - Mapmaker - related to your career?"

Harran turned to regard the young spell caster. "It was. Several generations before me also had that name. We were gifted with an exceptional ability to make maps of the underground passages in the mountains. Our skill with map making was highly sought after by high-ranking dwarves. I was the king's personal mapmaker - a distinct honour among my people."

"You said 'was'," said Amelia. "Don't you make maps anymore?"

Harran chuckled. This girl was young but astute. "I do, but only as a hobby. I am the leader of my people now."

"What do they call you now?" asked Amelia.

"King Dracon."

"What does that mean?"

"It's short for 'dragon conch.' It's an artifact I acquired that, when blown, calls all dwarves within earshot to arms. It is powerful enough to break any spell any dwarf is under and rallies them to my side."

"So your name changes with your job," concluded Amelia.

Harran nodded. "My earlier ancestors were known as Tunnelmaker before we switched specialties and became Mapmakers."

"Do you have mapmakers that work for you now?" asked Amelia.

"Yes," said Harran. "One of my chief mapmakers is called Rebecca Mapmaker. She happens to have an uncanny ability to find gem deposits."

"That's interesting," mused Amelia. She lapsed into silence to digest this information.

They shared other stories for a few hours before Harran tensed and pointed into the distance. "Is that what I think it is?" he asked suddenly.

Amelia looked where he pointed and squinted. "Yes," she said finally. "That appears to be a dragon."

A moment later, the beast dove to an unknown destination and disappeared from view behind some trees. A few moments later it reappeared and flew around in a tight arc and descended again. Then it reappeared and repeated its tactic. After it rose from the treetops the next time, smoke could be seen rising after it. The dragon did not give up. It dove two more times before departing the scene. It appeared to have a large object in its mouth as it flew away. By now the black billows were rising from the forest floor.

"We should alert the others," said Harran, rising.

"One moment," interrupted Amelia. She took out her orb and concentrated. The milky surface swirled but Harran could not make any sense of the patterns and designs it emitted.

After a full minute of watching the orb, Amelia looked up at the dwarf and shook her head. "We won't be able to do anything about what just happened without altering things. It's best to let it be."

"I'll let Kazin decide that," growled the dwarf. He tromped down the mountainside.

Amelia got up and followed. She was surprised at the trust the dwarf had in the old mage. She concluded they must have been through a lot of adventures together.

The camp was aroused and Harran relayed what he had seen. Kazin looked across the forest below and could see what he was talking about. The black smoke was rising and blowing to the southeast. He listened with interest as Amelia told him what her orb had relayed to her. Then he nodded in satisfaction. "Amelia's right. We can't run to the aid of everyone who is in trouble like we are used to doing. It is not up to us to interfere, even though it feels wrong. That's going to be the hardest part of this quest. We are not supposed to be here, so we shouldn't intervene."

Sherman was about to object but Kazin raised his hand. "We can, however, investigate what happened and learn from it. We might even be able to offer minor assistance as long as it doesn't change history." He looked questioningly at Amelia, who nodded.

"I can determine in advance if that's acceptable. The orb has allowed me to do minor things before without incident."

"That settles it then," said Kazin. He glanced across at the smoke, which was not as black and billowing as before. "It would be safer to walk from here. I'll fly us down to the base of the mountain. The sun is on the other side of the mountain now, so we will be covered from being spotted by its shadow." He turned to Sherman. "How long do you figure it will take us to reach that village?"

The warrior squinted in the direction of the smoke. "I'd say we will arrive at sundown if we leave right away."

"Alright," said Kazin. "Let's pack up."

As the others went to collect their gear, Sherman came up to his old friend. "Kazin, can we talk a minute? Alone?"

"Sure," said Kazin. He led Sherman a short distance away. When he turned to the warrior, he was disturbed by the big man's agitated expression. "What is it?" he asked in concern.

"I - well," Sherman hesitated and looked down. Then he steeled himself and looked up into the old mage's blue eyes. "You're going to hate me."

"Why?" asked Kazin quietly.

Sherman slowly drew his sword from its scabbard and held it out for the mage to see.

"What is it?" asked Kazin, confused.

"Can't you see?" asked Sherman. His hand began to tremble. "It's the wrong one!"

It took a moment for Kazin to grasp what his friend was saying. Then it dawned on him. He bent closer to examine the weapon. It was indeed the wrong sword. "No!" he whispered in dismay. His eyes were wide as he looked into Sherman's face. "How is that possible?"

Sherman swallowed. "I don't know," he stammered. "I - I guess I was in such a rush to help you in this quest. I was excited. I didn't check to see if it was the right sword." He patted the scabbard at his side. "This is the right scabbard. Somehow the magical sword must have been switched with this one. I haven't used the magical sword in so long, I -," he broke off, helpless to continue.

Kazin let out a long sigh. "Well, it makes no difference now. You have what you have. We'll have to carry on without it. I only hope it isn't the object that is the cause of our troubles."

Sherman clenched his teeth in anger. "I should have noticed. The magical sword was lighter than this one. I should have noticed that right away." He shook his head.

"Don't beat yourself up about it, Sherman," said Kazin, seeing his friend's anguish. "You probably didn't notice because every sword feels light to you. With your strength, it's not a surprise. You could carry ten swords and they would all feel light to you. Besides, the hilt on this sword and the magical one both look very similar. I had to look closely to see it myself."

"But our quest could be a waste of time," lamented Sherman.

"It's not a waste of time," said Kazin sternly. "We have a lot of things to investigate before we call it quits. I still think it's someone, and not something, that is the cause of our trouble."

"It's probably me," muttered Sherman.

Kazin put a reassuring hand on Sherman's shoulder. "I seriously doubt that, Sherm. If anything, you're the one who's going to correct the problem."

Sherman smiled wanly.

While everyone was packing, Amelia pulled Harran aside. "Is Kazin going to transform into a dragon?"

Harran nodded and regarded the red-haired mage. He realized she had never experienced Kazin's transformation before. "Yes. It's a little intimidating at first." He paused. "Come to think of it, it's always a little intimidating. You never really get used to it."

"Are we going to - to ride him?" Amelia looked nervous.

The dwarf winked at her. "Don't worry. We won't let you fall off."

Amelia took a deep breath and looked over at the dragon mage who was conversing with the big warrior. "Oooh!" she said breathlessly.

Chapter 6

Sir Galado awoke with a pounding headache. He opened his eyes but everything was dark. Slowly, his eyes became accustomed to the dark and he noticed a faint glow on his right. It was the sword. Then everything came back to him in a flash.

He had been riding on the back of the griffin moving at incredible speed, the wind rushing loudly in his ears. The griffin had flown in a straight path, sure of its destination - or so he had hoped. After a few hours, they had reached the north shores of North Lake where the griffin had landed to give the soldier a break to rest and eat. Then they had been off again. From the air, the lake had seemed to stretch on forever. After another several hours, the griffin had shrieked, causing the dozing Galado to look ahead. In the distance, he could vaguely make out the form of a dragon as it dove straight down toward the surface of the lake. Then it had vanished from sight. Since Kazin was the only known dragon mage of his time, Sir Galado had assumed it was he and Sherman who were the ones who had gone down. The griffin never slowed until it reached the spot where the dragon had last been seen. It had then begun circling the area where the dragon had gone down. Below, Sir Galado could make out a giant whirlpool. It swirled with tremendous force, drawing in the surrounding water into ever faster spirals until it vanished in its center. He had wondered at the sheer size of the whirlpool. How the lake had managed to retain its water level with this whirlpool sucking so much of it away was beyond him. The griffin had then circled closer to the whirlpool where Galado could hear it rumbling like an angry beast. How could anyone - including Kazin in his dragon form - possibly survive such a force of nature without getting crushed? He had suddenly realized his mission was a failure. He had been too late. There was no way he could reach Sherman now.

He had looked at the sword safely strapped to his side and had moved to straighten it on his hip. A sudden movement by the griffin had caught him unawares and Sir Galado lost his hold on the great beast. Helpless, he had fallen toward the hungry whirlpool. The griffin had given one last cry - barely audible above the roar of the whirlpool - before Sir Galado plunged into its depths. Then everything had gone black.

Now, he looked around using the faint light of the sword, thankful he was still miraculously alive. There was nothing but darkness on all sides. He reached into his pack, which was half slung over one arm and soaking wet from the water, while, amazingly, his clothing was dry. After a brief search in the faint light from the light of the sword, he withdrew some wildhorn leaves. They were called that because each wildhorn plant consisted of two leaves curved up like a minotaur's horns. These plants were unique in that they allowed anyone who ate them to temporarily see better in the dark. They were poisonous if too many were ingested at once, and the elves - whose eyesight was already very good - could not tolerate them at all. Any elf who ate these leaves could go blind with just a few.

Moments after eating some of the leaves, Sir Galado could sense, more than see, that his eyesight had sharpened. But it was still dark.

"Now what?" he muttered. He rubbed the back of his head and felt a large welt where he had obviously bumped it against something. He rose unsteadily to his feet and looked at the floor, but could not see what it was made of. It was smooth and dark, and the light from his sword would not reflect off it. As he moved his sword around to see his immediate vicinity, he noticed it went slightly brighter when he held it off to one side. It would go dimmer when he swung it in a different direction. Electing to use that as a guide, he moved forward slowly in the direction in which the sword gave off the most light.

He walked for a good twenty minutes in this way and finally came to a door set in a frame in the middle of nowhere. Sir Galado examined the door closely and examined the inscriptions across the top on both sides. The warnings made the hair on the back of his neck stand on end. Should he open it? The side indicating the past was likely the side Sherman would have used. The big warrior had said he was going back in time. Sir Galado looked behind him uncertainly but knew he could not go back. He couldn't stay in this dark place forever either. He had no choice but to carry on, and that meant to step through the door to the past. He could only hope he would wind up where Sherman had gone.

He cautiously approached the door and grasped the knob. It was stuck. He tried harder to turn the knob and was about to give up when the sword in his free hand flashed. With sudden ease, the knob turned and the door swung open. Cautiously, Sir Galado stepped through.

It was lighter here, kind of white and foggy. The ledge was small and two posts beckoned to one side. The posts led to a swinging bridge that swayed in some unseen breeze. The creaking noise it made was a little unnerving, but Sir Galado was not fearful. He had encountered such things previously in his lifetime. What did cause him fear was the obviously magical aura of this place. He didn't like magic because of what it had done to those he cared for. To him, it was a force of evil. Nevertheless, he had to cross the bridge. He glanced back and noticed the door had vanished. Brushing aside any foreboding feelings, he stepped onto the bridge.

The silence was broken two or three times by an eerie shriek, but Sir Galado kept going. He didn't want to tarry here any longer than necessary. He was a good three quarters of the way across when he stumbled over a broken slat. It snapped off the rest of the way with a loud 'crack' and then all hell broke loose. Black bat things dove down on him and threatened to knock him over the rope railing of the swing bridge. The bridge shook with approaching footsteps and some zombies appeared from beyond the mist like some hideous apparitions.

Before they got close, a dark cloud swung down toward the man. To the cloud, this was almost too fortuitous to comprehend. Here was the opportunity it had been waiting for! Without thinking about it, the cloud dove toward the man, hoping to take control of the man and control the body for its own nefarious ends. But the cloud had missed examining the man for magical energy, otherwise it would have noticed that the sword the man wielded was created from a powerful magic. As it closed on the man, the cloud was inextricably drawn into the tip of the sword, where it was absorbed without resistance.

As the cloud encountered the good spirits housed within, it clashed with the good magic. The sword swirled as the balance of good and evil fought for dominance. To Galado, with his limited experience and understanding of magic, the sword was reacting magically to the danger he now faced.

The zombies were now nearly upon him, and further contemplation of the sword was removed from Galado's mind. He swung the magical sword easily, striking several bat things before having to contend with the approaching zombies. As his sword struck each of the zombies, a shadowy wisp of light emerged from the falling bodies to be drawn into the sword's edge. These auras added to the dark portion of the sword's swirling colours, making the sword coalesce with more darkness than light.

Seeing this enraged the bat things and threw them into a frenzy. The spirits under their control were being stolen one by one and drawn into Sir Galado's sword! They attacked the hapless soldier with such vehemence he had to retreat. As he backed away from the approaching throng on the bridge and the aerial foes, he didn't notice the lone zombie who approached from the destination side of the bridge. It quietly laid a hand on the soldier's shoulder and squeezed with incredible strength until it drew blood. Sir Galado opened his mouth in agony but no sound came out. The zombie moaned and released its spirit into the soldier's open mouth as its old host body collapsed. Sir Galado's mind exploded into a thousand tiny lights as the spirit fought him for control of his body. He mindlessly thrashed about with his sword, taking down two more bat things and drawing the spirits from several more zombies into his sword in the process.

Suddenly his body convulsed, and he turned with renewed energy to face the end of the crosswalk which was not far away. Nothing stood between him and the door. With super human strength, he bounded toward the doorway with incredible speed. As he yanked the door open, he could hear the shrieks and cries of dismay behind him. The sounds stopped abruptly as he stepped through the opening and slammed the door after him.

The daylight was blinding and it took a good five minutes for his eyes to adjust. He squinted at his surroundings. There was a low valley before him with some scrub brush dotting the landscape. He didn't know where he was but didn't care. He took a deep breath and let it out again. He had forgotten what it was like to breathe fresh air. Sir Galado's mouth twisted into a distorted smile. He was alive again! It was now time to go and stop his untimely demise from taking place! With an insane laugh, Sir Galado bounded down into the valley.

No sooner had he gone a short distance when there was a deep rumble beneath him and the ground shook. He staggered to a halt and fell to his knees as an earthquake of significant proportions caused him to become unsteady. It lasted a good full minute before the quaking stopped. When it had subsided, he rose back to his feet and charged ahead again. But once again, his gait became unsteady and he tumbled headlong onto the ground. This time it was not a result of an earthquake. After he rolled to a stop, he sat up groggily and shook his head. Galado wondered what was going on. Where were all these strange thoughts coming from? Why was -? The world spun and he fell to his back as a sudden dizziness swept over him. A crooked grin appeared on his face again and a laugh that was not his own emanated from his lips.

At the same time, an earthquake rumbled across the valley.

Chapter 7

rch Mage Gresham looked around at the drawn faces of the high-ranking mages around him. Sleep appeared to have abandoned everyone these days. The war was taking its toll on them all and there seemed to be no end in sight. They needed an advantage that would give them an edge. Something they could have that the enemy could not steal, buy, or duplicate. New magical items and inventions only lasted for a while before they were taken from the dead soldiers and used against those who had created them. If the item was particularly potent, it was studied by the enemy mages and duplicated or modified for their own purposes. Most of the magical items eventually came up against a powerful spell caster from either side, who used their magic to neutralize the weapon or shield. This resulted in an overconfident maneuver by the one wielding the magical item, only to discover its magic had failed. This often resulted in fatality, since the magic was no longer there to be relied upon. With the weapon, helmet or shield neutralized, they were no different from ordinary soldiers.

Magical rings, it turned out, were the most potent weapons. Giving the wearer super human strength, accuracy, courage, or speed, rings were the most practical invention for the battlefield. Enemy mages had a more difficult time stopping the advance of someone with magical enhancement generated by rings than any other form of magic. It was harder to isolate a ring-wearer than a magical weapon wielder. To confuse the enemy, the Black Tower mages handed out hundreds of identical rings to every soldier. Some contained magic, but most did not. The enemy could not tell the magically enhanced soldiers from the ordinary ones by just a glance at their fingers. They had to watch each soldier very carefully to ascertain who was magically enhanced. More often than not they used neutralizing magic to neutralize a soldier, only discover the soldier never wielded magic. This waste of magic was a strain on their own magical reserves.

Arch Mage Gresham sighed and removed his pointed dark blue hat. It was creased from continuous use and the tip was bent. He scratched his head with other hand and patted down his black wavy hair. He put his hat back on and cleared his throat. When he opened his mouth to speak, a hammering noise from somewhere within the building interrupted him. He waited until the noise stopped and proceeded to speak.

"The enemy has been pushed back for now. We have control of the west bank of the Jackal River again. However, I think it's premature to celebrate. They keep coming up with more creatures to drive us back again. The various roving bands are beginning to join together into one force under the command of a powerful warlock. It's still unknown who or what he is, but he seems to be rallying all of our enemies under one banner."

"At least he hasn't got the support of the dragons," said a female voice. It was the voice of Arch Mage Penna, second in command next to Gresham. She was a middle-aged woman with brown hair and penetrating pale blue eyes.

"Yet," muttered another mage. It was Arch Mage Toele.

Mutters echoed around the table as another round of hammering emphasized the point.

When the hammering ceased, another arch mage piped up, "My work with orb development is looking promising. We are another step closer to harnessing the dragon's life force."

"What will that accomplish, Brendan?" scoffed Toele. He was an older mage with grey hair and a long grey beard. His wrinkled face gave his sour disposition an almost cruel look.

Brendan frowned. He did not like Toele, and didn't need to prove himself to the older man. Toele had a tendency to look down upon the younger mages among them.

"Go ahead," urged Gresham. "I think we'd all like to hear of your progress with the orbs." He gave Toele a withering stare and the old mage leaned back and raised his hand in a mock gesture of defeat.

Brendan shook off his anger and let his enthusiasm for his project take over. "We were able to successfully turn away a dragon that was intent upon razing a town to the south. It was just preparing to fry some cattle in a pasture when my associate held up the orb and cast the spell we had devised. The dragon lost its train of thought and failed to emit its fiery breath. Furthermore, it lost altitude and crashed into the ground!"

"Did you capture it?" asked another mage. It was Arch Mage Violet. She was a younger arch mage with blonde hair and blue eyes. She was very interested in Brendan's project and Brendan was more than happy to receive attention from the attractive mage. He was himself handsome to the ladies with light brown hair and large brown eyes. He smiled, revealing perfect white teeth.

"No. Unfortunately, the crash landing of the dragon caused my associate to lose his balance and he fell, dropping the orb and losing his concentration on the spell. The dragon regained its composure and flew away. It didn't return. The farmer was very relieved, and invited my associate to a celebratory feast in his honour."

"It sounds like you were able to at least distract the dragon," said Penna.

"But do you really think the orb can control a dragon?" asked another arch mage. It was Arch Mage Belham, a chubby, balding man with a jolly disposition, especially when food was present.

"I do," said Brendan resolutely. "It's only a matter of time before we capture a dragon. We just have to establish a bond between the dragon and the orb."

"I think I may spend some time working with you on this project," said Gresham. "There may be a way to link the dragon to the mage via the orb, rather than to the orb itself."

Brendan blinked. "I hadn't thought of that." He recovered quickly. "I appreciate any assistance I can get."

Gresham smiled. "Very well. We'll let Violet help you as well. She has come up with unique ideas in the past. With both of you on the same project, you may make headway more quickly."

Brendan blushed and Violet smiled.

Gresham turned to Arch Mage Belham. "How goes the ring production?"

Belham smiled. "Very well. We are churning out more magical rings than ever. Soldiers are lining up in droves to obtain one."

"Is it still effective in confusing the enemy?" asked Gresham.

Belham laughed. "You bet! The generals that have returned from the front say they have seen enemy creatures stealing rings from the dead, thinking they are all magical. When they do come across one with magical enhancement, they tend to fight one another for it. It distracts them from the fight and makes them an easy target for our soldiers. It's probably the reason for our recent successful engagement."

"Very good," nodded Gresham. He turned to Toele. "How is the magical weapon production coming, Toele?"

The old mage straightened as though he were elsewhere with his thoughts. "What? Oh, yes. The magical weapons are coming along, but slowly. It doesn't help that the caravans of goods from the Dwarven Mountains are frequently being attacked by roving bands of ogres. As most of you are aware, the dwarven convoys must pass through ogre territory to reach us. This requires increased numbers of security escorts to protect them. Although we have offered assistance in this area, the dwarves have declined to accept our help. It is a matter of honour to them to protect their own convoys. Our assistance would shame them into looking like they can't deal with the problem themselves. Despite this, most of the dwarven crafted weapons are still backordered anyhow. Apparently, King Hammarschist wants more gold. Again. If he keeps increasing his prices, we'll be broke before the war ends."

"Can't we manufacture the weapons ourselves, or obtain them from somewhere else?" asked Arch Mage Penna.

Toele shook his head. "Our weapons are not crafted with the same quality as the dwarven ones. As a result, most of the time our weapons are not capable of retaining magic. It takes a fair amount of magical effort to endow a weapon with magic. If the weapon is too impure, we are just wasting our time and energy. The magic will just not be absorbed. As for other weapons, the ones of elven manufacture would work, but they take longer to order because the elves are so far away.

Moreover, they don't generally manufacture very many from high quality tempered steel. They prefer to manufacture and use bows. We still have a number of bows to endow with magic, and another shipment will be arriving soon. The one disadvantage is that magic on wooden weapons fades over time. The only wooden weapons that retain magic indefinitely are the ones made from ancient trees, usually more than two hundred years old. The elves refuse to sell weapons of that grade since they consider such trees to be sacred."

"That's why we have to recharge our staves from time to time," finished Arch Mage Gresham.

Toele nodded. "Correct."

"Very well," said Gresham. He looked around at the assembly. "Is there any other business to discuss?"

"When is the construction of the tower going to be completed?" asked another arch mage.

"There is still a long way to go," sighed Gresham. "We keep having to stop work to fend off dragon attacks. The interruptions are causing inconveniences with the work crews, but the delays are unavoidable." Gresham smiled grimly. "But once the tower is complete, the magical shield we set around it will repel any dragon attack. We will finally be able to work in safety." As he finished talking, the hammering noise resounded around them again. "Meeting adjourned!" yelled Gresham above the din.

✗　　✗　　✗　　✗　　✗

The warlock surveyed his army as he stood in front of his tent. Black, brown and drab coloured tents and shelters dotted the valley below him, interspersed with smoke and flames from cooking fires. A kind of mood emanated from the valley, a mix of anticipation, anger, revenge, and bloodlust. The assemblage consisted primarily of orcs and goblins, disgruntled human mercenaries, and lizardmen. More of their kind joined them daily, desiring the spoils of war and other benefits associated with the battle. A size of this gathering was more expensive for the human enemies they faced than for the warlock. It was fortunate that the orcs and goblins relished the taste of human flesh, and if there was not enough to go around, they would eat the corpses of their own kind who had fallen in battle. The warlock made sure to allow them the spoils of war to keep up morale. Besides, he was not interested in those things. What was important to him were power and success. The failure of the past few days irked him, but he was patient. The further west his forces were pushed, the further the humans were from their home bases. This stretched their supply lines to their limits. He could only hope that the ogres to the north would strike those supply lines soon, thereby cutting off the advancing forces of humans.

He clenched his teeth angrily. Why did the ogres have to operate independently? Why couldn't they join forces with him? But he knew they weren't intelligent enough to see that if he could coordinate their forces to move in unison with his own, he would be able to secure a victory that would benefit everyone. Even the smallest ogre was five times as powerful as a human, and one ogre armed with a club or mace could easily compensate for a well-armed human wearing a ring of strength. They were nearly twice the size of a human and built far more solidly. The warlord chuckled. So were their skulls. There wasn't much room for a brain. So far, his calls to meet with the ogre chieftain had gone unanswered. Still, he would continue to try. Eventually he had to get through the chieftain's nut of a skull.

Roving bands of trolls to the south were causing havoc with the humans as well, but those isolated raids were minor compared to what they were truly capable of. If only he could find their leader, if indeed there was one. He could turn them into a force to be reckoned with.

Another force the warlock was trying to rally to his side was the minotaurs. They had long had tensions with the dwarves, and were always looking for an excuse to go to battle. They loved to fight, perhaps more than any other race the warlock knew. They were just as big as the ogres, and fought with ten times more ferocity. They were also more intelligent. Their society was more structured than the rabble he now controlled. To have them join him would be a boon to his entire army. But they were east of the entire human colony. They were so far east, in fact, that they were on the other side of some impenetrable terrain. Separating them from the humans was a low

71

jagged mountain range with gaseous vents that were unbreatheable to any who ventured too near, and a vast swampland that was virtually impassable. Any who ventured into this area rarely returned, and stories of what survivors had encountered bordered on the absurd and ridiculous, with stories of strange creatures to hallucinations and visions. To get to the humans, the minotaurs would either have to send a fleet of ships south into the Bay of Barlin, where elven and human patrols abounded, or circle north through a pass in the mountains patrolled by giants similar to humans. Then they would have to travel over a cave-riddled mountain range inhabited by the dwarves, right into the dense forested section just south of the mountains where the ogres were encamped. This meant the warlock had to have the ogres on board first, because otherwise they would regard the minotaurs as a threat encroaching on their territory. They would surely come to blows unless they had a common goal.

The warlock sighed and looked up into the sky. It was a dying shade of red as the sun faded, giving way to the moon and stars. From above was where this war would be decided. Whoever could get the aid of those infernal dragons would have the winning hand. He knew the humans were trying just as hard as he to control them. Whether they became allies or served him by some other means, victory would be his. He would gladly offer up his army as an offering to them for his victory. They could feast on all the combatants from both sides for all he cared. Too bad they didn't like the taste of orcs and goblins.

A servant came out of the tent to contact the warlock. It was a creature half orc and half goblin. It had all the physical characteristics of an orc but the mind and attitude of a cowardly goblin. "Sir, the commanders are waiting."

The warlock turned to him with a scowl. "I know that! I'll be there when I'm ready!"

"But - what should I tell them, Sir?" asked the servant fearfully.

"I'll be right there," snapped the warlock, and waved him away.

"Yes, Sir," answered the servant, who quickly disappeared back into the tent.

The warlock waited a few more minutes and then followed.

The tent was large and was sectioned off in several places. The front portion was fairly wide and had a table adorned with a map of the region. Seated around the table were various commanders of the forces in the valley below. There were four lizardmen commanders, three orc commanders, two goblin commanders, and one human mercenary commander. They all looked up as the warlock entered. To them he appeared large and intimidating. He was a good six and a half feet tall, with wide shoulders and muscular limbs. His facial features were rugged, with a long, pinched nose, an ugly scar on his right cheek, and eyes that were deep and black. His mouth was drawn in a scowl that left creases on his face which enhanced his dour expression. He had a black mustache and goatee, which he often stroked when deep in thought. His commanders knew better than to interrupt him when he did this.

The warlock looked around the torch-lit room and waited as each commander saluted him. Then he sat at the table's head and folded his hands on the table.

"So, gentlemen," he began, "what is the latest report?"

"The squabbles among my forces have subsided," said one orc. He wiped his hand across his mouth as some spittle escaped his deformed face. He had the wide mouth of an orc, and his two bottom fangs pointed up at an angle, but his face hung at one side, evidence of an old battle scar. "The magical rings we recovered have been distributed by lot. Those who have one in their possession will keep them as long as they live, and are banned from acquiring more."

"Good," said the warlock. He looked at the others. "Has this worked for the rest of you?"

"Yes," responded the commanders in unison.

"Good," repeated the warlock. "We will use this method after each battle."

"I still think the higher-ranking commanders should be entitled to one outright," objected a goblin commander. He was particularly dark green for a goblin, and his pointed ears protruded from a shiny brass helmet undoubtedly acquired from the latest skirmish. The warlock found it odd that the creature could find a helmet that actually fit its tiny head.

"The lot determines who will own one," stated the warlock sternly. "You have to lead by example."

The goblin looked down but said nothing further.

"Has anyone discovered an easier way to identify magical ring wearers?" asked the warlock.

"We are still working on that," said a lizardman commander. "We hope to have found a spell capable of doing that soon."

The warlock frowned. "Well, keep trying. It's important that we find a solution."

"Yes, Sir," said the lizardman.

"Our attempts to lure the dragons into the battle continue," interjected another lizardman.

"And?" asked the warlock.

"We have established a dialogue with one of the dragons, but there is no interest yet."

"We must convince them it's for their own good at all costs," insisted the warlock. "Use whatever means necessary to get them to see things our way."

The lizardman commander nodded. "We're trying."

"Well, try harder!" snapped the warlock.

"Yes, Sir."

"There is news of an approaching horde of cyclops," said the mercenary commander. "They come from the northwest. We don't know their intentions yet. The scouts were fearful of approaching them."

The warlock smiled wickedly. He had almost forgotten about the one-eyed creatures. Their ability to paralyze their prey by convincing them to look into their eye was legendary. "I suspect they want to join the party. When they arrive, tell their leader I would like to see him personally." He paused, and then added, "Tell your men that whoever takes on this task will be rewarded with a magical ring."

"I thought you said the lot determined who got to have a magical ring?" growled the goblin commander from earlier.

The warlock looked at the goblin with a gleam in his eye. "Then now you have your chance to get one without waiting for your name to be drawn."

The goblin looked away.

"Shall I cast a spell on you to remain impervious to the cyclops' gaze?" offered a lizardman commander.

"That's not necessary," said the warlock. "That kind of magic is at my disposal." He knew this irritated the lizardmen. He liked to keep them guessing as to his magical ability and prowess. He also wouldn't dare to let one of those creatures cast a spell on him if he could help it.

"We should keep their army slightly separate from ours," cautioned the mercenary. "Otherwise they could paralyze our people by accident."

"Agreed," nodded the warlock. The others nodded in agreement.

At this point the warlock pointed to the map on the table before them. "Here is the location of the human army. As you can see, they are well fortified. What we have to do is force them away from that location to come after us." He pointed to another spot on the map. "We can lure them into this valley north of Boot Plateau. It is bordered by a cliff face one side and a forest on the other. There they will be in a prime position to be ambushed. We should move the lizardmen into the cliffs to attack long range with magic. Mulder," continued the warlock, referring to the mercenary commander, "you will position your men in the forest to prevent the humans from retreating into the forest for cover. You can use the cyclops contingent to catch them off guard and paralyze them so your men will have an easy kill."

"Provided the cyclops chief agrees to this," interrupted Mulder.

"I'll be persuasive," said the warlock with a cruel grin. "Just leave that to me."

Mulder nodded.

"I'll also give you one contingent of lizardmen to hold back their mages and make them wary of entering the forest," continued the warlock.

"I suppose we get to be the ones who have to lure the humans into the valley," said an orc commander sullenly. "Why do we always have to take the brunt of the attack?"

The warlock smiled beguilingly. "Because your forces are the only ones who can handle such a task. Your race is slightly bigger and stronger than the humans. Can you imagine how long the lizardmen or mercenaries would last if I made them do it? We would be defeated in a matter of hours!"

The lizardmen hissed in anger and Mulder frowned. The orc commanders grinned at this compliment and the warlock smiled inwardly. His comment had the desired effect. A goblin commander giggled.

"Besides," added the warlock, "you'll have the help of the goblins. How could you lose?"

The goblin winced and the orc commanders snorted. "How indeed," muttered one.

"When do we get started?" asked one of the lizardmen commanders.

The warlock smiled. "Your enthusiasm is delightful, Saliss. We will start moving first thing in the morning. Have your scouts sent out immediately to find the best areas from which to attack."

Everyone nodded.

"If you have any questions, ask now or wait until we move out," said the warlock.

No one said anything so the warlock dismissed them. When they had left, he called for his servant. "Gorc! Gorc!"

The goblin-orc appeared at a shambling run. "Yes, Sir?"

"See to it I am not disturbed until the arrival of the cyclops leader."

"Yes, Sir," said Gorc. "Shall I post sentries?"

"Of course!" snapped the warlock.

"Yes, Sir!" said Gorc, saluting. He hurriedly left the room.

The warlock entered an inner chamber and picked up one of several scrolls from a small table with a candle perched in an ornate holder. In the flickering light he opened it and scanned its contents. His eyes narrowed as he read. "If only I could have more time to study these scrolls," he mumbled. "Once I master this magic, I would be invincible! An army of undead would be unstoppable!" He blinked distractedly. "What if I could revive a dragon?"

A cruel grin spread across his face.

Chapter 8

he air was rather cool due to the mountains behind them cutting off the setting sun and casting longer and longer shadows over the forest. The companions bundled up with whatever extra clothing they had with them and increased their pace. It was just beginning to get dark when they caught a whiff of the smoke from the dragon attack.

Kazin halted the group and looked around at them uncertainly. "I almost forgot we're in elven territory. They don't generally like strangers in their lands."

Sherman looked around warily. "I'm surprised the elven patrols haven't found us by now."

"They probably have," muttered Harran, fingering his axe nervously. "They just haven't shown themselves yet."

"I don't think so," said Amelia quietly. She had pulled out her orb and was looking at it intently. "There is no one nearby, anyhow."

"The orb can tell you that?" asked Olag.

Amelia nodded.

"They may have gone to help the villagers when the dragon struck," suggested Zylor. "They likely have their hands full."

"I suspect you're right, Zylor," said Kazin. "But we can't take any chances. I'll have to change your appearance for a while."

Zylor nodded and held up his amulet which hung around his neck. "I figured you would say that."

Kazin got ready to cast a spell on Zylor to change him into a human when an idea struck him. "You know, it would probably be a good idea to change you into an elf instead. None of us are elves, and the villagers might be really suspicious about a group of strangers barging into their midst without an elf escort."

"Good idea," said Harran.

"Too bad we all couldn't look like elves," commented Sherman. "Even one of us not being an elf would attract too much attention in my opinion."

Kazin thought about that for a moment. Then he brightened. "It's doable."

"How so?" asked Amelia.

"It's easy," said Kazin. "I'll transform Zylor first. His amulet will maintain the spell for as long as he wears it or until he uses his weapon in combat."

"Don't forget my shadow," interrupted Zylor.

"That's right," nodded Kazin. "Zylor's shadow will still be his real shadow, so it's best that he stays away from the light."

"That takes care of one of us," said Amelia.

"Sherman has the invisibility ring," continued Kazin. "We won't have to worry about him."

"Good idea," said Sherman. "That way I can keep an eye on everyone without being seen."

"What about the rest of us?" asked Amelia.

"I can cast magic on us to make us look like elves," said Kazin. "Just stay relatively close to me so it's not so hard to maintain the spells."

"But -," stammered Amelia, "that spell can only be cast on one individual at a time. There are four of us left - you, me, Harran and Olag. You can't cast all four spells at once and maintain them too!" She paused and added, "Can you?"

Kazin smiled and bowed. "I can and I will."

Amelia's mouth dropped. She was too speechless to respond. A mage capable of casting four spells simultaneously was unheard of. She was impressed when the mage had transformed into a dragon and flown the group to the base of the mountain. Now he was about to perform another seemingly impossible feat - four spells simultaneously. Casting two spells at once was common, and three was not uncommon. But four? Amelia had newfound respect for this old mage. She wondered what he had looked like when he was younger. She would make a point of inquiring about that in her orb.

When everyone was ready, Kazin began. First, he changed Zylor into an elf. Then he let go of the spell and the amulet retained the minotaur's newly created image. Then the mage transformed Harran, Olag, and Amelia. The orb atop his staff flared brightly. Then he transformed himself, and his staff and orb were replaced by a bow.

"We can't have my staff blinding everyone when we enter the village," explained the mage.

"That wouldn't do," agreed Harran. He was a small stocky elf and could easily pass for an adolescent. He scratched his bare chin self-consciously. "It even feels like my beard is gone."

Sherman chuckled. "Good thing, too. I can't even imagine an elf with a beard."

Amelia giggled. "That would be funny."

"Alright," interrupted Kazin. "Let's get going. I suggest someone else does most of the talking. I've got my hands full."

Sherman could tell from his friend's voice that he was under some strain from the spells. He popped on his invisibility ring and disappeared from view. "Follow me."

"Uh," blurted Olag. "How do you propose we do that?"

Sherman reappeared a few feet away. "Sorry," he said sheepishly. "I guess someone else has to lead the way from here on in."

Amelia giggled again and the others chuckled.

Zylor shook his head. "I'll do it." He trudged off into the bush with Harran and Olag behind him. Kazin followed. As he passed Sherman, he patted him on the shoulder. "I'm glad you're watching our backs. Be on the lookout for anyone who might be paying extra close attention to us."

Sherman nodded. He waited until Amelia had passed and put his ring back on. Then he waited a few moments to see if anyone was following them without their knowledge. Amelia's orb had told her the area was clear, but he wanted to confirm it for himself. Once he had confirmed the orb was correct, he stealthily stepped into the forest after his friends.

As the companions stepped into the village, they were surprised to see most of the villagers calmly clearing debris in the torchlight, while others went around offering food and water to those who worked. In fact, most of the debris had already been care of. No one seemed overly excited or stressed. It was as if they dealt with dragon attacks on a regular basis. It occurred to them that with dragons being common in this era, dragon attacks were commonplace as well.

Most villagers who saw them didn't give them a second glance, but one who appeared to be in charge came up to them.

He lowered his hood, revealing a youthful face and pointed ears. He gave them a faint smile. "Welcome travelers. My name is Brand. I'm the mayor of this village. We've just about finished cleaning up from a dragon attack earlier today. As it happens, you're in luck. The inn is unscathed and there are some rooms available should you require any." His accent was a little difficult to understand, so Amelia elected to speak for them. "Thank you. We have traveled far today. We could use a rest."

Brand nodded. "Right this way, then." He led them to a building that was built tightly between a group of trees. As they passed through the front doors, the smell of cooking and the light of the fireplace made them immediately feel at ease. The room was cozy compared to the cool evening outside.

"Please make yourselves comfortable," said Brand. "Forgive me," he added, "but I have to oversee the cleanup. Perhaps we can talk later." With a nod and a smile, he left them.

Tables were situated every few feet and were various lengths. The group chose one capable of holding six people and sat down. Zylor and Harran sat at one end facing each other. Olag sat in the middle and Kazin sat next to him. Amelia sat beside the dwarf.

"Someone mind pulling a chair out for me?" murmured a deep voice quietly.

Amelia jumped. She had forgotten Sherman was invisible. She pulled a chair back and it creaked as the big warrior sat down on it.

"Anyone interested in having an ancient meal before bed?" jested Kazin.

Harran groaned. "I was, until you reminded me about the 'ancient' part."

"It's perfectly safe to eat," assured Amelia. "Some of the older dishes are rather tasty."

"I take it you've eaten in the past before?" guessed Zylor.

"That's right," said the young spell caster. "I've found that eating locally prepared food doesn't seem to affect the future. It's the amount of gold you pay for it that is more likely to be a problem."

"Speaking of which," added Olag, "who's buying? I have no currency."

"I had anticipated that," said Kazin. His voice was less tense as he got used to maintaining his spells, but the strain was still evident. He pulled a pouch from his cloak and tossed it on the table. "That should cover our costs, and then some."

"Maybe we should just find some rooms and get some rest," suggested Amelia. She didn't like the idea of Kazin straining himself while they ate.

He shook his head. "No. We need to eat. I can hold these spells all night if I have to."

Olag hefted the sack of coins. "What if our gold runs out before our quest is finished?"

Zylor snatched the bag from his hands and tossed it to Harran. "It won't if we find someone responsible to handle it," he growled.

Olag looked hurt by the insult.

"But what if he's right?" asked Sherman as quietly as he could. Although the inn appeared to be empty save the elf at the counter, he wasn't going to take any chances.

Kazin shook his head. "We won't run out. The sack is magical."

Harran looked at the sack in his hands incredulously, his eyes wide. "You mean - the sack is one of those ones that never runs out of coins?"

"Precisely," said Kazin. "And don't ask me where I got it."

"Shhh!" shushed Amelia as she held a finger to her lips. "Not so loud! The waitress is coming!"

"Don't forget to order for me," whispered Sherman in Amelia's ear. She jumped but said nothing.

The waitress was an attractive young elf with chestnut brown hair. "Good evening. Are you all interested in dinner?"

"Yes," said Amelia. "What do you recommend?"

The waitress smiled. She rattled off a list of several choices and they ordered. Sherman squeezed Amelia's arm to indicate his choice and she ordered the larger portion. The waitress was surprised that Amelia wanted so much but didn't argue.

Then she asked with a wide smile if anyone wanted some milk beforehand to whet the appetite. Olag almost gagged at the suggestion and Harran winced. "We don't often offer it on our menu," added the waitress, "but a shipment has recently arrived from the human settlements to the north." The elves had never experienced milk from cows until the human settlers had arrived. It was considered a special treat for them.

"I'll have one," said Amelia. She didn't want the waitress to think they were strange.

"Me too," said Kazin. He gave Amelia a thankful look.

"I'm in the mood for a dwarven ale," said Harran.

"Me too," said Zylor.

"Same," said Olag.

Amelia felt the squeeze on her arm. She hesitated but Kazin knew what was up. "I'll have an ale as well," he stated.

The waitress looked at him curiously. "Instead of milk?"

Kazin smiled. "I'll still have the milk. Who can resist? But an ale for afterward sounds refreshing."

The waitress grinned, satisfied, and left for the kitchen.

"I've heard of tales about such an artifact," whispered Harran as he jiggled the sack. "But until now I've never really believed it existed."

"It's not something anyone would want to create," said Kazin.

"Why not?" asked Olag. "I would think it's something everyone would want to have."

"When part of the spell used to create it requires the death of the spell caster him or herself?" asked the old mage in elven disguise.

Amelia gasped. "Is that true? Someone died to create the sack?"

Kazin nodded.

"Why?" she pressed. "What could it possibly benefit him to give his life to make the sack? He wouldn't be able to spend it."

Kazin nodded. "From what I was told when I was in training in the Tower of Sorcery, a mage took it upon himself to try to create the sack anyway, thinking he could avert death in the process by adding some spell components and some necromancy magic. In theory, his spell modifications were foolproof. So when he was ready, he performed the spell in secrecy. He succeeded - partially. The sack was created, and he lived. For three days he boasted, spending his gold flippantly wherever he went. Then he noticed something was wrong. His body began to decay. His hair fell out, and his skin wrinkled and fell away. He paid healers to heal him but they were unable to help. In shame, he went to the clerics in the white tower and offered them the sack of endless coins in exchange for making him well again. But try as they might, they couldn't help him. Soon he became so weak and suffered from so much pain he couldn't leave his bed. It is said that he was like that for two weeks, alive but with a corpse for a body. A true zombie. At the end, his mind left him and they buried his seriously decomposed body in a deep grave. Many clerics claimed he still lived within that corpse, only he couldn't respond."

Amelia shivered. "That's a horrible story."

"What happened to the sack?" asked Olag.

"The white tower returned it to the black tower where it was stashed away. Mages were banned from repeating the spell. The spell itself was hidden away, never to be revealed again." Kazin shrugged. "That's all I know."

Amelia pointed to the sack. "Is that -is that the sack?"

Kazin smiled. "I can't say."

Amelia shuddered.

Their milk and ale were served and talk turned to lighter things. Before their food arrived, a few more people came in and placed orders. They appeared to be workers who had cleared debris and were done for the day. They cheered up noticeably as their milk was served.

The food finally arrived and everyone stopped talking to savour the delicious elven meal. Fortunately for Sherman, his place was near the wall so his plate was concealed from the other people in the room. He ate quickly but warily, making sure to keep his invisible head close to his plate to minimize the movement of his utensils. The plate was close to Amelia, so anyone glancing over would think it was hers. She elected not to eat and savoured her glass of milk.

Kazin, who sat across from Sherman, did his best to push his glass of ale away from him so Sherman could access it. It was a little more difficult for the warrior to ingest the ale without being seen, but he managed to do it unnoticed.

When the waitress came back for the dishes, she noticed Amelia's empty plate and gave her a strange look.

"I was hungry," explained Amelia. She patted her belly. "Now I'm full. It was delicious."

The waitress smiled and left with the dishes.

"You could have left her some, you know," chided Kazin to the empty space before him.

Sherman burped. "Sorry."

Amelia elbowed him and he winced.

"So now what?" asked Olag.

"We have to obtain information about the world beyond the elves' borders," explained Kazin. He nodded toward the quickly filling inn restaurant. "Let's mingle."

"Can you hold your spells while we're doing that?" asked Amelia, concerned.

Kazin nodded. "As long as everyone stays within the building. If anyone has to leave for whatever reason, let me know and I'll try to increase my spell power."

Everyone nodded.

"Let's not all get up at once," suggested Harran. "That would look strange."

"Good idea," said Zylor. "Some of us should stay and pretend we're having a conversation."

"You can guard the sack," said Harran. He tossed it to the minotaur, who was doubling as a tall, slender elf. Harran got up to wander around.

Kazin was already underway, bearing down on an elf at the bar who appeared to be a traveler who was not in his home village. He sat next to the individual and nodded to him as he sat down.

"Greetings."

"Greetings," responded the stranger.

"You don't look like you're from around here," said Kazin.

The stranger shook his head and took a swig of his ale. "No. I arrived with my caravan yesterday and delivered my goods to the village."

"What were you carrying?" asked Kazin.

The stranger waved toward the occupied tables behind him. "Take a guess."

Kazin took a glance behind him and returned his gaze to the stranger. "You brought milk?"

The stranger nodded. "Personally, I hate the stuff, but it brings in good money."

Kazin chuckled. "I know what you mean. Some of my friends are the same way."

The stranger held out his hand. "Shilar."

Kazin shook his hand, noticing his delicate elven hands make contact with Shilar's. "Kazin."

"Interesting name," commented Shilar.

"I didn't have a choice," said Kazin.

Shilar laughed. "Me neither."

"Are you staying long?" asked Kazin.

Shilar sighed. "I was due to depart this afternoon, but the dragon attack set me back. Two of my wagons were set on fire. I barely had time to get the containers of milk off in time. With the wagons destroyed, I had to sell the milk containers to the village at a discount to get rid of them." The crowd behind them erupted into a raucous laughter and Shilar winced. "I had hoped to get my shipment further inland where I could fetch a better price, but the dragon attack spoiled all that."

"Do you have any supplies left?" asked Kazin.

"Two of my wagons survived the dragon attack," said Shilar, "but only one still has containers of milk. The other one has herbs specifically designated for a town south of here."

Kazin nodded. "So where do you do most of your trade?"

Shilar snorted and took another swig of ale. "With humans, of course. But it's getting harder to do business these days."

"Why?"

"Haven't you heard? The war is all anyone is talking about these days."

"War?" asked Kazin. When Shilar gave him a look, he added, "My companions and I have been on a quest for some time and have just returned. Any news is new news."

85

Shilar nodded in understanding. "Well, as far as I can tell, there is a war going on between the humans and a sizeable number of evil creatures who see them as a threat. Ever since the humans sailed in from the east to settle in these lands a couple of generations ago, tensions have been building between them and the existing inhabitants. As far as we elves are concerned, it's a good thing the humans arrived. The evil creatures north of here have raided and pillaged our towns for generations. The raids were starting to get more frequent and deadly. Now they leave our borders alone for the most part. The humans are dealing with them instead. What surprises me is how resilient the humans are. They're building cities, farms, and even have a mage tower under construction - all this despite the raids being carried out by the evil creatures and the attacks by the dragons. And more troops continue to arrive by sea."

"Oh, really?" mused Kazin. He had forgotten the humans had come from the east. In his day, ships did not arrive from the old lands. They had stopped coming since the end of the dragon wars. Any vessels that had gone east to discover why had never returned. Contact with the old lands had been severed at that point in time, never to be reestablished.

"It seems magic is a new art to them," added Shilar. "Any humans coming to the new land are immediately checked to see if they possess any magical inclination. If so, they are directed to join the mages or clerics to learn the art of magic. After that they are enlisted in the army to fight against enemy spell casters." He grimaced. "Their blatant use of magic is offensive. Do you realize they use it for anything they wish?"

"You don't say," exclaimed Kazin, feigning shock.

Shilar nodded. "It is the most wasteful thing. At least our race reveres the ability and uses it only when necessary. Maybe the humans will learn the hard way that they cannot try to cast healing spells when their power lies with black magic, or the other way around."

Kazin nodded. "To do so will leave them capable of doing both kinds of magic, but at reduced power. They will become grey mages."

"Precisely," said Shilar.

"So what kinds of creatures are they fighting?" asked Kazin.

Shilar shrugged. "The usual. Orcs, goblins, lizardmen, even human mercenaries."

"Other humans?" gasped Kazin.

"That's right. Apparently some humans have other ideas about the situation. It's even rumoured that the enemy's lead general is a human. He's capable of magic, too."

"Interesting," mused Kazin. "What about the dragons?"

"What about them?" asked Shilar.

"Whose side are they on?"

Shilar laughed. "Their own of course! You didn't think they would actually take sides with anyone, do you?"

Kazin gave a bashful grin. "I guess not."

"So tell me," said Shilar, "what are your plans, Kazin?"

Kazin scratched his head. "I think my companions and I might take a journey up north to check out these humans for ourselves. They seem like an intriguing bunch."

Shilar shook his head. "I'd think very carefully about that. The roads are very dangerous. I have a security force that accompanies my caravans wherever I go. Bandits and roving bands of creatures are commonplace. Trolls in particular are a nuisance in these parts. They've been acting agitated and erratic lately."

"I'll keep my eyes peeled," promised Kazin. He held out his hand. "It was nice meeting you, Shilar."

Shilar shook his hand. "Good luck."

Kazin returned to his table to find Brand the mayor talking to the group.

"Ah, there you are," exclaimed Amelia, seeing the mage. "Brand was just telling us about the best routes to travel in these parts, and where to obtain various herbs that grow naturally in this area."

"Excellent," said Kazin. He noticed that Zylor and Olag appeared bored and were working on their second glass of ale.

"Well, it was good to chat with you all but I must discuss tomorrow's events with some of my people. I hope you have a delightful stay." He bowed and left.

"What a boring man," muttered Zylor.

"Zylor!" berated Amelia. "He was just trying to be friendly."

Olag yawned and Amelia glared at him, eliciting a laugh from the minotaur. He slapped the skink warrior on the back, causing him to choke on his latest mouthful of ale.

"Serves you right," muttered Amelia.

Zylor just laughed harder.

Harran returned from mingling just then. "Well, all I could find out was that dragons are an occasional nuisance and that unified spell casting of shield magic helps reduce the damage they cause, especially if they can get everyone gathered close together."

"That's a good idea," remarked Amelia. "It's easier for villages to put everyone inside one building and protect that building than it is to protect the entire village."

"That's why this part of the village appears to be unscathed," added Harran.

"I learned about dragons too," said a disembodied voice. Amelia jumped again at Sherman's voice but he continued without stopping. "I was listening in on a conversation between a couple who have a son working in the human's realm. He sent a letter to them recently telling of a dragon attack on his village. The dragon was about to blast a number of cattle with its fiery breath when it crashed into the ground. When it recovered, it took to the sky and flew off in a daze. A couple of mages were seen shortly after in that same spot milling about. Apparently they were doing some kind of test. It looked as if they were trying to control the dragon, but he's not sure."

"That's probably what they were trying to do," said Kazin. He told the others of the war between the humans and the other races. "Whoever can get the dragons to fight for them can gain a major advantage in this war."

Harran gave a low whistle. "So we've arrived in time for the dragon wars."

Everyone was silent as the impact of that statement sank in. The world was about to go into an upheaval that would be so catastrophic that the landscape would be forever changed. No one knew what would cause this, but they all knew that it happened during the dragon wars.

Kazin took the sack of endless coins from Zylor and was about to go and order rooms for them all when cries could be heard outside.

An elf came barging into the room and everyone stopped talking to see what was up.

"Trolls!" he cried. "Trolls are attacking the village!" He turned and ran back outside. The inn became a flurry of activity as the guests ran and evacuated the room to hide or find weapons. When everyone had left, the companions looked at Kazin in alarm.

"We cannot interfere!" reminded Amelia in a hushed voice.

Kazin swallowed. "Amelia's right. We're going to have to make a break for it. We have to get out of the village!"

"Flee?!" exclaimed Zylor. He slammed the table with his fist. "I will not flee!"

"Like Amelia said," said Kazin sternly, "we can't interfere. It could alter the future."

Zylor growled.

"We'd better act fast," admonished Harran. "If anyone sees us sitting here doing nothing, they'll suspect something is up."

They all got up and headed for the door.

"Sherman, see if the way is clear," ordered Kazin.

The door opened slowly and Sherman peeked outside. The commotion was louder out here. Elves were battling trolls using swords and magic.

"If we stay to the left," said Sherman, "we'll stay in the shadows. That way appears to be clear."

"Let's go," said Kazin. He turned to the minotaur. "Under no condition are you to draw your axe, Zylor. To do so will cause your appearance to revert to normal."

Zylor growled. "Then I don't see why you brought me on this quest." Nevertheless, he obeyed and followed Kazin out the door.

"Harran, you take point," instructed Kazin. "Trolls can only be defeated if their heads are cut off, and you're the only one armed with an axe other than Zylor."

Zylor growled again but said nothing.

"We have to hurry!" urged Amelia. She was gazing into her orb. It was a light pink in colour. She groaned. "We may be too late already."

"What do you mean?" asked Kazin from ahead of her. He did not slow his pace.

"The orb glows like this when history is changing. We must have done something to alter it!"

"We did nothing unusual," said Kazin. They had by now successfully ducked out of the village and were on a path that was washed in moonlight. This allowed them to move quickly and safely, since Kazin could not light the way with his staff.

Suddenly, a troll appeared in front of them, blocking the way. It was tall, about six or seven feet, and its arms hung down to its knees. Its body had a dark greenish cast similar to an orc. Its face was ugly, with ripples and creases overlapping one another, practically covering the slits where its eyes were. It opened its mouth and drooled in anticipation as it saw them coming.

Harran braced himself to deal with it, but out of nowhere a sword materialized and swung in an overhead arc. With incredible accuracy, it sliced through the troll's neck and the spittle splattered as the head flew from its shoulders into the brush at the side of the trail.

"Swords work just as well as axes," panted Sherman. The troll's body thumped to the ground and dark ooze leaked from its neck.

The companions stepped past the body and Amelia wrinkled her nose at the stench. They moved at a brisk pace for another ten minutes before halting to catch their breath.

"I'll have to fly us to a safe location far away from here and we'll have to sleep under the stars tonight," said Kazin.

"At least we had something good to eat," commented Sherman.

"I don't understand," muttered Amelia. She was sitting on a log and looking into her orb. It was now glowing with a darker shade of red than before.

"What is it?" asked Olag.

She looked up at them with a perplexed expression. "It's not right. According to my orb, the village is going to be destroyed."

Kazin put a gentle hand on her shoulder. "Then that's as it should be. We can't change history."

Amelia shook her head. "You don't understand. That village was never destroyed in our history. It became a prosperous town and a valuable trading center for the elves. According to my orb, if it disappears, it will not be rebuilt, and the loss of this village will set back the trading with humans for generations. Then there will be considerable changes to history. For one, it's the town where the unicorn first appeared to the elves. If that event didn't take place - well, you know the consequences."

Kazin blinked. "You mean that village was going to become the town of Jandal?" He remembered the town when in his past he had arrived with the companions that were with him at the time. Among them was the unicorn, who had persuaded the elven king to assist the humans in a war.

Amelia nodded. "This isn't supposed to be happening. The town was victorious against all intruders, including trolls. But somehow they're losing. It can't be happening!"

"It wouldn't surprise me if they lost," commented Olag. "Did you see how many trolls there were? There weren't enough elves in the village to fend off that many trolls."

"What do you propose we do?" asked Harran.

Kazin canceled his image spell on the group and they appeared as themselves, except Zylor, who still had his amulet on. The mage gave Amelia a curious look. "Are you proposing we help the villagers?" As if in response, Amelia's orb became a darker red.

Amelia consulted her orb for a moment and then looked up into the mage's face. "It cannot be allowed to happen. The village is supposed to survive."

"She must be toying with us," muttered Olag. "She wants us to interfere and change history for her benefit."

Amelia shook her head resolutely. "I don't want you to, but the orb -." She sighed. "We probably can't do anything about it anyway."

Kazin clenched his jaw and looked around at the companions. His gaze stopped on Zylor the elf. "How do you feel about a little free for all, Zylor?"

A slow evil grin spread across the elf's lips and he drew his weapon. Instantly, he reappeared as himself and his grin widened. "Anytime you're ready!"

Amelia stood up. "It's probably too late. By the time we run back there, the village will be lost."

"Who said anything about running?" asked Kazin. He stepped back a few paces and transformed himself into his dragon form. Then he lowered his wing. "Hop on. We're going for a ride."

In moments, he jumped into the air with the companions aboard. From the air, the village looked closer than they had expected. Below, they could see the village as flames erupted from several buildings.

"I'm going to land in the main courtyard," said Kazin. "Everyone get off and stick together. Remember that trolls regenerate very quickly. They can reattach their arms and legs within seconds, so always try to decapitate them. That's the only way to kill them short of magic. Merely stabbing them accomplishes nothing. I'll cast a shield to protect you from any elven arrows and magic."

"What for?" asked Amelia. "We're helping them."

"They don't know that," said Kazin. "As far as they're concerned, we're attacking them too."

"Would you trust a bunch of strangers who entered the fray?" added Olag.

"Good point," admitted Amelia.

"You'd better find cover until we're finished," put in Sherman. "I can even loan you my ring if you like."

Amelia glared in the direction of the disembodied voice. "Speak for yourself, warrior. I can take care of myself!"

Kazin landed in the midst of the commotion and the companions hopped off. The elves, who were down to several heavily armed groups fending off the trolls, cried in dismay upon seeing the latest intruders. A bunch of assorted creatures accompanied by a dragon was the straw that broke the camel's back. The elves prepared to flee for their lives. But what happened next caught everyone off guard. The earth suddenly trembled as an earthquake struck, causing many to lose their balance and fall down. It lasted only about twenty seconds, and no sooner had it subsided when a minotaur and dwarf charged into a group of trolls and hacked their way through them with such vehemence that they were lost from sight by flying body parts. A disembodied sword flanked one side and took care of any trolls who tried to circle around the minotaur and dwarf.

The elves took heart from the strange sight, and turned to continue their barrage of the approaching trolls. Their magic set some trolls on fire and stunned others to allow the elves armed with swords to finish them off. Many trolls wandered around with numerous arrows protruding from their flesh. All the arrows did was slow them down.

It was one of these trolls who had lost an arm from Zylor's axe. It stooped down to pick up its severed limb and reattached it to attack the minotaur from behind. A well-placed arrow from Olag penetrated its eye and it cried out in pain. This alerted Zylor to its presence and he turned and sliced off its head in one smooth motion, his muscles rippling with the effort. He looked Olag's way and gave a thankful nod. Olag immediately fired another arrow and it flew over Zylor's shoulder, embedding itself in another troll's eye. Zylor responded quickly and parted its head from its shoulders. He could thank the skink warrior later.

Kazin was back in his human form, having examined the option of remaining a dragon and then discarding the idea. The village was too concealed in the forest, and blasting enemies with his fiery breath would more than likely cause considerable damage to the village. Being a human mage would ultimately prove more beneficial. His magic was still powerful, and could be directed more accurately in such close quarters. He began casting lightning bolts into a different group of trolls who had some elves cornered between two buildings. As the trolls fell, the elves were able to fight their way back out into the open.

Amelia was dealing with a third group of trolls who were terrorizing some elves who were trying to stay out of the fight. There were two elves armed with swords at the doorway to a house and the elderly, women and children were huddled fearfully inside. The two elves fought desperately and were obviously tiring with the effort of keeping the trolls at bay. Amelia cast a 'haste' spell to improve their reaction time. They began to fare better and the trolls closest to them were bewildered with their renewed energy. Then Amelia created holes in front of the trolls just where they stepped, causing them to fall down. The elves pounced on them to slice off their heads. Two trolls spotted Amelia and headed her way, so she cast a wind spell, and they were forced to bend their bodies to push against the wind. Still they came on, so she magically created holes in the ground in front of them. The sudden lack of wind that was caused by the spell change caused them to lurch forward, and they promptly tripped and fell.

Kazin was impressed with Amelia's magical skill, but came to her rescue by incinerating the trolls with his lightning magic.

By now the elves were pressing the remaining trolls back. The tide was beginning to turn.

Shilar was fighting with his guards near his remaining wagons. They were having a difficult time with another group of trolls. One of the wagons had been overturned and a white liquid had made the ground turn muddy. This made the battle difficult for both sides. Olag was firing arrows into the trolls as quickly as any elf, and Shilar gave the skink warrior a strange look. Sherman waded into the fray, satisfied that Zylor and Harran were doing alright on their own. With deftness and strength, he sliced through one troll after another, giving Shilar's men the upper hand. They soon began going on the offensive, driving the trolls back.

Harran's ice axe did some of the most spectacular damage, instantly freezing trolls where they stood as it swung past them. This enabled the elves to knock down the bodies and shatter them into thousands of tiny fragments.

Amelia caught Kazin's attention. She pointed to her orb, which had lost its reddish tinge. "We did it!" she exclaimed. "History is back to normal!"

Kazin looked around. With the advantage clearly on the elves' side, he rallied his companions and they quickly melted into the forest as quickly as they had come. As they left, a small earthquake shook the ground for about a minute.

The tremor was enough to trip up the remaining trolls, and the more dexterous elves pushed them back into a tight group in the courtyard. Any who tried to escape were hacked to pieces by angry villagers. The trolls were fighting desperately now, but the villagers were too angry with them for the damage they had caused and the lives they had taken. Not one was left standing. When the last troll had fallen, the villagers cheered in victory. They looked around for their rescuers in order to thank them, but none were to be found.

The unknown rescuers were celebrated in songs and tales told over generations, but soon the songs were altered and then forgotten, as fact became myth. The story was just too bizarre to be true. The only known lasting record of the event was captured in 'The Adventures of Shilar, the Traveler', whose adventures during his life in the Dragon Wars bordered on the mythical. Accompanying the documents was the sketch of a creature not seen since in the elven realm. It was considered a figment of Shilar's imagination, and caused much debate about the truth of his stories. Ironically, it looked exactly like Olag.

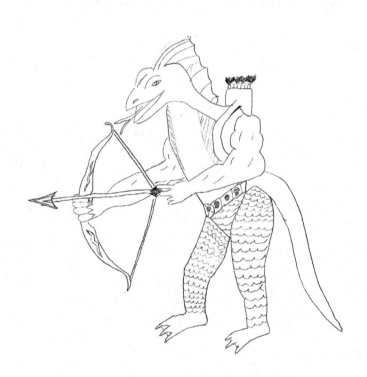

Part II

The Inter-
ference
Begins

Chapter 9

alado swiveled his head warily as the bandits surrounded him. His disheveled appearance made him look less capable with a sword than he was.

"Give us the sword, old man," jeered one bandit. He was the biggest of the five, and obviously their leader. "We don't want to hurt you." He had been admiring Galado's obsidian black sword.

"Yeah," added another. "Leave the swordplay to the experts. What do you need such a sword for anyway?"

"And those boots are too good for you too," said another.

"Don't make this hard on yourself," said the first one. "You're outnumbered."

"Back off!" growled Galado. He took a step toward one of them. At that instant, one of the other bandits lunged at Galado, but he easily sidestepped the attacker, sending him sprawling into one of his partners. He didn't watch the outcome of that move as another bandit swung his sword at him. Galado parried and thrust the opponent backward.

"You've got good reflexes," commented the big bandit. "But you don't seem to understand you're outnumbered. Come on, guys!" He lunged at Galado along with his entire crew.

Galado's training and instincts took over. He parried several blows before seizing an opening and pierced one opponent in the chest. In the next motion, he pulled his sword back and parried another blow while sidestepping an attack from the side. A ball on a chain whistled past his head and smacked into the head of another attacker. That man went down like a sack of grain, but not before Galado's sword pierced his chest.

Galado stumbled backward and fell as he tripped over his first victim, and it was fortunate he did, because the big bandit's sword whistled by scant inches from where his head had been a moment ago.

A glimpse of a ball and chain was enough to spur Galado into motion. He rolled aside just in time to avoid the spiked ball as it thudded into the ground beside him. In one smooth motion, Galado rolled to his feet and lunged at the fifth attacker, ducking under his axe and landing a solid thrust at the attacker's side. The axe wielder collapsed as blood gushed from his side. His weapon fell from his lifeless fingers as he sagged to the ground with a grunt.

Galado parried a blow from the big bandit and then ducked as the spiked ball whistled past him again. Annoyed, he shoved the big bandit away from him and swung his sword at the ball and chain guy. The opponent ducked in such a way that only the blunt side of Galado's sword struck him with a loud crack. But it was enough. The man's skull shattered and he fell in a lifeless heap. Galado turned to face his last attacker.

"You killed my friends!" growled the bandit through clenched teeth.

Suddenly, Galado's sword vibrated and glowed. Streaks of shadowy light shot from it directly into the bodies of the dead bandits. One of them slowly rose to his feet.

The big bandit was startled. Then he grinned. "I thought you were dead, Tim." He turned to Galado. "As you can see, it's not easy to kill us off," he sneered. He lunged at Galado, but the experienced soldier parried and shoved him back again, his muscles rippling with the effort.

Then another bandit got to his knees, and then stood up.

"You too?" said the big bandit. "I thought for sure -," his voice broke off as the others in his party all stood, one by one. Even the axe wielder with the gash in his side was standing. "I - I don't understand," said the big bandit uncertainly. His companions encircled him, and before he knew what was happening, they were upon him. There was nothing he could do to defend himself. They hacked into his body without mercy or concern and he soon lay in a broken heap, his blood watering the dry soil where he lay.

Galado was entranced by what he had just witnessed. Somehow, the light from his sword had revived these bandits. He looked uncertainly at these strange men.

"Fascinating," said one of the bandits as he looked at his hand. "This body has more flexibility than my original body used to have. Too bad my skull is in such bad shape."

"I can see better," said another bandit. "I never knew the world could look so clear."

"This body is overweight," complained another one. "I'll have to find a better one."

"Me too," said the fourth one. He was poking at the open wound in his side where the blood was clotted.

They all looked at Galado, who tensed.

"Where to, Boss?" said one.

"Boss?" repeated Galado.

"Sure," said another one. "You saved us from that eternal hell back at the time-line crosswalk. We follow you now."

Galado blinked in surprise. The insane grin spread across his face again. Without a word, he turned and walked in the direction he had originally been traveling. The four bandits looked at one another and shrugged. Then they ambled after him. The body of the dead gang leader was left for someone else to bury. One thing Galado had not noticed as he led the way was that his sword was a little lighter in colour than before.

It was already dark when Galado and his crew arrived at a small town. The bandit with the ripped open side was struggling to remain upright. A saloon was located at the edge of town and sounds from inside indicated that it was very busy that night. A man stumbled from the entrance and staggered away. He turned into a dark alley between the saloon and a closed leather shop, where he began to fumble with the clasp on his pants. His back was turned to the newcomers as he moved out of sight.

"Excuse me," murmured the bandit with the torn side. He moved forward as quietly as he could toward the drunken man in the alley. A few moments after he vanished from sight, a struggle could be heard despite the noise from the saloon. Several minutes elapsed, and the group wondered what had happened. Then the drunken man emerged and staggered up to them.

Galado placed his hand on his sword, but the drunken man held up his hand. He opened his mouth and belched loudly. Then he tried again. "It's O.K., Boss," he slurred. "It's only me." He pointed back over his shoulder. "My last host still had one good arm, so I strangled this guy. I thought it would be a good way to keep all the body parts intact. This body should last me a while."

"Good thinking," said another bandit.

"I'll get the next one," said the ball and chain guy as he gingerly touched his crushed skull. "I can't very well run around with a deformed skull without questions being asked."

"Oh, I don't know," said the portly bandit. "You could always act stupid or something. You have a good excuse with that body."

The ball and chain guy growled. "You have a body that will give you a good excuse to squeal once I'm finished with you."

"Enough!" said Galado. They all looked at him. "Our first concern is to find a place for the night." He looked around at them. "Let's pool our resources and I'll see what I can find."

The others fumbled in their pockets for any loose change.

"We're in luck!" exclaimed the drunken man. "This guy was loaded!" He held up a pouch of coins.

"Good," said Galado. "We'll secure some rooms with that. The rest of you should go and find some fresher bodies if you need them, or at least some clean clothes. You look like a bunch of bloody brigands - with emphasis on the 'bloody' part."

The others looked down at their blood-stained clothes and agreed.

"Good idea," said the portly brigand. He nodded toward the closed leather shop. "I think a quick shopping trip is in order."

"Don't take anything that could be traced back to the store," admonished Galado. "Stick to things that are commonplace. Check clotheslines for suitable clothing. Used clothing will not attract nearly as much attention."

"Right," answered one bandit.

"We'll meet back in front of the livery further down the street," added Galado.

"Why not here?" asked one bandit.

"Because this place will probably be crawling with people," said Galado. He pointed to the dark alley. "Someone is bound to find the body sooner or later."

"Right, Boss," said the ball and chain guy. "When I find my replacement, I'll be sure to hide the body."

Galado nodded. "Very good. See you in one hour." He turned to go down the street with the drunken man in tow. The drunken man was tossing the bag of coins in the air and catching it again as he went, and managed to drop it on the third toss. As he stooped to pick it up, Galado shoved him down and took possession of the bag himself. "We need this!" he growled. He turned and stalked off angrily.

The drunken man struggled to his feet and brushed himself off. "Sorry, Boss!" He staggered hurriedly after Galado.

A couple of hours later, Galado and his team entered one of the two rooms that Galado had rented for the night. As he gazed around at the new bodies that his group had acquired, he deduced that their undead bodies needed no sleep. He himself was the only one who required rest. In hindsight, he realized that two rooms were not really required, but at the same time having two rooms for five men avoided suspicion.

"Tomorrow we head south and west," said Galado. The men simply nodded. They needed no reasons to do what Galado wanted. He didn't explain that was where his true body was, and that it drew him like some sort of magnet. It was only a matter of time before his true body would be killed and he would be thrust into the endless death of the time line that he had escaped. It was up to him to prevent that death and jump back into his own body to complete his goal.

"We'll have to move quickly," continued Galado. "I realize I'm holding us back with my mortal body, but I expect to leave first thing in the morning as planned."

The men nodded again.

Galado looked around at the men and scratched his head. "It's going to be hard to tell you guys apart every time you take another body, so I'm going to number you and that's how you are to report to me." He pointed at the former ball and chain wielder. "You're number One. It's up to you to make sure the others are all present when we move out."

Number One nodded.

"You're number Two," pointed Galado. "And you're Three and Four."

The men nodded again.

"It's time I got some sleep," concluded Galado. "If you're planning to make any noise, go into the second room I rented. One, you take first watch."

"Right," said One.

The men all got up and left the room.

Galado lay back on the bed and sighed. His men didn't have the difficulty he had. Their bodies had no spirits to content with. He had a live body with a remarkably resilient spirit who constantly fought for control. That spirit was supposed to have been left behind in the time-line, but something had gone wrong. Galado had felt it was something to do with the sword. There was a magical bond between the spirit of Sir Galado and the sword that prevented them from being separated. Unfortunately, killing this body like his team was doing was out of the question. To do so would instantly send his spirit back to the unending death of the time-line, simply because his take-over would have been a failure. There wouldn't be an opportunity to take over another dead body like his team was doing. His spirit was not stored safely in the sword like the others were. The only safe jump for his spirit would be to jump into his true body when he prevented his own untimely death. That was his ultimate goal. Then the body he now possessed could be disposed of. Galado thought about the dilemma as he fell into a fitful sleep.

In the morning, he found his men in the next room playing cards. He sent One to get supplies - not a lot considering he was the only one who needed to eat or drink - and took the others to purchase some horses. They had just enough money to complete the deal. They could have killed the stable master, but everyone was on high alert with several murders being reported in the town.

At the stables, they were just getting ready as One came to them with the supplies. He was putting the supplies into his saddlebags when one of the villagers came up to him.

"Hey Ned! I was wondering where you were! You better get home quick. Your wife's worried sick about you since you didn't return home last night. Especially since the rash of deaths last night. One happened right outside the saloon where we were drinking last night!"

"Uh," stammered One. "I'll be home as soon as I can. Tell my wife not to worry."

The villager glanced at one of the other bandits and lowered his voice. "Since when do you hang out with Oscar?"

"It's a long story," muttered One.

The villager shrugged. "Well, I haven't got time right now. You can tell me tonight after work - if your wife lets you out."

One laughed nervously. "You got it," he said to the retreating form of his host's friend.

"We'd better get going," urged Galado.

The group mounted their horses and rode calmly out of town.

A few hours later, they caught sight of a caravan heading in the same direction as they were. It was a coach with four mounted guards riding escort.

"Fancy caravan," said Four.

"Must be rich," added Three.

"If we needed more money," said Two, "this would be the time and place to get it."

"What do you think, Boss?" asked One.

Galado grinned wickedly. "Why not?"

As they neared, the security detail spotted them and stopped the caravan.

"Let me do the talking," ordered Galado. He rode forward and nodded to the guards. "Greetings."

The security guards did not respond.

"What, no voice?" asked Galado.

"Be on your way," ordered one guard.

Galado turned to him and slowly rode up to him. In the meantime, his men moved into a surrounding formation. One moved to the front of the caravan near the coach driver.

"I suggest you stand down," said Galado calmly.

"What seems to be the problem?" said an older voice from the coach.

The guard in front of Galado turned back to the coach to respond. "There are some -." His voice broke off as Galado's sword penetrated his chest. In apparent slow motion, he fell lifeless from his horse to the ground.

The other guards looked to see their comrade on the ground, and Galado's men responded in that instant, attacking with silent ferocity. The guards were well trained, however, and fell into their role quickly. One of them came charging at Galado, but was no match for the skilled soldier. Galado parried one sword thrust and went on the offensive, easily stabbing his opponent. In the next instant, he dismounted and charged for the coach. One glance told him One had dispatched the coach driver and had seized control of the coach.

Galado kicked open the coach door and sprang inside. The old man rose to his feet, a dagger in his hand, but Galado's long sword made quick work of him. As the old man fell, screams assailed Galado's ears. He whirled around to face three ladies in white dresses. Their features were similar enough that he guessed they were related. As he raised his sword, their screams bombarded his ear drums. Before he could silence the noise, a huge, resistant force took hold of him. "No!" a loud voice yelled. It was his own. "You cannot use my body to do this!"

Galado's sword hand wavered as he fought for control. His vision clouded and he convulsed. "I will do it!" he growled through clenched teeth. He was no longer in control of his body. His sword hand reacted as if possessed. A swishing noise filled his ears and the screaming faded into the distance. Several moments passed and finally he opened his eyes. Sir Wilfred Galado was revolted by what he saw. Before him lay three beautiful ladies in white, blood stained dresses, their eyes open as though the last thing they saw was too dreadful to bear. The vision was so horrific, Sir Galado clenched his eyes shut and fell to his knees. He let out a loud wail of sorrow.

"See!" said a voice inside of his head. "See what you did? If you hadn't interfered -" Sir Galado's body convulsed again as the two spirits fought for control. When Galado reopened his eyes, it was not Sir Galado. It was the evil spirit once again. Galado rose to his feet, oblivious to the carnage around him. He laughed a sinister laugh. 'That should teach the original spirit', he thought.

The Sword of Dead began to shimmer and vibrate. Shadowy lights shot from the weapon and into the bodies in the coach, as well as the two guards he had dispatched outside. As before, the spirits from the sword seized control of the bodies and brought them to undead life. Also, as before, his sword lightened somewhat again. Now it swirled between dark and light.

The three women got up, as did the old man. They looked at one another with hideous grins.

"At last!" exclaimed one of the women. Her voice was only a whisper, since Galado's sword had cut her voice box.

Galado opened the coach's door to see guards standing before him. At first he was alarmed, but then he realized two of them were new spirits from the sword, while two of them were now part of his original crew. Only Three was still in his earlier form. When Three saw Galado looking at him, he shrugged. "No bodies left to take." A look over his shoulder confirmed One had taken the body of the coach's driver.

"Very well," said Galado. "Let's dispose of the bodies and be off." He looked over his shoulder at the old man and the women. "Old man, you will be called Five. Ladies, you will be Six, Seven, and Eight." He turned to the two new guards. "You will be nine and ten."

"Yes, Sir," said Ten. "We'll help with the disposal of the bodies."

Galado nodded and turned to the occupants of the coach. "You should pretend to be the owners of the caravan. Just keep out of sight. Your bodies are not really presentable with all the blood and wounds. We'll let you find some suitable replacements as they present themselves."

"We'll try to find some clothing to change into," said the old man. "It will hide some of our injuries."

Galado nodded and turned to Three. "You do the same. I'm sure some of the guards' clothing will fit."

Three nodded. "Right."

In less than half an hour they were off, an innocent looking caravan with three guards riding in front and rear, including Galado. He had also found some guard clothing so he could fit in with the rest of them.

Chapter 10

azin and his companions wandered quietly into the southern human port town of Malley. It was still dark, with the rising sun's light only a dim grey glow on the eastern horizon. They had landed under cover of darkness west of the city in an unpopulated area. With minimal noise, Kazin had let the companions off his back and transformed into his human form. Zylor was turned into a human warrior with the magic being maintained by his amulet. It was Olag's turn to use the invisibility ring to keep him concealed. That left the group consisting of several humans and a dwarf, not an uncommon sight in the human's realm.

They wandered quietly through the town as shop owners awakened and opened their businesses for the start of a new day. Some security patrols marched through the streets but none noticed Kazin's group, and if they did, they gave no indication that anything was amiss. Noises could be heard as ships were unloaded with passengers from the old world who had come to start a new life here among the early settlers. A few mages could be seen on the pier anxiously waiting for the passengers to disembark. They were eager to find people who were potentially capable of magic, and had all sorts of incentives to lure those newcomers to join the mage or cleric guilds for training. Many would undoubtedly join, having no source of income. Joining a guild would allow them to obtain a means of support while they established themselves in the new world. Some would be disappointed when it was discovered they had no innate magical ability. But it didn't hurt to find out.

Kazin yearned to ask the newcomers about the world they had left behind. Most of the information he had researched regarding the old world was sporadic and incomplete. It was as if the old world had faded from memory and existence in his time far into the future. Much of the histories had been lost after the dragon wars. Even books from the old world were not to be found. Books, it turned out, were not light, and therefore were not allowed on board when people came to the new world with a limited allowable amount of baggage. But history of the past was secondary to the current quest. No amount of history would be saved if the world in the future was allowed to disappear. Kazin had to stop that aberration first.

"I could use something to eat," grumbled Zylor.

"Me too," said Sherman.

"The shops are opening," said Amelia. "It won't be long now." She glanced at Sherman. "I think I'll eat your share this time."

Sherman reddened and was glad it was still dark.

Harran smirked. "You owe her one."

"I smell food," murmured the invisible skink warrior. "It smells like bread."

Zylor sniffed the air. "This human nose doesn't work so well but I think you're right. It's coming from over here." He led them to a bakery just off the main street.

When the baker saw them coming, he smiled happily. "Greetings! You're my first customers. You get to try the freshest bread of the day!"

"Smells good," remarked Kazin. He withdrew his pouch of coins. "How much for six loaves?"

The shop keeper's eyes widened. "My, my, my! You must be hungry!"

"We're planning to eat some now and take some with us for later," explained Amelia.

"Of course," said the baker happily. "But you'll have to wait a few more minutes. I haven't got that many prepared yet."

"No problem," said Amelia with a pleasant smile. "We'll wait."

The baker nodded and went to check on his oven.

The sky brightened as the sun revealed itself through an opening in the cloud cover, and sounds of a town coming to life emphasized the coming of dawn. A military recruitment booth was set up down the street and two soldiers prepared to enlist any interested newcomers.

"It's not the first thing I would want to sign up for after arriving in a new country to start fresh," commented Amelia.

"That's a matter of perspective," responded Zylor.

Amelia shot Zylor a glance and shook her head. "Only a minotaur would say something like that."

Zylor grinned.

A leather shop across the street opened for business and the shop keeper came outside, yawning. A number of newcomers wandered into the street fresh off the boat in the harbour. When the shop keeper saw them, he scrambled back into his shop. A moment later he reemerged with a wheeled cart displaying a number of leather items that he had crafted, including belts, varying harnesses, and bags. A few newcomers paused to examine the wares with interest.

"That hand bag is made from the hide of a dragon," boasted the shop keeper to a lady who was admiring the soft texture of the bag.

"A dragon?!" shrieked the lady, dropping the hand bag on the ground in surprise.

The shop keeper calmly picked up the bag and held it out to her. It seemed he was used to the reaction. "Yes, a dragon. Don't worry. It won't bite." The lady, intrigued, reached out again to handle the bag. "Dragons are a common sight in this land," continued the shop keeper. "We use dragon hide for all sorts of things."

"If only you knew," said Kazin beneath his breath.

"I'll bet that bag would be kept under lock and key in our time," commented Harran. "It would fetch a hefty sum indeed."

"No doubt," said Kazin.

"Your bread is ready," said a voice behind them.

Kazin turned and paid the baker and the companions moved away to make room for the baker's next customers, who had undoubtedly followed their noses to the scent of fresh bread.

They found a quiet area to stop and eat beside a jewelry shop, and Olag ducked into the shadows to eat his piece of bread without being spotted. After they had eaten, they wandered onto the pier to watch as more newcomers disembarked. Mages and clerics moved rapidly among the people, handing out invitations to try out for the guilds. The invitations included many incentives which would be offered to successful candidates depending on their magical aptitude. Those who showed interest were directed into the waiting wagons destined for the Tower of the Stars just east of Malley.

Amelia went to mingle with the crowds to obtain a copy of the invitation and returned to show it to the others. They studied it intently for a few minutes.

"You know," mused Kazin, "it doesn't mention anything about a war. These people are not being told everything they ought to know."

"Someone should inform them," said Amelia.

"It certainly can't be us," said Kazin sternly.

Amelia sighed. "I know." She paused to look into her orb but nothing was out of the ordinary.

"Do you think the war has something to do with our quest?" asked Sherman.

"I wouldn't be surprised," said Kazin.

"Maybe we could find out more about the war if we followed the wagons to the Tower of the Stars," said Sherman.

"I'm thinking the same thing," said Kazin, "but I don't think we should follow the wagons."

"What do you mean?" asked Harran.

"I think we should ride the wagons," said Kazin.

"You mean, sign up for the guilds?" asked Amelia.

Kazin grinned at her. "Sure, why not? It beats walking."

"They'll never let a dwarf on the wagon," said Harran. "Everyone knows dwarves don't have magical abilities."

"We'll just have to make you look human for a while," said Kazin.

Harran rolled his eyes. "Here we go again."

"It'll only be for the ride," said Kazin. "I'll change you back again when we get to the tower."

Harran sighed. "Very well. Let's find a spot out of sight of all these people."

He and Kazin departed, and when they came back a few minutes later, everyone was shocked. Not about Harran, who looked like a stocky human with dark hair and eyes, but about Kazin. The mage appeared as his younger self, an image they all knew well except Amelia, who was caught off guard by the attractive blond haired, blue-eyed man approaching them. She blushed as his blue eyes looked into hers. She suddenly experienced some feelings deep inside her that she had never experienced before. "Kazin?" she whispered in awe.

Kazin smiled. "What do you think? Do I look like a naive young man looking for adventure?"

"I remember a time when that was actually true," smiled Sherman, who noticed Kazin still had a slight limp.

Kazin laughed. "I guess it wasn't that long ago for you, Sherman."

"How so?" asked Amelia, confused.

"Right now I appear like I was many years ago," said Kazin. "But the way you saw me earlier is how I look now. When I came to ask for my friends to aid me in this quest, I appeared older than they remembered, because I came from the distant future to recruit them in their time. I am much older because I come from further into the future."

"I see," said Amelia.

"We'd better hurry," urged Olag suddenly. "The last of the wagons is preparing to leave."

The companions hurried to scramble aboard. There were still several places available to sit and Kazin patted the seat next to him.

"Sit here, Olag," he murmured in a low voice.

"Thanks," hissed the invisible skink warrior.

Amelia sat to Kazin's right while Harran, Zylor and Sherman sat across from them.

The ride was uneventful but bumpy, and the mages and clerics came around to get their names to submit to the testers at the Tower of the Stars. The companions gave fictitious names since they planned to sneak away upon arrival.

Star City was the city where the Tower of the Stars was located. It was named after the reef formation at the entrance to the Bay of Barlin where it entered the sea. The reef formation was called Ten Star Reef, and the ten reefs were beacons to inbound ships of the new world beyond.

Although the wagon made good time, it was well into the day when they arrived in the city. The tower was immediately visible, located high up on a mountainside overlooking the Bay of Barlin and the reef formations beyond. Gasps of awe were heard as the newcomers looked up at the impressive tower. They had obviously not seen it as they had passed it in their ship during the wee hours of the morning. The tower had turrets along the walls with cylindrical buttresses on the corners, and the center rose well beyond the buttresses like a giant square turret with many levels. The lower levels were larger than the ones above them and balconies sat atop the levels beneath. There were six levels in all, and the top was adorned with a flag bearing a crest not familiar to the companions.

"It's definitely not the same as what I remember," said Sherman.

Harran's eyes widened and he pointed to the left. "Where is the mountain range? This can't be the same place. The mountains are not high enough!"

"That's because things changed during the dragon wars," explained Kazin. "Most of the tower was destroyed when the upheaval took place, and the mountains were formed around that time. The dwarves lived in the mountains to the north and migrated to the new formations after the dragon wars. That brought a whole new era of prosperity to the dwarves, who were rapidly running out of valuable minerals and gems."

"Of course," said Harran, nodding. "I remember all the ancient digs in the northern mountains."

"They're not ancient at the moment," said Kazin. "I'm sure there are plenty of dwarves working those mineral deposits right now."

"Interesting," said Harran thoughtfully.

The wagon came to a halt and Kazin and his companions hopped out. It was learned that the Tower of the Stars was where the white mages currently operated from, and where new mages of all types were evaluated as to their magical aptitude and inclination. Everyone was led along a path toward the tower, but no one was monitoring the convoy of potential new recruits. It didn't take much for them to make a break for it, and they worked their way down to the commercial part of the city. It was just past noon and vendors were excitedly preaching their wares. The town was bustling with both locals and visitors, many who had arrived by boat in the local port.

They paused at a warehouse with a dark alcove so Kazin could transform Harran back into his bearded self. Kazin opted to remain his young self at Amelia's request. Then the companions entered an even busier marketplace. Everything was being sold from exotic foods to goods from other lands, especially articles of elven or dwarven origin.

Amelia chose to withdraw her orb and saw a pinkish glow in its depths. "Something is not right about this place. We have to be careful."

The companions remained alert as they moved through the marketplace.

At one point they passed a dwarven vendor who shouted, "Spirit blades! Come get your spirit blades! Dwarven quality and craftsmanship, enhanced with magic! Lightweight and solid! Come get your magical spirit blade! The Sword of Dead! Expert magic, expert craftsmanship!"

Sherman paused mid-stride and a shiver ran down his spine. Olag bumped into him and cursed quietly. Sherman turned to look at Kazin and knew the mage had heard the same thing.

"What's wrong?" asked Amelia.

Sherman had already turned to examine the dwarf's display of swords. Dozens of swords lined the table where the dwarf presented his wares. They were chained together to prevent theft. One glance at the swords caused the big warrior's shoulders to slump. Most of the swords were exactly identical. He could not tell one from another.

"Well?" asked Kazin quietly beside his friend. "What do you think?"

"Um, guys," interrupted Amelia, tugging at Kazin's sleeve. She lifted her cloak to reveal the orb as it emitted a dark pink glow.

"Sherman?" pressed Kazin, unfazed.

"It's the same as the sword I was supposed to bring," said Sherman sadly. "They all are. I had no idea it was so common."

"I don't think your sword was common, Sherman," said Kazin, eyeing the arrangement before him. He looked up at the dwarf, whose thick black beard and hair almost covered his face. "Which one is the 'Sword of Dead'?"

The dwarf became evasive. "I don't know. They're all magical, but some are more potent than the others. Take your pick. You might get lucky and get a good one."

"Why did you call it the 'Sword of Dead'?" asked Kazin. "Where did you come up with a name like that?"

The dwarf shrugged again. "It's what the mage who made it called it - I mean them."

Kazin became alert when he heard the slip. "So there's only one 'Sword of Dead'?"

"They're all magical," hedged the dwarf.

"Where is the mage who enhanced these swords?" asked Kazin.

"He's dead," said the dwarf sadly. He caught Kazin's stare. "But I didn't kill him!" he pleaded. "He was my partner! He - he died right after he put magic on the - the -."

"Sword of Dead," finished Sherman.

Now the dwarf was sweating. "Listen. I'll give you a sword at half price! It's a great deal! I made them myself. You won't regret it!"

Amelia elbowed Kazin. "Don't!" she hissed.

Kazin ignored her. "You don't mind if I check if they're magical first, do you?"

"Go ahead," said the dwarf, "but I won't unchain them unless you're going to buy one."

"Agreed," said Kazin. He held up his staff and chanted. Approximately half of the swords emitted a faint glow. "It looks like some of them aren't magical at all," said Kazin, eyeing the dwarf with a dark expression.

"But some of them are," said the dwarf excitedly, pointing to the glowing swords. It seemed he was happy to see some of the swords were actually magical.

"It's hopeless," said Sherman with a sigh. "How can we tell which one it is? Half of them are magical."

Kazin increased the intensity of his spell and the swords with a higher level of magic glowed with greater brilliance.

"Now we're down to six choices," said Sherman with a little more enthusiasm.

Kazin increased his magic some more and one stood out with a more powerful brilliance yet.

"That's it!" cried Sherman. He reached out and touched it reverently.

"Kazin canceled his spell. "We'll take that one."

Amelia groaned.

The dwarf was looking at Kazin with a strange expression, as were some nearby shoppers. "You're good with magic for a young guy," he said slowly. He lowered his voice. "You know, we could go into business together. I could give you a commission on the swords if you can prove to the customer it really is magical."

"No thanks," said Kazin.

"Just unlock the sword," urged Sherman.

The dwarf did as instructed and Kazin paid him. He even let the dwarf have Sherman's old sword to get an additional discount. He hoped it would compensate for the removal of a sword so history would not be altered.

Sherman hefted the spirit blade and felt a strange tingle run down his arm into his entire body. He didn't know it, but the sword melded with its new owner and created a bond that would never be broken. The warrior hefted the blade. "It feels right." He looked at Kazin. "But how can we be sure it's the same one? The real one is still at home."

"It existed before our time," said Kazin, "so it could very well be the same. Remember how you found it the first time. It was lost for a long time before you handled it. For all we know, you won't be bringing it back to your time when we go back. Some magical swords create bonds that last forever if you're the first one to own or wield it. You won't know its true capabilities until you use it. Either way, it has a strong magical signature, so it's a good blade."

Amelia glared at the two friends as they left the vendor and regrouped with the others. "You guys just blew it!" she snapped. She tugged out her orb and held it up. "Now you changed -," her voice broke off. The orb was back to its clear colour. "I - I don't get it," she stammered.

"It looks like they were supposed to buy the sword," commented Harran.

Amelia pocketed the orb again. "It doesn't make sense," she mumbled, red-faced. "It just doesn't make sense."

Chapter 11

ack in the humans' military compound, a young man named Paul was busy drawing sketches. Paul was a slender youth with long, brown hair. He was not heavily built, and as such was not very effective when it came to fighting. His specialty was more along the lines of artistry. Painting was his favourite method of expression, and he took advantage of his skills to make a modest living doing sketches of various things for people. He was still quite young when he and his parents migrated to the new land, but his passion for painting increased dramatically upon his arrival. The new races of people he encountered - the dwarves and elves – were interesting to talk to and make sketches of. His parents weren't enthusiastic about his hobby but tolerated it anyway.

Then things changed. War had broken out to the west and able fighters were required. Both of Paul's parents were seasoned fighters in the old lands, and this call to arms was something they could understand and relate to. With the added incentive of decent wages, they vigorously applied with the military, and took their son along, telling him he would learn along the way. But Paul was not interested in fighting. He just wanted to paint and sketch. Ordinarily, he would have been expelled from the army, but his parents managed to prevent that from happening. This was primarily due to their status. Paul's mother was known to several important people within the military, who knew of her battle prowess in the old lands. Subsequently, she was immediately selected to become one of the three top lieutenants under the general. Paul's father was chosen to be one of the infantry division commanders. He could have gotten a higher position himself because of his experience, but he preferred the tactical challenge of leading the infantry divisions and chose to remain in that role. For Paul's parents, one factor separated this war from the constant wars they had endured in the old lands. The enemy they now fought were primarily non-human. This made the fighting seem more like a defense of their new homes against sinister creatures that threatened to destroy them.

Paul was not enthusiastic about the prospect of fighting. He remained behind at the soldiers' compound while his parents eagerly marched or rode with the army. They were obviously disappointed in their son's lack of interest in fighting. It wasn't until the first injured soldiers returned that his interest was piqued. Reports of strange new creatures reached his ears.

Steeling himself, Paul resolved to go out with the next contingent of soldiers to see for himself. Once he got to where the fighting was underway, he was excited to see the hordes of orcs, goblins, lizardmen, and others. Here was something new and interesting to sketch! He quickly found a secluded spot well away from the fighting and began to make sketches of the various creatures. As luck would have it, the enemy was being pressed back and the fighting moved westward. A field of dead people and creatures lay sprawled across the valley, with human clerics and their assistants scurrying to find any injured humans they could heal or save.

Paul crept from his hiding spot and cautiously approached a dead orc. Its face was ugly, by human standards, but it was very interesting to behold up close. It's pressed back nose was moist with mucus and its greenish face looked like it was scowling. Its eyes were half open and glazed over. Its tongue drooped from the side of its mouth where one of its bottom teeth protruded up past its cheek. The protruding bottom teeth were long, and stopped level with the nose. How these creatures ate their food with those teeth like that was a mystery to Paul.

Oddly, Paul was not repulsed by the visage of the creature, or the stench or the fact that it was dead. He studied it with a detached curiosity and withdrew his sketch pad and writing implement. Then, with great care, he began to draw.

✕   ✕   ✕   ✕   ✕

Lieutenant Holden entered the meeting hall and saluted the arch mages who had assembled for the meeting. He was dressed smartly in a blue and black uniform and held his pie-shaped lieutenant's hat in his left hand. His hair was short and light brown and he had bright grey eyes over a pointed nose. His mouth was firm and unemotional. He waited to be asked to speak.

"Thank you for seeing us," began Arch Mage Gresham. He gestured around the table. "We are all eager to hear of news from the front lines."

More than two thirds of the arch mages were present. The rest were away, either assisting the army's mages or on other errands. Arch Mage Penna was gone to the barracks to oversee operations involving mages in the front lines. And Arch Mage Brendan was away working on the orb project.

The lieutenant cleared his throat. "Thank you, Sir." He turned so he was in a position to address the entire assemblage. "As you may have heard, we were making an offensive move against the enemy hordes. With fresh supplies we marched west and encountered only light pockets of resistance. It seemed the enemy was unprepared for an assault and we pursued them just north of the Boot Plateau. The enemy fled and we charged forward with the advantage. We had scarcely entered a pass north of the boot, when it became evident this flight was just a ploy to lead us into an ambush. Lizardmages appeared behind the rocks on the north face of the plateau's cliffs and began to assault our forces. Coming down the pass from the west were the enemies we were originally pursuing. They had turned and were joined by the bulk of their forces in one giant wall of creatures. Exposed, we were driven back into the forest to the north of the pass where an equally potent force was lying in wait. Human mercenaries, interspersed with magic wielding lizardmages, fell upon us. Our mages managed to counter the attack at first, but soon came upon a new enemy. We had known little about them previously, but soon learned how dangerous they actually were." The lieutenant looked around at the attentive assembly of mages. "We encountered a contingent of cyclops."

Gasps and murmurs were heard around the table.

"Please, describe these creatures," prodded Gresham.

"Well," said the lieutenant, scratching his head, "they have a thick yellowish green skin and stand around six and a half feet tall. They are similar to humans, and only wear loin cloths. As you've probably heard from the dwarves, they have only one eye situated in the middle of their foreheads. The tales of their ability to paralyze are also true. We lost many good soldiers and mages who looked into those creatures' eyes and became paralyzed on the spot. This left them vulnerable to attack and we were subsequently driven back into the opening in the pass." The lieutenant shuddered. "It was hard not to look into their eyes. Every instinct makes us want to look into the enemy's face, but to do so with these creatures is fatal." Holden withdrew a piece of parchment from his cloak and presented it to Arch Mage Gresham. "We have an artist within the army who has been making sketches of some of the creatures we have encountered. This is a sketch of a cyclops."

Grasham examined the photo and passed it around the table for the others to look at. "Very striking image," he commented. "This artist has talent."

"What happened next?" asked Arch Mage Toele. He was seated forward at the table with his hands clasped in front of him.

Lieutenant Holden continued. "It was around this time when a fortunate thing happened - well, mostly fortunate. A flock of dragons appeared in the sky and decided to get involved. There were so many of them that the sun was blotted out and the sky darkened. I've never seen so many of them gathered at once. They flew down into the pass and incinerated both enemies and allies alike. Lizardmen who attacked them with magic from the cliff face were singled out and burned, along with the poor souls in the pass. Some of the forest to the north was also set on fire.

"Continuing the battle was pointless for both sides by then," continued Holden. "The enemy retreated to the west and we went back to our base in the east. The dragons disappeared as quickly as they had come. The forest fire they started was still visible in the distance after we left."

"Do you think the dragons got involved in order to stop the war?" asked an arch mage.

Lieutenant Holden shook his head. "It's hard to say, but I don't think so. It was as if the dragons were enjoying the torment they were causing among those on the ground."

Arch Mage Gresham sighed. "I see why you say it was fortunate. Had the dragons not appeared when they did, our forces would surely have been decimated."

The lieutenant nodded. "Yes. We may not be so fortunate the next time. The reports on casualties confirm that the dragons killed more enemies than allies. But our losses were also great. This particular battle was a draw. No one came out ahead, except the dragons."

"Were no dragons shot down?" asked one arch mage.

Holden nodded. "Yes. There was one dragon shot down by lizardmages. It landed in the pass and crushed a number of orcs in the process. At least two other dragons were injured but they flew away from the battle."

"Our forces will have to regroup quickly, in case our enemies decide to press their attack, now that we are on our heels," commented Toele.

"We're in a defensive stance right now," said Holden. "The clerics are frantically tending to the injured, and those who are able are manning the defenses. But I'm sure the enemy has their hands full with injuries as well. I don't see them attacking any time soon."

Arch Mage Gresham looked around the table. "Are there any more questions for the lieutenant?" No one answered so he turned to Holden. "Thank you for your report, Lieutenant Holden. As always, we appreciate your updates of events on the battlefield."

Holden nodded, saluted, and left the room.

Gresham turned back to the assembly. "It appears we are battling two enemies at once. Does anyone have any suggestions about how to deal with the dragons?"

"Is there a way we can establish a warning system to alert us to a dragon attack?" asked Arch Mage Belham, who had been silent until now.

"Arch Mage Penna has an eagle as a familiar," said Toele thoughtfully. "If she can use it to scan the area of a battle, it could spot the dragons approach well before they arrive on site."

"That's a good idea," said Gresham. "If we could get all the mages with birds as their familiars to scan important sectors, we would at least get some forewarning of the approach of dragons."

"I can gather the master mages and have them do a survey to find any mages who have an aerial familiar," said an arch mage. He was a tall, wiry man with straight dark hair and a mustache. His real name was Arch Mage Sallow, but he was known as 'The Teacher' because he was the one who did training for the master mages who in turn taught the new recruits. His interaction with other mages made him popular and well known among the guild. "Once we find a number of mages equipped with the appropriate familiars, we can send them on scouting missions."

"Very well," said Gresham. "I suggest you get started as soon as the meeting is adjourned."

Sallow nodded.

"We should look into practicing a combined shield spell for our troops," suggested another mage. It was a stout mage with short brown hair and had dimples when she smiled.

"That's a good idea too, Arch Mage Doris," said Gresham. "I'll have that passed along to Penna with the next caravan out to the barracks."

"We could combine the magic with the clerics," added Doris. "It has been proven that shield magic is common between black and white mages."

"I'm sure we can do something there," said Gresham, "as long as the clerics aren't needed to perform healing, which is their primary function."

"Of course," smiled Doris, her dimples clearly evident.

"Any other ideas?" asked Gresham.

With no response, Gresham moved on. "On a lighter note, the tower is nearing completion. We will be able to cast a defensive shield on the building by the end of the week."

Enthusiastic murmurs and head nodding emanated from the assembled arch mages.

At this point an aide came in and whispered in Gresham's ear.

The arch mage thanked the messenger and straightened in his seat. The assembly, anticipating further news, quieted.

"We have some interesting news," stated Arch Mage Gresham. "It seems we have succeeded in taming our first dragon!"

Gasps escaped the lips of those in the room.

"Do you have proof of this?" asked Arch Mage Belham.

"Indeed we do," said Gresham. "Apparently Arch Mage Brendan is waiting in the courtyard with evidence of his success." Gresham looked around at the other mages. "We have been invited to see for ourselves." He rose. "Let's not keep him waiting."

The mages all rose and exited the meeting room. They reappeared at one of the tower's exits leading to the courtyard. The sun shone brightly in the sky and the surrounding edges of the courtyard were occupied by mages poised to shield everyone from potential attacks. But this was all ignored in favour of the magnificent and intimidating sight before them. It was immense, larger than any other creature any of them had ever seen up close before. Its wings were folded back along the length of its reddish golden scaled body. Its tail waved back and forth and its head turned on a long, flexible neck to observe the newcomers with interest through reptilian eyes.

The arch mages returned the gaze with awe and wonder.

Arch Mage Brendan stood close to the creature's side and turned to greet his visitors. He was so small next to the reptilian beast that some of the arch mages were startled to catch sight of him when he moved. He held in his right hand a glowing white orb.

"Hello!" he exclaimed, his face beaming. "Welcome!" He indicated the dragon behind him. "This is my friend, Burnett!"

"It has a name?" asked Toele. He, like many of the others, looked uneasy despite the sizeable security provided by the mages surrounding the courtyard.

"Oh, yes!" said Brendan with a smile. "Each one has a name, just like humans do."

"How do you know?" asked Belham.

Arch Mage Violet, who stood nearby, answered. "Apparently, the magic in the orb allows telepathic communication between the mage and dragon. It is the necessary ingredient in the magic of the orb that we had overlooked previously. Without it the orb would not work."

"And this allows you to control the dragon?" asked Toele incredulously. He still couldn't believe this giant beast was under Brendan's control.

"For the most part," said Brendan.

"For the most part?" asked Toele. He looked nervous again.

Brendan smiled again. "The dragon is an intelligent creature. In order to get it to obey, you have to reason with it."

"So you can get it to do what you want as long as it agrees to it?" asked Belham.

"Pretty much," said Brendan.

"Excellent work!" exclaimed Gresham. "This could prove to be a turning point in the war if we can get more dragons to support us willingly."

"That remains to be seen," muttered Toele. "I doubt that dragons would be willing to fight one another."

"We'll see," said Gresham. He turned to Brendan. "How many dragons are under control of an orb right now, Brendan?"

"Only two," said Brendan. "My associate has one under control in Arral."

"But several more orbs have been created and are ready to be used as we speak," added Violet. "We expect word from other mages within days."

"Excellent!" said Gresham. He pointed to the majestic beast before them. "Perhaps we can have a demonstration?"

Brendan grinned. "Of course!" He turned to the dragon and appeared to be deep in thought for a moment. Then the dragon lowered its wing and Brendan climbed onto its back right behind the head. He held on tight and the great beast stretched out its wings and launched itself into the air. It flapped its wings with a slow, methodical rhythm. Brendan and his dragon swerved in a long arc and dove back toward the courtyard. They flew in a low trajectory and surged over the assembled mages with incredible speed. Most of the mages ducked instinctively as the dragon and rider flew past. Several mages had even cast a shield spell to protect everyone from a potential attack.

The attack didn't happen, and Brendan and Burnett rose back into the sky. The dragon let loose with a flaming fireball, much to the delight of the spectators. The fireball fizzled out before hitting the ground a safe distance away. Then the dragon and rider swung back to the courtyard where the dragon opened its wings and slowed its descent. By the time the dragon reached the courtyard, it was going slowly enough that it could come to a running stop. As the dust settled, Brendan climbed back down to the ground via the dragon's wing.

Several mages cheered as he stopped to take a bow.

"Well done!" exclaimed Gresham.

"Impressive!" added Belham.

"I think we ought to make preparations to equip more mages with dragon orbs," said Gresham to the others.

"I recommend we assign orbs only to mages with a higher level of magic," said Brendan, as he strode toward them from the dragon. "It takes a considerable amount of concentration to maintain control of the dragon even when you're just flying through the air. My associate has the rank of master mage and he can barely control his dragon. Anyone with a lower rank than a master mage should not attempt this."

"Concentration to hang on?" asked an arch mage.

"Concentration to maintain control mentally," explained Brendan. "The dragon is quite intelligent and always tries to seize control of its actions. If you haven't got good enough mental control, the dragon will choose its own actions and convince you that it is in charge. It will then control you instead of the other way around. It could potentially find a way to seize the orb for itself and regain its freedom, leaving you in a vulnerable position. If you become separated from the orb, we don't yet know what could happen, since the orb links you to the dragon. It could even mean death." Brendan shrugged. "We just don't know right now."

"Understood," said Gresham. "We will limit the orbs to arch mages and seasoned master mages for now."

"And those who don't mind heights," added Belham.

Gresham chuckled. "Of course."

"How do you recommend capture of a dragon?" asked an arch mage.

Brendan turned to her. "Once you have learned the magic associated with the orb, you will be given one and then it would be a good idea to position yourself in one of the remote villages where dragon attacks are common. Sooner or later, one will appear in search of easy prey in the form of farm animals. Then you must confront the dragon with the magical spell you have learned while holding the orb in front of you. If you succeed, the dragon's life force will channel into the orb and the dragon will not harm you for fear of damaging the orb. To do so would kill it."

"So you keep the orb with you at all times?" asked Belham.

"Yes," said Brendan. "A good practice is to mount it atop your staff." He held his out so the others could see it.

"Excellent idea!" exclaimed Gresham. "It can't be lost so easily that way."

"It was Violet's idea," said Brendan, turning a smiling face to the fair-haired mage.

Violet blushed.

"Have you thought about how you're going to fight other dragons?" asked Toele.

Brendan frowned. "Yes, but I have no answer for that as yet."

"How do you care for such a creature?" asked Arch Mage Doris. "It must surely have an appetite."

"We have thought of that," responded Violet, "since that's when the dragon is hardest to control. They do indeed eat an enormous amount of food. Brendan has an arrangement with his dragon to let it fly north to an area where dragons like to feed."

"How do you know it goes north to feed?" asked Toele. "For all you know, it goes to the nearest human settlement to gorge itself before coming back."

Violet shook her head. "While giving the dragon permission to feed, Brendan had given it instructions to leave the human settlements alone. While it was gone, we watched for signs that a dragon attack had occurred in a human settlement. As yet there have been none. A few dragons have been spotted in towns south of here, but each of those times Burnett was with Brendan."

"That's good," said Gresham, "but we should continue to monitor this going forward, particularly if we manage to control more dragons."

"Absolutely," said Brendan, "but once you get to know one of these magnificent creatures, you'll know they are as good as their word."

"Telepathically speaking," said Belham with a wink.

Brendan laughed. "I suppose you're right."

"One other note," added Violet. "Brendan's dragon will only venture a certain distance for a certain time before it feels strongly inclined to return to where the orb is located. It cannot stay away for long, no matter how hard it tries."

"That's good," said Belham. "That way we know they will always return."

Gresham rubbed his hands together. "Well, I think it's time to get into action. We have much to do in the next short while."

"I'll rearrange the magical ring factory to accommodate more orbs," said Belham eagerly.

"If you need more people I'll get Arch Mage Tesa to assemble a team to help," offered Gresham.

Belham blinked. He had an affinity for the short, stout mage. He had worked with her on several occasions and enjoyed her company. "I'd love the help!" he exclaimed.

Gresham grinned. "I thought so." He gave a few additional instructions to some of the others and then everyone headed off to their respective tasks, leaving Brendan and Violet in the company of the dragon, along with the mages on security detail.

Chapter 12

A few days had passed and the companions were heading north after stopping briefly in Ridholm. Kazin was disappointed in how little information he had gleaned from the locals. It seemed everyone in that town was too busy to talk. But he did learn a few things about the old world that many of them had left behind.

Apparently, there had been many years of drought, and food was extremely difficult to come by. Nations were constantly declaring war on one another only to discover the territory they were fighting for was just as dry and barren as their own. People quickly became disillusioned about the fighting when they discovered the people in authority were the only ones who benefitted from the spoils of war. They abandoned the army in droves, much to the disappointment of power-hungry leaders who offered substantial gold and silver to their people to fight for them. They didn't realize that even money could not buy food that did not exist. The people instead used their money to buy one way fares on ships destined to a new land where food was reported to be abundant. Even the rumours of having to fight unusual creatures and dragons seemed more appealing that staying where they were and starving while their leaders decided what rations to hand out on a daily basis. At least they would have something to fight for in the new land.

The shipping companies were the ones who had profited the most from the arrangement. They had plenty of business, and the influx of currency meant they could manufacture additional ships at a record pace. They even manufactured warships for the Barlin Shipping Company, named after Admiral Barlin, who had been the first human to sail into the Bay of Barlin and discover a lush, soil rich land that was ideal for a new settlement. The admiral returned a second time with a number of settlers supported by a military force and the first settlement took hold in the new land. Later ships brought cattle and poultry, and from then on there had been no stopping the wave of newcomers.

Alliances were forged with the dwarves and elves, and trade was established. Magic was an entirely new concept, and the elves were astounded when they learned that many humans were capable of this ancient art. From there, human mage guilds were formed and evolved into the form that currently existed.

But that was all history. The only thing they could establish regarding their mission was that it probably had something to do with the war and the upcoming upheaval to the world as they knew it.

Now they traveled along a dusty road that was used primarily by patrols as they moved between various guard posts situated along the perimeter of the humans' realm. This was the route they had decided upon after much deliberation. Amelia had cautioned them time and again about the need to distance themselves from any unnecessary encounters that could change the future. There had already been too much interference as far as she was concerned. Thus the less-traveled path was chosen, and here they rode on horses they had acquired in Ridholm.

Kazin did admonish the need to reach the war zone, however, and no amount of non-interference should stop them from going there, since, as he put it, the threat to the future had to be stopped. And he would do whatever was in his power to destroy it. He had no choice but to interfere when the time came.

Amelia was not pleased about that threat, but conceded it was the only way to deal with the problem.

Because they were effectively going the long way, they were all in agreement that they should make haste. What they hadn't counted on was the dense fog that had wafted in from the east. The gaseous vents on the jagged peaks to their right were poisonous if one was too close to them, but they were far enough away that the gases were diluted to a harmless level.

Zylor was in the lead on a very large horse. Ordinarily, he would have opted to run alongside the others. Minotaurs on foot could easily keep up to mounted riders provided the horses weren't galloping at full speed. They didn't have any use for horses in general, except for the purposes of food. But it wouldn't do for him to be without a horse should they come across a patrol or some travelers. He was thankful for the thick fog. This meant he did not need to be under the annoying spell that made him look human. Should someone happen along, Kazin could quickly cast the spell on him and the amulet would take over, concealing his true identity once again.

A noise to his right caused him to reign in his horse and hold up his hand. His horse's breath steamed in the cool, damp air, a testament to its overwhelming load.

Because of the fog, Sherman, on a large horse as well, nearly bumped into the minotaur before realizing he had called a halt. The others pulled up behind them and Zylor explained that he had heard something.

After a few minutes of waiting, he shook his head in exasperation. "Maybe it was just the wind." He spurred his horse forward and the others followed quietly.

Less than a minute later Zylor called a halt again. He snorted. "There's something out there," he growled. "I smell it."

"What is it?" asked Harran.

Zylor shook his head. "I've never come across the scent before. It's - irritating."

"Maybe it's the gas," suggested Olag. "That's not a scent you've experienced before. I can smell it too."

"No," growled Zylor. "It's the scent of a creature of some sort. My instincts tell me it's extremely dangerous."

Olag snorted. "How can you tell it's dangerous if you don't -," he broke off.

Everyone turned to the skink warrior as his eyes widened in alarm. His spiked fins stiffened and his nostrils flared. "I see what you mean, Zylor. I just caught a whiff of it. I'm chilled to the bone and I don't know why." He turned to Kazin. "Don't you feel it?"

Kazin shook his head.

"Maybe someone cast a spell on us," suggested Sherman.

"Then why aren't the rest of us affected?" asked Harran.

Kazin did a 'spell check' spell and the orb atop his staff glowed purple. "That's strange," he muttered.

"What is it?" asked Amelia.

"There is magic in the area, but I've never encountered this kind before," responded the arch mage quietly. "I should know what this magic is, but I don't recall -."

A scream suddenly broke the still air. A moment later it was repeated.

"Someone's in trouble!" exclaimed Sherman. He fingered his sword nervously.

"It came from over there," added the dwarf, pointing to the right.

"We should go help!" said Sherman through clenched teeth.

Amelia cleared her throat and everyone turned to look at her. She held up her orb. It was glowing with a dark pink. "I think not."

The scream sounded again and everyone turned to the old mage. Kazin swallowed nervously. "We must ignore it. Let's move on."

They hesitated, but there were no more screams. Zylor cursed and spurred his horse forward, muttering under his breath. One by one the others followed until only Amelia was left. The group was just fading from sight when her orb turned a dark red. The further away the others rode, the darker it became. It also began to vibrate - a new feature that had never occurred before. The orb vibrated more and more violently and started to heat up.

"Guys, wait!" cried Amelia. She spurred her horse forward to catch up with the others. "Stop!"

They all turned to the spell caster as she galloped up to them in a panic. "The orb is telling me - us - not to ignore this - whatever it is. Riding away from it makes it worse!" For added effect she held up her orb. It was a brilliant red.

"But we're not supposed to interfere -," objected Olag. He was quite happy to be heading away from the danger.

A scream sounded again, still off to the right, but a bit further back where they had first heard it.

"I say we check it out," said Sherman resolutely.

"I'm with you," growled Zylor.

"We'll all go," said Kazin, "but proceed with caution. There is magic in the air and it could be a ruse of some sort."

"I'm inclined to agree," seconded Olag. "Whatever it is, it's not to be trifled with."

The orb in Amelia's hand began to pulse. "I think we'd better hurry," she urged.

Sherman was already in motion, with Zylor and Harran on either side of him. Kazin urged his horse forward with the others in order to keep up.

It took only a few moments before they reached the edges of the jagged territory where the land rose up in jutted peaks that marked the beginning of 'no man's land'. To travel further meant risking death. The gaseous vents and treacherous terrain, along with the stories of no one returning from this territory alive were reason enough to stay away.

"That's funny," muttered Harran. "I didn't realize we had ventured so close to this area."

"Neither did I," grumbled Sherman. "The fog must have caused us to travel off course."

"No doubt," said Kazin. "I did notice the fog was getting thicker."

A scream sounded again, this time much closer. One of the horses whinnied and the others became skittish. Amelia cast a spell on the horses which immediately calmed them.

Zylor dismounted. "The horses aren't going any closer. We'll have to leave them behind."

"Someone will have to stay with them," said Kazin as he and the others followed suit. "We can't risk them being scared off."

"I'll stay," offered Olag.

"Very well," said Kazin.

"We can tie the reins to these outcrops so you don't have to hold them," suggested Harran. He tied his horse's reigns around an obsidian stalagmite-shaped rock that protruded from the ground at an odd angle. The others followed his example.

Within moments everyone was ready to proceed. Just then another scream sounded, followed by a short cry.

"I'll lead the way," said Harran. No one argued. His instinct with finding his way in the mountains was legendary.

As the skink warrior watched the others disappear into the mist, he suddenly realized he was going to be alone with only the horses for company. He didn't want to face the dangers the others were about to face, but being alone was just as bad. Olag hoped they wouldn't be long. Suddenly a thought struck him and he shuddered. What if they didn't come back? What if they succumbed to whatever was casting those spells and he was left to fend for himself? He certainly couldn't go to the humans for help, and his own kind wouldn't even recognize him. He would be a freak of nature, and would be shunned by everyone. The skink warrior would truly be alone. Olag groaned inwardly and chided himself for going on this quest. It was a bad idea. Only one thing gave him hope. That was the knowledge that the group he now traveled with was the most courageous, savvy, and capable crew he had ever encountered. They had gotten out of some extremely dangerous situations before. This was no different. If anyone could come back from this current undertaking, it was they. Besides, they were his friends. They were also honourable. They would never abandon him. Somehow he had earned their trust, and he wasn't about to let them down either. They were in this together.

With a sigh of resignation, the skink warrior hunkered down between some smooth outcrops and opened a can of trail rations to distract his troubled mind. At least he still had possession of the invisibility ring should he need it.

Harran crept forward slowly. He pointed ahead of him. "I see the outlines of a cave," he whispered. "We must be close."

The others crowded around him and squinted into the fog. Suddenly, the fog lifted slightly, revealing a strange sight. Left of the cave entrance was a dry, lifeless tree. Bound to it was a young woman in a tattered dress. Prodding at her with some sharp sticks were a pair of orcs. They were drooling and gurgling in glee every time they succeeded in eliciting a moan or cry from their captive.

Sherman drew his sword and started forward with Zylor at his side when Kazin cried, "Stop!" They looked questioningly at the mage.

"It's an illusion!" said Kazin. "It's not real!"

The woman screamed again and Sherman winced. "Are you sure? It sounds awfully real to me."

Suddenly Harran began to jump around uncontrollably. "Get them off me! Get them off me!" His legs were covered in red ants.

"Ignore it!" yelled Kazin. "It's not real! It's only illusion!"

Then a giant bat swept down on the mage from above. Instinctively, he swatted it aside with his hand and felt it slash his arm. He cursed at his reaction. "It can't hurt you unless you believe it's real!"

Meanwhile, Harran was still hopping around and the warrior and minotaur were on their way to deal with the orcs. Amelia was using magic to deal with the giant bats as they became more and more numerous. One bat swooped down on Kazin again, but this time he closed his eyes and took a deep breath. Nothing happened. As the bat made contact with him, it vanished. The illusion had no effect if he refused to believe in it. Now he had to convince his friends of that. He walked over to Harran and held him firmly by the shoulders. "They're not real!" he yelled into the dwarf's face. By now the dwarf's legs were entirely covered with large red ants. "Ignore them! They're not real!" Kazin repeated.

Harran squeezed his eyes shut and repeated. "They're not real. They're not real." As quickly as the ants had appeared they vanished. The dwarf opened his eyes and breathed a sigh of relief.

"That's how you resist," said Kazin. "Don't believe the illusion is real."

Harran nodded.

Kazin glanced back at Amelia as a giant bat struck her and vanished. She had heard Kazin and was tuning out the illusions. She gave the arch mage a wan smile and nodded. "I'm ok."

Kazin heard a clash behind him and spun around to see Sherman and Zylor engaging the orcs in combat. Strangely, the orcs had acquired swords and shields. Even more alarmingly, they seemed to increase in size, becoming larger every moment. Within seconds they were bigger than even the minotaur.

"Sherman! Zylor! They're not real!" cried Kazin, running over to the struggling fighters. Perspiration beaded Sherman's forehead as he fought in desperation against an ever growing foe.

The warrior fended off blow after blow, having changed from attacking to defending tactics.

"It's not real, Sherman," said Kazin loudly. He stepped into the apparition as it swung its sword at him. In an instant the orc vanished, and Kazin was unharmed. Kazin resolutely stepped into Zylor's opponent and it also vanished.

The minotaur lowered his axe, his breathing ragged. "I could have taken it," he growled.

"Kazin, behind you!" yelled Amelia.

Kazin turned just as the creature lunged into him, sending him sprawling. "A harpy!" cried Kazin, struggling to his feet. "Let's get out of here!"

The creature, with a hag's head and a bird's body, circled for another attack.

"Is it real?" asked Sherman.

"That's what's been creating all the illusions!" cried Kazin.

"Then let me at it!" yelled Sherman, lunging forward to intercept the gruesome creature.

"No, Sherman!" cried Kazin. "Those creatures are powerful! Even magic won't affect them!"

Sherman ignored him, slashing and parrying with the enraged beast. Zylor tried to get closer to the combatants but there wasn't enough room to gain access. The harpy used its wings to fight from the edge of a precipice, and Sherman was dangerously close to losing his footing on the smooth rock surface.

Kazin didn't know what to do. He suddenly wished Olag was present to use his arrows. It was the only effective way to deal with such an aerial beast. Harran and Amelia watched the epic battle in amazement. The harpy easily avoided every slash of Sherman's sword, twisting out of the way with the ease of a fly. Her wings swung her in close enough for her to claw at the warrior's shoulder and in the same wing beat she swerved away from another useless strike by the warrior.

Suddenly Kazin had an idea. His magic wouldn't work on the harpy, but it would work on Sherman. He chanted his spell and pointed his staff at Sherman's sword. In the blink of an eye it vanished. Sherman was too busy to notice and swung his apparently empty hands at the harpy. The creature wasn't sure what to expect and didn't move in time. Sherman's invisible sword sliced clean through one of the harpy's wings and then back through one of its legs.

With a scream not unlike the ones they had heard earlier, the harpy fell to the ground at Sherman's feet. As it lay there, it changed its form to one of a beautiful woman in torn clothes.

Sherman raised his sword and then hesitated, breathing heavily.

"Finish it!" yelled Kazin. "It's illusion!"

Sherman closed his eyes and swung downward. The scream that echoed throughout the region sent a chill through the spine of every living being within earshot.

"That's disgusting," rasped Sherman, looking at the ghastly corpse before him, with a hag's head and a bird's body.

"I'm amazed that we never encountered such a creature before," murmured Zylor.

"That's probably because they went extinct after the dragon wars," said Kazin. He had come up to them to be sure the creature was indeed dead. "Either that, or they left the region like the dragons did, for reasons we can only guess."

"Good thing too," muttered Sherman. "They're nasty creatures." He turned to Kazin. "How did you know the orcs were an illusion, Kazin? We just got here and you started hollering at us that none of it was real. How did you know that?"

Kazin grinned sheepishly. "Remember when my staff turned purple and I couldn't figure out what that meant? That's because I forgot that purple usually signals that illusion magic is being used. I very rarely encounter illusion magic cast by someone else, even though I use it frequently myself. For instance, I use illusion magic to make Zylor appear human. But once I saw the scene with the orcs, I became suspicious. Both the human woman and the orcs were out of place here. That's when I remembered the significance of the purple colour of the orb on my staff. It had to be illusion magic. I knew that's what it was, but not what caused it - until the harpy attacked me. Harpies have extremely powerful magic, particularly when it's related to illusion. That's why it's so realistic. Until now, I've only ever seen them in books that we studied in the tower when I was an apprentice. But once you see something like that, you don't ever forget it."

Voices behind them caused the trio to turn around. Harran and Amelia were standing at the cave entrance peering inside. Amelia's orb was shining with a bright white light.

"What have you got?" asked Kazin as they walked up to the dwarf and spell caster.

Amelia straightened and looked at Kazin. "As soon as the harpy was slain, my orb stopped glowing red. As I got closer to this cave, it started glowing white."

"What does that mean?" asked Sherman.

Amelia hesitated. "Well, it only ever does that in one place - in my father's study. It has a tendency to light up whenever I wish to examine one of his magic scrolls. I've occasionally had to lend it to my father because he finds the light helpful when he studies spell scrolls."

"It sounds like you have an artifact that is partial to spell scrolls and spell books," said Kazin. "It's not unheard of for artifacts to be drawn to certain things. The various spells and spell components used to endow the artifacts with magic tend to polarize the item toward certain things. Your orb was probably enhanced with magic using a number of different spells from a number of different scrolls and spell books." He pointed to Sherman's sword. "Sherman's sword has a tendency to do severe damage to undead creatures. Somehow spirits are related to its creation, hence the term 'spirit blade'."

Amelia gaped at the arch mage with new found respect. He was very knowledgeable when it came to magic. She made a point to learn what she could from this man.

"So Amelia's orb is saying there's a spell scroll nearby?" asked Zylor.

"I'll bet it's in there," said Harran, pointing into the cave mouth.

Kazin moved forward and did a few spell checks. One for the presence of other creatures, one for magical warding, one for illusions, and one for magical or mechanical traps. Finding none, he gave the ok to enter the cave. "Just don't touch anything until I check it to make sure it's not cursed," he admonished. Having said that he lit his staff and led the way in. Zylor, not being interested in magical treasures, offered to keep watch outside.

The cave entrance opened up into a dingy cavern where several short tunnels and alcoves were apparent in the gloom. All of the tunnels were short and most were dusty from lack of use. Those ones ended in dead ends or fissures where light wisps of poisonous gas emanated. They hastily vacated these areas and concentrated on the only two tunnels that did seem to be used. These tunnels led to small caverns where the harpy obviously had made her home. The first one they examined was equipped with logs and boulders set in some sort of furniture arrangement. Some of the boulders were used as tables, and others were set in a pattern meant to be a hearth, with smaller rocks piled around in a circular pattern to prevent cooking fires from spreading. Some left-over meat from some unknown source was still in the homemade fire pit and flies swarmed the contents.

Amelia gagged. "Uggh! That's disgusting!"

"Not a healthy diet, I'd say," remarked Sherman.

"I don't expect the harpy had much choice," added Kazin. "There's not likely very much to eat in these parts."

A metallic crash made them all jump in surprise.

"Where's Harran?" asked Sherman, looking around anxiously. The light provided by Kazin's staff and Amelia's orb cast strange flickering shadows on the wall around them.

Kazin muttered under his breath, remembering suddenly that dwarves could see well in the dark, being adapted to cave life. He led the others from the first room back into the cavern where the tunnels branched off. They saw Harran emerging from the second tunnel they hadn't examined yet.

The dwarf grinned at them sheepishly. "Sorry. I bumped into some rusty armour in the other room. It must be the harpy's storage room. There is a bunch of things in there she must have accumulated over the years from some unwary explorers."

"Let's take a look," said Kazin. He held his staff aloft as he led them into the second cavern. The rusty armour Harran had bumped into was in a haphazard pile to the left and was indicative of everything else in the cavern.

"It looks like harpies like to be sloppy," remarked Harran.

"It's not like they have a lot of guests," added Amelia.

"Unless they have you over for supper," joked Sherman.

Amelia shuddered. "I don't like creatures who eat people."

"I'm sure they'd like you," chided Sherman, "with a little seasoning, of course."

Amelia glared at Sherman and he laughed. "I'm just kidding."

"Alright, you two, knock it off," said Kazin. "Let's just give this place a quick scan and then we'll get out of here." He coughed. "The gases aren't something we should be breathing for long." He cast a spell to see if anything was cursed or protected by magic but nothing showed. "It's all safe," he declared.

They wandered around and kicked things aside in the hopes of exposing something useful.

As Amelia approached the back of the cavern, her orb brightened. "There's something here," she called. The spell caster began to go through the contents on the floor at her feet and Kazin joined her.

"Aha!" she exclaimed jubilantly as she shook the contents of a ratty old robe to the floor. Among the items lying there was an old, weathered spell book with most of the pages torn out. She carefully picked up the book and opened some of the pages. The characters were severely faded but appeared to be elven letters and symbols.

Kazin had lived among the elves for a time so he leaned in close to examine the words. "Hmm," he mused. "I know some of the characters, but many of them look unfamiliar."

"This book is very old," said Amelia very quietly. "I recognize some of the symbols from an old elven dialect long since forgotten."

Kazin looked at the young, red haired spell caster curiously. There was a certain attraction he suddenly felt for her but he shook it off. Perhaps the gas in the air was getting to him. He was far too old to experience such feelings. "How far back in time have you gone?" he asked.

Amelia smiled up at the arch mage sweetly. "Oh, a fair ways," she said vaguely. She had a soft expression and Kazin was hypnotized for a moment.

"There's some jewelry over here," interrupted Harran.

They went over to examine the items the dwarf had pointed out. There was a pouch containing bracelets, necklaces, and rings.

"It probably isn't of much use to us," said Kazin. "We don't need items to sell for gold with our magical pouch of coins handy."

"Why don't you check them for magic?" suggested Amelia.

Kazin shrugged. "Why not?" He cast his spell and nothing showed. "I guess that answers that question."

"Wait," said Harran. He withdrew a dark green ring from the pouch. "I thought I saw this ring sparkle when you did your magic."

Kazin sighed and repeated his spell. Sure enough, the ring emitted a number of very tiny sparkles. "Hmm," said the arch mage, scratching his beard thoughtfully.

"What is it?" asked Amelia.

"Usually magical items emit a continuous light when I cast this spell on them. I've never encountered a response like this before."

"Maybe it's cursed," said Sherman.

Kazin shook his head. "No. It's not cursed. But it is magical."

"Someone should try it on," suggested Amelia.

Harran held the ring out to Amelia. "Ladies first."

Amelia looked at Kazin.

"Go ahead," said the arch mage. "I can remove any negative effects with magic, should it be required."

Amelia slowly took the ring and put it on her finger. She immediately looked younger and more radiant than before. Any wrinkles she had were gone.

Sherman whistled. "You look beautiful."

"Indeed," murmured Kazin. The gases were definitely having an effect on him.

"I don't feel any different," said Amelia. She removed the ring and immediately looked like her former self again. The mage held the ring out to the others. "Someone else try it on."

Harran put the ring on and instantly looked many years younger. His beard became darker and his face became less weathered. After everyone commented on his appearance, he removed the ring and passed it to Sherman, who also looked more youthful under the ring's spell.

Then the ring ended up on Kazin's finger. He appeared just as he did when he made himself appear younger in the town of Malley.

"I think you should keep the ring," said Amelia with conviction. "It makes the biggest difference on you."

"She's right," agreed Sherman. "It feels a lot more like old times when you look like that."

Harran shrugged. "It makes sense to me. I did notice it made me feel a bit younger too, but maybe that was just my imagination."

Kazin noted that the ring did make him feel younger. He sighed. "Ok. I'll keep it. But let's conclude our business here. Our quest is far more important than rings of youth. We've lost some valuable time with this entire diversion."

Amelia held up her orb, which had dimmed after the discovery of the spell book. "At least the orb is no longer red. We did the right thing by eliminating the harpy. History could have been altered had we left it to terrorize others who ventured too close."

"Don't you think it's odd that our interference corrected history instead of altering it?" asked Harran.

"And it's not the first time," added Sherman, looking pointedly at the red-haired mage. Amelia reddened.

"It could be that we are already in the process of correcting history," put in Kazin. "The orb might be telling us to react instead of the other way around. We'll have to take it one step at a time." He turned and headed back to the tunnel leading out of the cavern. "Right now we should find a safe place to regroup and concentrate on healing any wounds we've incurred."

But Harran's question bothered him too. He was all too aware of the danger that he and his companions could alter history with one wrong move or action. Could they actually be the cause of the whole problem in the first place? That was a distinct possibility. Only time would tell. Kazin shook his head at the irony. Time would tell all right, in his own future.

Chapter 13

alado rose stiffly after a fitful night where he battled for control of his body. The original spirit seemed to come out of the depths every time he wanted to get some sleep. It knew that was when his control was weakest. He still did not understand why the original spirit was not left behind at the time travel bridge where it was supposed to be. What could possibly be causing such an unbreakable bond? He ground his teeth in frustration. He needed to get his true body soon. That was his priority.

It was still well before dawn when Galado got dressed and went down the stairs to the main level. The house was lit with expensive oil lamps and Galado's crew was busy finishing preparations for departure. They were in the estate of the wealthy merchant, which belonged to the old man who had been slain in the coach.

Some documents in the coach had indicated the address in the next town where he resided with his three daughters. After seizing control of the coach and guard's bodies, they had made their way straight to that destination.

Upon arrival, some men had opened the gates leading to the estate. Two of Galado's men had quickly dispatched the gate keepers while Galado and his crew had ridden boldly up to the house. They had dismounted and barged into the house led by Galado, where he and his entourage had then made quick work of the staff. Catching everyone off guard, the operation had been swift and mostly noiseless.

There was only one thing that had not gone according to plan. The doorman who had been preparing to open the door for his master had been stunned by Galado's intrusion. He had been about to object, when Galado's sword pierced his chest. He had sagged to his knees as Galado pulled the sword free. Then he had fallen over and his eyes faded, while blood appeared at his mouth. In the meantime, Galado's men and women had swarmed into the house in order to dispatch the rest of the unwary staff. Galado had waited for the inevitable surge of energy from his sword to enter the dead doorman's body, but none had come. A faint laugh had echoed in his brain and whispered in hoarse glee. "Hah! You can't use that trick anymore! You're out of souls! Hee, hee, hee!" Galado had tried to shake the voice from his head. He had grimly set about looking for other people to slay, only to discover the voice was right. There would be no more spirits joining his army.

After the gruesome work had been done, he had issued some orders to his crew. Then he had used the luxurious dwelling to bathe and shave, and then found a comfortable bed in order to get some rest.

Now, as he emerged in the dining room, he saw eight of the ten of his army present in various bodies, waiting patiently for his arrival.

One man, dressed in sentry garb, rose and beckoned to the table where a warm meal sat waiting. "Help yourself to some food, Boss. Everything's under control. Three and Five have the gate house under control. No one will interrupt us."

"I take it you're One?" asked Galado, acknowledging the guard.

"Yes," said One.

Galado nodded and sat down to have breakfast while the others watched. It was an odd feeling, but he knew they no longer needed food to sustain themselves.

While Galado ate, he formulated a plan to reach the front lines of the human army and then make his escape to the other side. It was just as well his crew was not too large. Stealth would play an important role in the days ahead. He looked up at One. "Do we have enough horses and weapons available?"

One nodded. "Yes."

"Supplies?"

"Yes. We packed as per your orders last night."

"Bodies?"

"Stashed under the hay in the stables."

"Good," said Galado. He finished his breakfast in silence and rose to his feet. "Does everyone have a body that is presentable and will last a while?" As he spoke, he noted the three women among them. He approved of their battle attire and weapons. The old man must have had an impressive armoury to draw from. The women looked just as ready for battle as the men.

"We do," said One. "In fact, some of us are finding we can make the bodies last a little longer than at first. It's a matter of getting used to the new body each time."

"Good," said Galado. "We have several days' ride ahead of us. I do not want to waste time."

"What should we do about the estate?" asked one of the women.

"We lock it up so no one can enter," said Galado. "The longer it takes to discover what happened here, the better. We should be long gone by that time."

The woman nodded.

"Let's be ready to leave in twenty minutes," said Galado.

"Right, Boss," said One. He turned to the others. "You heard him. Let's get cracking!"

Less than twenty minutes later the gang emerged from the estate grounds on horseback. They exited the gates quietly and locked them securely behind them. The estate was close to the edge of town, so they had no difficulty emerging onto the road heading in a westerly direction. As they widened the gap between the town and themselves, they increased their pace. One led an extra pack horse with basic supplies, gold and food for the 'Boss'. No one looked behind them or felt the slightest remorse for the deaths they had caused. All that mattered now were Galado's objectives.

✕   ✕   ✕   ✕   ✕

The warlock closed his spell book and took a deep breath. The spells were starting to blur before his eyes. Perhaps a short break would clear his mind. He needed a temporary diversion and got one just then when he heard a timid knock on the curtain support post.

"What is it, Gorc?" asked the warlock.

Gorc jumped in surprise - not that the warlock knew it was he, but that he wasn't being berated for his interruption. "Um, Sir, there's a messenger here to see you," stammered the goblin-orc.

"Who is it?" asked the warlock.

144

"Um, it's um," stammered Gorc. The warlock still hadn't yelled at him.

"Out with it, you useless creature!" snapped the warlock. "Maybe you'll talk better without your tongue getting in the way! Should I tear it out for you?"

That was more like it. "An ogre is here to speak with you," managed Gorc.

The warlock straightened in his chair. "Did you say 'ogre'?"

"Y-yes, Sir," stammered Gorc.

"Why didn't you say so?!" growled the warlock. "Show him into the main command room. Tell him I'll be there shortly."

"Yes, Sir," said Gorc. He bowed and left hastily.

The warlock's pulse quickened in anticipation of this encounter. This was the meeting he had been waiting for. If his plans concerning the ogres panned out, he would have the upper hand in the war. It was time to sweet talk the ogres into supporting his cause. All he had to do was find out what they wanted and offer it to them. They weren't a complicated race; they were just as greedy as the others who now served him. It was just a matter of exploiting that greed for his own purposes.

He quickly put on one of his better robes - a shimmering metallic blue cape of elven silk that could not be torn, sewn over a stainless lightweight chainmail. The chainmail was not visible or noticeable to anyone, and was barely noticeable to the warlock himself, thanks to the magic he had applied to it making it virtually weightless. He smoothed his hair and mustache, and stroked his goatee. Then he made his way into the conference room where the ogre commander stood uncertainly.

The warlock stewed at Gorc's ineptitude. "Please! Have a seat!" he beckoned to his visitor. "You've come a long way and should have a rest!" He looked over his shoulder and bellowed, "Gorc! Have some food and drink brought in for my guest!"

"Yes, Sir," squeaked a weak voice from the next room.

The warlock turned his attention back to the ogre, who was already sitting down. The ogre removed his cap and the warlock was astounded to see that the ogre was in fact a female, with light brown hair which fell down to her shoulders in a straggly mess. Her hard features and helmet had made her appear like one of the many males of her species. But then male and female ogres were difficult to tell apart under normal circumstances anyway.

Regaining his composure, the warlock sat opposite his guest and displayed a beguiling smile. "So, to what do I owe this pleasure?"

The ogre did not smile back. "I am Commander Becka, and I come to make a trade."

"A trade?"

The ogre nodded. "We have a common enemy in the humans. For some time now we have been trying to thwart the humans by interfering with the flow of weapons from the dwarves. When successful, we succeed in accumulating finely crafted weapons and armour which, as you know, are unequaled in strength and durability."

"I applaud your efforts," said the warlock. He was surprised to note the sophisticated level of speech from this ogre. Most ogres spoke in short, blunt phrases. This one had a higher level of intellect than he had imagined possible from these creatures. He would have to watch his step. "Please, continue."

The ogre nodded. "We have gotten to the point of storing large numbers of these weapons and armour, including helmets and shields; more than we require ourselves; yet our campaign rages on."

"Continue," said the warlock. He was interested in finding out where this was leading.

"Recently, the dwarves have been increasing their security around the convoys of goods, forcing us to gather in larger numbers," continued the ogre. "This is making ambush nearly impossible. As a result of our numbers, we are spotted well in advance. Then the dwarven guards send a signal to the convoy and they make haste in another direction. Since they are on horseback, we are unable to catch up to them. Our speed is no match for them and they use that to their advantage." Becka shrugged. "Occasionally we get lucky and corner them in an area where the going is difficult, but their scouts ensure this doesn't happen often. And when we do engage them, the fighting is fierce. Our warriors grumble because there does not seem to be a point to their efforts. The humans continue to battle on. Even skirmishes along their northern border are going nowhere. They have numbers on their side, as well as magic."

"I see your dilemma," said the warlock.

At this point Gorc came in with a tray and placed a hot meal in front of the warlock and his guest. Then he poured two glasses of elven wine before swiftly departing.

"So, commander," began the warlock as his guest dug unceremoniously into her food, "how can I be of help?"

Becka gave the first inclination of a smile. "I noticed your forces are a little under equipped for this war." She took another bite of her food. "You could use some better weapons and armour."

"Indeed," said the warlock slowly. The ogre was not exaggerating. His army's weapons were sub-par. He took a bite of his own food so as not to appear concerned. "And what can I offer in exchange?"

Becka swallowed her food, obviously enjoying the flavour. "We need something to give us an edge in our struggle. It would be useful to have access to magic. That would not only even the odds against the human guard posts, but would make it possible for us to stem the flow of weapons from the dwarves. Even though the dwarves are naturally more resistant to magic, we could use the magic in other, more creative ways."

The warlock grinned inwardly. So that was it! The ogres did not wield magic, and wanted some to increase their chances of success! He ate some more food, using the pause to think of what to say. "Ok," he said as he stroked his goatee. "Perhaps we can come to an arrangement. What did you have in mind?"

Becka nodded. "We will give you our surplus weapons in exchange for a contingent of lizardmages. The magic will go a long way in slowing down the shipments of weapons to the humans you now face."

The warlock frowned. "I can continue my campaign regardless of what weapons we wield. It doesn't matter to me what the enemy uses. We will kill them for their weapons if need be. We'll get them one way or another. My problem is the numbers of humans we have to deal with, not their weapons."

"Then we have no deal?" asked Becka. Her expression was dour.

The warlock held up his hand and grinned. "Don't be so hasty! I didn't say that!"

"Then what do you propose?"

The warlock smiled gently and calmly took another bite of food. "I value your efforts more than you know, commander. I propose that you supply us with your weapons while I provide you with a contingent of lizardmen you requested, with the added assurance that you combine your forces for an attack on the human guard posts and villages situated along their northern front. There will be minimal magical resistance since they will all be concentrating on my forces here."

Becka blinked. Then she spoke slowly. "Such an undertaking will be difficult. As I mentioned earlier, our numbers are too small to overcome that of the humans." The warlock frowned but the ogre continued. "However, we could probably succeed with the backing of an extra contingent of lizardmen. Just having them there will give our warriors the confidence they need to succeed."

The warlock thought for a moment and then smiled. "We have ourselves a deal!" He rose and held out his hand. The ogre rose also, making him feel small in comparison. She was a good foot taller than he. She took his hand into her giant one and shook it.

The warlock raised his glass of wine. "A toast to our new alliance!"

Becka, not used to such a delicate glass, gingerly took it in her gargantuan hand and held it up. "A toast."

They both downed the contents.

"If we succeed in driving back the humans," continued the warlock, "we can join forces and you won't have to worry about being outnumbered. After this undertaking, you are welcome to join the winning side; under my command, of course."

Becka grunted. "If this works, you have our allegiance." She put down her glass. "I ride out in the morning."

"I'll have your spell casters ready to move out when you're ready," assured the warlock.

Becka put her helmet back on and trudged out of the tent, her helmet squishing past the top of the opening. Entering at that moment and looking tiny compared to the previous guest was Gorc. He looked nervously over his shoulder. "The new contingents of orcs have arrived, Sir, along with two contingents of lizardmen."

The warlock smiled. "Just in time, Gorc. Just in time."

"Sir?" said Gorc nervously. His master's good mood was unnerving.

"Tell the lizardmen to re-supply and prepare to move out first thing in the morning. I'll give them their instructions shortly."

"Yes, Sir," said Gorc. He left the tent not relishing the idea of telling the lizardmen that they were moving on so soon. He hated their hissing of contempt whenever he was sent to give them instructions. They obviously resented a creature like him giving them orders. Furthermore, he had to wake one of the lizardmen commanders to accompany him with the orders so they would realize the orders were legitimate. Newcomers in particular would never believe what he said otherwise.

Chapter 14

Arch Mage Gresham could scarcely believe he had done it, yet here before him stood a menacing, fire-breathing dragon. The bronze giant towered above him like a giant elven tree, blocking out the sun with its massive head. The reptilian eyes never blinked once, and the nostrils flared as a result of the exertion expended in trying to resist the spell. Gresham's own breath was ragged from the magical spell, and adrenaline still flowed through his veins even now. It was an exciting experience for him. He never would have believed he could accomplish something of this magnitude with mere magic, yet here he stood, with a magnificent beast under his control.

"Well?" said a voice inside his head. Instinctively he looked around for the speaker, though he should have known the source of the voice.

"Are you just going to stand there like a fool or are we going to do something? I'm kind of hungry right now, so I'm going to find something to eat." The dragon looked across the field at some grazing cows.

Gresham shook off the strange feeling created by the dragon's telepathic voice and mounted the orb atop his staff in the specially designed tripod clasp that Arch Mage Violet had made for him.

The dragon watched this action with great interest. It was the object that housed its spirit. How it worked it did not know, but the mage had control over it. All it knew was the orb was an item to be protected at all costs. To lose it or damage it could mean death.

When Gresham had the orb securely affixed to the staff, he looked up at the dragon. "We will deal with your hunger, my friend. But first I would like to know what to call you. Do you have a name?"

The dragon wasn't interested in small talk, but knew somehow that it was expected to comply with the mage's wishes. It wanted to get the upper hand in its relationship with this magic wielder, so it bent its head close to the mage and breathed out its name slowly, as if it was preparing to fry the puny human on the spot. "Hooraath," hissed the dragon.

Arch Mage Gresham was shaking in his boots, but outwardly kept his composure. He wrinkled his nose. "Well, Horath, you ought to do something about your breath. Perhaps your diet needs to be changed."

Horath recoiled away from the mage. He was shocked at the puny human's impertinence. "Why, my breath is absolutely fine! Your nose is obviously too puny to distinguish good odours from bad ones!"

Gresham chuckled. "Obviously my puny nose works better than your massive one." To prevent the conversation from deteriorating he added, "but bad breath aside, I'm pleased to make your acquaintance, Horath. I'm Arch Mage Gresham, but you can call me Gresham."

"Hummph," said the dragon. "Sounds almost like 'greasy ham'." He lowered his head to the mage but a bit farther away this time. "You wouldn't happen to have any ham for me to eat, would you? North of the mountains there are prairies full of wild boars. They are so tasty!" The dragon pulled his head back. "I could devour dozens at a time!"

"Then why are you bothering with our cows?" asked Gresham.

The dragon tossed its head casually. "They're here, aren't they?"

"But they belong to us," said Gresham. "We raise them for milk and food."

"That's not my problem," stated Horath.

"It is now," said Gresham with an edge in his voice.

"How so?"

"Because your priority will be to defend the herds of cows, as well as humans and villages, against others of your kind."

Horath exhaled sharply, leaving a puff of steam in the air. "You can't be serious!"

"Oh, but I am," said Gresham. For added effect he reverently rubbed his fingers over the orb on his staff.

Horath jealously eyed the orb. "You pit me against other dragons? I could be killed!"

Gresham knew he had to proceed cautiously. "From what I can tell, dragons don't die so easily. They are a very resilient and intelligent race. You know when to stand down or flee if the odds are against you. You don't do things rashly; you put thought into your actions."

"That much is true," said Horath proudly.

"Besides," added Gresham, "I would never put you into a position beyond your capabilities."

Horath flinched in surprise. "Really?"

"Really," said Gresham. "We're linked in more ways than you can imagine. You are too valuable to me."

"I am?"

"Absolutely," said Gresham. "In fact, I've considered your hunger before I even captured you." He pointed over to the other side of the field. "There's a cow over on that side of the field that I've purchased for you. It's only one, but it should tide you over until you can find some proper food somewhere where there are no people around."

Horath looked across the field and then back at Gresham. "For me?"

Gresham smiled. "Yes."

"And you won't try to stop me?"

Gresham shook his head. "It's yours."

Horath turned and prepared to launch himself into the air.

"You'll find that I put thought into my actions as well," said Gresham. As Horath sprang into the air, the mage called after him. "We'll make a good team, you and I." He could only hope that his statement was true as the dragon flew toward his meal.

Elsewhere, Arch Mage Belham had been in a village not far from Sorcerer's Tower obtaining supplies for magical artifact production when a dragon had been sighted at the edge of town. He had hurried to the scene with the orb he had been given earlier that day and did the spell as he had been instructed. To his surprise, the spell had worked, and he had captured himself a female red dragon.

Fillith, as she was called, had a sense of humour that rivaled his own, and an appetite that only he could appreciate. She was considerably overweight, yet she soon convinced him to purchase an additional cow to satiate her hunger, and he was more than happy to oblige. In exchange, she offered to take Belham for a ride once she had finished eating. At first he had been nervous, clumsily climbing onto her back and trying to get comfortable. He laughed at his own awkwardness. Fillith must have been ticklish, because his awkward movements caused her to laugh as well. This resulted in Belham being bounced around, making them both laugh even more. As they took to the sky, they were both in tears they were laughing so hard.

After a while, though, they settled down and Belham marveled at the view below them. He hung onto Fillith's neck, his hands finding a comfortable spot where the scales joined. The arch mage had the time of his life. He enjoyed it so much he rode Fillith all the way back to the tower where he prepared to land in the courtyard as Brendan had done. The security guards and mages were alarmed at first, and Belham had to do several passes, yelling at the top of his lungs that he was not a threat, before he was given a signal that he was clear to land. He made a mental note to design some sort of password that could be given for a friendly dragon approaching the tower so there would be no confusion in the future.

Belham had to bring his supplies inside, so he left Fillith in the company of the guards with strict orders not to hurt anyone or damage anything. She was a big hit with the guards who were on duty, allowing them to get near and touch her scales and claws. To their delight, she even spoke with a few of them and joked around with them. Unlike Horath, Fillith was not bothered by the fact that her life essence was in the possession of a human arch mage. Her easy-going nature was a testament to the fact that not all dragons were ruthless, bloodthirsty, self-centered creatures. They were actually very intelligent and highly emotional, and could wreak havoc when things did not go their way, but they were mostly fair and cool-headed when one got to know them. How they managed to communicate with all of the various races in their own languages was a mystery that no one could solve. So it was simply attributed to some form of inherent magic on the dragons' part. In fact, it was learned that magic use acted like some sort of magnet, drawing dragons within a certain radius to investigate. When Fillith had been captured, she was being drawn to a couple of master mages who were practicing their art in a field so as not to bother anyone. Fillith had been innocently circling the mages when Belham had appeared and captured her life force in his orb.

Fillith had everyone's attention for about three hours, but that changed when a speck was spotted in the sky to the south east. As it got closer, it was identified as another dragon. The guards scurried to their posts and Belham was alerted. He came running into the courtyard out of breath and flustered.

"Oh, dear!" he panted. "I - I guess we have to do battle with the intruder." He looked at Fillith. "Um - I'm going to have to ask you to deal with -."

"The dragon," finished Fillith. She eyed the approaching dragon warily. "Ok then," she growled. "We'd better get moving. Hop on, Belham." She lowered her wing to let him climb on.

"What - me?!" squeaked Belham. "Are you sure -?"

"Just get on!" snapped Fillith. "You know magic, don't you? Having you with me improves my odds considerably. Now hurry up!"

Belham scrambled up to Fillith's neck, mumbling, "I don't think this is such a good -."

Fillith didn't give him a chance to finish. She launched herself into the air with a speed that belied her girth. "Oh, stop worrying!"

"But what if the other dragon decides to fry us with fire?" complained Belham. Fillith's speed made it difficult for him to maintain a secure hold.

"Don't you know shield magic?" asked Fillith. "I thought you were a powerful mage!" The approaching dragon increased rapidly in size.

"Of course I know shield magic," retorted Belham. He had a good grip now and was peering ahead at the oncoming dragon. It was very light in colour. Sunlight reflected off its wings displaying pure white scales. He wondered what sort of dragon it was.

"An albino!" hissed Fillith.

"A what?" asked Belham.

"A white dragon," explained Fillith. "They don't fry their prey like I do. They freeze them with ice breath."

"Ice breath?" repeated Belham weakly.

"Yes. What magic do you have at your disposal to combat ice magic?" asked Fillith.

"The best way to deal with ice magic is with fire magic of equal or greater intensity," said Belham. "I know quite a few spells that are based on fire."

"Good," said Fillith.

"But why don't you fry the dragon with your fiery breath?" asked Belham. "Your flame will be more powerful than my magic."

"That is true, but when two fire breathing dragons clash - as is the case most times - if one spews fire, the other can do the same. Fire dragons are naturally more immune to fire, but fighting like this could seriously injure or kill both of the dragons. Thus, dragons often clash with teeth and claws instead. But in this case, when dragons of opposite types fight, we use our ability to cancel out the opponent. If I spew fire, the ice dragon will cool off my magic with its ice breath before my flame reaches it. The resultant effect is a blast of hot steam at best. The same holds true if the ice dragon fires first. My flame will heat the ice breath and neutralize its effect. The only way to score a hit would be to catch the other dragon off guard so they don't have an opportunity to fire back. If we clash with teeth and claws, it causes pain and distracts the opponent, so flame or ice breath has a chance of doing damage. That's why I told you having you along will improve our odds. After you shield us from the first ice breath with your magical shield, you have the opportunity to go on the offensive immediately before the other dragon can prepare another shot. Any damage you do will distract it and I can hope to get in another shot of fire before there is any retaliation. It's all about getting in the first shot. The one with a successful first shot usually wins."

"It sounds like you've done this before," said Belham.

"Once or twice," muttered Fillith vaguely.

By now the approaching dragon was only a few hundred yards away. Belham readied himself for a shield spell but hesitated when he saw something unusual. Straddled across the white dragon's neck was an object that looked strangely - human. The figure straightened as Belham got closer and he could see the individual's hand raise into the air. At the same time, the white dragon veered away to the left.

Fillith adjusted her flight path to follow but Belham called out to her. "Wait! There's someone on that dragon!"

"I see them," said Fillith. "Do you know who it is?"

Belham squinted as they neared.

"Tell me soon or I'll attack!" snarled Fillith.

Then the figure on the back of the white dragon raised both arms and waved them back and forth. At the same instant the figure's hood flew back revealing blonde hair. He recognized the figure instantly. It was Arch Mage Violet.

"It's a friend!" cried Belham. "Stand down!"

Fillith veered away and let a small fireball loose as she exhaled. She looked back at her rider. "That was close!"

Belham sighed in relief too. He had almost attacked a fellow arch mage. He had enough excitement for one day and told Fillith to return to the tower.

As they turned, Violet and her mount pulled up alongside. "Hooray! You got one too!" she cheered.

"I almost fried you!" shouted Belham sternly. "I thought your dragon was a threat until I saw you!"

"Sorry!" called Violet. "I'm glad you held off long enough to see me!"

"I'm surprised you didn't shoot at me too!" said Belham.

"I saw your dragon rise from the tower's courtyard," said Violet. "I figured your dragon was one of ours, but I didn't know if it would see me as a threat or not - until I saw someone riding her. Then I knew I had to show that my dragon was under control and being ridden, and wasn't on a mission of destruction. I was counting on you to see me."

"I did see you," said Belham, "but I couldn't identify you until we were almost on top of you. My visual range is not much different from the dragon's attacking range."

"We'll have to be wary of that sort of thing when we get into combat," said Violet. "We don't want to be attacking each other."

"That's for sure," said Belham. "Now I know that if I see a dragon with a rider I should proceed with caution. I did notice you shortly before we were within attacking range, even though I couldn't identify who you were yet."

"That's good," said Violet. "It gives us a few extra seconds to react."

"Your white dragon is quite rare," commented Belham. "Now that I know your dragon is on our side, it won't be hard to identify you from a distance."

"That's true," said Violet, "but be aware that there are other ice dragons out there too."

"True enough," admitted Belham. He pointed to the tower's courtyard which was nearly below them. "I'll land first and give you a signal when it's safe for you to do so."

"Right," said Violet. "Myst and I will circle around until then."

Belham landed in the courtyard with Fillith and told the guards the white dragon was a friend. Then he gave the signal to land.

The white dragon was all the rage for a while, and Fillith sat in her corner quietly, clearly not impressed by the attention Myst was receiving. Belham consoled her by talking to her and getting to know her better. They had only been together for half a day, yet he could feel a kinship with the great beast. With evening wearing on, she hinted that she was getting hungry again. Belham himself was getting hungry and knew what the dragon felt like, so he gave her permission to fly north to feed on some wild animals. Before he let her go, he had a fluorescent red ribbon prepared and gently affixed around her neck. He instructed the night watch commander to look out for this ribbon and allow the dragon to land back in the courtyard when she returned from her foraging. A similar ribbon was prepared for Myst in case she decided to fly off in search of food. Being a white dragon, Myst hardly required a ribbon, but as Violet had pointed out, there were other white dragons out there too.

And so the dragon riders became an integral part of the world's history henceforth.

Chapter 15

he fragile figure awkwardly lurched forward, its single arm flailing for balance. One leg was longer than the other, causing it to walk in a wide arc. Soon it came to a smooth boulder that was too high for it to climb. It stopped and wobbled uncertainly for a moment before negotiating reverse motion with its legs.

"What have you got there?" asked a voice softly.

Amelia paused from her experiment to look at the young face of the speaker. She smiled up at him. "I'm glad you kept your ring on, Kazin."

Kazin smiled back. "I've noticed it makes me feel younger. This ring does more than just alter my appearance. I've rarely encountered an artifact that has multiple magical functions. The spell caster who made this was very talented."

"Spell casters in the past often wielded stronger magic than those in the future," said Amelia. "That's why magical artifacts are more common in this era."

"Do you know why this is the case?" asked Kazin.

"No. Do you?"

Kazin sighed. "No. That's one mystery I haven't figured out yet." He pointed to the log Amelia was sitting on. "May I join you?"

Amelia smiled in spite of herself. "Of course! Make yourself comfortable."

Kazin sat down and stretched out his legs. As usual, he was wearing his sandals, which was common footwear for mages. He pointed to Amelia's stick man. "I see you're experimenting with animation magic."

"Is that what it's called?" asked Amelia. Her stick man had regained its composure and was slowly walking back toward them. "I learned it from the magic book we found."

"Remarkable!" said Kazin. "It's a good thing you have some familiarity with the old dialect."

Amelia stole a sideways glance at the blonde mage beside her. "Thanks to you."

"What do you mean?" asked Kazin, returning her gaze.

"The tips you've given me over the past few days were a great help," explained Amelia. "Especially the information about concentration, mental discipline, and the art of letting the words and meaning of the spell sink in. I used to be in too much of a hurry to say and cast the spell, but your approach works better. Now I take the time to study and understand the spell and you know what? I can cast the spell much more effectively. The spell is less likely to go wrong too."

"That's great!" beamed Kazin. "You're a fast learner."

"It's the teacher," said Amelia, blushing.

Kazin nodded toward the stick man. "Your friend is about to get into trouble." As he spoke, the stick man moved within a step of Kazin's foot. Then, with an exaggerated swing of its leg, it stepped on one of Kazin's toes.

"Hey!" cried Kazin.

Amelia broke into a fit of laughter.

The stick man put its weight on its front leg and was about to lift its other leg when the front leg slipped off Kazin's toe and embedded itself in between two toes. It wobbled uncontrollably and flailed its arm wildly. This comical reaction caused Kazin to break into laughter along with Amelia and they soon had tears streaming from their eyes.

At last Amelia reached for her stick man and released it from its predicament. She examined it briefly before tossing it aside. "That's enough, little man," she giggled.

Sherman called from behind them to let them know the horses had been watered.

Kazin wiped his eyes. "It's time to move on. The horses are ready."

Amelia nodded. "Let's go."

They rejoined the others and everyone mounted their horses.

The jagged peaks were now behind them as they made their way westward. They were just south of the Velden Iron Mine on their way to Trent. The sun was shining overhead and there was a gentle breeze out of the north.

Within an hour, they came to a narrow gully bordered by a gently sloping hill on either side. The road went right through this gully. It was an excellent place for an ambush, so Harran rode ahead to scout out any potential danger. He was stopped in the middle of the gully when they caught up to him.

"Any sign of danger?" asked Sherman.

Harran shook his head. "All clear." He pointed to a spot off to the side where a makeshift cross protruded from a pyramid of stones. "It looks like someone was recently ambushed here, though. We'd better be alert just the same."

"Let's go then," growled Zylor. He scanned the surroundings intently. He was hoping for some action. It had been too quiet for too long as far as he was concerned.

"Wait," said Amelia. "My orb is vibrating."

They turned to her as she withdrew her orb. It was pulsing with a very light pink colour. It brightened when she held it toward the pile of stones.

"I'm not digging through that pile of stones!" growled Zylor. "That place belongs to the dead who lie there!"

"He's right," agreed Harran. "We shouldn't disturb it."

"I wouldn't dream of it," said Amelia curtly. "But something is out of place here. Whatever happened here was not supposed to take place. History has been altered, but it's not bad enough to affect the long term future."

Kazin scratched his head. "So something happened here that wasn't supposed to happen," he mused. "If that's the case, whoever or whatever caused this event is still out there. This could be important, or it could merely be an anomaly. We'll have to watch for clues as we go forward." He turned to Amelia. "Keep an eye on your orb, Amelia. Watch for any other signs that things aren't the way they should be."

Amelia nodded. "Right."

"Too bad that thing doesn't track what's causing the changes to history," said Olag. "That would be more useful."

"That's a good suggestion, Olag," said Kazin. He turned to Amelia. "See if you can figure out a way to use the orb to track the thing causing the anomaly."

"I'm not sure -," began Amelia.

"Remember the training I gave you," admonished Kazin. "If you keep applying a different technique to an artifact, it may respond differently. I'd guess that orb is fairly old, and you said yourself that spell casters in the past wielded stronger magic. That orb may have qualities that you don't even know about. Just take the time to study it. It'll come to you."

Amelia nodded uncertainly.

The companions moved swiftly through the gully with Harran and Zylor scouting ahead. There was only room for two abreast, so Kazin led the rest of them with Sherman at his side, while Amelia conversed with the skink warrior at the back.

"So Kazin," said Sherman in as quiet a voice as he could muster, "do you think it's wise to trust Amelia's orb? I still don't know if the orb is telling us what she claims. Could she be making the orb change colour so she can manipulate what we do?"

Kazin stared at his friend in shock. "Why do you say that, Sherman? Don't you trust her?"

Sherman reddened. "Well, it's just that I'm not sure if your judgment may be affected. You guys are hitting it off really well, and maybe you just aren't looking for those kinds of possibilities."

Understanding dawned on Kazin's face as Sherman spoke. He laughed in a friendly way and slapped Sherman's muscular arm. "Sherman, you are a valuable and loyal friend. Most people wouldn't see things like you do, and if they did, they would be afraid to say anything. You have the courage to bring things into discussion even if there's a chance of retribution. Yes, Sherman, there is a spark of interest between us, and I haven't felt this energetic in a very long time, but I haven't lost my judgment. This quest is too important for distractions. Nevertheless, I'm only human, so if you sense that my judgment is wavering, I'm relying on you to bring me to my senses. Don't be afraid to speak out. It's vital to our mission."

Sherman nodded solemnly.

"As far as the orb," continued Kazin, "yes, someone could potentially manipulate what it does, but I can tell when that's happening without question. Granted, Amelia practices some arcane magic that I don't fully understand. It kind of reminds me of druid magic. Either way, I can sense when magic is being used versus an artifact that is reacting on its own. It's actually a little easier for me than an ordinary mage because I'm part dragon as well. Dragons are drawn to magic. I should know." He smiled at the big warrior. "But thanks for questioning things. It's important to distinguish what we know from what we assume."

They heard laughter behind them as Amelia and Olag shared a joke. Kazin was happy they got along. At first he wasn't sure they would because Amelia was part mermaid. Perhaps it was easier for Olag to overlook because she looked more like her human father. At any rate, the team needed to learn to trust one another.

They suddenly caught up to Zylor and Harran. They had cleared the gully and were looking down into a valley where a village was visible to the left and a road branched off to the right. The minotaur was obviously disappointed about not finding any foes to battle.

At this point, Kazin had to make Zylor appear like a human amid the usual grumbles of protest, while Olag donned the ring of invisibility. His reins were given to Amelia so she could appear to be leading a pack horse.

The companions rode down to the intersection where a sign indicated the road going north led to Velden Iron Mine, and the south led to the village of Shara, en route to the city of Velden itself.

"We go south," said Kazin. "I'm sure once we reach Velden, there will be a road leading west." Without another word he spurred his horse forward. The rest of the group followed.

Within the hour they reached Shara. Since the sun was now getting low on the horizon, they decided to obtain some rooms at an inn where Amelia claimed the orb reacted ever so slightly but didn't even turn pink. They had some time, so they decided to check out the local tavern for some food and drinks and to find out any news. They tied their horses to a hitching post in front of the inn and opted to go to the tavern on foot because it wasn't very far from one end of town to the other.

The tavern was large. It was meant to accommodate the burly miners who lived in the area. Tonight the tavern was busy, but the atmosphere was rather gloomy. A number of villagers eyed them suspiciously as they entered.

"I wonder if it was such a good idea to come in here," murmured Sherman as Harran led them to a vacant table.

"If anyone asks, we're just travelers passing through town," said Kazin.

"I'd wager they don't get too many travelers this far north," put in Harran.

"You're probably right," agreed Kazin. "If they press us for more information, we'll have to tell them we just finished escorting a shipment of supplies to the guard posts and the convoy chief had no more need of our services since he was heading back to Malley empty handed. We took a different route because we heard there was work in Velden."

"That sounds plausible," nodded Harran.

The companions settled back and ordered some food and ale. Amelia promised Olag she would stash some of the food in her cloak for him to eat later.

"Ok," whispered the invisible skink warrior.

After they had eaten, they went to mingle.

Sherman sat at the bar beside two men who had somber expressions. They were having ales and spoke in hushed tones so Sherman could hardly hear.

"I still think the ones who killed Ned and Oscar were the ones who murdered the strangers in town," said the first fellow. He had big ears and bushy grey eyebrows.

"But you saw it yourself," argued the second man. "He left town with Oscar. You know as well as I do that Oscar was a crook. He only ever looked after himself." The second man was younger by a few years and had a wiry build. His black hair was thinning and his face was creased with many lines. Both men had big, callused hands, indicative of mine workers. They obviously worked in the Velden Mine.

The first man sighed. "I know, but I can't see Ned as the killing kind. I've known him for a good ten years, ever since he came to work at the mine."

"People change," said the younger man.

"Maybe Ned got involved with Oscar's crew because they were blackmailing him about something," suggested the first man.

The younger man nodded thoughtfully. "I can go along with that. Good men can easily get into trouble that way. Maybe Ned had no choice but to go along with them."

"It would be just his luck that he would ride out with them when they ran into a fatal end," said the first man. He wrinkled his bushy eyebrows. "But I still don't understand some of the details the undertaker mentioned when the bodies were brought back to town. For instance, if Oscar's crew attacked a caravan, why weren't the bodies dragged aside and buried? Why were they just left where they were?"

"They may have run into another group of bandits," suggested the second man. "Thieves have no respect for the dead."

"If so," argued the first man, "why were there no other casualties? The only bodies that came back were the ones that I recall seeing with Oscar. Only one or two of Oscar's men were not among them. I distinctly remember a fellow with a thick black mustache. He definitely wasn't among them."

"Maybe he escaped," suggested the second man.

"Or he was working with the ones who killed Ned and Oscar." The first man scratched his head. "Maybe Ned and Oscar were betrayed. That man with the black mustache definitely wasn't from these parts."

"Could be," responded the second man.

"And what about the cause of death?" asked the first man. "They were all strangled. How is that consistent with armed bandits?"

The second man frowned. "That I can't figure out. The only thing I can think of is that the undertaker was mistaken. The ravens did a fair bit of damage before a caravan stumbled upon them. Some of those bodies were pretty ravaged."

"That could be." The first man sighed sadly. "Ned's wife is taking it pretty hard. She said some bitter things about him the morning he rode out. But it's obvious she still loved him dearly."

The second man patted him gently on the back. "I'm sorry about your friend. If it helps, I'll join you at tomorrow's funeral."

The first man nodded. "I'd appreciate it." He downed his glass of ale and rose. "I'd better get to bed early tonight. The funeral takes place first thing in the morning. The mine foreman wants everyone to be at the mine ready to work by noon."

The second man nodded and finished his ale. "Good point. I'm going to hit the hay too." He rose and followed his friend from the tavern.

Sherman downed his glass and ordered another. From what he could gather, there was a string of murders that had taken place in this village. He would have to keep an eye out for a man with a black mustache. He got up and made his way back to his table where Harran was talking about the murders that had taken place in the village. They were talking freely since most of the villagers were retiring early for the night, no doubt to get ready for the funeral. The nearest people still in the bar were well out of earshot.

According to Harran, four bodies were found in different parts of the town. All except one were hidden out of sight, the last being discovered just that morning. They were all strangers. It was the reason the people in the village were on edge, especially where strangers were involved.

Olag continued by relating what he had learned as an invisible eavesdropper at another table. Some local men had ridden out to Velden a few days ago with some strangers and three of them were found later that day by a small caravan. Ravens were swarming their bodies and the caravan people chased them away. They would have prepared a burial mound, but one of the escorts recognized the men and convinced them to return the bodies to the village for a proper burial. As luck would have it, there was a mage associated with the caravan, and he was able to freeze the bodies for transport. When they got to the village, the undertaker was summoned. He inspected the bodies and determined they were all strangled.

"Strangled?!" blurted Zylor. "All of them? Are you sure?"

"That's what they said at the table," said Olag.

"Isn't that a little odd?" continued the minotaur. "You would think they were stabbed or something. Maybe the occasional one would be strangled if neither combatant had a weapon. But all three?"

"That is indeed unusual," mused Kazin thoughtfully. He had been listening intently the whole time and seemed deep in thought. He turned to Sherman. "What did you find out, Sherm?"

Sherman smiled at his friend's way of saying his name. It used to irritate him, but now he had grown accustomed to it. The big warrior retold what he had heard, including the part about the man with the thick black mustache. "I think we should be on the lookout for that man," added Sherman. "He could be trouble if we cross paths."

Kazin nodded. "That could be. If he's a gang leader, he could cause all sorts of trouble for us."

"We can't let that distract us from our goal," reminded Amelia.

Kazin turned to the red-haired mage. "Good point. But I want to make sure these events aren't related to our goal. I'd like you to consult your orb often from this point forward. We know the death back in the gully was not correct according to the historical time line. We're just lucky it wasn't drastic enough to change history. If it was, we would already be too late to change things back to how they should be."

Everyone fell silent as the thought of potential failure permeated the air.

Kazin laughed. "Sorry. I didn't mean to put a damper on things."

"But you're right," said Harran. "We could easily fail if we merely wait for something to go wrong as a sign that history has been changed. We have to be pro-active."

"But how do we do that?" asked Sherman. "How can we determine when something is about to change history, without knowing when it actually happens?"

"Good question," said Kazin. "The only thing I can think of is that whoever is causing history to change - and I'm fairly certain it's a 'someone' and not a 'something' - is going to impact everything around them to some degree or other. That will cause Amelia's orb to react. Everything they do or touch will be affected. The orb reacted slightly at the inn. Perhaps whoever is altering history has been there. We don't know this for sure, but it stands to reason that if that individual was a stranger in town, he would have stayed at the inn."

"And there's only one inn in town," put in Amelia.

"Precisely," said Kazin.

"So we use the orb to track the culprit who's affecting history," stated Olag.

Kazin nodded. "Yes. We have to follow the trail that person is leaving in their wake."

"If there's even a trail to follow," growled Zylor.

"That's what we have to find out," said Kazin.

"How do we know we aren't too late to do anything already?" asked Olag.

"I think the orb is the answer to that question, Olag," said Kazin. "If we were too late to change things, the orb would probably do something drastic. From what I've studied about orbs, they tend to shatter if the magic reaches a certain limit. Dragon orbs often shatter when the dragon dies. In this case, the orb might vibrate and turn such a dark red that the orb can no longer contain the magic, causing it to shatter."

Amelia gasped. "Are you serious?!"

Kazin shrugged. "I can't say for certain, but that's my best guess."

The red-haired mage looked down at her orb and rubbed it lovingly with her fingers. "I'd hate for that to happen. This orb is priceless."

"That's just another reason to stop whoever is changing things from causing a permanent change," said Kazin.

Amelia looked up at Kazin as the realization of his statement sank in. She now realized that even the preservation of her orb banked on stopping someone from changing history.

Sherman yawned. "How about if we get some rest and start on this trail first thing in the morning?"

The next morning it was foggy and damp as the companions emerged from the inn's breakfast restaurant. Sherman led the dwarf, minotaur-turned-human and invisible skink warrior to the horses and they started filling the packs on the horses with supplies. Meanwhile, Kazin and Amelia watched a small procession of people as they marched past on their way to the cemetery. A dozen and a half mine workers carried three coffins on their broad shoulders. They were well built and shouldered their loads with ease. Sherman looked up from his work and recognized two of them as the two men who were at the bar the previous evening. One woman following the miners sobbed and wiped a handkerchief over her face. Everyone else marched behind the coffin bearers in silence.

As the procession passed, Amelia tugged at Kazin's sleeve. He looked down as she lifted her cloak. Some of her breast was accidentally showing and it took a moment for him to realize what she was actually trying to show him. The orb pulsed in her hand, emitting a pinkish glow. He nodded in understanding.

"How serious is this as far as history is concerned?" asked Kazin quietly so as not to disturb the procession.

Amelia ducked around a corner and withdrew her orb where passersby would not see. She concentrated on the orb for several minutes. At last she lowered her hand with the orb and her face turned pale.

Kazin, who had followed her, saw the reaction. He gently touched her arm and spoke softly. "What is it? What did you see?"

The red-haired mage turned to look into Kazin's eyes. Her own eyes were sad, and tears welled within. "This town -," began Amelia. She blinked the tears from her eyes and wiped her robe across her face to clear the tears that resided there. She spoke again, with more determination. "This town is going to be overrun by ogres. The people in the coffins died before they should have, but they would have been killed not long from now regardless. Anything they would have done from now until the ogres arrive was not enough to change history. Almost all of the inhabitants of this town will die when the ogres attack. They won't be ready. The town will be destroyed and will not be rebuilt." Tears welled up in Amelia's eyes again. "They won't stand a chance. Their deaths will be brutal. The ogres will show no mercy. It's - horrible." She broke off and turned away.

Kazin thought about the time when he was growing up. He recalled his geography lessons and realized that this village did not exist in his time. It wasn't even mentioned. This village was not only destroyed, but it was forgotten as well. History had made no mention of it. He shuddered. Fate could sometimes be very cruel.

Amelia turned back to the mage and he could see her composure was restored. She was now angry. She pointed after the procession. "Those men who died before their time might have died anyway, but their untimely death means that someone has interfered with history. You wanted to know if these mysterious deaths were related to your quest. I believe they are. Someone is out there killing people. Sooner or later they will kill someone who matters."

Kazin nodded thoughtfully. "I agree." He and Amelia went to their horses where the others waited patiently.

"Where to, Boss?" asked Sherman lightly.

"Velden," said Kazin decisively. He mounted his horse and spurred it forward. The others followed. Before they rounded a bend in the road, Kazin took one last look back at Shara, a village that would soon be forgotten by time itself.

Chapter 16

he warlock shook with the effort of the spell, his visage stern and determined. The dead rodent did not move. Unwilling to admit defeat, the warlock tenaciously tried the spell again, using a slightly different inflection and a different set of spell components. He blotted out everything around him so that the only thing that existed besides himself was the dead rat. The magic of the spell began to transform the air around him as he neared the completion of the spell. Something within him snapped, and a small amount of force from deep within himself surged toward the inert form before him. At last, the rat stirred. The whiskers twitched and the dead eyes opened. Everything about the magic felt right as the warlock completed the spell. The rat stood on all fours and observed its master with a dull expression. The rat appeared to be waiting for instructions. The warlock rejoiced inwardly at his success.

He gave it a verbal command to see what would happen. "Walk!"

The rat began to walk across the room.

"Stop!"

The rat stopped.

"Walk!" commanded the warlock again.

The rat complied.

"Sit!" said the warlock.

The rat sat and observed him.

The warlock chuckled. The rat obeyed every word he commanded without hesitation. This instant response to his every command was a side effect he had not anticipated. The spell was more useful than he had imagined!

"Um, Sir?" said a timid voice behind him.

"What?!" exclaimed the warlock in surprise. He spun on the intruder. It was Gorc. "Gorc!" he snarled savagely. "What did I tell you about sneaking up on me?"

"Um, sorry, Sir," stammered Gorc. "I was just -,"

"I'm busy!" snapped the warlock. "Come back later!"

"Sorry, Sir," said Gorc. Seeing that the warlock was in one of his moods, he turned and left hastily.

The warlock turned back to his rat and was dismayed to see that his rat was lying dead on the floor once again. He swore and stamped his foot. Obviously, his spell still needed work. In order to be useful, his spell had to have a much longer duration. If a mere distraction was all it took to lose his subject, then it defeated the purpose of even casting the spell.

The subject had to last long enough to carry out his commands, as well as manage on its own without his supervision, possibly miles from where he currently happened to be. His goal was to resurrect a dragon and use it to create havoc with the humans. Unfortunately, undead creatures could not exist very far away from the spell caster who created them. At least, that's what the spell books he was studying had indicated. A dead dragon brought back to life would only be useful within his realm of magical influence. Outside of that boundary, the dragon would cease to be animated and return to its original lifeless state. If he wanted to achieve something far away from himself, he had to do it with a live subject.

The warlock thought about this for a moment. How could he control a live dragon? How could he direct its thoughts to carry out his commands? He looked at the dead rat on the ground before him. It had shown no hesitation in following his orders. There were no errant thoughts to interfere with his commands. It was a willing subject. The warlock scratched his head. The spell book had mentioned that dead creatures were the most willing subjects, once animated. Part of the spell he had cast was meant to animate the rat. The latter half was meant to control the subject. What if he used the latter half of the spell on a live subject? The spell book had indicated that this was difficult because of the errant thoughts of the living being. However, it didn't mention anything about clearing the subject's mind before attempting to control it.

He dashed back to his spell book and leafed through its pages, stopping on the page he sought. "Here it is!" he muttered excitedly. "How to clear a subject's mind; removing its memory."

The warlock looked up with a gleam in his eyes. That was it! Now all he had to do was find a subject to experiment on. He looked toward the exit curtain. "Gorc!" he called in a voice much more pleasant than before. "Gorc, come here!"

A few minutes later the curtain was tentatively drawn aside and the goblin-orc poked his head into the room. "Y - you called?"

The warlock rose and beckoned his servant to enter. "Come in, Gorc. You had something you wanted to tell me earlier?"

Gorc blinked. "Y- yes, Sir. I was just informed that a contingent of trolls have arrived from the south and wish to speak with you."

"Trolls?" said the warlock excitedly. He decided to postpone his experiment for the moment. "Is their leader among them?"

Gorc shrugged. "I don't know. The sentry said she had a hard time communicating with them because they all tended to talk at once. It seems they have no chain of command to speak of."

"I kind of had that impression," mused the warlock. "Did they figure out who to send back to me?"

"Yes," said Gorc. "They chose three of their number to talk with you, claiming three would be able to negotiate better than one."

The warlock chuckled. "With their level of intelligence, the entire contingent of trolls wouldn't be enough to do proper negotiating." He put his hand on Gorc's shoulder. "But let's keep that to ourselves, shall we?"

"Yes, Sir," said Gorc.

"Prepare the table for our guests," said the warlock. "They should be arriving soon."

"Yes, Sir," said Gorc.

The table was set and the warlock waited in the command center for his guests. It was not long before Gorc entered to announce the arrival of the trolls.

The trolls were larger than the warlock would have guessed, rivaling ogres in height, about six and a half feet tall. They were the same greenish colour as the orcs, but that's where the similarity ended. Their flesh sagged all over, making them seem uglier than any creatures who currently served under him. Their long arms were muscular and menacing, with brown hair barely masking the green skin beneath. The arms ended with hands twice the size of an ogre's. Long, sharp claws emanated from the tips of the fingers making an effective weapon capable of ripping and tearing. Their eyes were mere slits between sagging skin folds in their faces, and their cheeks and chins hung in a grotesque manner.

The warlock shrugged off a feeling of revulsion and smiled, beckoning them to sit at the table. They grunted and complied, eyeing the food speculatively. One of them immediately began to pick up the food with his gigantic hand and placed it into his mouth. Spittle dripped from the folds of skin under its droopy chin.

"Please, help yourselves," said the warlock warmly. "You've come a long way." The other two trolls began to eat sloppily and quickly finished off their meals. The overlapping folds of skin covered any evidence of sexual orientation on their naked bodies. The sagging breasts all looked alike. When the guests had finished eating, the warlock opened the conversation. "So would you like to tell me what the reason is for your visit? I hope you have come to offer your aid in my battle against the humans."

The trolls responded in unison, but the warlock tried to understand their response.

"The humans don't interest us," said one troll.

"They aren't important," said the second one.

"We have other battles to fight," said the third.

"Then why have you come?" asked the warlock.

"The elves are nuisances," said the first one.

"We hate the elves," said the second one.

"Elves are in our way," said the third.

"Their magic is hard to beat," continued the first troll.

"Magic - bad," added the second one.

"The dragons are drawn to magic," said the third.

"That's why the dragons interfere," said the first one.

"They are drawn to magic," said the second.

"It makes battle difficult," said the third.

"What?!" said the warlock. "Dragons are drawn to magic?"

"Yes," said the first one.

"They are aroused by magic," said the second.

"We need magic to win," said the third.

So that's why the dragons had always appeared out of nowhere when the fighting began! The battles with the humans had been getting more and more magical in nature, and the dragons more numerous. The warlock wondered why his lizardmages had never discovered this. They were always reminding him how intelligent they were, yet these simple trolls have discovered something relevant about the dragons that he could potentially use! He put the information to the back of his mind for further examination later. "So," he said slowly, "you want to obtain magical aid from me."

"Yes," replied the trolls together, nodding excitedly.

"We hear you have magic," said the first one.

"You are known for your magic," said another.

"We want your magic," said the third.

"And what do you offer in exchange?" asked the warlock.

The trolls looked at one another.

"What do you want?" asked one.

"What do you need?" asked the second one.

The third one shrugged.

The warlock stroked his goatee thoughtfully. "I have an idea. What if you help me defeat the humans, and then I'll have my entire army assist you in eliminating the elves for good?"

"Won't work," said the first one, shaking its head.

"No time," said the second.

"Our lands will be overrun with elves by then," said the third. "They have declared war on us."

"They have?" asked the warlock. This was an interesting development.

"They have," nodded the first troll.

"We beat them to it," added the second one.

"They didn't expect it," said the third.

"But they are fighting with magic," said the first troll.

"If it wasn't for magic, we would have finished them," said the second one.

"Magic would put them back in their place," said the third.

"I see," said the warlock. He stroked his goatee again. After a moment, he spoke. "Unfortunately, I cannot spare any magic wielders without depleting my own forces."

"Then we wasted our time," said the first troll.

"This is pointless," said the second one, rising.

"That's too bad," said the third, rising to its feet as well.

The warlock held up a hand. "Hold on! I haven't finished." He beckoned to the table. "Please, sit."

The trolls sat back down.

"I can arrange something that will work for both of us," said the warlock. "I can supply some magical items to aid you, and I'll even spare some lizardmen to do magic for you, but you will have to give them command of your forces to help you to do the most damage to your enemies. Your success can only be assured if you have an organized army. The lizardmen are clever and have the ability to outsmart your enemies."

"So you'll help?" asked the first troll.

"Sounds good to me," said the second.

"I like it," said the third.

"I will, however, expect an equal trade for my lizardmen," said the warlock. "For every lizardman I give you, I want a strong, capable troll to fight for me here against the humans."

The trolls looked at one another again.

"This works for me," said the first.

"I think that's fair," said the second.

"Good enough," said the third.

The warlock smiled. "Then we have a deal!" He rose and held out his hand. The trolls took turns shaking his hand and then left the tent, jabbering excitedly with one another. How they listened to each other while talking at once was a mystery to him. Thankfully that was not his problem.

It was time for a lizardmage to command his own battalion. Saliss was the most qualified among the lizardmages, and the most dedicated to this war, so it would fall to him to command the trolls and keep them in line. Communication with those creatures was something he would have to figure out. With Saliss in command of the trolls, the warlock could coordinate the attacks of both his forces and Saliss' to coincide and do the maximum amount of damage.

Fighting on two fronts was not something he particularly desired, but keeping the elves occupied was a good way to prevent them from deciding to assist the humans. Furthermore, if Saliss could get the trolls to split up and attack the elves from the north as well as the south in a pincer movement, the northern contingent had a good chance of becoming involved in conflicts with the humans, who were merely on the other side of the Jackal River. All the warlock had to do was run some of his forces south of the Boot Plateau and march for Claw lake. From there he could have Saliss' forces secretly join him and go to attack the human army's encampment from the south. It wouldn't be a surprise attack - undoubtedly human scouts would be watching his meager forces every step of the way - but the addition of trolls at the last minute would catch them off guard. Combined with the bulk of his forces from the west, the warlock had the upper hand. If the lizardmage Harse, who had been assigned with a number of other lizardmen to the ogres north of the human settlements, managed to time his own attacks properly, the humans would surely be thrown into turmoil.

The only problem with that scenario was that the ogres still had command of their own forces. But they were tired of defeat. They needed a leader who could bring them results. It was up to Harse to try to manipulate the ogres to attack where and when he suggested. If Harse could prove that his decisions and timing were effective, the ogres might just look to him to lead them. Then true progress could be made on the northern front. Only time would tell if this strategy would pay off.

The warlock wrung his hands in anticipation as plans formed in his mind. He would summon Saliss first thing in the morning. As for right now, he had an experiment to perform.

"Gorc!" he called. "Gorc, where are you?"

Part III

Multiple Objectives

Chapter 17

s the companions neared the town of Velden, black smoke could be seen on the horizon.

"What do you suppose is causing that smoke?" asked Sherman

"It could be from a dragon attack," suggested Olag.

"I didn't see any sign of a dragon in the air," said Amelia, "but that doesn't mean there wasn't one here a little earlier."

"We'll find out when we get closer," said Zylor.

The group quickened their pace. As they got closer, most of the smoke had dissipated, but a small waft of smoke still emanated from somewhere on the far side of town. Within the town's limits, people could be seen calmly going about their daily business. No one paid any heed to the smoke.

"I guess it must have been an isolated house or barn fire," remarked Sherman. "A dragon attack would have been more serious."

"You're probably right," said Kazin, "but we'll find out what it was all about nevertheless."

"Our quarry was here," added Amelia. She was looking at her orb. It was a pinkish colour again. "Something here isn't quite right."

"We'll have to be cautious," said Kazin. "We don't want to alert the one we're after that he or she is being followed. They may panic and run if they get wind of someone being onto them. If that happens, it may become very difficult to track them down."

"Are we going to get rooms for the night?" asked Zylor. He obviously wanted to get away from being a human warrior for a while.

Kazin looked at the sun's position and nodded. "We might be here for a while to look for clues that were left behind by our quarry. It will be sundown by the time we finish looking around and asking questions. We should book rooms just in case, but depending on our progress, we may have to depart rather quickly."

"In that case," put in Harran, "I should purchase supplies now before the shops close for the day."

"Good idea," said Kazin.

"I'll book the rooms at the inn," offered Sherman. "I can also coordinate with the stable master regarding the horses."

"I'll go with you," said Zylor.

"Very well," said Kazin, withdrawing his money pouch. He passed some coins to Harran and then tossed the bag to Sherman. "Guard that with your life."

"Don't worry," said Zylor. "I'll protect him."

Kazin laughed. "No doubt, but who will protect you when you turn back into your real self?"

"That's where I come in," said Sherman.

"I need no protection!" retorted Zylor. Then he nodded. "But you are right. I will restrain myself. But once the rooms are secured, I will remove the amulet and release the spell. I need to be in my true form or I will explode!"

Kazin nodded. He knew the strain the minotaur was under to be suppressed all this time. He started to wonder about the viability of having the great beast along.

Zylor turned to the dwarf. "Harran, see that you purchase a larger quantity of dried meat this time. I use more than my current human body requires."

"Ok," nodded Harran.

"You guys do what you have to do," said Kazin. "The rest of us will see what we can learn about this town and the fire." He looked toward the apparently empty pack horse. "Unless you would rather stay in a room with Zylor?"

Olag hissed. "No. I will go with you. Being invisible, I can learn things you may miss."

"Good point," said Kazin. He pointed to the nearby inn. "We'll meet in front of the inn in, say, two hours?"

"I won't be able to attend," said Zylor, "unless you come to change my appearance first."

"Of course," said Kazin.

With that, the companions parted ways.

Harran rode with the others for a while until they neared the shop section of the town where all sorts of goods were bought and sold. He bid farewell to the others and turned to a meat vendor shop. In front of the shop he dismounted and tied his horse to a hitching post. Then he went inside to the potent aroma of meats of all sorts. There were steaks, ground meat products, sausages, and dried meats. It was to this last section he went. The prices advertised were reasonable - not that he didn't have enough gold; Kazin had given him plenty to work with. The dwarf grabbed what he thought they would consume, but then thought better of it and took extra, remembering Zylor's request. His hands were nearly full as he passed the sausages, and the aroma of one of the flavours caught his attention. He paused to grab a handful of these as well, thinking that the others would like a bit of variety on their journey. Then he brought them up to the counter to pay for them.

The vendor was a friendly bald man who teased Harran about his appetite but also commended him about his selection.

Harran took the ribbing good-naturedly and paid for his meat.

Meanwhile, a figure in the shadows, who had been watching the dwarf intently since his arrival, exited the front of the store hastily. Neither the shop owner nor Harran noticed.

Back outside, Harran packed his purchase of meat securely in one of the saddle bags on his horse. Then he untied his horse and rode it along a street with stores on both sides. He saw an attractive sign in front of one of the shops advertising herbs and remembered that Amelia was looking for some spell components and healing herbs. He checked his pockets and found the list she had given him earlier that day. He approached the store front and dismounted, tying his horse to the hitching post nearby.

Next to the entrance an old, weathered man sat on a portable cot and held out a bowl. "Alms! Alms for the poor!" he croaked with a shaky voice.

Harran hesitated. He was going to toss the man a coin but remembered that any unnecessary action could cause a change in history. The hesitation was only momentary, however. He tossed the man a coin anyway. One coin in the beggar's life would not likely make much of a difference.

"Thank you so much!" said the beggar as Harran passed by and entered the shop.

He quickly found what he needed and even purchased some wildhorn leaves that were sealed in a jar. Personally, he despised that herb because he was allergic to them and they made him sneeze, but they were useful for a variety of reasons. Their primary use was to help whoever ingested them to see better in the dark. One danger, though, was that if too many were consumed at once, they also caused blindness. Another use for this herb was for various spells that black mages and clerics were able to cast. The wildhorn leaves, by themselves or in conjunction with other spell components, would allow the spell caster to obtain different results for the myriad of spells at their disposal.

With that purchase completed, Harran exited the shop to store the supplies with the horse. He was about to launch himself back into the saddle when he heard the sound of tin being hammered. Next to the herb shop was a shop specializing in cookware. Curious, he wandered over to the shop and peered into the window. A number of implements and cookware were on display. Recalling that the frying pan his entourage had been using was getting worn out, he decided to see if he could find a nicer one available here.

The dwarf entered the shop and waited for his eyes to adjust. Unlike the herb shop, where it was bright and welcoming, this shop was dark and uninviting.

"Can I help you?" said a voice nearby.

Harran turned to see the proprietor standing behind a counter, observing him. It was a dwarf. He was an older fellow with a long grey beard. His face was weathered and his hairline was receding. His mustache made up for the lack of hair on his head. It was thick and bushy and tended to quiver when he spoke.

"Yes," said Harran. "I'm looking for a new frying pan."

"You've come to the right place," said the dwarf. He gestured to the shelf at the side of the room. "There are some on display over there."

Harran moved over to the shelves to take a look at the merchandise while the proprietor eyed him up and down.

"You know," said the owner, "I've got some better merchandise in back."

Harran turned to the owner and suddenly realized the proprietor was assuming he was a wealthy traveler. With his shiny chainmail and helmet, and his sharp looking axe in its holster, he probably looked wealthy compared to the normal traffic that frequented this shop. He decided to play along to see what the proprietor had for special customers. "May I take a look?"

"Certainly," said the proprietor. He turned and entered a storeroom behind him. A moment later, a young dwarf emerged and ran hastily around the counter and past Harran to go outside. About ten seconds later, the proprietor returned and looked around. "Is he gone?"

"The dwarf who ran out of here like his pants were on fire?" asked Harran.

The proprietor nodded. "That would be him. That was my son. Oh, well. I shouldn't have sent him on an errand right then. The item I wanted to show you is in a location that is too awkward for me to reach." He reached around to his back and rubbed it gingerly. "My back is too stiff these days. My son is small enough to access it, but now he is gone." The owner peered at Harran. "But you would be able to get at it." He waved Harran forward. "Come. I'll show you where it is. I'm sure you'll be pleased with the quality."

Harran shrugged. "If it's not too much trouble."

"Not at all," said the proprietor. "Not at all."

Harran approached the store room and the proprietor let him enter ahead of him. He wrung his hands nervously as Harran passed and Harran caught the nervous movement out of the corner of his eye. He half turned, expecting something strange was going on, when his helmet was suddenly whisked off. At the same instant, a heavy object came crashing down on his head. Stars showered his vision and a metallic tone clanged into the recesses of his brain. As the blackness of unconsciousness took over, he heard a voice he hadn't heard before say, "What do you know? It IS good quality!"

Meanwhile, Kazin, Amelia, and Olag investigated the fire that had initially drawn their attention. It was a barn-like structure within an estate that had burned down. People were scattered around the building as the remnants smoldered, and some appeared to be mourning.

Others used pails of water to prevent the fire from spreading to the surrounding buildings.

A man yawned as he exited the property and Kazin waved him down. "What happened here?" he asked.

The man shrugged. "I wish I knew. Most of the people in the estate - the ones who lived and worked here - were found dead. Their bodies were discovered thrown together under the hay in the stables."

Amelia gasped and put her hand to her mouth. "No!" she whispered.

"Apparently, someone who works at the estate reported to work after a short time off and couldn't get a response at the gate. He went into town to get help and they broke in only to discover that no one was around. Then one of the searcher's dogs was acting all agitated near the stables so they went in and discovered the bodies under the hay."

Kazin forced back his revulsion. "Did you see the bodies?"

The man shook his head. "No, thank goodness."

"So you don't know how they died?"

The man shook his head. "No."

"How did the fire start?" asked Amelia.

"We did that," said the man. "It was better to burn the bodies where they lay."

"Why?" asked Amelia. "How many were there?"

"A lot," said the man. "Most of the residents and staff were among the dead from what I heard."

Amelia gasped and looked at Kazin in horror.

Kazin's face was grim. "Do you know how long ago the bodies were lying there?"

The man shook his head. "No, but one of the elders mentioned that they weren't dead too long because the bodies didn't smell bad enough to have lain there for long. He figured maybe one or two days at the most."

Kazin asked a few more questions but didn't glean any more information. He thanked the man and waited until he was out of earshot. Then he looked at Amelia. "What does your orb show?"

Amelia withdrew the orb and, sure enough, it was a dark red.

"It looks like we're on the right track," said Kazin. "Our quarry has been killing again."

"That bastard!" snarled Amelia. "We have to catch him - fast!"

"We'll have to keep an eye on his impact on history too," said Kazin. "Sooner or later he's going to kill someone important, even if it's only a woman who's supposed to give birth to someone who may be important in a future generation. The repercussions could be devastating."

"Oh, he's making those kinds of waves alright," said Amelia. "My orb is kind of vague at the moment, as though the future is uncertain."

"That's not a good thing," said Kazin with clenched teeth.

Olag's horse shifted and Kazin looked at the pack horse. "Olag?"

"I'm back," said the skink warrior.

"I didn't even know you were gone," said Kazin. "What did you find out?"

"The townsfolk made a list of the names of the dead and compared it to a list of the names of the people who worked at the estate. The names all matched with the exception of only one body."

"One of the bad guys, perhaps?" asked Kazin.

"Maybe," said Olag. "He wasn't identified. The villagers then made a list of the remaining staff that weren't present among the dead and rounded them all up for questioning. According to the list that was posted, they only found the people who were not on duty at the time of the killings."

"And the ones who were?"

"That's the weird part," said Olag. "There were only ten people on the list who could not be found, and they all should have been on duty. Yet not one of them could be found for questioning."

"Maybe their bodies weren't discovered yet," said Kazin.

Amelia shuddered. "Or they could have been kidnapped for ransom."

Kazin considered this. "That's unlikely. It would draw too much attention. I don't think our quarry wants to be found. He'll move to a new area rather than being discovered."

"I found out one other tidbit of information," added Olag. "I overheard some people talking, and I don't know how accurate their information is, but they said that many of the victims had been strangled."

Kazin gave a low whistle. "That's the trend we have been seeing."

"We should go and report our findings to the others," said Amelia. "It will take us a while to get back to the inn."

"Good point," said Kazin. The inn was back on the other end of town.

He led the way back across town to find Sherman lounging on a bench in front of the inn.

"It's about time," yawned the warrior upon seeing them approach. He rose and stretched. "So, what did you find out?"

"We'll wait until everyone is assembled," said Kazin. "I take it Harran isn't back yet?"

Sherman shook his head. "I haven't seen him."

"Funny," said Kazin. "He didn't have that much to buy."

"Maybe he's trying hard to bargain with some of the vendors," joked Sherman. "You know how dwarves are when it comes to buying stuff."

"True enough," said Kazin. "We'll give him a bit more time."

Since Sherman was dying to hear what they had found out so far, Kazin led him inside the inn so he could tell Zylor at the same time. He left Amelia and Olag to wait for Harran to return.

The minotaur was sitting on a bed looking like his usual self when the mage and warrior called to him through the locked door. He rose and unlocked the door to allow them to enter and then locked it behind them. It wouldn't do for an unwary person to accidentally enter the room to see a minotaur standing there. Zylor appeared much happier in his usual form. He had removed the amulet and it rested on the night stand.

Kazin briefed them on their discovery and both Sherman and Zylor appeared relieved that they were still hot on the trail of their quarry.

"I still don't know why they would choose to go through the effort of strangling their victims," said Sherman. "A quick sword thrust is much quicker and more efficient."

"Strangling is a cowardly way to fight," growled Zylor. "They must sneak up behind their victims while they are unaware of their presence. They should stand and face their opponent and look them in the eye. If we catch up to them, I will show them how true hand-to-hand combat works!"

"Actually, Zylor has a good point," said Kazin.

"Hand-to-hand combat?" asked Sherman. He looked confused.

"No," said Kazin. "I don't mean that. I mean the part about strangling. Don't you think it's odd that most of the victims were strangled? I can see a few of them being surprised from behind, but most of them? It doesn't make sense."

"You're right," said Sherman. "You would think that many of them would become alerted to the danger and at least put up a fight."

"It is unusual," agreed the minotaur. "There must be a reason for this."

"Well, we'll find out eventually," said Kazin. He looked at the minotaur. "Zylor, we'll find a place to eat and return with some food a little later. Are you ok here?"

Zylor snorted. "No one will bother me here. I have already slept for a bit. You go and do whatever you have to do."

Kazin nodded. "Very well. We'll be back." He and Sherman went back out to the inn's entrance where Amelia paced nervously. When she saw them, she walked up to them and displayed her orb. "Something is wrong! When Harran didn't show, I decided to try using my orb to see if I could find him and it started to vibrate!" she showed the orb to the others and they could see its pinkish colour. Kazin placed a finger on the artifact and could feel the vibrations that Amelia was talking about.

"Harran is long overdue," said Olag, who was still invisible. "He should have been back by now."

Kazin swore. This was something he had not foreseen. "We'll have to search for him."

"We should search together," said Amelia. "If we separate, we might run into a trap. For all we know, the strangler or stranglers are still in town and know we are after them."

"I sure hope not," rumbled Sherman. "I was hoping surprise would be on our side."

Kazin scratched his head. "We need to cover ground quickly. It would take ages to cover the entire town in one group. If we split into two groups, we can cover twice the territory, while still having someone watching our back."

"Make it three," said the skink warrior. Everyone turned to the invisible voice. When he spoke again, everyone jumped because he spoke from behind them. "I can move more stealthily on my own like this," said Olag. "I may come across people talking and learn something vital that wouldn't be learned if I searched with any of you."

"Good point," said Kazin. "You go ahead and see what you can find out. Sherman, you accompany Amelia and try some of the shops on the south end of the vendor district."

"What about you?" asked Amelia.

"I'll get Zylor and we'll check the north district."

"You could come with me," suggested Amelia sweetly.

Kazin shook his head. "I'd be better off going with Zylor. I'm the only one who can transform him into a human warrior. If he gets out of hand, I'm the best one equipped to deal with it."

Amelia looked dejected but said nothing.

"And who's going to watch your back?" asked Sherman. "If we lose you, we'll all be stuck in this point in history."

"I'll be fine," assured Kazin. "Zylor learned a lot from you. He should be able to handle it, even if he turns into a minotaur for a short period. I can change him back into a human and tell people I turned him into a minotaur on purpose."

Sherman sighed.

"And if you're worried about losing me, stay close to Amelia. She has knowledge of time travel. She can help you get back home."

Amelia reddened. "I'm not leaving without you."

"Of course not," said Kazin, smiling. Then his face became serious. "Now go!" he ordered. "We don't have time to stand around talking! Harran could be in real danger! We meet back here at sundown!"

Sherman nodded and he and Amelia raced for the stables to grab some horses. Meanwhile, Kazin bounded up the stairs. He hastily explained the problem to Zylor, expecting some resistance to the plan, but the minotaur instantly grabbed the amulet and threw it around his neck, waiting for Kazin to transform him into a human warrior. Then they bounded down the stairs and ran for the horses themselves.

Hours of fruitless searching turned up nothing. Kazin and Zylor entered various food related shops starting at the north end of town and worked their way toward the center of town. All of the shopkeepers gave the same answers. Either they had no dwarven customers that day, or, if they did, none of them matched Harran's description. Granted, most dwarves looked alike to most humans, with long beards and weathered faces, but none wore a horned helmet and chain mail.

Kazin was beginning to despair. It was getting late and some of the shops were starting to close up for the day. Then Zylor stopped suddenly and pointed.

"That looks like Harran's horse. I distinctly remember his horse was brown with a white leg."

Kazin looked where Zylor pointed. A horse was tied to a hitching post in front of a shop. As they neared, they could see it was an herb shop.

"I guess I'm wrong," said Zylor upon seeing the shop. "It's not a food vendor."

Kazin stopped and looked at the pleasant-looking warrior at his side. "I just remembered! Amelia had asked Harran to pick up some herbs! We should have been checking those vendors too!"

Zylor groaned and looked back the way they had come. "It's too late to go back and check those shops. They'll all be closed by now."

"But maybe this one is still open," said Kazin, starting forward again.

He and Zylor entered the shop and the owner looked up from her desk in surprise. "Oh! I was just about to close up."

"Sorry," said Kazin, "but we're merely looking for some information. We're looking for a friend. He may have been in here to purchase some herbs."

"He is a dwarf," added Zylor as politely as he could.

"Oh!" said the vendor, nodding. "I had a dwarf drop by earlier today. I don't often get dwarves as customers."

Kazin gave Zylor a quick glance. "What did he look like?"

The vendor chuckled. "Why, like a dwarf, of course!"

"What was he wearing?" asked Zylor impatiently.

"He wore a helmet and chain mail," said the vendor. "A very pleasant fellow."

Kazin and Zylor exchanged excited glances.

"Can you remember which herbs he bought?" asked Kazin.

"Hmm, let's see now," said the vendor, thinking. "If I recall correctly, he bought some healing herbs and a jar of wildhorn leaves." She glanced between the two men. "Is he the one you're looking for?"

"I think so," said Kazin. "When did he leave your shop?"

"Oh, it was several hours ago now, I would say," said the vendor, "probably shortly after noon."

"Thanks so much," said Kazin. He and Zylor stepped outside and observed the horse.

"It must have been him!" exclaimed Zylor through clenched teeth.

A beggar staggered toward them. "Alms! Alms for the poor!" He held out a bowl with gnarled, shaking hands.

"Get lost!" snarled Zylor.

The man cringed and moved on, obviously used to being rejected.

Kazin had already moved toward the horse and examined it closely. It paid him no heed and merely shook its mane.

"It's his horse," said Zylor behind him. "It has to be."

"But why would he just abandon it?" asked Kazin. He reached for the saddle bag and opened it. Inside was a large selection of dried meats. "That's more than we need," commented Kazin.

"I told him to buy extra," said Zylor. He clenched his teeth angrily. "He came through for me and where was I when he needed me? Cowering in a room in an inn!"

Kazin contemplated some sausages he had found and recalled how the dwarf liked his sausages. "Don't let it bother you, Zylor. You couldn't have known." He went to the horse's other side and opened the pack to reveal a stash of herbs. Among them was a jar of wildhorn leaves.

"You shouldn't touch what ain't yours!" said a frail voice a short distance away. It was the beggar.

"I told you to get lost!" snarled Zylor, stepping forward threateningly.

The beggar stepped back but Kazin intercepted the warrior. "Hold it, Zylor." He turned to the beggar. "Do you know who owns this horse?"

"You shouldn't take what don't belong to ya," mumbled the beggar. He turned and started walking away.

"Wait!" cried Kazin. He caught up to the beggar. "I'll pay you for information! It could be a matter of life or death!"

The beggar stopped. "Wh- what do ya wanna know?"

"Was the owner of the horse a dwarf?" asked Kazin.

The beggar nodded. "A mighty good one, at that."

"Was he wearing a helmet and chain mail?"

"Yup."

"What happened to him?" asked Kazin anxiously. By now Zylor was beside them.

The beggar shrugged. "I dunno." He pointed to the shop behind them. "He went in and didn't come out."

"The herb shop?" asked Zylor.

"No!" said the beggar, waving his hand dismissively. "The cookware shop."

Zylor and Kazin looked at the shop adjacent to the herb shop and then at each other.

"You said he never came out?" asked Kazin.

"That's what I said," said the beggar. "You deaf or somethin'?"

Kazin threw a handful of coins at the beggar and sprang after Zylor, who was already halfway to the cookware shop. The door was locked and they tried to peek in the window past the items in the window display.

"I'm going in," growled Zylor, circling back to the door.

"Zylor, don't -," began Kazin.

Zylor kicked in the front door and barged into the shop with Kazin in tow.

A small torch was lit by the front desk but no one was present. Zylor's intrusion was loud enough, however, and a storeroom door at the back opened. Emerging from the room was a dwarf with a bushy mustache and a long grey beard. Upon seeing the intruders, he started in surprise. "What! What is the meaning of this?! Can't you see I'm closed?"

Zylor took two long strides - longer than his human form should have allowed - and grabbed the dwarf by the collar.

"Zylor, wait!" pleaded Kazin, running to try to intervene.

"I'm looking for a friend of mine!" snarled Zylor. Even for a human he looked fierce. "He's a dwarf!"

The dwarf winced and would have gulped if Zylor hadn't had his shirt squeezed so tight. "I don't know what you're talking about!" he rasped.

"Yes you do!" growled Zylor. "Talk!"

"Zylor -," cautioned Kazin.

"Talk!" repeated Zylor. He loosened his hold just slightly.

"I haven't seen any dwarves," said the dwarf.

"That's not what we heard," said Kazin. It was obvious the dwarf was lying despite the intimidating man threatening him.

"Well, I haven't seen any dwarves recently," insisted the dwarf.

"The beggar outside saw him come in here," said Zylor.

The dwarf laughed. "And you believe him? Are you daft?"

A low growl emanated from deep within Zylor's chest as his rage began to build up.

Kazin had an idea. "I'll give you one more chance to tell the truth. If you don't, I'll turn my friend into something that any dwarf would have nightmares about."

The dwarf snorted. "You can't make me talk! I've got connections. My people will come for you at night when you're sleeping and pay you back. You'll see. We own this town!"

"Zylor," said Kazin, "it's time to show him your poker face."

Zylor smiled. He slowly drew his axe from its sheath on his back. But it wasn't his axe that frightened the dwarf. It was the grin on Zylor's face. The smile widened into the toothy grin of a minotaur. Zylor grew in size to his true height, making the dwarf seem puny in comparison. The dwarf struggled to get free, even as he was lifted off the ground by a hairy, clawed fist. The dwarf's squeal of fright was cut off as Zylor tightened his grip further. The minotaur's hot, fetid breath was nauseating to the hapless dwarf.

"I would talk if I were you," said Kazin firmly. "There's no telling what my friend will do. My magic has a tendency to go awry from time to time. I guess I still need practice."

Zylor loosened his grip on the dwarf so he could speak. "I'll talk! I'll talk!" pleaded the terror stricken dwarf at last.

"Then talk!" breathed Zylor in a quiet, menacing voice.

"Your friend was here!" said the dwarf hastily. "Some of my contacts - they spotted your friend in town wearing chainmail from the king's personal guard. None of the king's personal guards ever leave the dwarven realm. They are always on duty. So my contacts figured he was a defector or a thief. Either way, there would be a healthy reward for his capture. They followed your friend to my shop and ordered me to lure him into the back where they ambushed him and took him away."

"Where did they take him?" snarled Zylor.

"Back to the dwarven realm, of course," said the dwarf. His mustache quivered nervously.

"When?" asked Kazin.

"Several hours ago," said the dwarf. "They left with one of the many dwarven convoys that deliver weapons to the Tower of Sorcery and the human guard posts. The returning caravans carry some human goods and the gold that the weapons were sold for. They are heavily guarded. The return convoys travel quickly. In two days your friend will be at one of the entrances to the dwarven mountains. Beyond that, the dwarves won't let you past. You might as well forget about your friend. You'll never see him again."

"How do we track the convoys?" asked Zylor.

The dwarf shook his head, his mustache quivering. "I don't know very many details about the convoys. I do know they use different routes to confuse the roving bands of ogres, but that's all."

"Where do the convoys gather before departing?" asked Kazin.

"I don't know," said the dwarf, "but caravans are coming and going regularly. You just have to be at the town's north gate to see them depart."

"How many caravans leave per day?" asked Kazin.

"That depends on the volume of goods being transported," said the dwarf. "Some days there are as many as twelve convoys. The last couple of weeks have been brisk. I'd say at least ten convoys have come and gone today alone."

"Are there any more convoys departing today?" asked Zylor.

The dwarf turned to regard the minotaur who towered over him and nodded. "I'd wager that there is another one or two leaving before nightfall."

"Ok, Zylor," said Kazin at last. "You can let him down now. We have what we came to find out."

A look of disappointment crossed Zylor's features as he put the dwarf down and re-sheathed his axe.

"I'll have to change you back to your original form, Zylor," said Kazin. He chanted and Zylor immediately returned to his human form.

Zylor frowned and turned to the door. Kazin waited until the warrior had stepped past him and turned to follow when the dwarf called out. "You'll pay for this! My contacts will deal with you like they did with your friend!"

Zylor turned and looked past Kazin with a sadistic grin. "I hope they try! Once we dispose of them, we'll know exactly who to come for next!"

"I really think it's in your best interest not to mention us to anyone," added Kazin. "I'd sure hate to see harm come to your son because of your stupidity!"

"H - how do you know I have a son?" stuttered the dwarf.

"He's been watching his father through the opening in the storeroom doorway," said Kazin. "I'm sure you'll have some explaining to do."

The dwarf spun to look behind him and just caught sight of his son ducking out of sight. Then he turned back to the front door which stood ajar, the hinges all but torn off. The unwanted guests were gone. The dwarf's face was white as he contemplated his next move. He decided right then and there not to say anything about this incident to anyone.

Kazin and Zylor returned to the inn with Harran's horse. The others waited anxiously out front and looked hopeful when they saw the extra horse. Kazin ushered them into one of the rooms and filled them in on what they had uncovered thus far. Everyone was disappointed at the circumstances surrounding Harran's disappearance.

"We have to get him back," said Amelia.

"How do we do that?" asked Sherman. "It will be difficult to track him down."

"Why don't you change into a dragon and we can fly after the convoy?" suggested Amelia. "Surely we can catch up to them quickly."

"The problem is which route did they take to the dwarven mountains?" said Zylor. He was now in his original form, having removed the amulet. "If they go a different way each time to avoid the ogres, we would be flying around aimlessly."

"Besides, it's too dark," added Sherman.

"But that's the best time to go," argued Amelia. "We could fly under cover of darkness and look for the lights of the convoys. It would be easier to find a light in the darkness that a dark convoy in the daytime."

"They don't use torches," said Olag. He had removed the invisibility ring since he was in the relative safety of the room away from any prying eyes. "They avoid using torches for travel and don't even make campfires when they pause to rest in order to avoid detection by the ogres."

"How do you know this?" asked Amelia.

Olag shrugged. "I found out by listening to a couple of dwarves in a tavern."

"You were in a tavern?!" asked Amelia. "You were supposed to be searching for Harran!"

"What better place is there to find out information?" retorted Olag.

"What else did you find out?" asked Kazin.

"Apparently there is another dwarven convoy scheduled to depart the town this evening," said Olag. "The meeting place is at a book store, of all places. It's located on the north end of town."

"Did they say if they had a prisoner to transport?" asked Sherman hopefully.

Olag shook his head. "No. This convoy is traveling light. They will merely be transporting gold obtained from the sale of dwarven weapons. But they did say dwarven civilians are welcome to go with them for security reasons. There will be some construction engineers who have recently completed work on the Tower of Sorcery who will be heading home with the convoy."

"We could follow them," suggested Sherman.

"I doubt if we could keep up without being noticed," said Zylor, "if they travel as fast as the dwarf told us."

"And we can't exactly join them," said Sherman.

"Not unless we were all invisible," admitted Olag.

"What do you think, Kazin?" asked Amelia.

Kazin looked at her. "What does your orb tell us?"

Amelia withdrew her orb and studied it. As she concentrated, the orb's colour varied its reddish hue. At one point it turned dark red and she looked up at the companions. Her face was strained. "I'm sorry, but if we go after Harran, we will lose track of our quarry and he will change history. Our only chance to stop him is contingent on us following his trail. If we go after Harran, we will lose that trail and our quarry will be unstoppable."

Zylor pounded his fist on the table beside him. "We will not abandon Harran!"

"And what does the orb tell you about Harran? Will he escape his captors? Will he find a way to rejoin us?" asked Kazin.

Amelia studied her orb. It turned dark red again. She looked up and her face was haggard. "No, he will not escape on his own. If we don't free him, he will change history as well. The orb shows that we still have a chance to free him if we respond quickly."

"Then that is what we will do!" stated Zylor fervently. He gave Kazin a defiant look. "If history is altered by the one we seek, we can still go back to our own time and live our lives as we ordinarily would have before this quest began."

Kazin shook his head. "I wish it were that simple, Zylor, but if history is changed now, everything after this can be affected. I can't guarantee your own time will not also become affected somehow. Even small changes can have considerable repercussions."

"Then we must have caused some of these changes ourselves by now," said Sherman.

"If that were so," said Kazin, "Amelia's orb would indicate that."

Everyone turned to the red-haired mage.

"Well, both of you are right," said Amelia. "We should have made some sort of impact on history by now, however small, but we haven't. I don't understand why this is, but it's true."

"But either way, stopping the one we seek will be pointless if we don't rescue Harran," objected Olag. "Amelia just said so earlier."

"What if we pursue both objectives?" asked Kazin. He nodded at Amelia. "Will your orb show if that's possible?"

Amelia sighed. "That's going to be difficult, but I'll try." She consulted her orb again and long moments passed. The orb colour wavered with varying shades of red but did not go to a dark red. At last, the mage paused and looked up. "According to the orb, it's possible to succeed at both objectives. Barely. The odds are against us."

"How do we do it?" asked Sherman.

Amelia shook her head. "It's not that specific. It only shows me that it can be done."

"I don't like it," muttered Sherman. "United we stand, divided we fall."

"True," said Kazin, "but if we don't separate, this whole expedition is a failure."

"If the orb is to be believed," added Olag.

Amelia shot him an angry glance.

"I believe the orb," said Kazin. He looked at Amelia once more. "If we succeed, will our whole group be able to reunite? I wouldn't want half of us lost in time."

Amelia sighed and consulted the orb again. A few minutes later she looked up again. "There's a good possibility we will reunite. Ultimately that depends on how we fare with our goals."

This time it was Kazin's turn to sigh. Then his face lit up. "Of course!" He withdrew his miniature pouch and used enlarging magic to increase its size. Then he searched through it and pulled out several rings which he placed on the table. "These rings," he explained, "I brought along for just such an occasion. I anticipated that some of us would get separated. In hindsight, I should have handed them out earlier. Then we wouldn't have been in such a predicament in the first place. These rings allow the wearer to magically transport themselves to the one wearing the master ring, in this case the one I'm putting on right now." He slid a ring onto his finger. Then he handed one out to each of the others, except Amelia. "I'm sorry," he apologized. "I wasn't expecting any additional companions on this journey."

"But you have one left," said Amelia, pointing to a left over ring on the table.

"That one is for Harran," said Kazin. "Whoever finds him has to give him this ring and it will allow him to be magically whisked back to me with the others."

"How do they work?" asked Olag.

"When you're ready to come back to wherever I am," instructed Kazin, "you rub them continuously with your finger for five seconds."

"Why so long?" asked Sherman.

"Because that eliminates activating the ring by accident," said the mage.

"There's one problem," objected Zylor, holding up his ring in his giant hand. "It's too small for my fingers."

"No it's not," said Kazin. "It's magical. It will fit any finger you choose to put it on."

The minotaur looked doubtful as he tried to slide the ring onto his finger. But as Kazin had promised, it slid onto his finger perfectly. "Remarkable!" exclaimed Zylor in fascination.

"But now the real question that's on everyone's minds," said Sherman. "Who's going on which quest?"

Everyone looked expectantly at Kazin as he considered. "Well," he said at last, "the only way to track our original quarry is using Amelia's orb, so Amelia has to go on that quest, and since we are in human territory, the best one to send to protect her is Sherman. As far as the quest to find Harran, if the trail leads to the mountains, Zylor is best equipped to find his way through the dwarven tunnels. The training you received from Harran previously is an asset that cannot be overlooked."

"Good," said Zylor. "I would have gone after the dwarf anyway."

"That's what I figured," said Kazin. He turned to Olag. "The ring of invisibility makes you an asset either way, Olag, but I think you should go with Zylor."

Olag looked at the minotaur without enthusiasm but Zylor merely grinned back.

"The ability of stealth is paramount if you are going to free Harran," continued the mage. "And if I change Zylor - wait a minute! I have a better idea! Zylor has a tendency to draw his weapon too readily, so if I transform him, he will be prone to returning to his original form at an inopportune time. But if I transform you, Olag, into a dwarf, you can blend in with the dwarves who are heading home with the caravan. As long as you refrain from drawing your weapon, you'll remain a dwarf indefinitely. Zylor can protect you, and stay nearby while wearing the invisibility ring!"

"You mean - you mean I could have had a turn at wearing the ring of invisibility all along?" exclaimed Zylor. "I always thought it was because my fingers were too big!"

"Um, I suppose you could have had a turn," stammered Kazin, "but I just thought that you didn't want to wear it because it wasn't particularly honourable to do so."

"Being invisible is cowardly," agreed Zylor, "but this time I'm doing it for Harran. His life is at stake. In my current form I would never be able to get close. With the ring there is a chance."

Olag reluctantly passed the ring to Zylor. Just to be sure, the minotaur tried the ring on - and disappeared. Then he reappeared as he removed the ring again.

"That's a lethal combination," remarked Sherman.

"What about you, Kazin?" asked Amelia suddenly.

"I will have to proceed with the original quest," said Kazin. "I fear our adversary is particularly dangerous, and I will need all of my magical power to stop him."

"Good," said Sherman.

When everyone looked at him, he added, "Um, I mean it's good that he's coming with me. It's easier to keep an eye on him that way."

"Ditto," said Amelia with a twinkle in her eye.

Kazin addressed Zylor and Olag. "Take what supplies you need. We can purchase more in the morning." He passed Harran's ring to Zylor. "See that Harran gets this." Then he gave Zylor's amulet to Olag and cast a spell on him, making him look like an ordinary dwarf. His quiver of arrows was altered to look like a pack with tools for making concrete.

"Remember," admonished Kazin, "don't draw your weapon, and you will continue to look like a dwarf. That will ensure you will get passage into the dwarven mountains if that's where Harran was taken, which is very likely. Good luck to both of you."

The minotaur and skink warrior/dwarf shook hands with everyone and Zylor put on the invisibility ring. Then they departed.

Kazin looked at the remaining companions. "Well, I think we should take advantage of the rooms and get some sleep. We'll need our wits about us tomorrow. I hope that Zylor and Olag find a way to get some rest riding with the caravan."

"I still don't like our odds now that we're split up," said Sherman.

"We might make better time as a result," said Amelia. "Smaller groups tend to travel faster."

"Let's hope that's true," said Kazin. "We've already lost some valuable time."

Chapter 18

arran awoke with a start as his body jostled violently and the sound of creaking and hooves filled his ears. He raised his head briefly, but the world spun and his head throbbed in tune to the horses' hooves. It felt like he had awoken from a night of heavy drinking. Fervently he hoped this was a bad dream, but it didn't stop. Another bounce caused him to land on his elbow and a sharp pain engulfed his senses. This was no dream. In agony, he tried to sit up and take note of his surroundings. It was daylight, perhaps mid-morning, and he was riding on a wagon as it sped down a rocky road. He squinted between the bars of a cage to catch sight of a considerable number of horses ridden by dwarves. Most of the dwarves were armed, consisting mostly of males, with a smattering of females, who were undoubtedly children of the fighting classes of dwarves. They were brought up in military fashion, and were trained just as well as the males. Interspersed with the fighters were a number of civilian dwarves, who rode with their heads held just as high. They were experts in their trades, and had no shame in being non-fighters. Some of the more ambitious ones carried weapons, and, even though their combat skills were not at the same level as the trained fighters, they would surely put up a fight regardless.

One of the military types nudged a civilian and muttered something. The dwarf in question looked over at the wagon that Harran rode in. Seeing Harran awake, his eyes lit up and he moved his horse so it ran beside the wagon. The dwarf had a bushy black beard and wore a long grey coat. He appeared to be a business dwarf of some sort, possibly a merchant.

The wagon lurched again and Harran had to hold onto the cage to steady himself.

"So!" drawled the dwarf with a slightly high-pitched voice. Just looking at him one would not have expected that kind of voice. "I see you have awakened."

"Yes," said Harran slowly. "What are you doing to me? Why am I caged?"

The business dwarf chuckled. "Don't be coy with me. You are either a coward or a thief. Either one is punishable by law." His face darkened. "Either one is also dishonourable."

"You're mistake," said Harran angrily. "I'm neither. What gave you the idea I was a coward or a thief?"

The business dwarf laughed. "Surely you jest?"

"I see no humour in this!" snapped Harran, slapping his cage.

The business dwarf chuckled. "We'll just let the authorities decide your fate. Once they see your chain mail, they'll confirm your identity. If you are the owner, you'll be punished for abandoning your post. If you're not the owner, you're a thief, and will be dealt with accordingly. There is no way out for you. But for me there is only the reward of bringing you in. Personally, I hope you are this General Ironfaust, as the armor indicates. It will fetch me a tidy sum indeed! But if you aren't," the business dwarf shrugged, "I will still receive a reward. I can't lose! Maybe the real General Ironfaust will reward me for returning his armour!" He chuckled again and shook his head.

Harran took a few moments to digest what he had just heard. Then it dawned on him. The chain mail he had brought back in time with him originally belonged to a dwarf who lived in this era and was part of the king's personal guard. Once endowed with the task of the king's personal guard, a dwarf had to stay near the king, and could only leave the realm if the king did. Later in time, this dwarf - Ironfaust - had no more need of his chain mail, so he passed it onto someone, who in turn gave it to Harran the last time he had gone back in time. Not sure whether that item had a bearing on the alterations to history, Kazin had asked Harran to bring it along on this quest. Unfortunately, someone had noticed the chain mail and recognized it for what it was. They had suspected it was out of place, and laid a trap for the unwary dwarf. And now here he sat, riding in a cage to be turned over to the authorities in the dwarven realm.

Harran cursed and sat back in despair.

The business dwarf chuckled gleefully upon seeing Harran's reaction.

Harran contemplated his situation. His armour had landed him in trouble, and if he was turned over to the authorities, they would surely involve Ironfaust. What would Ironfaust do when he saw his chainmail? What if he wore his chainmail when he confronted Harran with identical chain mail to his own? What would happen when an object made contact with itself from the future? Could it occupy the same space in the same time? Kazin had warned of potentially dire consequences if this happened. Now, due to his lack of caution, Harran was in a position to cause such an event! Furthermore, his ice axe had been taken. He had to find it or it might fall into the wrong hands. It had the potential to change history as well. He put his head in his hands in despair.

Another heavy jolt from the wagon brought him back to the present as his wagon struck another boulder. A loud crack was followed by a snap and the entire wagon tilted to one rear corner, threatening to topple Harran's cage to the ground. A grinding noise confirmed that one wheel had broken and the dwarf driving the wagon cursed and yanked sharply on the reins to halt the horses.

The wagon lurched to a precarious stop amid a choking cloud of dust. The driver climbed off the wagon while the surrounding dwarves rode up in concern. Several dismounted and ran to inspect the damage.

Harran's cage had been mounted to the floor, but several of the lighter crates had bounced across the wagon onto the ground. Two had split open and the contents were strewn about on the ground. Things became a flurry of activity as the dwarves hurried to deal with the damaged wagon. This delay, with potential roving bands of ogres in the vicinity, was not a welcome situation. They had to work fast.

Harran was impressed with the dwarves' efficiency. It was as though they had trained to deal with this. Ignoring Harran and his cage despite his offers to help, they moved the heavy crates of gold to the front right corner of the wagon. This caused the weight on the wagon to shift to that corner, thereby lifting the damaged rear left of the wagon off the ground. By combining the tools on the wagon and those of the civilians, the dwarves worked together to remove the remnants of the broken wheel from the axle. A spare spiked wheel, previously fastened to the wagon's side, was installed on the axle in place of the damaged one. In the meantime, some civilians re-packed the damaged boxes and a carpenter nailed them shut. When the wheel was changed, the boxes were loaded and the weight was once again centered properly on the wagon. Within half an hour they were ready to depart, when one of the civilians called out and pointed to the other rear wheel of the wagon. One of the spokes appeared to be broken, and upon closer inspection, it was discovered that two spokes were damaged and were very close to snapping off. A brief discussion ensued and most of the dwarves with construction background agreed it would be better to repair the damage now rather than risking another wheel breaking off, since they had no spare one left to replace it with. The military dwarves didn't like this, but deferred the decision to the experienced dwarves. While the repairs ensued, the military sent out scouts in every direction to watch for ogres.

The repairs required that the wheel be removed, so the dwarves had to move the weight to the good corner to allow the removal to take place. Repairing the wheel was no easy task because they needed parts to join the broken spokes back to the wheel rim. The dwarves who insisted the repairs be done immediately justified their decision when they cut pieces from the discarded wheel because they were already formed to the right shape. While they worked, some civilians went to a nearby stream to water the horses. The wagon's horses were also given water from pails that were carried back from the stream. The repair took an hour and a half and the loading and shifting of crates and boxes took another twenty minutes.

Finally they were underway. Everyone, including Harran, had a chance to eat during the operation, so the military dwarves decided to ride straight through the day and into the night to make up time.

It was a rough ride for Harran and his head still throbbed. He must have passed out a few times during the night because the sky lightened in the east sooner than he would have expected.

The sun was just appearing over the horizon when he heard a strangled cry up ahead. More yells could be heard as the wagon altered course and started to pick up speed. It had been going at a brisk pace for hours, and the additional speed put additional strain on the repaired wheel. A splintering sound came from the wheel and the driver slowed the wagon in anticipation of another accident. He anticipated correctly as the wheel made another splintering noise before breaking apart. The wagon's horses were reined in and the driver turned to the back of his seat to obtain a short sword. Then he jumped to the ground. A short distance away yells could be heard as the dwarves clashed with a contingent of ogres who had ambushed them.

"Let me help!" cried Harran as the driver ran past. The driver looked up at him briefly and then shook his head. "I haven't got the key." He turned and ran to join the attack.

Flashes of light could be seen as magic wielders made their presence known. Dwarves did not wield magic and neither did ogres, so Harran hoped it was Kazin and his companions coming to aid him. But that hope was dashed when the business dwarf came into view.

"Damned lizardmages!" he panted. He briefly looked at Harran as he scanned the wagon's contents. He climbed up onto the broken wagon and tried to lift one of the boxes. It was too heavy for him. "My gold!" he wailed. "I'm ruined!"

"Let me out!" cried Harran desperately. He needed to get out of there in a bad way.

The merchant looked at him and his eyes lit up. "Wait! I can't take the gold, and I can't take you, but I can take your armour and axe!" He rummaged around the wagon for a moment. "Aha!" he cried. He held up a bag. "This is it!" He jumped down from the wagon and tripped as the weight of the bag made him lose his balance. Harran's helmet flew from the bag's opening and rolled under the wagon. The dwarf scrambled back to his feet. He started forward, but came to an abrupt stop. Appearing from ahead were two ogres. Nervously, the dwarf looked around in a panic. Then he dumped the sack and picked up Harran's ice axe. With great effort, he hoisted it over his shoulder in preparation for the inevitable.

The ogres approached the armed dwarf confidently. They knew he was not a battle-hardened dwarf by his appearance. In their opinion he was easy prey. As they got close, the dwarf swung the ice axe with great effort. He swung too soon, but the axe did what it was made to do and solidly froze one ogre in its tracks. But the second ogre was far enough away that it was not affected. In two large strides it reached the dwarf, who was off balance and struggling to bring his axe into a backhanded swing. All it took was one solid punch with its meaty fist for the ogre to end the life of the desperate dwarf. The dwarf crumpled to the ground without a sound. The ogre looked between its counterpart and the ice axe a couple of times before deciding to take the axe for itself. Lumbering away, it ignored its frozen partner and went in search of other prey. Apparently it did not notice Harran in the cage.

Harran watched all this in dismay, not making a sound for fear of getting himself killed. Images of what the unauthorized ice axe would do to history plagued his mind. He held his head in his hands and wished all this was a bad dream, but he knew it was not.

Battle cries and yells raged on around him for another twenty minutes or so before the din died down. The victors were obvious as a number of ogres came into view of the wagon. The sun was visible through the trees and reflected on their dumb, emotionless faces. When they spotted Harran, some of them started forward in anticipation of another kill, but a shouted command halted them in their tracks.

An ogre wearing a helmet and chain mail appeared and strode past the others to peer at the dwarf in its cage curiously.

"What is it?" hissed another voice. A lizardmage wearing a black cloak ambled forward to see what was going on.

"A dwarf," said the ogre chieftain, pointing at Harran.

The lizardman glanced at the ogre chieftain. "Obviously." He looked back toward Harran curiously. "Interesting," he said, drawing out the 's' sound. "I see we have ourselves a dwarf in captivity. Why is that, dwarf? Answer, or we finish you like your brethren!" He gestured behind him.

"It is strictly a misunderstanding," said Harran. He didn't elaborate.

The lizardman chuckled. "It must be a serious misunderstanding for them to have you locked up! I think you did something very bad for that to happen. I think your precious honour has been compromised. Am I right?"

"My honour is none of your business!" snapped Harran.

The lizardman chuckled again. "Oh, but it is!" He turned to the ogre cheiftain. "Start getting the crates of gold and other items of value. Leave the human merchandise unless you need it. We have a good haul today."

The ogres began emptying the wagon, paying no heed to Harran in his cage. One ogre even stopped to pick up the bag containing Harran's chain mail.

The lizardman redirected his attention to Harran. "You have three choices, dwarf. I could kill you, I could leave you here to be found by the dwarven patrols - if they find you in time - or I could salvage your honour."

"How?" asked Harran, although he was sure he didn't want to know.

The lizardmage smiled - or what passed for a smile. "By doing something for me."

"I would never do your bidding!" spat Harran.

The lizardmage chuckled. "The way I see it, if I let you free, you will be honour bound to repay me. So, in exchange for your freedom, I want you to do something for me." The lizardmage paused before continuing. "On the other hand, since the other dwarves had you caged, you must not be an honourable dwarf. Maybe I shouldn't be negotiating with you."

Harran saw through the lizardmages' manipulation tactics, but he knew this conversation was also keeping him alive.

By now, most of the wagon's valuable contents had been removed. The ogres had no difficulty carrying the crates away into the forest. The wagon's horses were freed and chased into the forest as well.

"What do you want me to do?" asked Harran stiffly. He had to look interested to keep the conversation going as long as possible, yet appear as though he was affronted by what was being asked of him. Maybe he could talk his way into being released from the cage. It was a remote hope, but it was all he had going for him.

The lizardmage hissed gleefully. "I was hoping you would see it my way. I want you to -," he was cut off as an ogre came running into the clearing, out of breath.

"The patrols are coming!" he panted.

"Dwarves?" asked the ogre chieftain.

"Yes," said the messenger. Even as he spoke, a horn could be he heard not far away.

The lizardmage hissed. "We were spotted! I told you to stay out of sight!"

"How many?" asked the chieftain.

"Many!" said the messenger.

"How many!" snapped the lizardmage irritably. "Are there more of them than us?"

The messenger considered for a moment. "Yes! They are many more! They are all riding!"

"Military patrols," snarled the lizardmage. He turned to the ogre chieftain. "Have your army fall back! We need to regroup!"

The chieftain was not pleased but turned and gave the order anyway. A war horn sounded again.

"Too close!" hissed the lizardmage. He began to run into the forest after the ogres who had carried away the crates, but stopped and looked at Harran. He raised his staff to cast a spell. A third horn sounded. It was much closer this time. Harran was obviously not worth the time or effort of a spell with enemy troops bearing down on their position, so the lizardmage turned and melted into the forest.

It wasn't long before the sounds of horses could be heard. The dwarven army reined in nearby and voices could be heard as the dwarves examined the primary battle area. Some patrols were dispatched and two mounted units rode in the direction of the raided wagon. It didn't take them long to come across Harran sitting forlornly in his cage in the mostly empty wagon.

One of the patrols whistled and a number of mounted soldiers rode into the clearing to witness the scene. One of them was the patrol leader, judging by the red feather protruding from his helmet. He dismounted and approached Harran.

"Who are you?" demanded the patrol leader.

Harran rose to his feet. "Harran Mapmaker, at your service," he answered, giving a stiff bow. "It's good to see you."

"What happened here?" asked the patrol leader. He ignored Harran's small talk.

"We were ambushed by ogres," said Harran. He pointed to the empty wagon beside him. "They took everything of value, including the gold. It's too bad you weren't a bit earlier. They just left."

"Shall we pursue them?" asked one dwarf that Harran surmised was the second in command.

The patrol leader shook his head. "No. Once in the forest, they have the advantage. We will be slowed down by the horses. They won the battle this time. How many were there?" he asked Harran.

"Several dozen," said Harran, "although I'm sure there were others."

The patrol leader nodded. He eyed the cage Harran was confined in. "How did you end up in that cage?"

"I - I was knocked unconscious," said Harran awkwardly. "I woke up in here." He didn't want to admit to being captured. It was not honourable to be taken by surprise.

"Are there any survivors?"

Harran shook his head sadly. "I don't think so." It was unlikely any were left alive. They would have fought to the death and he would have died with them if we would have been able to. But he also knew deep down his quest for Kazin was far more important - even more important than his honour. Suddenly it occurred to him that there was no one alive who could identify him as a prisoner any longer.

"Why didn't they kill you like the rest?" asked the patrol leader.

Harran shrugged. "I don't know. You arrived before I could get the lizardmage to tell me anything useful."

"Lizardmage?!" exclaimed the patrol leader. "Did you say lizardmage?"

"Yes," nodded Harran. He looked confused.

The patrol leader exchanged glances with his second in command.

"That explains the burn marks on the trees and ground, and the burned dwarves," said the second in command.

The patrol leader nodded and turned back to Harran. "This is serious business. If the raiders are using magic, the king must be warned immediately! Our tactics need to be altered to deal with this."

He turned to his second in command. "Prepare to return home. We must make haste!" To another he added, "Free Harran. He comes with us."

Several dwarves equipped with axes approached the cage and quickly shattered the wooden bars to free the prisoner. Harran stiffly climbed to the ground. A glint under the wagon caught his eye and he spotted his helmet. He quickly bent down and retrieved it. As he straightened up, a dwarf came up to him with a horse. Harran gratefully accepted it and mounted it expertly. Then he rode over to the patrol leader who was still issuing commands. He turned and eyed Harran's helmet keenly. "Nice helmet, for a mapmaker."

"I purchased it a while back," said Harran. "It got knocked off before I was knocked unconscious."

"These things happen," said the patrol leader. He excused Harran's feeling of dishonour with that comment. Had he been a military dwarf, he would have been reprimanded, but he was merely a mapmaker, so it was excusable.

If only he knew, thought Harran.

"Sir," interrupted Harran when he thought it was a good time to ask, "Are you certain you need me to report to the king? Surely you don't need me to tell him about the lizardman?"

The patrol leader eyed him suspiciously. "It would be better to give him a first-hand account of what transpired here. Why? Are you afraid of talking to the king? Most dwarves would envy the chance to speak freely before the king!"

Harran considered the comment and realized there was no way out of it. If he pushed the subject, he might arouse suspicions that could portray him as not being on the up and up. Going to the dwarven realm was not what he wanted, but to refuse to go was too suspicious by far. He laughed lightly. "I guess I am a little nervous."

The patrol leader laughed and slapped him on the back. "Don't worry, my friend! He's not a bad fellow once you get to know him!" He squinted at Harran. "You know, he looks a lot like you." He turned away to direct the removal and burial of the dwarves who had been slain.

Harran shuddered, knowing he was soon going to meet his distant ancestor.

A couple of hours later they were under way. Harran looked back at the wagon as they departed. Up to this point, he had been going to the dwarven realm as a prisoner. It was ironic that he was still going there, but this time as an ally. Either way, there was no escape.

Chapter 19

ylor gripped the chariot tightly with both hands as he bounced along the rugged trail. At first he ran alongside the dwarven convoy, but the dwarves made haste at maximum speed. This pace was too much for even the minotaur to keep up with, so he sprang for one of the two-wheeled chariots and let the horses do the work. They were powerful horses, and the crates piled upon the chariots were filled with heavy gold, so the large minotaur was an almost unnoticed additional weight for these horses to pull.

Things were a little easier for Olag, who rode one of the available horses that were used for the trek back to the mountains. He easily passed as a dwarf who specialized in concrete work and was not asked any uncomfortable questions upon his arrival. For the first part of the journey he could feel Zylor's presence beside him, but a mumbled comment about tiring and jumping on one of the chariots informed him that the minotaur needed a respite from his run. The skink warrior made a point of riding near the chariot in case Zylor should wish to communicate with him, but conversation was minimal, partly due to the fact that the other dwarves were potentially within hearing distance. Their mission was too important to take any unnecessary chances.

So the first day went quickly and a brief halt was called at dusk to rest and water the horses.

Olag moved to a spot far enough away from the dwarves so he could talk with the invisible minotaur. From what they could gather so far, they were on the shortest route back to the dwarven realm.

"If Harran took any of the other routes," said Zylor quietly, "we will be gaining on him."

"Unless he took the route we are currently on," said Olag.

"Then we are still on his trail," said Zylor.

"If he even came this way," said Olag.

212

"Oh, he's headed back to the dwarven realm alright," said Zylor. "The dwarf I interrogated confirmed that much."

"If we get to the mountains too late to catch up with Harran, we will have to enter the dwarven realm to find him," said Olag.

"Then that is what we will do," said Zylor fervently. There was no hesitation in his voice.

Olag sighed. "I just hope we don't get found out."

"Just leave the fighting to me," said Zylor. "Kazin was right to change you into a dwarf. I would never have remained in that form for long enough to have done any good."

"Just don't get too carried away," cautioned Olag. "We're not here to change history. We just have to find Harran and bring him back."

A dwarf suddenly whistled, signaling everyone to prepare for departure. Olag passed Zylor some dried meat and a sausage which promptly disappeared into Zylor's invisible pack.

The convoy surged ahead again, but more slowly due to the darkness. The dwarven guides unerringly led the convoy through the night, and another break was called at dawn near a stream. The dwarves dismounted and stretched. Some of them prepared breakfast while others tended to the horses. The military dwarves went on short patrols to secure the area. An hour later they were off again.

The sun rapidly rose overhead and it was close to noon when an alarm sounded from the dwarves riding point up front. With practiced skill, some military dwarves redirected the chariots and civilian dwarves to cover. Olag was among those who were directed to keep quiet and concealed.

Zylor was under no compunction to hide while something was afoot. Seeing that Olag was safe, he bounded ahead to see what all the fuss was about.

The convoy had stumbled upon a contingent of ogres who had been camping at the edge of the trail. Cooking fires still smoldered among the trees while the front running dwarves already clashed noisily with their foes.

The ogres were unprepared for the attack, and hastily regrouped to meet the assault. The confusion was short-lived and they retaliated just as the remainder of the dwarves joined in the fray.

Although outnumbered, the dwarves were more experienced fighters. They outmaneuvered the ogres and toppled their bigger adversaries by striking their legs out from under them. Once down, the ogres were helpless against the sharp dwarven axes.

But the dwarves began to lose on one front. A menacing ogre wielding an ice axe was swinging his weapon wildly, freezing several dwarves at a time and then shattering their frozen statues where they stood. Zylor saw this and knew he had to react. He made his way toward the offending ogre.

Meanwhile, Olag successfully snuck away from the civilian dwarves to scout around the enemy encampment. The ogres were too busy with the attacking dwarves to notice him in the background. Among the ogres' belongings were a number of crates. Some of the lids were open, revealing gold and silver coins, probably stolen from a previous dwarven caravan. Bags of assorted belongings were scattered around the area, but Olag only scanned a few of them, finding the contents too raunchy and repulsive. As he walked, he stumbled over one bag and heard a metallic noise emanate from within. He stooped to pick it up and shook its contents to the ground. What he saw made the invisible fins on his head stand up. To be certain, he picked up the item to examine it more closely. There was no doubt in his mind it belonged to Harran. He looked around sharply in the hopes of catching sight of the dwarf, but he was nowhere to be seen. Olag's spirit sagged. Where was Harran, and why was his chain mail here among the ogres? Was Harran still even alive?

Back in the battle, Zylor faced his opponent, all too aware that invisibility was no defense against an ice axe. He warily circled to the ogre's side, drawing his weapon slowly and carefully. As expected, his weapon became visible to the ogre. The ogre was momentarily surprised, but was intelligent enough to bring his axe back to his shoulder in preparation for another swing.

Zylor, satisfied that the ogre was aware of his presence, knew it was now honourable to fight the monster. With a vicious swing, he brought the axe around in a high arc and mesmerized the ogre with the motion. It gaped at the oncoming axe and could do nothing to avoid the weapon as it sliced its head from its shoulders in one fluid motion.

Greenish blood squirted from its neck as it collapsed to the ground in a heap, dropping the ice axe in the process.

At the same time, an earthquake struck again, similar to the last one that had happened when the companions were in the elven realm.

Some nearby dwarves were fascinated by the sight and took heart, charging into the fray with battle cries. To them, it was the gods who had intervened on their behalf.

A lizardman, who had been concealed behind some trees and was using magic to enhance the speed and strength of the ogres, had also seen the mysterious axe as it eliminated the ogre. He hadn't expected to come across a magic wielder among the dwarves. He stepped from cover and sent a lightning bolt in Zylor's direction.

"Zylor!" cried Olag loudly above the din. He had also seen Zylor's accomplishment, and was situated in a spot where the lizardmage was visible to him.

The minotaur turned to where he heard Olag call to him, and out of the corner of his eye he saw the lightning bolt coming at him. He ducked to avoid being hit, and the bolt whizzed past his head and struck his axe. The weapon exploded into a thousand tiny fragments, slicing into his hand in the process. Oblivious to the pain, Zylor looked to where the bolt had originated to see the lizardman duck back behind the trees. His gaze would have been malevolent had he been visible.

Olag watched as the lizardman chanted a spell and disappeared from sight. He cursed inwardly. If he wasn't restricted from using his weapon, he would have filled the lizardmage full of arrows before he could escape.

Zylor, being weaponless, instinctively looked around for a weapon. His eyes rested on the ice axe. Without hesitation, he picked it up and sheathed it so it disappeared from sight. There was no need to use it as the dwarves were now in control of the battle. The ogres were on the run. The sounds of battle lessened.

As quickly as it had begun, the battle was over.

The dwarves who were killed were buried with a short service, and the carcasses of the ogres were thrown into a ravine. The injured were tended to and readied for the trip home. The newly acquired boxes of gold were added to the chariots, and extra horses, which previously bore dwarves, now assisted in pulling the overloaded chariots. It would slow down the caravan, but there was no complaining. Dwarves loved their gold. It was worth the effort, even if that meant a delay in getting home.

Some dwarves speculated about the disembodied axe and the unexpected earthquake, but all were happy it was on their side. Some even attributed it to the intervention of the gods. The god of war must have intervened on their behalf. The motivation alone of the presence of the axe was enough to give them an edge in this battle. But the matter that was more of a concern was the disappearance of the ice axe. A thorough search of the general area turned up nothing. It was finally determined that a fleeing ogre must have picked it up and ran off with it, not aware of the value of its find. Either that, or the explosion that was seen shortly after the appearance of the other axe meant that the gods had taken the ice axe in payment. An act like that was something the dwarves could fully appreciate.

Zylor pulled Olag aside and obtained a bandage to wrap around his damaged hand. He chose to wrap the bandage himself and, as he did, it also became invisible, ensuring his identity remained hidden. As he worked, Olag led him to a spot a short distance away from the others. He opened a pack and told the invisible minotaur to peek inside. A soft groan indicated the minotaur had seen the artifact.

"Harran's?" he rumbled softly.

Olag nodded. "I'm sure of it. But I don't know where he is. I looked all over, but there were no dwarves present in the raiding party."

"With all the crates of gold lying around, I'd say his party was ambushed," said Zylor. "I'll bet this ice axe was his too. I haven't seen any of these around, even though Kazin thinks they were common in this era."

"He wouldn't have given up the axe without a fight," said Olag, shaking his head sadly. "I can only surmise he is dead along with the convoy he was traveling with."

Zylor growled, but it was a different sound than any Olag had heard before. It was more of a growl of sorrow, if that was possible. "Remember," said the minotaur thoughtfully, "Harran was kidnapped. It stands to reason that his weapon and armour were taken away. We don't know for sure that he is dead."

"But if his caravan was robbed - and it appears that it was - the dwarves would have died trying to defend all of that gold," objected Olag. "They would have fought to the death."

"Maybe so," growled Zylor, "but Harran knew the importance of our quest! He would not have sacrificed his life for gold - or anything else for that matter! If anything, he would have found a way to escape and come back to us."

"Perhaps," said Olag, "but whether he was killed, or managed to escape the fate of the other caravan, what are we supposed to do now? Do we continue to look for him or return to Kazin? And if we continue to look, where do we look?"

"I think we owe it to Harran to keep looking for him," said Zylor, "at least for now. We can return to Kazin in an instant with the rings he gave us, so time is on our side. But if we go off on our own, we would have no more success than finding a needle in a haystack. If we stay among these dwarves, we may gather clues to his whereabouts. Staying the course should yield the best results."

Olag sighed. "Ok. But I think this is going to be a waste of time."

"If you do not wish to help, I will simply go alone," growled Zylor. "I will not abandon Harran!"

"I don't want to abandon him either!" snapped Olag, "but the evidence points to him being dead!"

"I am not convinced," growled Zylor. "If you do not believe he is -."

"Hey! I miss him too!" snapped Olag. Aware of drawing undue attention, he quieted his voice. "We'll continue to search for now. I hope you're right and he is still alive. Like you said, we have time on our side. We can probably be more successful finding Harran than finding Kazin's elusive strangler anyway. At least we know what our quarry looks like."

Olag felt a giant reassuring hand on his shoulder. "Thank you," mumbled the minotaur. "You'll see that I'm right. Harran is still alive."

The skink warrior heard the minotaur as he trudged off to be on his own. He felt the minotaur's agony in that statement. It was more a statement of faith than one of fact. He could only guess what the minotaur and dwarf had been through in previous adventures. Some of the stories he had been told were amazing in their own right. But it was the untold ones that created the bond between the minotaur and dwarf. Those stories were not divulged. Those were the ones that bonded them as the best of friends. Once again, Olag felt privileged to be a part of these companions. What they saw in him - a mere skink warrior - was beyond him. He was supposed to be their mortal enemy, yet he was trusted as one of them. What's more, he enjoyed their camaraderie. Once again, he felt the desire to help. He didn't want to let them down; not now, not ever. Was this what it was like for them? Did they always feel like this? Was he becoming like them? Olag decided he liked the feeling. For the first time in his life he felt like he belonged. He decided right then and there that he would do everything in his power to preserve his friendship with these unlikely companions. They were worth fighting for. They were worth protecting. They were worth finding. He turned and strode confidently back to his horse. It was time to saddle up.

Chapter 20

he town of Trent was bustling with activity as Kazin, Sherman and Amelia entered via the eastern road. It was getting toward evening, but Kazin was determined to cover lost ground and didn't want to stop for the night. He stopped at an inn to see if any travelers, particularly large groups of ten or so, had stopped in from the east. The innkeeper informed them there were no large groups, and her only occupants for the last few nights were tradesmen - mostly dwarves, military personnel, and traveling vendors. She urged them to check other inns as there were a few on this end of town.

Kazin thanked her and did as she suggested. It didn't take long to find them, and those innkeepers all claimed to have the same kind of clientele. Amelia's orb confirmed that their quarry had not set foot in those places.

As they left the last inn, Sherman spoke up. "What if they didn't stay here? What if they went straight through?"

"It's possible," admitted Kazin.

"Then we should be checking the stables," continued the big warrior. "When I used to travel as a caravan guard, and we were in a hurry, we would only stop at a town to trade in our horses for some fresh ones."

"Wasn't that costly?" asked Amelia.

Sherman nodded. "Sure, but with the time it saved in getting the goods delivered, it was often well worth it. A couple of days less to pay an entire crew wages meant more profit for the merchant."

"Good point," said Kazin. "It wouldn't hurt to check out the stables in this end of town."

The trio approached one stable and an old, grizzled stable master greeted them. "Come to trade in your horses?" A quick look behind him revealed a handful of tired looking horses.

"No, thank you," said Kazin politely.

"Ah, well, my selection is a little limited right now," said the man. "I expect a good dozen or so back in the next few days. If you're still in the neighborhood, check with me this time tomorrow. I might have more to show ya."

"Sure," said Kazin. "But while we're here, have you seen any large groups of travelers come into town to change out their horses? Say, ten or so people?"

The man shook his head. "Naw. But you can check with some of the other stables. There's one on your left almost as soon as you enter town. He's got a bigger supply than I do. He specializes in larger groups." He put the back of his hand beside his mouth and added with a whisper, "but he's a lot more expensive."

"Thanks," said Kazin. He looked at Amelia who had peeked into her pocket at her orb. She looked up and shook her head.

Kazin led them to the stables that the older man had suggested, and from a distance they could see some horses prancing about in the fenced grazing area beside the stables.

As they neared, Amelia gasped. "Kazin!" she whispered. "I recognize the brand markings on the sides of some of the horses! They look like the symbol that was on the gates of the estate where those bodies were found!"

Kazin squinted at the horses. "I believe you're right."

"Look," said Amelia. She held up her orb. It glowed with a light pink.

"Let's see what we can find out," said Kazin.

They approached the gate of the stables where a middle-aged man with slick black hair came out to meet them. He smiled, revealing a couple of missing teeth. "What can I do for ya?" he drawled.

"We're looking for a group of ten or so people that came from the east," said Kazin.

"I get lots of groups coming and going all the time," said the man. "Can you be more specific?"

"Um, one of them had a thick black mustache," said Kazin.

The man's grin widened. "Oh, yeah! I remember that one. He rode in yesterday afternoon with a bunch of others. Except for him, the rest of them looked kinda ill." The man pointed over his shoulder at the horses in the yard. "He traded in some damned good horses for the ones that I had. Said he was in a hurry; didn't have time to stop." The man chuckled. "Not only did I get some better horses, I got top dollar for the ones I sold him! He said money was no object! Can you believe it?"

"Where were they headed?" asked Amelia.

The man scratched his head. "Now, that's the funny part. They rode into town, but came ridin' back out this way a few minutes later. I heard him mumbling about there being too many mages in town. They charged out on the east road and veered south. The fool didn't even stop for supplies - I seen that they didn't have much when they changed horses. He'll regret it later on, especially with some of them being sick and all. There ain't no supplies for miles down that way, unless he happens across some farmers kind enough to sell them something."

"Why was he nervous about the mages?" asked Kazin.

The stable master shrugged. "I don't know. There are lots of mages around because of the tower in the west. They often come here to replenish supplies."

"I see," said Kazin. He looked at Sherman. "It looks like we won't be spending the night. Should we exchange our horses?"

Sherman nodded. "We rode them pretty hard. It would be a good idea to change them."

The stable master grinned again. "I've got some excellent horses available. But they won't go cheap."

"Money is no object," said Kazin. "Give us your best ones."

Twenty minutes later, the stable master gleefully jiggled his pouch of coins as the companions rode off with three of the horses that had originally belonged to the estate in Velden. Taking the stable master's advice, they rode into town to replenish supplies before heading south out of town.

"It's too bad," said Kazin. "I would have liked to have gone to see Sorcerer's Tower. I'm curious to see how much it's changed."

"It could still happen," said Sherman.

The companions rode hard into the night and Sherman, with the aid of Kazin's lit staff, followed the road skillfully, navigating around muddy areas and up and down sharp inclines with practiced ease. When the horses grew weary, Sherman guided them to a secluded spot away from the main road near a stream. The horses drank thirstily, as the steam from their breath emitted from their flaring nostrils. Amelia suggested they get a few hours of sleep before continuing on and elected to take the first watch. She awoke Sherman a few hours later and he in turn woke Kazin. Kazin was going to take the next watch, but Amelia woke up and said she didn't want to sleep any more anyway. Sherman didn't have a problem with that as he was not tired either, so it was decided they continue on their journey. After a quick bite, they mounted their horses and returned to the road leading south.

The sun was just preparing to make its debut to the east when the companions crested a small rise to glimpse a small farming village before them. It nestled among some rolling fields dotted with forested sections that followed hidden streams.

They paused to take in the beauty when an unusual sight caught their attention. An object appeared high in the sky above the village. The morning sun's rays glinted off the side of the object with shiny, bronze flashes.

Amelia gasped. "A dragon!"

The dragon swooped down, but not at the village. It aimed for a spot just to the west. It swooped close to ground level and then rose back up into the air. It seemed to waver for a moment before plunging back to the ground. This time it did not return to the air. Some trees blocked the view, so the companions didn't know what had happened.

Kazin shuddered.

"What is it?" asked Amelia, noticing his discomfort.

"There is a powerful magic at work here," said Kazin. "I've never sensed anything so - disconcerting."

Nothing further transpired, so the companions continued their ride toward the village. They warily watched the tree line where the dragon had disappeared in case they needed to run for cover. They had not gone more than several hundred yards when the dragon reappeared. It soared high into the air in a large arc.

"Is it just me, or is there someone riding that dragon?" asked Kazin.

Sherman squinted. "I can't tell. Your eyes are better than mine."

The morning sun got brighter and the dragon swung around to head back toward the ground. Amelia called out. "He's right! There is someone riding that dragon!"

"That explains the magic I felt," said Kazin. "Unless I miss my guess, that dragon is being ridden by a mage. We're in a time when mages are capturing dragons with dragon orbs. What we are witnessing is one of the first dragons being tamed by magic!"

"That's incredible," said Sherman. "Except for you, Kazin, I've never known anyone to control a dragon before - except that you change into a dragon physically."

"Dragon orbs are a new invention in this era," said Kazin. "We are likely to see more dragon riders in the days to come. Dragon mages like me come a little later when dragons die for various reasons while their life essence remains intact in the orb."

"He seems to be having fun," interrupted Amelia, pointing. The dragon was flying erratically and finally dove back down again, this time heading for the village. Suddenly it let loose with a blast of fiery breath, striking a building on the outskirts of the village. In an instant the building was ablaze.

"That wasn't very nice," remarked Sherman. "He could have shown off any number of ways without causing damage."

The dragon circled around and blasted another building. The mage on its back was waving his arms wildly.

"I don't think he's showing off," said Kazin suddenly. "He looks as though he's lost control of his dragon!"

"Oh, no," wailed Amelia. "What does that mean?"

"It means," said Kazin smugly, "that the mage will have to get control of his dragon soon or he will be controlled by the dragon. If he's using an orb - and that's the only way he could be riding one now - he's linked to the beast. There is no severing the connection, except by death."

"Oh, no," said Amelia again. She consulted her orb. It was faintly pink.

Suddenly, another dragon and rider appeared from where the first one had emerged. It swung east to confront the renegade dragon, which had already set a third building on fire. Riding this new bronze dragon was a figure with a pointed hat.

"Where'd he come from?" asked Sherman. "We should have seen him earlier."

"I suspect he was on the ground since we crested the rise," said Kazin. "He was probably involved in capturing the other dragon. Now he's going to intervene to try to stop the renegade from doing any more damage."

The trio watched the aerial battle in fascination. The dragons circled one another several times before the renegade blasted at its counterpart with fire. The mage on the bronze dragon put up a shield that prevented the flames from doing any damage and then lowered his shield to shoot a lightning bolt into the renegade dragon's flank. With a shriek, it spun away with the second dragon in pursuit.

Then the mage riding the renegade dragon turned and shot a lightning bolt back toward the second dragon. The mage was not prepared for the attack and turned to steer his mount to the side to avoid the bolt, but it struck the dragon's right wing. The searing pain made the bronze dragon howl and it banked away sharply, causing its rider to lose his grip and slide down to the injured wing.

Seizing the advantage, the renegade dragon turned to attack its counterpart and clawed its right side with its long talons. The mage wasn't in a position to cast any spells to aid his mount and the dragon screamed in pain again. It dove for the cover of the trees to escape the wrath of the renegade dragon. Ironically, the dragon rider never lost his hat in all of that commotion.

Sensing victory, the renegade dragon screamed in delight and soared back into the sky. It circled around in preparation to redirect its energy back at the village.

Meanwhile, the bronze dragon landed in a field and staggered to a halt, with the mage hanging on for dear life.

"Uh, Kazin," said Amelia.

He turned to the red headed mage. "What is it?"

She held up her orb. It was bright red. "I just consulted the orb. According to this, the renegade was not supposed to prevail."

A shriek drew their attention back to the sky. The bronze dragon was airborne again. It flew erratically, its injured wing obviously causing a great deal of pain. Its rider was urging it on.

"It looks like he's back in action," said Sherman.

Amelia consulted her orb again. "This isn't good," she said.

"What is it?" asked Kazin.

"If the bronze dragon confronts the renegade dragon again, he will lose, and his rider will die."

"Then that's what must happen," said Kazin.

Amelia shook her head and pointed. "If that dragon rider dies, the war will be lost and history as you know it will be changed forever. That dragon rider is one of the most crucial individuals in the war."

"Are you saying we have to intervene?" asked Sherman.

Amelia's face reddened. "According to the orb, we are in this time in history and we are the only ones who can correct the current problem." She turned to Kazin. "According to the orb, we are a part of this history. It took me a long time to come to that conclusion, but it's the only thing that makes any sense. We are a part of this era, whether we like it or not. That's why we haven't changed history despite all of the things that we've done so far. Under normal conditions we should have changed history dozens of times by now, but we haven't."

Another shriek sounded as the two dragons clashed again. It was not looking good for the bronze dragon and its rider.

"Alright," said Kazin. "We'll discuss this more later." He took a few steps away from his friends and transformed into his dragon form.

"You're not going without me," growled Sherman. He bounded up Kazin's wing to find a spot on his back.

"I'm going too," said Amelia. She climbed up Kazin's wing and the warrior's strong arm swung her up beside him. The startled horses were left to graze in the field beside the road.

"Let's show that wise guy how real battles are fought!" cried Sherman. He brandished his Sword of Dead.

Kazin sprang into the air and shrieked, enjoying the feeling of being a dragon once again. He had been repressing the sensation for quite some time. The cry was loud enough to distract the renegade dragon as it was about to deal another serious blow to the bronze dragon. The mage riding the bronze dragon, seeing the new approaching dragon, knew he was outmatched, so he guided his dragon below the renegade and fled in the opposite direction.

The renegade dragon, feeling confident, swung around to face the newcomer, shrieking in delight. Its rider howled in glee, feeding off the dragon's emotions. The dragon was in complete control.

Kazin flew straight at the renegade dragon. "Get ready to throw up your shield, Amelia," he instructed. "If that dragon unleashes flames, I want everyone to be safe. I'll concentrate on getting close enough for Sherman to strike with his sword, and if that mage tries something, I'll deal with it. Be prepared to drop the shield on my command."

"Right!" said Amelia above the rushing of the wind in her ears.

As the two dragons neared one another, Kazin was surprised at the size of his opponent. It was a fair bit larger than himself. He concluded it was probably an older dragon, but one with a strong will. The mage was undoubtedly not strong enough to overcome that will.

As expected, the renegade dragon blasted Kazin with fiery breath. Amelia's shield easily directed the heat away. A moment later, the renegade mage shot a lightning bolt at Kazin and his riders. The bolt was harmlessly deflected aside as well.

"Now!" cried Kazin. Amelia dropped the shield as Kazin swung close to the other dragon while Sherman prepared to swing his sword. The renegade dragon made a sudden movement, trying to slash at the warrior, but Sherman was ready. He swung his sword and sliced clean through one of the dragon's extended claws.

The dragon shrieked as it suffered its second injury. Angered, it circled around for another pass, but not before Kazin shot off a weak fireball at the enemy mage. The mage was struck squarely on the back, but ignored the pain while his cloak caught on fire.

Kazin turned to confront his foe again, but this time the opposing dragon opted to make a close in attack with its claws. Kazin anticipated this and told his riders to hang on. As the dragons came together, Kazin and the other dragon reared back and sank their claws into one another's chest. They snapped at one another with their giant jaws. Locked in combat, they frantically flapped their wings to retain altitude.

As they struggled, Sherman climbed to a spot where he could slash at one of the other dragon's exposed claws. Another lightning bolt from the enemy mage would have knocked him off his mount if it wasn't for Amelia's protective shield. No more magical spells came from the enemy mage as he finally noticed his burning cloak and hastened to deal with that problem.

Amelia saw what Sherman was trying to do and had the foresight to cancel the shield spell just as Sherman's sword struck true, severing another claw from the renegade dragon.

The dragon was unprepared for this and let go with that clawed foot. This unanticipated motion caused it to lurch to the side so rapidly that its rider lost his grip and tumbled from its back. The mage gave a weak cry as he fell, his cloak still ablaze. It was a moment before the renegade dragon realized what had happened. Remembering the orb in the mage's possession, the dragon pushed itself away from Kazin and dove to try to rescue the mage.

As Amelia looked down, she was shocked to see how much altitude they had lost while battling. She could see the falling mage as he fell, and knew that his dragon would not be in time. Thankfully Kazin turned so that she could not see the last few seconds when the mage hit the ground.

A piercing shriek from the renegade dragon was enough to inform them of the mage's death.

Kazin circled slowly as he watched the dragon land by the mage's inert body in the field below. A few minutes passed as the dragon examined the body. Then it cried out one last time and threw itself on top of the human mage. It never moved again.

"Is it - is it dead?" asked Amelia.

Kazin flew back to a safe distance from the village. "I think so. The orb must have become damaged in the fall. Without it the dragon's life essence has been lost. If the orb was intact, the dragon could have taken it and survived."

"That's so sad," said Amelia woefully.

"That's the price of the magic," said Kazin. "When I obtained my dragon orb, the dragon died, but the orb was still intact and contained its life force. That's why I was able to meld with it and become like it.

If I die and the orb is still intact, whoever takes it over will have the same abilities as I have." Kazin stopped speaking in order to land in a grassy meadow a short distance from their horses. His passengers slid and jumped to the ground. Then he transformed back into his human form. His face and chest were cut and bleeding.

"Kazin!" exclaimed Amelia. "You're hurt!"

"They're only minor wounds," said Kazin. "That's another thing I share with the dragon."

Amelia was about to tend to his wounds when the ground shook as an earthquake struck the area. It didn't last long, but it caused the horses to whinny and jump. They were already skittish with Kazin's arrival as a dragon, and Sherman was hard pressed to settle them down.

Amelia was finally able to tend to Kazin's wounds and deftly took care of the worst of it. She was concerned about the earthquake and wondered out loud whether it might have something to do with them and their quest.

"Perhaps," said Kazin. "The landscape as we know it is going to change drastically from what it is now. The question is when."

"We should ask some of the upcoming villagers what they think," suggested Sherman. "Maybe earthquakes are normal in this point in history."

"You're right," said Kazin.

As they prepared to saddle up, the bronze dragon came into view. The rider saw them and gave a command to his mount. It landed awkwardly nearby because its wing was still damaged. The rider quickly dismounted and approached them while Sherman worked to calm the horses again.

"Greetings, strangers!" he called. "Have you seen a dragon fly past?"

"We saw a couple of them," said Kazin evasively. He looked at Amelia, who shrugged. She didn't know if Kazin should give away his identity.

"I could have sworn one of them landed around here somewhere," said the dragon rider, looking around.

"One landed somewhere over there," said Sherman, pointing to the area where the renegade dragon went down.

"I saw that one," said the dragon rider, "but I was looking for the one that won the fight. It flew over here somewhere."

"If it landed around here we would have noticed it," said Amelia.

The dragon rider's eyes narrowed. "To be sure." He studied Kazin's bloody face. "You're hurt."

"I fell off my horse as I watched the battle," lied Kazin. "I'm ok."

The dragon rider grunted. "Are you a mage?"

"I know some magic," said Kazin unhelpfully.

"Why aren't you at the tower?" asked the dragon rider.

"I'm going to see some sick relatives," said Kazin. He was referring to their quarry, whose companions looked sick according to the stable master in Trent. He pointed at Amelia. "My sister came to get me because she knows the way." Amelia knew the way because of her orb. But he knew the dragon rider didn't know these things.

"I see," said the dragon rider. He didn't sound convinced. "Well, if you come across the dragon or its riders, find out who they are. Then report back to the tower to see me. Just ask for Arch Mage Gresham."

"Ok," said Kazin.

"Right then," said Gresham. He took off his hat, tried to straighten the kinked tip - unsuccessfully - and put it back on his head. "Have a safe journey." He turned and went back to his dragon. As he climbed back on his mount he said, "Let's go, Horath. We'll tend to your wounds shortly."

The great beast launched itself back into the air, but not before giving the companions a shrewd glance. It appeared he didn't trust these strangers either.

As they flew back to the first dragon, it occurred to Arch Mage Gresham that the strangers didn't even show any interest in Horath. It was as though they had seen dragons up close before. Anyone else would have been awed by Horath's presence, not to mention the fact that a mage had apparently tamed him. He looked back at the trio as they became small specs in the distance. The warrior with them looked about the right size to be the one who had ridden the dragon to his rescue, and the red-haired mage could have been the other rider if his eyes were to be believed. The blue cloak was not a common colour for a robe, yet the second rider wore an identical blue robe. What were

229

the odds of that? Did the redhead have possession of an orb in order to control a dragon? But where was the dragon? It was too big to hide from Horath's keen vision, yet it was simply gone. And what of the injured young mage? How did he fit into the picture? One would think his companions would be cut and bleeding, not him. Perhaps he had been casting spells from the ground. Maybe in the process he did fall from his horse as he had claimed. Gresham shook his head. He had a feeling he would run into that trio again.

But right now Gresham had the problem of finding a way to deal with cleaning up a failed experiment. The handful of mages assisting with the experiment should already be on site by now. The master mage's body would be returned to the tower for burial. But disposing of the dragon's body would be a challenging task. Thankfully, the nearby village was known for having experts in tanning hides and manufacturing leather goods. Hopefully, the value of the dragon's hide would make up for the buildings that were damaged by the renegade mage and dragon. Also, Horath needed healing. The cleric among his group would have her hands full. Thoughts of the work ahead raced through Gresham's mind and he soon forgot about the strange trio in the field.

Chapter 21

lag and Zylor arrived at the base of the dwarven mountains near a cavern entrance to where the dwarven realm was located. It was heavily guarded by a large contingent of dwarven soldiers. It was fortified with trenches and barricades, and towers dotted the area, filled with expert dwarven archers. Even the mountainside itself was carved in such a way that from a distance it appeared like a giant castle wall with buttresses and turrets from which the defenders could fight. Overhangs were also factored in, to ensure protection from aerial foes such as dragons.

At the gate, the convoy was greeted by a dwarf adorned with shiny silver armour and colourful feathers protruded from his horned helmet.

"Password!" he called out.

A dwarf from the convoy rode forward. "Amethyst."

The guard nodded and turned behind him. "Open the gates!"

Giant iron gates opened outward, silently and smoothly, not a sound coming from the expertly crafted dwarven hinges.

The guard turned to the convoy leader. "You may enter. Follow me."

The procession moved forward and Olag steeled himself as he went along with them. He fervently hoped he and Zylor would not be found out. He nudged his horse forward in order to listen in on the conversation between the procession leader and the guard.

"Have you any news on your journey from the human lands?" asked the guard.

The convoy leader cleared his throat. "We had one encounter on the way here. We happened upon a large contingent of ogres who had been camping near our path. They hadn't expected our group to be coming along, and were unprepared when our scouts had come upon them. Our frontal forces had been able to dispatch a number of them before they could regroup and counterattack. By then all of our forces were engaged as we were trained, and we held steady under the onslaught. An ogre wielding an ice axe appeared, but the gods intervened.

"Oh?" said the guard. "How so?"

"Apparently an axe had appeared out of nowhere," said the dwarf. "I didn't witness it myself but others in my group had seen it. It severed the ogre's head from its shoulders and then an earthquake struck. Right after that, the mysterious axe exploded and vanished."

"Interesting," said the guard. "And what of the ice axe?"

The convoy leader shook his head. "We could not find it. Either the god had claimed it for himself, or an ogre had found it and run off with it."

"That's too bad," said the guard. "Are you sure magic wasn't involved?"

"It's doubtful," said the convoy leader. "If there was magic, it was on our side. Why do you ask?"

The guard scratched his beard. "Well, we just had a patrol come back from the furthest of our return paths from the humans' realm. They had come upon the scene of a convoy that had been attacked. The convoy had been defeated with the aid of magic, and the gold and valuables had been taken."

"The ogres we defeated had gold and valuables in their possession!" exclaimed the convoy leader. "It must have been the same group!" He pointed to the overloaded chariots. "Much of the gold you see is from our encounter!"

The guard looked back. "Well done! Your chance encounter has resulted in saving what was lost. The gods have surely been watching over us."

Olag could contain his curiosity no longer. He took a chance and spoke. "Excuse me, Sir, but you said earlier that magic was involved in the attack on the other convoy. How do you know this? Were there survivors?"

The guard looked at him curiously as he debated whether to answer a civilian.

"I had friends in that convoy," added Olag.

The guard's face softened. "Ah. I'm sorry to hear it. From what I was told, the patrol said they had seen signs of burning consistent with magic and there was one survivor who confirmed the presence of a lizardman. I don't know whether to believe the story or not, but if it's true, I think it may be an isolated incident. I don't think the ogres are smart enough to hire lizardmen. If they were, we would have encountered more magic when our convoys were attacked previously, and I haven't heard of anything like that so far except for this one incident."

Olag was ready to inform him of the lizardmage he had seen, but realized he may have been the only one in his convoy to see him. If he spoke about it, he would surely be questioned, and his background would be put under scrutiny. Instead, he asked, "Do you know who the lone survivor was?"

The guard shook his head. "No. All I know is it was a civilian. I think he claimed to be a mapmaker. He's been sent to relay his story to the king."

Olag's heart was in his throat. A mapmaker! Harran was a mapmaker. Could it have been he? "How long ago did he come through here?"

The guard scratched his beard. "About a half a day ago. Excuse me," he added as they approached the gate leading to the dwarven tunnels, "but I have work to do. The earthquake has done some minor damage to the battlements and I must oversee the repairs." He rode ahead with the convoy leader and they spoke to some tunnel guides. Arrangements were made to move the supplies and gold to wagons drawn by miniature oxen, a favourite breed of the dwarves.

During this time, Olag filled Zylor in on what he had learned from the guard.

Zylor seemed skeptical. "I don't know. What if the survivor was someone else? We would be going into the heart of dwarven territory for nothing. Besides, Harran wouldn't go interfering by talking to the king. That could change history, and he knows better than that."

Olag was surprised at Zylor's lack of faith. "What if he had no choice? The guard said he was 'sent' to the king. That implies he had no choice. If he's the only eyewitness who saw the lizardmage, he's the one who has to tell the king personally."

"If Harran was the sole survivor," argued Zylor, "he wouldn't have said anything about lizardmages in the first place."

"Unless he didn't know that they didn't know about them!" spat Olag. "Did you know the dwarves aren't aware of lizardmen being in these parts? I didn't. I saw one, and maybe you caught a glimpse of him, but no one else saw him."

"I don't know," said Zylor uncertainly.

"Do you have any better ideas?" snapped Olag. "I'm going to wherever the dwarven king is, because that's where Harran went. If you don't want to come along, suit yourself."

Zylor was surprised at Olag's vehemence. It spurred his bloodlust to kick in. "You are right. We haven't got any other leads. Let's do it!"

"Good," said Olag. "And remember, we have Kazin's rings to instantly teleport to his location if something goes wrong."

"Good thinking," said Zylor, "but there's one problem."

"What's that?"

"Do you know the way to the dwarven king's home?"

Olag grinned. "We just go where the gold goes."

Zylor laughed and slapped the skink warrior's back with an invisible hand. "Of course! I should have thought of that!"

There were still a few minutes before the gold was scheduled to depart, so Zylor and Olag came up with a way for Zylor to communicate silently without speaking. This was needed as the next leg of their journey would be cramped and any noise Zylor made was bound to expose his presence. So they worked out a series of taps where the minotaur could tap Olag to let him know certain things.

When that was sorted out, Zylor had Olag obtain some parchment and writing implements so the minotaur could draw maps of their progress through the mountain. That way they could backtrack and leave the mountains should the need arise. They even paused to confirm Zylor could use the writing implements and parchment without those items becoming visible to anyone other than Zylor. The minotaur was glad he had learned the skill from Harran. It was a skill that no other minotaur could boast about having.

Shortly thereafter they were underway. The light of day gave way to the darkness of the tunnels and Zylor inwardly thanked Harran again, this time for having the foresight to purchase sight giving wildhorn leaves before he was captured.

Olag didn't require any, being naturally able to see in low light conditions. The dwarves in the convoy traveled with torches and this was more than enough for them to see where they were going. Side tunnels appeared at intervals and here and there dwarves left the main convoy to go to other destinations. Olag and Zylor stayed with the oxen and carts, because they were destined for the king's treasury.

They stopped to take breaks at convenient intervals, and even encountered underground streams where they and the oxen could obtain fresh water. Zylor was thankful there were no tunnels that were too small for him to travel, although there were a few places where he had to duck his head to avoid hitting his horns on the tunnel roof. He followed the party at a discreet distance so as not to be heard, and the close quarters meant his scent could potentially be picked up if he was too close to another dwarf. Thankfully most dwarves had weak noses - almost as weak as humans - so he wasn't too worried about the latter.

Olag kept to the back of the group as well, providing a buffer between the invisible minotaur and the rest of the convoy. Any minor noises Zylor made were assumed to be coming from Olag.

At one break Zylor discreetly showed Olag his map of their current location. They were much lower in the mountains, and the temperature was considerably warmer as a result of their proximity to a lava flow that meandered along beside their path. The path appeared to have been cut into the rock many years ago, undoubtedly by dwarven craftsmen. The path was solid and smooth, and weathered only in areas where rock slides had made their mark over the centuries. Olag was impressed with Zylor's ability and commented on it more than once.

Zylor insisted it was amateur work compared to the maps he had seen Harran draw.

The rest of the trip was uneventful, and both Olag and Zylor were surprised to learn that they had reached the capital city of the dwarves within twenty-four hours. Zylor was slightly disappointed that there were no foes to fight, but concluded the dwarves had rid the area of monsters years ago. No threat could be expected so close to the dwarven capital. Indeed, there were no guards evident at the entrance to the city.

Once within the city limits, most of the remaining civilians in their party veered off to find their homes or the nearest taverns or inns. Zylor tapped Olag's shoulder and the skink warrior-dwarf turned off into a side street.

"We'd better not stay with the carts of gold," murmured the minotaur when they were out of earshot. "The guards might become suspicious."

"Agreed," said Olag. "But we have to follow them to get to the castle."

"I agree," said Zylor, "but it'll be tricky for me to keep up with mapmaking with so many side streets to mark."

"Maybe you should only mark the major routes," suggested Olag. "You can mark any unusual or memorable landmarks for additional reference."

"Good idea," said Zylor. He looked after the convoy. "We'd better get moving so we don't lose them."

Olag led the way, keeping a safe distance behind the wagons of gold. Zylor frequently signaled Olag with the arm signal when he needed to stop and mark the map. This carried on for about half an hour when they finally spotted the king's palace ahead of them. They stopped in awe of the incredible sight. The entire castle seemed to be made of gold. All of it, from the pointed spires to the walls, buttresses, and even the gate radiated its own golden light. It was as though a thousand torches were lit, reflecting off its surface, yet no torches could be seen.

The procession of carts was ushered through the gates, which closed silently again behind them.

"Well, now we know what they're using all that gold for," said Zylor.

"I'm sure not all of it is in use," said Olag. "I'll wager there is a sizeable stash of gold stored somewhere within those walls."

"But it's not the gold we're after," reminded Zylor.

"True," answered Olag, "but my guess is if Harran is anywhere to be found, it's somewhere within the castle. We have to find a way to get inside."

Zylor shuddered as he thought of the last time he had been in a dwarven castle. That time he had been a prisoner and had to break out. This time he was being asked to do the opposite. "I could take out some of the sentries. They wouldn't see me coming."

"Chances are that would set off an alarm," said Olag, shaking his head. "Then it would be impossible to do anything with all of the guards on alert."

"I'm open to suggestions," said Zylor.

Olag considered. He looked down at his satchel and an idea began to form in his head.

"Go on," urged Zylor intently. "You look like you're onto something."

Olag grinned mischievously. "I see my thoughts are more noticeable in this dwarven body. Yes, I do have an idea. I think a more subtle approach is required for this part. Follow me, Zylor, and on my cue make sure to squeeze past me to get inside past the gate."

Olag walked up to the gate where a sentry resolutely stood on guard. Two more sentries stood behind the gate watching the stranger approach.

"Good day," said Olag cheerfully. "I have a delivery for Hagen Ironfaust. He is one of the king's elite guard."

"I know who he is!" snapped the sentry. "Give it to me and I'll see that he gets it."

Olag shook his head. "He wanted me to deliver it personally. I made some modifications to the item and he needs to inspect it first. If it's not satisfactory, I have to take it back and make any necessary changes. Giving it to you will only delay matters."

"What is it?" snapped the sentry, obviously not pleased at being prevented from taking the item inside himself.

Olag withdrew the chain mail Harran had taken back in time with him.

When the sentry saw the chainmail, his eyes opened wide. He briefly inspected the engravings. "Where did you get this?!"

"I told you, Hagen entrusted it to me," said Olag calmly. "He wanted some alterations made and I made them. Do you want to call him out to explain his wardrobe changes to your satisfaction? I'm sure he'll be overjoyed to explain why he's gained weight and needs alterations made to his chain mail."

The sentry reddened. "No, no. That's not necessary." He turned to the guards behind him who were snickering at his predicament. "Open the gates!" he ordered.

The guards opened the gates and Olag smiled a charming smile at the sentry as he walked past. "Thank you." As he passed the inside gate, his pack got caught on the edge of the left gate.

Olag tugged at the pack. "Oh, my. It's snagged."

One of the inside guards sprang to aid Olag in freeing his pack. As he worked, the other sentries looked on. None of them noticed as Olag made a gesture with his fingers behind his back. A light tap on his arm indicated that Zylor had passed by.

The guard freed the pack and handed it to Olag. "Here you go."

"Thank you," said Olag with a smile. He waved to the outside sentry and then turned to go.

"Do you need any directions?" asked the other guard.

Olag turned back to him. "That's not necessary. I've been here before. Thanks anyway."

The guard nodded and helped his counterpart close the gate.

When they had gone around a corner out of sight of the guards, Zylor spoke. "You're smooth, Olag, very smooth."

Olag hissed at the compliment. "Thanks. But that was the easy part. Now we have to find Harran and get out of here. I don't want to be in this place any longer than I have to."

"Agreed," said Zylor.

Chapter 22

Arch Mage Gresham looked at the assembled mages and their mounts. The dragons varied as much as their masters. Some dragons were metallic in colour, ranging from red to bronze to green. Others were more drab in appearance, being mostly black or brown. Violet's white dragon contrasted with all the others, being the only white one among those assembled. Colour was not the only difference. Size and girth also distinguished them from one another. There were a couple of smaller, younger dragons all the way up to some larger, more intimidating ones. Some dragons were slender and flexible, while Belham's Fillith was rotund and bulky. It was an interesting cross section of the dragon population. There were fifteen dragons in all so far, and the count was growing.

Gresham had imparted information on the failed orb control attempt he had witnessed and all of the riders and dragons had listened intently to the story. It reinforced the importance of keeping both the rider and dragon protected from life threatening situations. It also proved how important it was to have complete mastery of the dragons. Some, like Belham and Fillith, had a strong healthy bond and therefore there was little strain for Belham to maintain control. Others had a more tenuous bond, particularly those with older, more experienced dragons. But even those dragons were heedful of Gresham's story, realizing how fragile their own existence was since it was now reliant upon the survival of their new masters. No one relished the idea of either the dragon or mage losing their life.

"Did you find out who the other dragon rider was who intervened on your behalf?" asked Brendan.

Gresham shook his head. "No. Whoever it was managed to disappear before I could catch up with them."

"Do you think they got hold of one of the orbs without our knowledge?" asked a female master mage. Her name was Sasha and she rode a large black dragon called Hess.

"It's possible," admitted Gresham, "but I can't say for sure."

"We have all orbs accounted for," said Violet. "There are none missing, except the one that was shattered when the master mage lost control of his mount."

"Are you sure?" asked another master mage with a green dragon.

"Definitely," said Violet. She looked at Brendan for support.

"She's right," said Brendan. "Our orbs are all accounted for. Whoever was out there was controlling a dragon using some other means."

Murmurs spread throughout the group and Gresham held up a hand to achieve silence.

"Be that as it may," he said, "we will need to concentrate our efforts on the war. If there's someone else out there, hopefully they see fit to show themselves again. We will need all the help we can get on the battleground."

At that instant, a horse rider came galloping up to the mages and their dragons at full speed. The rider reigned in at the foot of Gresham's dragon. It looked tiny compared to the massive dragon. Waving up to Gresham was Arch Mage Sallow.

"Sallow!" called Gresham in greeting. He quickly got off the dragon to speak with Sallow. "What news have you?" He spoke loudly enough for everyone to hear.

Sallow dismounted and walked up to Gresham. He took his cue from Gresham and spoke loudly as well. "I have received a number of reports from mages who have aerial familiars. Most of the familiars have returned from an extended flight out beyond our front lines and report that the enemy is preparing to move out. It looks like they are getting ready to make an attack on our forces. Their numbers seem to have grown, if many of the accounts are correct."

Gresham swore. "It looks like we won't have time to train for a fight. I was counting on getting some practice in before putting our mounts to the test."

"It will be a few days before the attack happens," said Sallow.

"That will have to suffice," said Gresham. "Have you found out anything else useful?"

Sallow nodded. "Several things. A handful of familiars came back with reports that a small group of the enemy is moving south around the boot plateau."

"That's strange," said Gresham. "We'll have to monitor their movements."

"They could be planning to strike at our base from the south as well as the west," suggested Belham.

"Could be," admitted Gresham, "but we are well fortified on that side, so a small force should pose no problem."

"Could they be planning to cross the Jackal River in order to raid our towns?" asked Brendan.

"I wouldn't put it past them," said Gresham. "We may have to set up ambush parties along the river on our side just in case. Thankfully, we have dragons that can scan the river very swiftly should the need arise. I'm sure they don't know we have dragons on our side yet."

"I have word from the elven territory as well," added Sallow. "Two of the familiars have returned from the south and apparently the fighting between the elves and trolls is intensifying. The elves look like they are being lured out of complacency and are starting to form organized troops."

"That might cause a delay in supplies from the elves," said Violet.

Gresham nodded. "That's more than likely. We've been seeing a drop in elven supplies lately. We'll have to make up the difference with weapons from the dwarves."

"That may change," said Sallow.

"Why?" asked Gresham.

"Three familiars returned from the north - one eagle and two ravens. All three report larger groups of ogres being present along the dwarven travel routes. This may hamper supplies from there as well."

Gresham swore.

"At least we have a fresh supply of magically enhanced weapons ready to transfer to our soldiers," said Belham. "We have our biggest stash of fire swords, lightning spears, and thunder hammers to date, and even have a number of ice axes ready to go. Not to mention another pile of magical and non-magical rings."

"That's good," said Gresham. "But we'll have to use them sparingly if we can't get any more dwarven crafted weapons to replace them. We'll have to increase the number of guards in the northern guard posts to counter this additional threat. We've repelled the ogres easily thus far with the magical support of a handful of mages, but if they come at us in increased numbers, we could be overrun. That means pulling away some of our forces from the front lines." He shook his head. "I really don't like the thought of fighting on two fronts."

"It sounds like the warlock has something up his sleeve," said Belham.

"No doubt," said Gresham. "So far we've been lucky the ogres are not fighting us in conjunction with the warlock, but that may have changed. If they found a way to unify their attacks, we could be in serious trouble."

"We should assume the worst," said Sallow.

"He's right," agreed Brendan. "We may need to spread out our dragon forces to keep each of our fronts balanced. Even one dragon attacking from the air can make a big difference."

"True," said Gresham, "but remember that there are other dragons out there as well. That is the biggest threat to all of us. We'll have to choose our battles carefully. If there's any doubt about a situation, it's best to retreat and protect ourselves and our dragons, because we are inexorably linked. If one of us dies, the other will die also. It would be better to escape and fight another day. Our link to our dragons is both lethal and fragile at the same time. We need to think in terms of both of our safety. Let's preserve this magical bond as best we can, and avoid getting into situations that could destroy us."

Murmurs of agreement rumbled through the assembled mages.

Chapter 23

arran was ushered into the assembly hall and instructed to sit to the side in an alcove overlooking the general assembly. He was told to sit and wait until he was summoned. Then the guards left him in order to tend to other duties. It was the first time he had been left on his own since arriving in the dwarven realm. He had tried to sneak away from the patrol group unnoticed more than once, but was spotted by sentries who had taken their duties seriously. Even the sentries on night duty had been impossible to evade. Harran had also run out of reasons for moving around at odd hours, his favourite being that he was an insomniac. After a time, he had resigned himself to the fact that he was going to see the king whether he liked it or not.

Now he was finally left alone, but there was good reason for the guards not to be concerned. The assembly hall was bursting at the seams with security guards. Even the king's elite personal guards were present in their golden chain mail. The styles were very similar to the chain mail Harran had brought back in time with him. There was no doubt they were the same vintage.

Seeing once again no avenue of escape - all exits were effectively covered - Harran decided to sit back and observe the chaos as dwarves milled about getting to their seats. Torches lined the walls at even intervals and reflected off golden beams, panels, and tapestries, creating a brilliant atmosphere that forced the darkness into the furthest cracks and corners. Bright red rugs were laid on twenty golden steps leading up to a dais that was furnished with a massive golden throne and a slightly smaller one to its left. The arm rests were inlaid with precious gemstones. Small stone tables were situated to either side of the thrones. These were engraved with symbols of various artifacts, interspersed with a variety of gemstones. Flanking these were some potted plants of a variety Harran was not familiar with. The pots were a chestnut brown in colour and engraved with elven symbols of love and fertility.

The seats of the assembled nobility were set up such that the seats in the back were slightly higher than those in front to ensure everyone had the opportunity to see what was going on. Those who sat in the back were obviously of higher rank as indicated by their clothing and the jewelry they wore.

Judging by the number of attendees, today's meeting was an important one. Scarcely a seat was vacant. Anticipation climaxed as a door behind the thrones opened outward. Two golden goblets were brought out and placed on each of the small tables. This was followed by an old, bald dwarf with a long, white beard who was dressed in a white robe lined with golden trim along the edges and the sleeve cuffs. He stood off to one side while two younger dwarves dressed in blue velvet robes and pointed hats with dark blue feathers appeared. They each carried horns fashioned from those of the miniature oxen. They positioned themselves on either side of the thrones just in front of the plants.

The audience quieted as the dwarves raised their horns to their lips. In unison they sounded their horns, playing an announcement melody. The sound was sharp and clear in the assembly hall.

When they were finished, they lowered their horns and the old man stepped forward. "All rise!" he commanded, beckoning with his hands.

The old man introduced King Hammarschist and his queen. Then the door behind the thrones opened again and two doormen entered. They stopped and held the doors for the king and the queen to enter the room. Following them were two of the king's personal guards. The doormen waited for the dwarves with the horns to exit the room and then quietly retreated themselves back into the back room, while the two guards remained in front of the doors.

All was silent as everyone watched the king and queen take their places on their thrones. Once they were seated, the old man gestured and said, "Be seated."

Everyone sat down.

The king was dressed in a handsome blue and yellow robe with golden trim. His crown was golden, with long, pointed spires protruding from the top. The tips of the spires were cupped so that each one could carry a gem of a different colour. The queen was dressed no less elegantly, wearing a lavender robe inlaid with gold and silver lace. She wore more jewelry than anyone else and easily outshone everyone else in the room.

But it was not all of this that grabbed Harran's attention the most. What made the hair on his neck stand on end was the king's physical appearance. If Harran had been twenty years or so younger, he would have been looking at none other than his own reflection! Harran had suspected he was descended from this king, but this only confirmed it. He looked around in a daze and noticed a guard staring at him. With a shock he realized he was still standing, so he hastily sat down.

A wine bearer appeared and poured wine into the king and queen's goblets.

Then the meeting was underway and the old man directed the proceedings by announcing each of the speakers to the king in their turn. The first few speakers brought relatively unimportant news, but subsequent speakers had more interesting things to talk about. Things like new mineral deposits, weapon production, and wealth accumulation through trade dominated these reports.

Things got really interesting when speakers came in to report on affairs external to the dwarven realm. The crowd was hushed when these messengers spoke, intent on learning the latest news from abroad.

One dwarf reported that the recent earthquakes had been more severe in the northeast. As a result, an entire section of the mountains had simply flattened out, opening a path into the minotaur's realm. Guards had been stationed there to watch for the enemy, but more guards were needed with the presence of ogres nearby. The king was understandably shocked at this news, as was everyone else, but was reluctant to commit troops to the area. He was more concerned about the dwarves who lived near the area. He ordered some troops to accompany medical teams to aid the injured and evacuate the communities affected by the disaster. Some miners were also assigned to go along should there be any cave-ins to dig through.

Another dwarf reported seeing a large group of dragons amassing for something, but he didn't know what their intentions were.

Another dwarf reported an increase in ogre attacks on dwarven convoys destined for the human lands.

At this news the king became angered. "I can't keep increasing the security on the convoys! The humans are already grumbling about our prices! If we add more security to our convoys, the price will go up, and the humans will stop doing business with us!"

"Maybe," said the dwarf, "but we are making more than 400 percent profit as it is. A few extra security guards -..."

"Enough!" snapped the king. "We shall hear no more of this." He signaled the old man, who dismissed the dwarven messenger and introduced the next speaker.

This time it was the patrol leader who had brought Harran here to this meeting. The patrol leader removed his plumed hat, revealing his thinning black hair. He stroked his beard nervously, worried the king might not respond well to his news after the last speaker.

With permission to speak granted, he reported his progress on the caravan routes. He got to the part where he had arrived at the location where a caravan had been ambushed by a band of ogres. The king was dismayed by the news but said nothing.

The patrol leader continued, explaining his findings and the potential presence of magic users among the ogres. "The burn marks on the surroundings and particularly the casualties most likely came from magical fireballs."

"How do you know this?" snapped the king. "Maybe a dragon got involved and blasted some fire at the people!"

The patrol leader bowed. "If it please your majesty, I have a witness. He was a lone survivor. He was knocked unconscious and the ogres missed killing him."

"Bring him to me," ordered the king.

Harran was brought to the king and he introduced himself as Harran Mapmaker. He was half expecting the king to recognize him, but the king gave no sign of recognition. The queen, on the other hand, gave Harran a shrewd stare.

"Mapmaker, eh?" said the king. "Do you have any areas of specialty?" He glanced over at his wife and then back to Harran. "My wife is keen to find more gemstones. New deposits are harder and harder to come by. In fact, we haven't found a new gem deposit in nearly two years!"

"That's why trade is so crucial to us these days," added the queen, speaking for the first time. "One of the best ways to increase our wealth is via trade with the elves and humans."

Harran shook his head. "Sorry, your majesty, but I'm just an ordinary mapmaker. I pride myself on the detail of my maps."

"Too bad," said the king. "Most, if not all, of our tunnels are mapped out. There isn't much work for your type these days."

"I've noticed," said Harran.

"So you've survived an ogre attack," stated the king. "Tell me, how did you manage to survive when everyone else was killed?"

"I would have died at their side," said Harran, "but I was knocked unconscious."

"Pity," said the king. "What did you see before you were knocked unconscious?"

"I was with the wagon," said Harran. "Just as the point guards alerted us to danger, the wagon driver and I took the wagon off the trail to try to keep the goods safe and away from the fighting. We heard the commotion around us and I saw flashes of light that was the result of fireballs."

"But you didn't see the fireballs themselves?" asked the king.

"No," said Harran, "but I know it was fireballs. It couldn't have been anything else."

"I'm not convinced," said the king flatly.

"Tell him what you saw when you came to," said the patrol leader.

"Yes," urged the king. "Tell me."

"When I came to," said Harran, "I was in a cage and some ogres were deciding what to do with me when -..."

"You were in a cage?" interrupted the king. "Whatever for? Why didn't they kill you outright? They've never taken prisoners before. Why now?"

The king was sharp, if stubborn, thought Harran. He had to be careful. "Apparently their leader wanted to ask me a few questions. You see, their leader was a lizardmage."

Loud murmurs spread through the assembly hall at this news.

"What?!" exclaimed the king. "Silence!" he roared at the assembly. The room quieted quickly.

"You actually saw the lizardmage?" asked the king.

"Yes, your majesty," said Harran.

"What did you tell him?" asked the king.

"Nothing."

"Nothing?"

"Nothing," said Harran. "He didn't get the chance to ask me anything because the dwarven patrol had just arrived and was engaged in battle with the ogres nearby. Apparently the patrol had caught them unawares and they were quickly driven away."

"Why didn't they kill you before they left?" asked the king.

"I was no threat to them," said Harran. "They had little time to react if they were to flee successfully."

The king sat back and mulled over the story. "Well," he said slowly, "there could have been a lizardmen among the ogres, but the way I see it, it's only an isolated incident. The ogres probably hired the lizardmage to do a job for them and he did it. Unless we see more evidence, I'm inclined to see this as just that - an isolated incident. An alliance between the ogres and lizardmen is a long way off."

"But, your majesty," began the patrol leader, "we've seen evidence of fire magic before! Only this time we have a witness!"

The king waved a hand dismissively. "I have spoken! Bring up the next speaker!"

As Harran and the patrol leader descended the stairs, a somewhat portly dwarf, the chief of the king's personal guard, stepped forward from his position at the bottom of the dais. "Your majesty, if I may speak freely?"

The king sighed. "Go ahead Ironfaust. I know what you're going to say."

The hairs on Harran's neck stood on end when he heard that name. He looked at the face of Ironfaust as he walked past and instantly recognized the chainmail the chief of the personal guard wore. He shuddered at the thought of nearly coming in contact with the man who wore the same chainmail that he would wear centuries later. It was a good thing he no longer had the chainmail in his possession.

The shuddering Harran felt did not stop and Harran was slow to acknowledge the fact that another tremor had occurred. It only lasted a few seconds, but it was enough to get the people in the assembly hall to murmur among themselves.

As Harran and the patrol leader walked to the back of the hall, Ironfaust continued his conversation.

"Your majesty, I think that you are underestimating the significance of lizardmages among the ogres. My spies inform me there are more lizardmages present in ogre territory than we realize. They've been keeping a low profile on purpose because they are preparing for an assault on the humans' northern settlements."

Harran wanted to hear the outcome of the conversation, but he was ushered from the assembly hall to a room down the hallway. The patrol leader told him to stay there until he returned to escort him from the castle. He stationed two of his guards in front of the door before going off on some unknown errand.

Harran sighed and sat down on a bench dejectedly. He fervently hoped he would be released soon so he could go and find Kazin and the rest of the companions. He was sure he had interfered in history, and Kazin and the others would not be impressed, especially since he had lost the ice axe and chainmail. But he knew they would not hold it against him either. It was a difficult quest as best, possibly an impossible one. Maybe they were in above their heads this time. The dwarf held his head in his hands and sighed again.

A thump at the door brought him out of his reverie. He looked up to see the door open and a young, friendly looking dwarf entered. Upon seeing him, the dwarf beamed. "Harran!"

Harran raised an eyebrow. "You know me?"

From out of nowhere a disembodied voice cried, "It is you!" Suddenly invisible hands grabbed Harran and lifted him high into the air.

The invisible guest let out a short laugh. "I knew we'd find you!"

"Zylor?" mumbled Harran in disbelief. "You can let me down."

Zylor laughed. "Sorry. I just had to get a closer look at you to make sure." He lowered the dwarf back to his feet.

"Give me a hand with these guards, Zylor," grunted Olag. He was busy trying to drag the unconscious guards into the room to get them out of the hallway.

Within seconds, the guards seemed to float into the room together, carried by the invisible minotaur.

"Just put them over there," suggested Olag, pointing to one side. He closed the door and faced Harran again.

"Olag?" asked Harran.

Olag grinned. "That's me, in the flesh, not in my scaly hide."

Harran slapped him on the shoulder. "You guys came for me!"

"Of course!" retorted the minotaur.

"Where are the others?" asked Harran.

"They're still pursuing our quarry," said Olag. "According to Amelia's orb, we had to split up. Apparently if we all went after you, our quest would have been unsuccessful. Similarly, if we didn't go after you, we would have failed as well. Our only chance of success was to split up like we did."

"Interesting," said Harran. "Is that why you were changed into a dwarf?"

Olag nodded. "Yes. I'm wearing Zylor's talisman so the magic will keep me looking this way unless I draw my weapon."

"And I am wearing the invisibility ring," added Zylor. "That way I can fight without having to worry about the magic Olag is under right now."

"I thought the ring was too small for you," said Harran.

"So did I," said Zylor, "but it seems the ring can change to fit the wearer magically." Zylor's voice became gruff. "Kazin didn't tell me this before, so I could have used it previously instead of being under a spell making me look like a human."

"Well, it seems to have worked out for the best this time," said Harran. "I'm glad you guys came."

"Here," said Zylor. "Have a sausage."

Harran looked to see a sausage placed into his hand. "Where did you get this?"

"It was in your pack when we found your horse near the herb shop," said Zylor.

Harran laughed. "Thanks. I'm kind of hungry anyway." He bit into it and smiled as the flavour sank in.

"I hate to cut this reunion short," interrupted Olag, "but I think we should get out of here pronto. We can catch up on things later. Zylor, have you got the rings?"

The rings appeared on the bench behind Harran. "Here they are."

"What are we supposed to do with these?" asked Harran.

"We simply put them on, rub them for five seconds, and we'll join Kazin via their magic," instructed Olag.

"OK," said Harran. "Let's do it. The sooner we get out of here, the better."

The trio put on the rings and rubbed them.

"That's funny," commented Olag after rubbing his ring for more than five seconds. "It's not working."

Harran gave up as well. "Zylor? Are you still with us?"

Zylor grunted. "It seems Olag is right. These things do not work."

They tried again without success.

"You know," mused Harran thoughtfully, "sometimes the mountains interfere with magic. This dwarven city is so rich in minerals and gold that it might be preventing these rings from finding where we should be going."

"That could be," said Olag. "According to Kazin, these rings are supposed to bring us to the master ring Kazin is wearing. If the mountain's walls are too thick or the city's minerals are too plentiful, then we may have difficulty getting them to function."

"Maybe Kazin is too far away," suggested Zylor.

"It's possible," said Olag.

"Then what are our options?" asked Zylor.

"We'll have to get clear of the mountains," said Harran. "We'll have to walk out of here."

Zylor groaned. "I was afraid you'd say that. Thankfully I still have the invisibility ring." He was not keen on being in the dwarven castle. "What's the plan to get out of here?"

"I was counting on the rings to do their job," lamented Olag.

"Somehow we'll have to fool the guards at the entrance in allowing us to leave," said Harran. "But they aren't likely to let us go without a plausible explanation, certainly not while the meeting is in session."

"Just create a distraction and I'll take care of them," snarled Zylor.

"That could cause an alarm," objected Harran. "It's bad enough these guards have been attacked," he added, indicating the guards nearby.

"They'll have a tough time explaining what hit them," said Zylor. "One minute they stood there and the next they were unconscious."

"Nevertheless, I will have escaped," said Harran.

"Then we'd better go while we have time on our side," urged Olag.

"Right," said Harran. He went to the door and peeked out. No one was in the hallway. "Let's go," he whispered. He was about to head away from the assembly hall but changed his mind. "Wait. I want to hear what's going on in the assembly hall for a few minutes."

"Harran!" cautioned Olag. But Harran was already on his way.

"He's got a mind of his own," said the minotaur quietly. "You have to get used to it."

Harran pressed his ears to the doors of the hall but couldn't hear clearly. "These dwarven doors are thick," he whispered. Cautiously, he pushed a door open a crack and peeked through the opening. There were two guards in front of the door, but they were watching the proceedings with rapt attention. Ironfaust was standing in front of the throne and the king and queen were not visible. There was a slight commotion as some of the nobles were objecting to the proceedings, but Ironfaust had the attention of most of the dwarves.

"My friends," he said loudly, "I have taken command out of a duty to my people. We are placed in a difficult situation. As you know, the earthquakes are making it harder to stay in the mountains in safety. We may have to consider fleeing to the outside world for a time. If that happens, we will need allies to coexist with. Trade with the ogres, orcs, minotaurs and lizardmen is out of the question. The elves, though allies, are too far away, and if we need help, they will take a long time to come to our aid. The humans are new to these lands, but they would be the only trading partners we will have. If we let them fall at the hands of the warlock and his allies, they will come after us next. I propose we back up the humans in their war so that the evil creatures do not prevail. Our combined forces have a good chance of driving back the hordes that cover the land now. Our forces are well trained, and that training is wasted if we cower in the mountains where our homes are in danger of being destroyed by earthquakes."

Shouts of dismay were drowned out by shouts of approval.

"I know this is extreme," said Ironfaust, "but the truth of the matter is we are not as secure as we used to be. We need to fight for our survival. We will need the humans as much as they need us. We need not abandon our homes entirely. We can take our riches with us, but we will need to establish a place for ourselves in order to safely store that which is ours by right. I do not know where we will wind up, but staying here is not an option."

More shouts and yells echoed through the hall as Harran slowly closed the door. "I've heard enough," he said. He turned to go back down the hallway.

The others followed quietly. They went down several corridors and Harran was about to take a right turn when an invisible hand touched his shoulder.

"We should go left here," whispered Zylor.

Harran blinked. "How do you -?"

A piece of parchment previously invisible was thrust into his hand. "My map shows the exit to be to the left," explained Zylor.

Harran studied it for a moment and then chuckled. "So it is. I taught you well, Zylor."

The companions went left and zigzagged their way back to the castle's entrance using Zylor's map. Miraculously, they never encountered anyone else. Before they rounded the final corner, they paused.

"Now we have to have a plan to get past the guards," whispered Harran.

"You could wear the chainmail of the king's personal guard and they wouldn't question you," suggested Olag.

Harran sighed. "I lost it, Olag."

Olag grinned and opened his pack. He withdrew the chainmail. "You mean this?"

Harran's eyes opened wide in astonishment. "How did you -?"

"You left this behind too," said Zylor. The ice axe appeared before the dwarf.

"I - I don't believe it! How did you guys find this stuff?"

"We'll tell you later," said Olag, "but right now I have an idea. Put on the chainmail."

Harran hesitated. "I don't think I should do that. That's what got me into trouble last time."

"Just trust me," said Olag.

"Listen to him," admonished Zylor.

Harran incredulously looked at the spot where Zylor should be standing. "What? I never thought I'd hear that from you, Zylor."

"Just do as he says," said Zylor.

"Just let me do the talking," said Olag. "If my plan fails, we still have Zylor's method as a back-up."

Harran rolled his eyes. "I can't believe I'm agreeing to this." Nevertheless, he donned the chainmail. Zylor sheathed the axe to keep it hidden from view again.

"Let's go," whispered Olag. When Harran was ready, he led the others around the last corner and confidently strode toward the gate. Thankfully, one of the guards was the same as before. Olag addressed him. "Hello again! It looks like I'll have to make a few more minor adjustments to Ironfaust's chainmail." Olag thumbed over his shoulder. "He sent his servant with me this time, since they are nearly the same girth. It should make my task that much easier."

Harran frowned at Olag's comment. Ironfaust was a fair bit fatter than he. But he nevertheless tried to look the part by pushing out his chest and gut.

The guard suspiciously eyed Harran, but could find no reason to suspect foul play. Begrudgingly, he looked over his shoulder. "Let them out. It's Ironfaust's tailor."

The other guards shrugged and did as they were told. When the companions were clear, the gate doors clanged shut behind them. In silence the companions walked several blocks before they paused to catch their breath.

"You took a big chance back there!" said Harran to Olag. "Do you know how fat Ironfaust actually is?"

Olag shook his head. "No, I've never seen him." He pointed to the chainmail. "But he must have fit into the chainmail at some point."

Harran conceded that it was true. Ironfaust was in fact wearing the chainmail at this moment in the hall. Perhaps he wasn't as fat as he thought - or Harran was fatter than he thought. The dwarf looked down at himself in shock. Then he shook his head. No. It occurred to him that the chain mail could be magically enhanced to fit the wearer like Zylor's invisibility ring. That must be it. If so, it would never need to be altered to fit someone else. He shook his head again.

Just then footsteps could be heard. Someone was running in the direction of the castle. The companions didn't have time to step into the shadows as a dwarf came running by. He saw them as he ran past and staggered to a halt when he saw Harran's chainmail. Turning back, he jogged up to them all out of breath and saluted Harran with the traditional dwarven salute - slapping his left shoulder with his right hand.

"Sir!"

Harran returned the salute.

The dwarf caught his breath before speaking. "News from the eastern front, Sir."

"Continue," said Harran.

"Scouts have returned from the east with the news. A portion of the mountains has been leveled, and the minotaurs are gathering to encroach on our territory as expected," said the dwarf. "If they attack, we will need our full forces to withstand their assault."

Harran and Olag exchanged glances.

"When do you expect them to attack?" asked Harran.

The dwarf shook his head. "I don't know. They are still gathering. But there are already enough of them presently to pose a threat to everyone on this side of the mountains."

Harran and Olag exchanged glances again.

"Do the ogres know they are coming?" asked Harran.

The messenger shook his head. "Doubtful. The scouts reported no sign of ogres in the area. They seem to be occupied south and east of our location. I suspect they are planning a major attack on the human communities. If the ogres knew of the minotaurs preparing an invasion of their lands, they would abandon their conquest of human settlements in order to defend their home regions."

"Thank you," said Harran. He had heard enough. "Repeat your message to the king at once!"

The dwarf saluted again. "Yes, Sir!" Then he ran off for the castle.

"The king is -," began Olag.

"I know," said Harran. "But he'll have to find that out on his own."

Moments later another earthquake struck. This time dust and small debris fell from the ceiling in a fine cloud.

Harran looked up. "I suspect the dwarves will be vacating this region of the mountains sometime soon, for one reason or another, whether it is war or geographical change."

"And the orcs and lizardmen, among others, will take over what's left of these mountains in the future," said Olag ominously.

Harran nodded. "It's sad but true." He looked back toward the castle in the distance. "It must have been a huge undertaking to disassemble the castle and take the gold with them."

A hand rested on his shoulder. "But they succeeded," said Zylor calmly. "They did what they had to do."

Chapter 24

The chanting by the throng of lizardmages was an ominous sound. The combined magic being called upon made the air crackle with static. The warlock and his selected group of lizardmages stood to one side of the throng, waiting patiently for the first one to appear.

"There!" hissed on of the lizardmages.

"Good!" said the warlock. He waited until the dragon was within range. Then he held up his hand and the chanting ceased. At this point the chanting began among the warlock's group. The rhythm of the chant grew in intensity while the curious dragon came closer. Then the warlock added his own voice to the chant. His powerful magic was noticed by all as he brought his spell to bear on the dragon. Too late, the dragon became aware of a spell being used against it. Too late, it shrieked and tried to veer away. The warlock completed his spell and paused. The dragon swooned and its head drooped. Lizardmages ducked and scrambled to make way for the dragon as it came down with a thunderous crash.

While lizardmages fled from the cloud of dust, the warlock ran toward it. He needed to reach it quickly to apply his next spell.

When he reached the site, the warlock was amazed - and pleased - to see the dragon disoriented but unharmed. The mind clearing spell had worked! Now the creature was open to mind control. He eagerly began chanting his next spell and enforced his will upon the great behemoth. When he finished his spell, he waited expectantly for a reaction. By now, some of the braver lizardmages had appeared and were ready to use defensive magic as per the warlock's previous orders to protect him should the spell fail.

The dragon turned its head slowly to the warlock and blinked. It did nothing, so the warlock commanded it to rise to its feet. The dragon obeyed. Then he commanded it to lie back down. It complied. He ordered it to raise its front right claw into the air. It complied without question. The warlock laughed gleefully. It had worked! His plan to control a dragon had worked just as he had hoped!

Then he stopped laughing and approached the dragon amid hisses of fear from the lizardmages. He went up to the dragon's head and stroked its neck. "You are a fine beast," he murmured. "I will now ride you." At this, the lizardmages hissed again. The warlock carefully climbed up the dragon's wing to situate himself on the giant creature's neck. "You will now take me on a short flight," he commanded, "and you will ensure that I do not get thrown off."

The dragon got to its feet and stretched out its wings. With a few graceful flaps, it launched itself into the air.

The warlock hung on tightly at first, but soon realized he could loosen his grip as the dragon rode very smoothly through the air. He decided he reveled in this kind of experience. This was how he wanted to get around.

Below he could see the tents and fires of his army. It was much larger than he had imagined, and he took delight in the vast army he controlled. Victory would now surely be his.

The warlock commanded the dragon to shoot out a flaming fireball and the dragon complied. The sky lit up and the warlock ducked as he and the dragon flew through the scorching flames. He would have to remember to tell the dragon to direct his flame to the side next time so they didn't get hurt in the process. With a shout of triumph, the warlock turned his dragon back to the field where the lizardmages waited. It was time to repeat the process so that each of his spell casting commanders could obtain their own mounts. He would ensure the dragons would obey him first and guarantee they would not harm him before handing control over to the commanders. He didn't trust lizardmages, but he needed them in this war.

The dragon landed easily in the desired area and the warlock dismounted.

"Prepare to draw in another dragon!" he ordered.

The lizardmages hurried to get in position for another attempt. The warlock wrung his hands in anticipation. This was too good to be true.

x   x   x   x   x

Galado surveyed his crew and their latest bodies. They looked much healthier than their previous bodies, which were well into the decomposition phase. But he had ordered them to make their previous bodies last as long as possible to avoid killing people and drawing attention to themselves. Thus they had gone west rapidly, and booked passage across Claw Lake to arrive south of the army garrison just west of the Jackal River. It was nighttime when they had encountered a patrol. The patrol consisted of eight people, two women and six men, who had stopped them to inquire as to their presence there. Galado had told them they were there to enlist, so the patrols had ordered them to follow them back to the base to sign up. As soon as their backs were turned, Galado's men and women had sprung into action. Within minutes they had new bodies to use. That left two of Galado's crew still in their old bodies.

After hiding the dead bodies and chasing off the extra horses, the entire group went back to the base, and were ushered in without question, since they were recognized as members of the patrol. From there they went straight for a short distance until they were out of sight of the guards at the gate. Then they curved off the main path to skirt the outside edges of the encampment.

By sheer luck, they heard noise off in some nearby bushes and stealthily investigated to find a couple having sex. Reacting quickly, they soon had the remaining bodies they needed to manage for a few more days.

"I've always wanted to have red hair," commented the woman who took over the body of one of the lovers.

The old bodies were quickly buried in that same location so they wouldn't be discovered. Two of Galado's men always made sure to bring shovels for this purpose.

"Now we have to blend in with the army for a while," said Galado. "We should try to find out battle plans, and work toward finding a way to get out of here and go further west. I will find my living self in that direction."

"We could volunteer to go on patrol to the west," suggested One. "By the uniforms of our patrol guard bodies, our arm bands have the same markings. We're probably assigned to go together whenever our patrol is ordered to go out."

"Good point," said Galado. "It looks like you're the leader of that group, judging by the star on your vest. You'll have to inquire as to your duty roster."

"Yes, Sir," said One.

"What about us?" asked the one who had the red hair.

"You two will have to stay with me for now," said Galado. "When the patrol gets permission to head out, we'll try to volunteer to go along and hope there will be no issues."

"You could pretend to sneak out to make love," smirked one of the others. The rest of the group laughed.

"That's not such a far-fetched idea," said Galado seriously. He turned to One. "You'd better check in with your commander. Let them know everything is fine and then look into the duty roster. Find out when and if you'll be assigned to patrol to the west. You may have to trade shifts with someone so we can get out of here sooner. I'll take our loving couple here and see if we can find one of their tents. I need to get some sleep. We've been traveling nonstop for three days."

"Right, Boss," said One. "Let's go," he said to the others. They rode off to the main path and disappeared from sight.

Galado and the two lovers rode for a while in the hopes of finding one of their tents, but to no avail.

At one point, a commotion in one part of the camp sent a number of people running to see what the commotion was all about. Curious, Galado and the others, who he found out were Six and Ten, hurried to see for themselves.

A crowd was gathered in an area near several campfires. Even before pushing their way through the throng, Galado and his team spotted what the commotion was all about. Towering above them was the fearsome visage of a dragon. Roughly shoving people aside, Galado accessed a better vantage point in front of the crowd. Standing before the dragon was a human mage. He had a pointed hat and a serious expression. He was talking to the crowd.

"With the help of a number of these dragons, we hope to improve our odds of success. Now we will be able to direct the dragon's wrath at our enemies!"

A number of those gathered cheered at this, obviously excited about having aerial support in their favour.

"There are not many of us yet," continued the mage, "but more dragons are being brought under our control as we speak. We hope to have close to fifty by the time we are once again engaged with the enemy."

Once again cheers were heard.

Galado was shocked. Fifty dragons? He had no idea the humans had managed to control one dragon, let alone fifty. This was something he did not know when he was preparing for battle against these forces. He had been killed before discovering this. With a shudder, he realized he was approaching the day of his untimely demise. He had to continue moving to find his original body quickly. Sleep would have to wait. He pushed his way back through the crowd with Six and Ten close behind.

He wandered aimlessly for a while and swore he could hear the laugh of the previous host of his body within his head. When he was tired was when that voice bothered him. He was not surprised. He needed to rest. Before long, One and the others came up to him.

"Well?" asked Galado.

One smiled. "Sure enough, our roster had us going out in patrol to the west. We are due to go out there the day after tomorrow."

"No good," said Galado. "We need to move sooner."

One frowned. "How soon?"

"Tonight," said Galado.

"Don't you want to sleep?" asked Six.

Galado shook his head. "There's no time. I have to reach my original body within a few more days. If I don't, I will fail to save myself."

"Understood," said One. "The next patrol to the west is due to leave in two hours. I will try to find their leader and see if they will trade shifts with us."

"Do it," commanded Galado. "Take your group with you. Maybe you can shorten your search with more of you looking."

One nodded. "Right, Boss." He was about to leave, but turned back. "Do you want us to take over the bodies of the next patrol if they don't want to trade?"

Galado shook his head. "It's too risky. Just try to be very persuasive."

"Right, Boss," said One. He turned and left with the others of the patrol.

Galado turned to the lovers. "See if you can convince the guards to let you find a secluded area outside of the compound. If they refuse, try sneaking out. Don't forget to obtain some weapons before you leave. It shouldn't look unusual if you leave with weapons, since there is no security beyond the gate. Once you're out, find a place where you can see the patrols coming and going and signal us when you see us leaving the compound. If you fail to see us, you will know we have failed to switch shifts. Then come back to the compound - and be sure to thank the guards so they are more likely to let you go out again another time should we have to do this again."

"Yes, Boss," said Six and Ten in unison. Holding hands, they left for the west gate.

Satisfied, Galado waited for One to return.

A half hour later, One came up to Galado and reported success. The patrol leader due to go out was not keen on the west run, especially while it was dark, and gladly switched with One, whose shift was in the daytime.

"Good," said Galado. "Only one thing remains. I will need an outfit similar to yours in order to blend in with your patrol. Hopefully one extra person will not stand out in a patrol of eight."

"I think we can manage both of those things," said One. "I know where our patrol is camped. There are sure to be additional uniforms available. As for our number, we can keep the guards busy with small talk. No one will take the time to count our number. If they do, we will be milling about out of formation to confuse them. Horses tend to be skittish when dragons are present."

Galado smiled. "Very good, One! It appears you've gotten yourself a body with a brain this time."

One smiled. "We're getting the hang of these bodies. It's not so bad, actually."

✗　　✗　　✗　　✗　　✗

Elsewhere in the compound, a young man named Paul was making a sketch of yet another dragon.

Chapter 25

azin circled the small clearing slowly as he prepared to make his landing. There wasn't a great deal of room to land, especially in the twilight of early dawn, but he managed it with a great deal of alacrity. Once he came to a stop, he lowered his wing to the ground to allow Amelia and Sherman to disembark. Once they were safely on the ground, he transformed himself back into his human form. He still wore the ring of youth as per Amelia's wishes and looked like a youthful mage freshly graduated from the Tower of Sorcery.

"This place will do for the night," said Sherman, looking around the clearing.

"There's a small stream just south of here," said Kazin, "not that there are any horses to water."

The companions had been nearly as far as the city of Arral when Amelia informed them they were losing ground on their quarry. It was evident from her orb that those they pursued were making time by not sleeping for the night, and in the process they were avoiding making any changes to the flow of history. In order to gain time, the companions came to the conclusion that they needed to risk flying instead of riding. With rumours rapidly spreading about dragons being ridden by mages, it was now less of a concern for Kazin to fly. If he were spotted from below, it would only add fuel to the rumours that they already knew to be truths. One of the only dangers would be if the mages below them considered them to be a threat and decided to do something about it. The other danger was if mages, who were trying to capture a dragon with an orb, unleashed a spell to capture Kazin without realizing he was already a dragon mage.

This concern was put to the test when that very situation had occurred as Kazin flew south around Arral to avoid detection by its inhabitants. Some mages far south of the city had been concealed in the woods and had brought their magic to bear on the companions as they had flown overhead. Kazin had lost his concentration and almost fainted, while his altitude suddenly dropped. Sherman and Amelia had been warned something like this could happen, and Amelia had reacted by raising a shield to protect Kazin from the magic below. Kazin had immediately recovered mentally, but had continued to lose altitude. Sherman hung on while Amelia had switched her spell from a shield to a haste spell. Kazin had been alert enough by then to mentally resist the spell from the mages, and he rapidly shot out of range of the spell casters below, much to their astonishment. Once clear, Kazin had turned back to Amelia and thanked her for her quick actions. From there, they had made wise use of the haste spell to cover ground more rapidly than before. After that, Kazin had found a place to land and he apologized for the rough ride. He had forgotten the mages of old had more powerful magic than in his time. From then on, the companions had unanimously agreed to travel only at night when humans would not be able to see well enough to cast such spells.

Now they prepared to make camp for the day in an area that was well away from any human habitation. Several tree branches were gathered to make a shady area where they could sleep.

Sherman took the first watch, knowing Kazin was exhausted from his flight, and Amelia had expended some energy with her spell casting. Shortly before his watch ended, he made breakfast and gave some to Amelia when he woke her for her shift.

Kazin was woken up later to relieve Amelia and he looked around their campsite curiously. Something was different. "That's odd," he said. "I don't remember the trees as being so dense this morning. The clearing was bigger. I'm sure of it."

Amelia smiled at him. "You're right. It was getting a bit too bright for you to sleep properly, so I called the trees in closer to provide additional shade. It also helped to cut out the wind that had picked up."

Kazin could hear the tree branches as the wind whistled through them, yet not a single gust could be felt in their sleeping area.

"Where did you learn to do that?" asked Kazin.

"Some of it was in the old spell book we found," said Amelia. "Unfortunately, much of that page was missing, so I had to improvise.

Your lessons in improvisation came in handy. Without your training, I wouldn't have been able to make it work."

"You are a very capable student," said Kazin, beaming. He rose, gave Amelia a kiss on the cheek, and then walked past the protective trees to find the stream and wash up before taking his turn with watch duty.

Amelia blushed as she prepared to get a few hours' sleep before dusk. Her dreams were romantic in nature, prevailed by a young, blond haired, blue eyed mage.

Kazin's watch was initially uneventful, but near dusk he heard a shriek that he instantly recognized as that of a dragon. Fully alert, he waited and, sure enough, he heard it again. Ordinarily it shouldn't have bothered him, but for some unknown reason it caused the hairs on the back of his neck to stand on end. Looking at his companions, he saw that they still slept soundly, so he put up some magical warding to protect them and prepared himself to investigate the sounds he had heard.

He transformed into a dragon and leapt quietly into the air. As he flew low over the trees to avoid being spotted in the day's dying light, he didn't notice the pulsing, red light of Amelia's orb as it peeked out of her cloak beside her blanket.

Kazin reveled in the wind as it rushed past him, cooling his reptilian body. It would be too easy to become a dragon full time. Only his mental discipline kept him from succumbing to that temptation. Many mages did not have that discipline, especially in this time in history, and they wound up controlled by the dragons they were supposed to be controlling. Those mages and dragons were extremely dangerous, and were ultimately chased down and destroyed by other dragons and their mounts, or other mercenaries hired strictly for this purpose. How Kazin had managed to control the dragon within his orb for so many years was beyond him.

Now he flew toward where he thought the dragon cries had come from. Peering intently through the long shadows cast by the trees below, he caught a glimpse of what could have been a dragon below. He also sensed a magic similar to the one he had experienced earlier when he had almost fainted. Choosing a suitable spot not too far away, he made his landing stealthy and silent. Then he became his human self again.

Quickly and carefully, he made his way to where the dragon was. As he got closer, he could hear voices. It was the voice of a dragon conversing with a mage.

Kazin cast a silence spell on himself and crept as quietly as he dared through the forest to get close enough to not only hear, but see the speakers as well. Once he got close enough, Kazin was surprised by what he saw. Not by the mage, who was an ordinary, middle aged man with dark hair and a traditional black cloak worn by black mages, but by the dragon. It was the tiniest dragon he had ever seen. It must have been a very young one.

"I didn't want one so young," grumbled the mage. "Go away!"

The dragon eyed the mage's orb warily. "I cannot! Please don't make me do that!" it pleaded. "I cannot abandon the orb!"

The mage swore. "I don't know how to reverse the spell," he muttered. "Remove your essence from the orb so I can draw in another dragon!"

"I can't!" cried the dragon. "I don't know how! It's your magic!"

The mage swore again. "Great. If I show up with you, I'll be the laughingstock of the entire conclave of mages!"

The dragon drew back in surprise. "What? Why? What's wrong with me?"

"You're a puny runt!" retorted the mage. "What use would you be to us?"

"I'm not a puny runt!" snapped the dragon. "I just haven't grown up yet!"

"Exactly," said the mage with a wave of his hand. "Now go away!"

"Not without the orb," said the dragon coldly.

"I can't do that," said the mage flatly. "If I do that, the arch mages would have my hide. Orbs are not easy to manufacture. The orb stays with me."

"And I stay with the orb," said the dragon firmly. "If you want to get rid of me, you'll have to part with the orb."

"I will not," said the mage. "Now be gone, or I'll have to use magic on you."

"I'll fry you on the spot if you so much as open your mouth to cast a spell," said the dragon.

"You can't hurt me!" said the mage scornfully. He held up the orb. "If you do, you'll destroy the orb and you will die!"

The dragon recoiled somewhat. "Maybe. But I'll die if I'm away from the orb anyway. Either way, it makes no difference to me. You, on the other hand - ..."

The mage shook his head. "You can't have the orb, so you might as well go away and die in dignity. Maybe then your essence will leave the orb and I can use it to find a real dragon to control."

The dragon straightened its neck. "I am a real dragon!"

"You give me no choice," said the mage. He did a quick chant and shot an ice bolt at the dragon's chest.

The ice bolt struck true and the dragon shrieked in pain. At the same moment, Kazin felt a stinging sensation in his chest. He doubled over in pain and fell down, revealing his presence.

The dragon glanced at Kazin and then back at the mage. "So!" he cried. "You are trying to trick me! Well, I'm not as useless as you think, mage!" With a great blast of flame, he spewed a sizeable fireball at the mage. Without time to react, the mage screamed and held his hands over his face instinctively, throwing the orb aside in the process. His hands were a useless means of protection as the fireball struck him. He was thrown to the ground and his body was consumed so quickly that he could not utter another sound.

The mage's body was still engulfed in flames as the dragon lunged beyond him to pounce on the orb. The orb was intact, pulsing with the dragon's life force. Gingerly, the dragon held it up to admire it. In so doing, it noticed Kazin, who had recovered from his mysterious pain.

"So," said the dragon slowly, "now that I have the orb, you cannot control me. You shall die the same way as your friend!" With that, he blasted another fireball in Kazin's direction.

Kazin casually deflected the fireball, his spell not even audible to the dragon. When the flames subsided, Kazin stood unharmed.

The dragon was taken aback. "What? How did you do that?"

"I used magic," said Kazin quietly.

"Well, you can't have my orb!" said the dragon, turning its claw to hide it from view.

"I don't want it," said Kazin. He held up his staff. "I already have one of my own."

The dragon eyed the orb on Kazin's staff and then looked at its own. "It's the same!"

At those words, the ground shook vehemently as another earthquake struck. The quake lasted for a good half minute and both Kazin and the dragon waited for it to subside.

"I want that orb too," said the dragon finally.

"You already have one," said Kazin. "You don't need another one."

"I don't care," said the dragon. "Give me yours and you won't get hurt."

"I can't do that," said Kazin.

"You saw what I did to your friend!" said the dragon, pointing to the smoking remains of the mage.

"He wasn't my friend," said Kazin. "I didn't even know him."

"I don't believe you," said the dragon.

Kazin shrugged. "Suit yourself."

The mage and dragon stared at one another for a few moments in silence.

"Well?" said the dragon.

"Well, what?"

"Give me the orb!"

"No."

Without warning, the dragon pounced on Kazin, but the mage vanished from sight at the last second. Scrambling to its feet, the dragon looked around.

"Looking for me?" asked a voice behind him.

The dragon spun to the sound and faced a grinning, young mage.

"I've been practicing that spell for a few dozen years," said Kazin, "but this is the first time I've ever needed it."

"A few dozen years?" said the dragon, perplexed. "But you're not that old."

"You shouldn't believe everything you see," said Kazin. "That last spell should have taught you that. I'm actually much older than I look."

Without warning, the dragon let loose with another blast of fire. Again Kazin batted it aside like a harmless fly.

Enraged, the dragon lunged again but stopped short, expecting Kazin to teleport himself away like last time. But this time Kazin didn't move. He didn't even flinch.

"You can't defeat me," said Kazin. "It's time to put your greed aside and go away. I don't want to hurt you."

Again the dragon lunged in Kazin's direction, but this time Kazin cast another spell as he teleported a short distance away. At the same time he fired a lightning bolt at the dragon's left side.

The dragon cried out as the projectile struck it and Kazin simultaneously felt a burst of pain in his own side. At the same moment, another earthquake struck just as fiercely as before.

Kazin stumbled around to observe the dragon, who was already in motion. This time the mage could only put up a shield as the dragon pounced on him. The impact of the dragon landing on the shield caused a great thunderclap and the ground heaved worse than it had ever done thus far. The heaving did not stop as both the dragon and Kazin fell to the ground in agony, both suffering from the pain of the lightning generated at their contact.

Kazin got to his feet slowly, as did the dragon. Neither could hold their balance very well. Fear was in the dragon's eyes as it regarded Kazin intently.

Then something dawned on Kazin and his eyes widened. "Is - is your name Filbar, by any chance?"

The dragon's eyes widened and it nearly fell down again, but instinctively opened its wings to maintain balance. Then it launched itself into the air with a shriek. "No!" it wailed. "You cannot know that my name is Filbar! It's impossible! Leave me alone!" The dragon then flew out of sight as fast as it could fly.

Kazin shuddered in the dying light of the dragon's flames around him. The quaking had finally stopped. It was impossible, but he had encountered the dragon he would become in the future - or his own past. That was why he had felt everything the young dragon had felt. When Filbar was in pain, so was he. Whatever happened to Filbar, happened to him. But that was not the worst of it. His

contact with himself - at least his dragon half - was not something that was supposed to happen. This encounter was what he had dreaded above all else. Contact with himself at the same moment in time could very well be the catalyst that caused his history in the future to fall apart!

Kazin looked at the charred remains of the other mage nearby. Was he supposed to be here to see Filbar? Or was it a mistake on his part? Kazin grit his teeth. He should have consulted Amelia's orb first.

The young mage shook his head sadly. What had he done? With foreboding thoughts, he transformed back into his dragon form and flew back to camp.

His companions were wide awake by now, having been roughly awoken by the earthquakes. They were anxiously awaiting his return. Amelia marched up to him once he had changed back into his human form, and was starting to demand an explanation from him about his whereabouts, but his serious, dark expression caused her tirade to fizzle out quickly. Even Sherman knew it was unwise to talk to him right then. Questions could wait.

Without a word, Kazin picked up his things and transformed back into his dragon form. He lowered his wing to the ground and the others climbed onto his back. Kazin launched himself into the air effortlessly and the trio flew off in silence.

Kazin didn't respond to the others' occasional query, so they left him to his thoughts and talked quietly among themselves. They wondered whether Zylor and Olag were having any luck in finding Harran. Sherman pointed out that if they had found him, they would have rejoined the rest of them by now using Kazin's rings. In his opinion, the search was continuing on.

Amelia conceded his point and fervently hoped they would succeed soon. The longer it took them to find Harran, the less likely they were to find him. Sherman hoped so too, but knew as long as Zylor and Olag hadn't come back yet, they hadn't given up either.

Amelia consulted her orb on their progress, but couldn't fathom whether they were succeeding or not. The only thing she knew for certain was that future history had not been rewritten - yet. Kazin flinched upon hearing this statement but said nothing. Amelia chose that moment to give a course correction to Kazin and the dragon complied.

"Something has been slightly altered west of here," said Amelia, hoping Kazin was paying attention.

"We're over a lake right now," remarked Sherman, looking down. He hated heights and held on tighter after his downward glance.

Amelia confirmed his statement as the moon momentarily poked out between some clouds to reflect off a shiny surface below.

About ten minutes later, the air became noticeably more humid and the moon slid out of sight for the last time.

"I do believe it's going to rain," commented Sherman.

Amelia pulled a water resistant cloak from her pack and wrapped herself in it. "I guess we couldn't have expected perfect weather all the time."

"We have had good weather up until now," agreed Sherman. He withdrew a proper cloak from his own pack. He had scarcely donned the cloak when the first raindrops could be felt stinging against his face.

"We're almost clear of the lake," rumbled Kazin at last.

"We're also getting close to where the orb is drawing us," said Amelia. "Just go north a bit. I'll let you know when we're at the spot."

Kazin flew for another twenty minutes before Amelia informed him they were almost on the spot. The dragon circled around to scout out a suitable landing place and glided toward a small field. The ground was wet but not enough to be muddy. Though it was still dark, Kazin's keen dragon eyesight ensured a safe landing.

Once on the ground, Sherman stretched while Kazin transformed into his human form and lit his staff. The bright white light was reassuring and warm in the damp rain, and Amelia was impressed by Kazin's ability to heat the area as well as light it up. Not only that, but he had erected a shield above them to prevent them from getting any wetter than they already were.

Kazin nodded at Amelia. "Lead the way."

Amelia consulted her orb and discovered it was a dark pink. It seemed to become darker when she pointed just south of their current location. She started in that direction and the others joined her.

Not more than fifty yards away, Sherman called a halt and pointed to a mound beside a small grove of trees. He led the way to it and kicked at the soil. "This has been fairly recently dug up. I'd say no more than a day or two ago."

Amelia's orb was darker now. In the darkness it was unnecessary to tell the others. The red glow was eerie to behold. "Something bad happened here," she said.

"It's a burial mound," said Sherman, poking at a section of the soil. "Whoever did this didn't care to do a neat job. It was done in a hurry."

"I'll wager it is the final resting place of some unfortunate people," said Kazin. "Our quarry has killed again."

"Yes," said Amelia slowly. She studied her orb. "I - I see eight bodies here. They look like they were in combat with a patrol unit for the army." She looked up at Kazin with a fearful expression. "They were all strangled!"

Kazin nodded grimly.

"Why would a patrol strangle people?" asked Sherman. "They would have been armed."

"Not only that," added Amelia, scratching her head, "but if these people died, our quarry would have been slain. Yet my orb says they're still out there. I don't get it."

"Maybe some of them were captured," suggested Sherman.

"Amelia," said Kazin, "can you make out the images of the people we're chasing?"

Amelia consulted the orb. After several minutes she shook her head. "It's no use. The faces keep changing. In fact, I see so many faces we must be after dozens of people."

"That's impossible," said Sherman. "If there were that many of them, someone would have been bound to notice and we would have little difficulty tracking them. There can't be more than a dozen."

"Sherman's right," said Kazin. "Maybe the faces you're seeing are the ones our quarry has killed."

"That's possible," admitted Amelia. "For some reason the orb can't distinguish between them."

"Well, keep trying," said Kazin gently. "You're doing much better at tracking our quarry, not to mention seeing what they've done. You couldn't do that with your orb a few days ago."

Amelia smiled wanly. "I guess you're right. The orb can tell me a lot more if I learn to master it properly."

"So what now?" asked Sherman.

"I think I'll fly for another hour or two," said Kazin. He turned to Amelia. "Where to?"

Amelia consulted her orb. Then she pointed north. "That way. There's a sizeable army in that direction. Our quarry went in that direction."

Kazin nodded. "Good. Once we're close, I'll set down and we'll proceed on foot. There should be some fresh supplies there, and I'm getting hungry."

"Me too," said Sherman. "Our stash is getting rather lean anyway."

It was nearly dawn when they were almost at the army garrison's south entrance. The rain continued as a light drizzle and the sky was still dark. At this point Kazin cast a spell on them so they all looked like ordinary civilians. Sherman's weapon and Kazin's staff were magically concealed.

At the gate they were asked a few questions, but since they didn't appear to be a threat, were let inside without a hassle. It took a while for them to find their way to the patrol master's tent, but the timing was good. The patrol master had just finished assigning duties to the patrols and was just sitting down to have breakfast.

Kazin inquired as to which patrols had gone to the south the past couple of days and nights. At first the patrol master was suspicious and evasive, but Amelia worked her charms on him and won him over with her story of wanting to find her brother, who was said to be on one of the patrols under an assumed name to avoid being found by his family. Finally the patrol master gave them the designations of the patrols who were on duty at the requested times. He then directed them to the area where the various patrols were housed. The companions left the patrol master's tent with six patrol designations and made their way to the appropriate area of the camp.

As they walked, they went past a hand-to-hand training area, a hospital where white robed clerics worked to heal injured soldiers, a stable containing horses as far as the eye could see, and a forge where weapons were being crafted or repaired. Beyond that they could see a cordoned off area where a number of dragons waited. They were no doubt dragons who were ridden by mages.

"That's an impressive sight," said Sherman. "I've never seen so many dragons in one place before. In fact, I've never seen so many dragons, period."

"That was normal in this time period," said Kazin.

"There's even a white one," said Amelia.

"An ice dragon," said Kazin. "Those were more rare, but just as dangerous."

Above them in the predawn light, a handful of dragons could also be seen, circling the camp slowly. Astride the dragons were mages who wore black cloaks and staves in their hands. Kazin shuddered, realizing that they could have been spotted landing near the south gate, but then realized the darkness that hid them from view worked both ways.

A few battalions of soldiers marched in unison as they were urged on by their commanders. The camp was so huge that Kazin couldn't even hazard a guess as to how many soldiers and mages there were.

They took a small detour to a spot where cooks were preparing breakfast for the troops. On the way they stopped by a young man who sat at a table with a stack of parchment piled on one side. On the free portion of the table was a partial sketch of a dragon. Amelia paused to look at the completed sketch on the top of the pile.

"Wow!" she exclaimed. "That's very realistic!"

The young man looked up from his work. "Thank you. I've been doing many sketches of dragons. They're my favourite. Would you like to buy one?"

"No, thank you," said Kazin. "But my companion is right. It is a very good sketch. You are very talented."

"Thanks," said the artist. He let Amelia browse through the stack for a few moments. Then the companions thanked the artist and continued toward the cooking area.

As they departed, the artist looked after them curiously. He sensed there was something unusual about these individuals, but couldn't place a finger on it. Then he shrugged and returned his attention back to his sketch.

No one asked any questions when the companions lined up with a number of early risers to get a decent helping of gruel. Famished, they ate everything on their plates before going back to the tent area where the patrols were housed.

When they got there, they spotted a large board with wooden slabs indicating patrol designations loosely swinging from various parts of it. The board was marked with columns designating north, west and south. Three rows of hooks hung below these marks. The top row was marked with the early shift, the next row with the late shift, and the last row with the night shift.

There were twelve patrol designations, each represented by some sort of symbol.

"Great," muttered Sherman. "We have to check half of the patrols to find out what happened a couple of nights ago. Why didn't we just ask the patrol master and be done with it?"

Kazin shook his head. "We don't want to raise suspicion by asking that directly. If the patrol master suspected we had something to do with it, we might have been questioned. By asking the patrols themselves, they'll assume we were told by the patrol master."

"I don't like all this subterfuge," grumbled the big warrior.

Kazin put his hand on Sherman's shoulder. "Patience, my friend."

"Well, we might as well get started," said Amelia. She pointed to some tents nearby. "Those tents have the same designation as one of the ones the patrol master has marked on his list."

"They appear to be off today," commented Kazin, looking at the board. "Perhaps we can find some of them already awake."

"Good," said Sherman. "Then they can answer some questions."

A few soldiers were milling about with plates of breakfast as the trio came up to them. Sherman took the lead asking them questions to see if they had heard of or been in a fight or skirmish south of the encampment within the last two days. No one knew of any such encounter.

"That's one down," said Sherman as they left those tents. "Five to go."

"They were telling the truth," said Amelia. "My orb didn't show anything out of the ordinary."

"Let's keep trying," said Kazin.

Three more patrols were questioned but nothing was turned up.

"Two left," muttered Sherman.

"And one of them is out on patrol," said Kazin. They had returned to the giant board and he looked it over. "That patrol is out in the west right now. They won't be back until the early shift relieves them from duty."

"That's still about an hour from now," said Sherman, looking at the dull sky. The rain showed no signs of letting up.

"We might as well see if we can find the fifth group," said Amelia.

They soon found the tents belonging to the fifth patrol on their list. The patrol leader himself sat outside his tent in a folding chair having a hot drink. The rain didn't seem to bother him.

"Hi," said Sherman politely. "Can we ask you a few questions?"

The patrol leader looked up at him and appraised Sherman's muscular figure. "Sure."

"We were just wondering if you might have encountered anything unusual in the last couple of days on your southern patrols," said Sherman.

The patrol leader took a sip of his drink and shook his head. "No. Why?"

"Just curious," said Sherman. "We just came from that direction and saw signs of some sort of skirmish. It's not important."

"Oh, really?" said the patrol leader. "A skirmish, you say?"

"The ground in one spot was torn up by many hooves and there were some pieces of torn clothing in the area," said Sherman. "We thought it might have been one of the patrols, that's all."

"Were there any bodies?" asked the patrol leader.

Sherman shrugged. "I didn't see any."

The patrol leader shrugged and took another sip of his drink. "Maybe you were mistaken. It could have been a group of horses disturbed by the earthquakes we've been having."

"Maybe," said Sherman. He turned to go but the patrol leader called to him. "Are you in the army?"

Sherman turned back to him. "No, but I'll be signing up."

The patrol leader smiled. "Good. When you do, ask to join the patrols. Then come and see me."

"I'll consider it," said Sherman.

The patrol leader nodded.

"That leaves one left to check," said Amelia, checking off her list.

"What do you mean?" asked the patrol leader, standing. He had overheard her and strode forward to look at her list.

"The patrol master gave us a list of the patrols on duty in the south in the last two days," explained Amelia. "We've spoken to all but one."

"This group here?" asked the patrol leader, pointing to her list.

"Yes."

"They're not here right now," he said.

"We know," said Kazin. "They're patrolling in the west right now."

"That's right," said the patrol leader. "My group would have been out there, but they wanted to trade shifts with us." He scratched his head. "Why they did that I don't know. That's the most dangerous area to patrol." He looked at Kazin. "I was glad to make the trade. My group needed the break. We'll be well rested when we get our next shift."

A group of horsemen suddenly rounded the bend and rode past. A patrol led by a heavy set woman rumbled by.

The patrol leader waved as she rode past and she nodded in response. "Helen's group will be relieving the one that's out in the west. If you follow them, you'll find the west gate. If you're lucky, you can catch the other patrol as they return from their shift."

The companions thanked him and followed the patrol led by the big woman, Helen.

Along the way, Sherman stopped to smuggle supplies from one of the food tents. A fat lady working there caught him in the act but fancied the big warrior, so she wound up helping him to pack a few extra bread rolls. Before leaving, he gave her a quick kiss on the cheek and ran off. She stood watching him, blushing shyly in the light of a nearby lantern.

"You're smooth," said Amelia, laughing.

"What?" protested Sherman. "At least some people know how important food is. Besides, she could be my great, great, great something grandmother." He turned and waved to the young lady, who waved back. Kazin and Amelia chuckled.

Amelia looked at Kazin and saw that he was in better spirits than before and was glad of the change.

As the companions reached the west gate, they discovered a small commotion in progress. The relief patrol was ready to go out, but the guards at the gate were holding them back.

"We can't let you go out until the previous patrol is accounted for," said the guard at the gate. He was a burly man with dark hair.

"But if something has happened to them we need to go and find them!" objected Helen, the patrol leader of the relief group. Her eyes were angry and unyielding.

"The procedure is to alert the standby patrol," said the guard at the gate. "I cannot let you pass until they are ready to accompany you."

"Then alert them!" snapped Helen. "Time is being wasted!"

"They've been summoned," said the guard. "You'll have to wait until they get here."

Helen swore and her horse whinnied impatiently.

By now a small group of soldiers had appeared and milled about nervously, chattering about the cause of the delay of the returning patrol.

"Move aside!" called a voice. "Move aside, please!" The mage Kazin recognized as the one with the pointed hat pushed his way to the front with a few other arch mages behind him. "What seems to be the problem?"

He was informed by the guard about the patrol that had not returned on time.

The mage nodded. "Has the standby patrol been notified?"

"Yes," said the guard.

As he spoke, a group of riders appeared and threaded their way through the crowd.

"It's about time," snapped Helen.

"Group seven reporting for duty," called the reserve patrol leader.

"Good!" said the gate guard, relieved. He gave Helen a nod. "Now you can go." He turned and gave the guards in his command a signal and the gates were opened. The two patrols turned and charged out of the compound, the muddy ground splashing the guards at the gate, much to their dismay.

Kazin noticed that the reserve patrol was additionally comprised of a few mages and clerics should their services be required on this mission.

The mage with the pointed hat turned to the arch mages with him. "Have any of your familiars spotted anything amiss out there?"

One of the mages shook her head. "Nothing has been reported to me. Even my own familiar came back around midnight and never saw anything of importance."

"Strange," said the mage with the pointed hat. He turned to the crowd and began shooing them away. "Nothing to see here, folks. Back to whatever you were doing. Be alert!" To the arch mages he said, "I think we'll run a patrol of our own."

Kazin and the others turned back with the crowd so as not to stand out. He didn't want to be recognized by the mage with the pointed hat.

"What now?" asked Sherman.

Kazin didn't have a chance to respond. A hand tugged at his sleeve.

"Kazin," said Amelia quietly. He turned to her to look into her big blue eyes. He would have been entranced had it not been for the concern those eyes held. She lifted her cloak to show Kazin the red, pulsing orb. "Something is happening out there," she said, pointing over her shoulder. "Our quarry is out there. I can feel it."

Kazin nodded. "I figured as much. We'll leave shortly, but first we should find a secluded spot. I'm going to have to try to make us invisible. Then, when we're clear of the compound, we'll make a break for it by air."

"Can't you make yourself invisible as a dragon?" asked Sherman quietly.

"No," said Kazin. "You know how when someone who is invisible draws their weapon and the weapon becomes visible? Well, the same thing holds true for a dragon mage. If an invisible mage becomes a dragon, that dragon is the weapon. Once I turn into a dragon, my whole body becomes visible since I am the weapon.

"How do you know that's what will happen?" asked Amelia.

"I tried it before," said Kazin.

"That's too bad," said Sherman.

"A little walk will do us good," said Kazin. "It won't take long to get out of sight of the gate."

"And how do you propose to get past the locked gate?" asked Sherman. "You said we're not flying out."

"We're going to levitate out of here," said Kazin.

"Levitate?" asked Amelia. "You can do that?"

Kazin nodded. "It's another spell I've been practicing. Ordinarily, it is a simple spell for druids, but not black mages. The spell I've discovered on one of my quests is meant for black mages, and differs significantly from the magic that druids use. It is much more complex, but it effectively does the same thing. I've never used it on multiple people before, but I'm fairly certain I can make it work."

"Fairly certain?" asked Sherman.

"If it doesn't work, I have other tricks up my sleeve," said Kazin.

"You never stop learning, do you?" asked Amelia.

Kazin turned to her and smiled. "That's one thing you'll learn about magic, Amelia."

"We'd better go quickly," said Sherman suddenly. "Daylight is not far off." He pointed to the brightening sky in the east. The others needed no further urging, quickening their pace accordingly.

Sherman noticed Kazin's limp again and hoped their quest was successful so that Kazin would walk normally again. He was more determined than ever to see this quest through.

Chapter 26

he patrol consisted of approximately three dozen orcs. To them, this puny contingent of humans was no match for them. What they didn't count on was the fact that these humans would not die. Numerous stabs and blows with their weapons did not prevent them from rising back to their feet to continue to attack. Instead of going on the defensive as any normal force would do when outnumbered, these humans came on with a reckless vengeance. Before long, orcs began to fall. These, too, rose back to their feet, only to attack the orcs nearest them. The confusion had the desired effect. The orcs were unprepared as orcs they had fought alongside moments ago were now attacking them instead.

Galado pressed his opponent back and his quick reflexes easily cut down the orcs, who were bigger but much slower than the agile human. He paused to look around as his team took over one orc body after the next. Their human bodies had long since been hacked beyond usefulness, and now it was all orcs against orcs. Galado wondered how his team could identify one another amid all the chaos, but they managed it somehow. They were also cognizant of Galado's whereabouts and went out of their way to ensure he did not have more orcs to face than he could handle. Indeed, Galado hardly broke a sweat with the handful of orcs he had dispatched. Now, as the last of the orc patrol battled for their lives, Galado's crew was more careful not to damage these last survivors as these would be the ones whose bodies they used henceforth. When the last orc was slain by strangulation, Galado's crew reported to him. They were a disgusting conglomeration of drooling, shambling orcs.

"This body is awkward," drooled one orc, moving about clumsily.

"So is this one," said another.

"But the arms are much stronger," said another, flexing its arm.

"You'll have to get used to them," said Galado. "When we get to the main army, there will be plenty of other bodies to try out."

"Good," said an orc beside Galado. "What are your next orders, Boss?"

"You're One?" asked Galado.

The orc nodded and grinned stupidly.

Galado nodded. "We continue west. We have to reach the main army."

"What about the bodies?" asked another orc.

"Leave them," said Galado. "Anyone coming upon this scene will assume the orcs won this battle, since they don't bury their dead. Any human patrols coming upon this scene will be leery about going further, once they see what happened to their patrol." He looked around at his crew. "It makes sense, since everyone still standing except myself is an orc. Besides, you'll have to act like orcs now anyway."

"Good," said a different orc. "Hiding the bodies was always extra work."

"What about the horses?" asked another orc.

Galado surveyed the carnage around him. Two horses were killed in the exchange, a third one lay on the ground injured, and the rest had run off. Galado's horse was only one of two unharmed horses still in the area. "We'll have to leave them," said Galado. "Orcs don't use horses." He went to his horse and swung himself into his saddle.

"How come you get to have a horse?" asked an orc.

Galado smiled at the creature who spoke. "I'm not an orc." His smile left his face. "I want all of you to head west. I'll take this horse north for a bit and then rejoin you a bit later."

"Why?" asked One. "Where are you going?"

"If I walked out of here with you," said Galado, "an alert patrol might spot my footprints among yours and wonder why a human is traveling with orcs. Orcs aren't known to take prisoners without some ulterior motive, so it would look very suspicious. By riding out in another direction, my tracks will simply appear as though a horse was fleeing the scene much like the others have already done. When I rejoin you later, we should be well beyond the safe zone as far as the humans are concerned." Galado waved his hand around him. "Once they count the number of dead humans in this area, it will be obvious the entire patrol has been slain. They won't be looking for any human survivors by then."

"Good point," said One. He looked at the others. "You heard the Boss. We head west on foot. Our bodies are much more powerful than the human bodies we had, so it won't be as bad as any of you think." He turned and trudged off in a westerly direction. The others followed, some of them grumbling quietly about having to walk.

Galado smiled. They were already acting like orcs without realizing it. He paused to kill the injured horse, not because he felt sorry for it, but because orcs never left anyone or anything alive. Then he led the other remaining horse from the scene in a northerly direction at a run. A short time later, he released the horse and continued riding his own horse in a northwesterly direction. This would continue for a while before he headed southwest to rejoin his group. As he rode, plans were formed in his mind as to how to get close to his real body in order to prevent his early demise. He yawned, but pushed thoughts of sleep from his mind. There was simply no time to rest.

✗　　✗　　✗　　✗　　✗

The warlock clenched his fists in anger. Why had Harse acted so soon? He should have waited for word from him first! The ogres were supposed to attack on his orders! Now he had to put his own plans into action sooner than expected. He turned to Gorc. "Tell the commanders we have to move out within the next few hours. We will move the entire army one day closer to the humans and break camp again. Hopefully this will keep the humans off balance while they try to figure out why we did that, and at the same time it will give our forces something to do so they will stop grumbling. The expectation of imminent war will make them happy. I expect word very soon from Saliss. As soon as his forces are in place with the trolls, we will sound the horn for the attack. It's time we got ready for the inevitable."

"Yes, Sir!" said Gorc nervously. He fled from the room to carry out his orders.

Chapter 27

arran wasn't happy about the delays, but there was nothing he could do about it. Several detours had to be made since the recent earthquakes had collapsed some of the tunnels. Fortunately, they had managed to get back onto their chosen route each time, but the last time was unnerving. It had taken nearly a day to catch up to where they had last left off. Furthermore, teams of mini oxen were traveling down the same tunnel as they were. They moved at their own speed. The oxen couldn't be rushed, but they had such stamina that they rarely needed to stop.

The convoy threaded their way along, destined for the heavily guarded mountain entrance that lay at the end of their journey. Harran was beginning to doubt whether Zylor's maps were correct, yet major intersecting passageways were marked amazingly accurately. The minotaur did an incredibly amazing job on his maps and Harran was determined to congratulate him on his work when he had a moment to speak to the invisible companion alone. The fresh air coming in from outside was the first indication they were nearing their destination.

"I smell rain," said Olag.

Harran nodded. "So do I. I can also feel the humidity. It must be raining outside."

About twenty minutes later, they finally reached the entrance. Then it took a good half hour for the oxen drawn carts to be redirected to where they could be unloaded. The companions were surprised when the carts were uncovered for unloading. The carts were laden with weapons, bows and arrows. There were even magical weapons among the loads, including ice axes similar to Harran's own weapon. It was during the commotion of the unloading and distribution of weapons that Zylor returned Harran's ice axe to him, while obtaining one from the carts for himself. No one noticed as the weapon disappeared from sight as soon as he sheathed it.

When the carts were out of the way, Harran, Olag, and the invisible minotaur moved past them to step outside. What they saw then made their jaws drop in astonishment. Beyond the fortifications on the mountainside was a vast army of dwarves. Harran had never seen so many dwarves assembled in one place. Even his army in the future paled in comparison to this.

Torches flickered in the drizzling rain, but did not go out as battalions grouped together in formation, waiting for something. A couple of high-ranking battalion leaders and lieutenants were conversing in hushed tones nearby when one glanced in the companions' direction. Upon seeing Harran, she nudged the dwarves closest to her and said, "At last!" She straightened up and gave the customary salute, right hand on the left shoulder. "All hail King Ironfaust!"

Her companions repeated, "All hail King Ironfaust!"

Harran looked behind him for a moment but saw no one. He looked at Olag, who returned the gaze with wide eyes.

"I think they're hailing you," said Olag quietly.

Harran looked down at himself as he realized too late his mistake. He had not removed Ironfaust's chain mail and now the soldiers in front of him thought he was Ironfaust! "Oh, no!" he groaned.

As word trickled down to the forces below a chant could be heard from the assembled dwarves. "Ironfaust! Ironfaust! Ironfaust!"

"Ah - I'm not -," began Harran too feebly to be heard.

"We could use the rings and get out of here," suggested Olag, close to Harran's ear.

"And how would the dwarves react when their king disappears right in front of their eyes," said Zylor. "I'm sure history would record that event."

Harran clenched his jaw as he spoke. "Zylor's right. I can't just vanish right now. If the real Ironfaust shows up, I can find an opening and try the ring, but not right now."

"What are we going to do?" asked Olag.

As if in response, the female lieutenant approached. She had to yell to be heard above the chanting, which continued to cascade down the mountainside. "What are your orders, your majesty?"

Harran looked into the lieutenant's eyes and had to admire her beauty, which was highlighted in her sharp looking uniform. "What is the scouting report?"

The lieutenant nodded and beckoned a young scout forward. "Report what you told me, master scout."

The scout saluted nervously. "Your- your majesty! The northern human guard posts have been overrun and the Velden Mine is under attack. By now it may already have fallen. The ogres have amassed into one large fighting group and are in league with a number of lizardmages. They are moving south next in order to attack the human settlements. The humans have most of their forces to the west to deal with the warlock. There is no way they can hold off the ogres for long, even if they have more mages to aid them."

"We must move at once," urged the lieutenant. "If we wait too long, we may be too late. Right now our forces have speed on our side. If we send the cavalry in first, they might slow the advance until the bulk of our forces arrive. This will put a significant strain on our cavalry, but it is the only way to slow the ogres down."

"Don't forget the minotaurs," whispered Olag to Harran.

Harran looked to the east where the sky was beginning to lighten. The mountains he was used to calling home did not exist yet, but even the low-level range he had seen the last time he was here had changed. Some parts of it had risen substantially, while others had fallen. The valleys were sure to contain large forces of minotaurs who were itching to get involved in the battle. If they got involved, even the legions of dwarves below were no match for the combined forces of ogres and minotaurs. If Harran led the charge to aid the humans, he would be leading thousands of dwarves to their doom.

This thought was not lost on Zylor. He placed a hand on Harran's shoulder. "I have an idea."

"Sir?" said the lieutenant. She had heard and assumed it was Harran who spoke.

"I have an idea," said Harran, "but let me converse with my advisor first." He pulled Olag aside where they wouldn't be overheard.

"What's your idea, Zylor?" asked Harran as he looked at Olag.

"I can't stop the minotaurs from getting involved," said Zylor, "but I can redirect their attention. I'll have to go and have a chat with the minotaur advance guard to do that. You'll have to go on without me. I can meet up with you later. If not, use the ring to get back to Kazin. We're clear of the mountains now so the magic ought to work. You just do what you have to do. The minotaurs will not be attacking the dwarves here."

Harran sighed. "Very well. Good luck, Zylor."

A hand momentarily touched the dwarf's shoulder and then the minotaur was gone.

Harran grasped Olag by the shoulders. "Well said." He turned to the lieutenant and spoke loudly. "We ride at once!"

The lieutenant nodded and proceeded to give orders to get the army underway. Before she left, she pulled an object out of her pouch and handed it to Harran.

He looked down at it as it was placed into his hands. It was a dragon conch. Harran's eyes widened at the sight of the object. A dragon conch was a seashell that had magical properties that benefitted the dwarves in a myriad of ways. When used in battle, it had the power to increase the courage of the dwarves on the battlefield and rally them to the one who blew on it. It also had the added effect of increasing the dwarves' immunity to magical attack. It was a revered artifact and was one of their most precious relics. "How - where did you get this?" asked Harran.

The lieutenant smiled. "It has been in the army's possession for many years. Didn't you know about it?"

Harran nodded. "Of course," he lied. "I just forgot. Excellent. We will make use of it soon."

The lieutenant left to get the troops moving.

Harran looked at the forces gathered below. "How could so many dwarves have been prepared for this so soon? We only just left the castle where Ironfaust was starting his revolt. Did these dwarves know what was going to happen?"

Olag looked at Harran. "You forget, Harran, that we were delayed several times by cave-ins. We spent almost two days just trying to get back to our route. There were undoubtedly many other routes to this location that were not as affected by the earthquakes. Another thing you forget is that news travels fast. Most of the dwarves you see here were probably closer to the mountain entrance than we were. There were many tunnels branching off to different communities well before the city with the castle. I suspect there will be many dwarves coming here after we are gone, including King Ironfaust himself."

Harran nodded. "You're right, Olag. My sense of timing is off." He shook his head and looked down at himself again. "I told you this chainmail was going to get me into trouble. If only I had removed it, I wouldn't be in this mess right now."

"I'm thinking it's fortuitous," argued Olag. "If Ironfaust is delayed too long, the humans will be overrun and history will be changed. Your error seems to be very timely indeed."

Harran turned to the pleasant looking dwarf beside him. "Are you saying that we are supposed to be doing this?"

Olag smiled a wicked grin. "It feels right, doesn't it?"

An earthquake brought them back to the matter at hand. The lieutenant came running up to them. "Your horses are ready!"

Harran checked to see that his ice axe was secure in its sheath and nodded. "Lead the way!"

✗   ✗   ✗   ✗   ✗

Scaling the wall and sprinting past security was easy for the invisible minotaur. He was delayed more by the navigation down the steep mountain face. His hand and footholds were not the greatest, being wet from the rain. An earthquake made his task more difficult. It caused him to lose his grip and slide down the mountainside in a shower of pebbles and rocks. Fortunately, the recent earthquakes made this a common sight along the mountainside and no one paid any heed to it.

The tumble to the bottom was rough but quick, and Zylor immediately got to his feet and dusted himself off. Then he got his bearings and turned to go east. Being cramped and plodding along in the tunnels was not his thing. Instead he yearned to run and stretch his muscles. So, after navigating around some dwarven barricades, he broke into a run. The rain splashed against his face and the wind blew against his body and it felt good. Suppressing a howl of glee, Zylor picked up speed and ran as fast as he could. He knew he could keep this pace for a few hours. His body was well toned and a good workout was long overdue. If only he could use his fighting skills.

✗　　✗　　✗　　✗　　✗

General Hyrock stood and stretched his aching limbs as he sent off the last detail of guards to their assigned areas of the fortifications. He was a burly dwarf with dark, curly hair and a well-trimmed mustache that was the envy of those who served under him. He had come back on duty as part of his rotation just as the new king led the bulk of the army south to the aid of the humans. His lieutenant was in charge prior to that and, as expected, things had gotten out of hand with the arrival of thousands of dwarven troops. It took a full hour and a half to reorganize his guards so they would be ready should the minotaurs or ogres take it upon themselves to attack. It wouldn't do to have disorganized dwarves defending their homes while the bulk of the army was out on a mission. His fortifications could potentially be the last stand for the entire dwarven realm. If his fortifications were breached, there was no one left to defend their realm from attack, or worse, looting.

Hyrock's lieutenant came up to him to inform him of new arrivals at the tunnel entrance. The lieutenant was a fairly young dwarf, as dwarves go, but his wrinkled face belied his age. The stress of having a command at such a young age had taken its toll.

Hyrock looked at his lieutenant as he spoke and noticed a look of uncertainty in his eyes. "You know what to do," said Hyrock. "Send the new arrivals south to join the army."

"But - I think you had better come and see these dwarves for yourself," said the lieutenant timidly. "There's - a problem. A big problem."

Hyrock sighed. "Alright. Lead the way, Sid."

The lieutenant led his superior officer to the cave entrance where a number of dwarves milled about in agitation. Right away Hyrock recognized the attire of the dwarves who stood there. It was a number of the king's personal guards.

Hyrock strode up to them and saluted. "Ah, gentlemen! I see you have found a route to the entrance! If you seek your new king, he has already left with the entire army. You will have to make haste to catch up with him."

A fairly large dwarf spun on him. He had fire in his eyes and his visage was one of wrath. "What?! What king?! I am the new king!" he hollered, pointing to himself. "I am King Ironfaust! Don't tell me Hammarschist was behind this!"

The hairs on the back of Hyrock's neck stood on end. He turned to his lieutenant. "Sid! What is he talking about?!"

Sid gulped. "Um, Sir, it wasn't Hammarschist - I've seen him before. It was another dwarf. He wore - he wore the same chainmail that he is wearing!" He pointed to Ironfaust.

Hyrock looked at Ironfaust, then back at Sid. "Are you sure?"

Sid nodded. "I'm sure of it. The chainmail was identical."

"How can that be?!" demanded Ironfaust. "My chainmail was specially crafted for me and me alone!"

Hyrock scratched his head. "Are you saying that an imposter is in charge of the army?"

"It must be!" shrieked Ironfaust. "No sooner have I become king when my authority has already been usurped! How could you allow this to happen?!"

Hyrock straightened. "Neither I nor my lieutenant can be blamed for this error! Neither one of us has ever seen you before."

"When the new king - I mean imposter - showed up," stammered Sid, "the army's lieutenants made the assumption that he was the new king, so I had no reason to question whether he was the one. He spoke to his advisor for a moment and then proceeded to give orders just like a king would. He had the whole army organized so efficiently that none of us questioned it."

"He had an advisor?" asked Ironfaust. He shook his head. "No matter. We'll get to the bottom of it. Give me your fastest horses. I will go after them."

"Unfortunately that won't be possible," said Hyrock.

Ironfaust turned on him. "What do you mean?"

Hyrock pointed to the stables at the base of the mountain. "All of the horses we had have been taken for the war. Any late soldiers have been sent to help the army on foot."

Ironfaust turned and cursed for a good thirty seconds. "I just don't believe this!" he wailed. He held his hands up to the sky. "Why me?"

"No point complaining," grumbled one of Ironfaust's entourage. He was also dressed in personal guard attire. "You wanted to attack the ogres right away anyway. We'd better get going if we want to make sure the army is doing what they should be."

Ironfaust finally calmed down. He stomped his foot in frustration. "You're right. Standing here accomplishes nothing." He turned to Hyrock. "We'll talk about this later. There are going to be some changes to the way we do things around here. Hold firm until we return."

Hyrock nodded and saluted. "That is my intention, Sir!"

Ironfaust and his group hoisted their flag and headed for the exit, joined by a small group of soldiers who had just appeared at the cave entrance.

As he left the fortified area, Hyrock spoke to his lieutenant without looking at him. "If that's the real Ironfaust, I'm glad he has to walk. It'll be good for him to get some exercise."

Sid chuckled.

✗　　✗　　✗　　✗　　✗

The commander lowered his looking glass. It was a similar unit to the ones the minotaur fleet used aboard their ships. "Yes," he said slowly. "The dwarves haven't got a very substantial force protecting their entrance."

Another minotaur, a lieutenant, grinned. "They underestimate us. Pity. I was looking for more of a fight."

"I'd say there's something more to this picture," said another lieutenant. He was the shortest of the three. He lowered his own looking glass and pointed to the southwest. "Something is happening over there."

The commander examined the area with his looking glass. "Yes," he said at last. "There is black smoke on the horizon. Something is afoot."

Minotaurs milled about as they prepared to move out. One of them stepped closer to the commander and looked across the way to view the valley below. His horns were much larger than any of theirs and the commander wondered why he had never seen this particular minotaur before. He himself was a few inches shorter than the newcomer. To see someone taller than he was rare.

"I wonder what's causing the smoke," said the first lieutenant.

"It's probably the ogres fighting with the humans again," said Zylor. "They're always fighting from what I've heard, lucky bastards."

The commander and lieutenants turned to the newcomer. He was not asked the question and it wasn't his place to answer, but his sheer size and his large horns were intimidating enough to prevent a rebuke by any of them.

"The ogres are at war with the humans," said the commander at last. "It is their territory we will be invading in order to reach the dwarves."

"So what?" retorted the first lieutenant. "If they object, I welcome their wrath!"

"Yes," agreed the short lieutenant. "If the dwarven mountains are so poorly guarded, it will be a bonus to wipe out the ogres in the process. The land will be ours for the taking!"

"There is a small group leaving the dwarven mountain," said the commander, peering intently through his looking glass again. "It appears to be a royal party, judging by the flag."

"Strange," said the first lieutenant. "Do they not see us? We could go down there right now and finish them off with little difficulty."

"I don't think they're worried about us," said Zylor. The others looked at him like he was crazy.

"How do you figure that?" asked the first lieutenant.

Zylor shrugged. "With all the earthquakes we've been experiencing, the dwarves are probably packing up and getting ready to leave their mountain. Attacking there will gain us very little. All we would succeed in doing would be to wander collapsing tunnels in search of left over treasure and gold."

"And what do you suggest?" asked the short lieutenant.

Zylor didn't flinch as he looked him in the eye. "There is no honour in killing dwarves who are fleeing their homes." He pointed to the billowing smoke in the distance. The rain had stopped and the smoke was becoming blacker and larger. "That smoke tells me a battle is raging over there. It's much more honourable to sink my axe into the thick skull of an ogre who is armed for battle. If a few puny humans get in my way, they'll die too. And unless I miss my guess, there will also be plenty of dwarves present to go around for all of us!" With that, he stalked off to join the other minotaurs who were getting ready to move out.

The lieutenants looked at their commander with astonished expressions. The commander laughed at them. "If only you could see yourselves! I only wish you could both display that kind of courage and ambition more often. It would make my job that much easier." His smile vanished. "Prepare to set out for the smoke. Where there's smoke, there's fire, but it's nothing compared to the fire in my veins once we go into battle!"

While the lieutenants scrambled to get things underway, the commander tried to seek out the mysterious minotaur in the crowd, but he was nowhere to be seen. He sighed. "Oh, well," he thought, "I'll no doubt see him in battle leading the charge."

Chapter 28

"This looks like a suitable area to change our mode of travel," said Kazin. They had successfully levitated over the west fence of the encampment and no one could have seen them leave since Kazin had made them invisible. He had used four spells simultaneously again - three to make each of them invisible, and one to levitate them over the fence. The fourth spell worked on all of them at once as long as they held onto Kazin. Amelia had expressed concern about being detected since there were so many mages in the encampment, but he assured her he had that possibility covered with a spell designed to prevent them from being detected. If that were true, then Kazin was casting and holding five spells at once, which was impossible. She just shook her head at this incomprehensible feat and resigned herself to holding on and enjoying the ride.

Levitating was an unusual experience. It felt like they were simply standing on air as they went, yet somehow Kazin moved them along at a smooth pace. They simply floated across to the expanse beyond the encampment and then lowered to the ground as gently as a leaf.

When they were on solid ground, Kazin let go of the levitation spell and breathed a sigh of relief. "Whew! That spell takes a lot out of me!"

Amelia looked at him in concern. She had enjoyed the experience so much she hadn't noticed the strain Kazin had been experiencing.

Kazin looked down at his feet. Even though he was invisible, he could feel his feet pressed into the mud up to his ankles. His sandals made sucking noises as he tried to lift his feet out of the mud. "I should have found a better spot to land."

"That's why I wear boots," said Sherman, chuckling.

"Mages need to travel light," said Kazin. "It's part of being a spell caster. Most shoes and boots contain some metal parts, such as buckles and shoelace eyelets. That metal can reduce the potency of spells, and ultimately be costly if the spell isn't powerful enough to work properly. That's why we prefer to wear sandals with leather straps, and robes with cloth waist straps. That's also why we don't use metallic weapons. It interferes with our magic. Even magic cast on metallic objects won't adhere for long unless it's refined properly. Besides, I don't get blisters like you do."

"That's true," admitted Sherman. "It could mean the difference between life and death if you're in battle and your footwear is causing pain. The distraction only has to make you take your mind off what you're doing for an instant. You could let your guard down and then it's too late."

Kazin looked around and sighed. "It's going to be a muddy walk for a little while. But once we get far enough away, I'll be able to get us off the ground and into the air."

"There's a grove of trees over there with a valley behind it," said Amelia. "If we can get over there, we can fly along the valley at a low altitude and avoid detection by the guards in the encampment."

"I'm more concerned about the dragons," said Kazin. He looked up at the lightening sky. "At least the dark rain clouds are keeping the daylight to a minimum."

"We'd better move," said Sherman. He started for the grove of trees Amelia had mentioned.

They reached the grove quickly and without incident, and Kazin transformed himself into a dragon. As he did, the magic that made them invisible disappeared. The others climbed onto his back and then Kazin took off. With a few strokes of his wings he was off, circling to the west. Amelia cast a haste spell on him and the trio shot off so quickly anyone potentially catching sight of them merely had to blink to miss seeing them vanish into the distance. Such a momentary glimpse would make any man question what he had seen.

The takeoff had the effect of disturbing a pair of ravens sitting in a nearby tree. They squawked into the sky and one of them turned to fly in the direction of the encampment. It had to report what it had seen, however improbable, to its magical master. The presence of its new mate, however, would be kept to itself.

Kazin streaked across the sky. He soon spotted the human patrol to the north and stayed clear of their visual range. Only when he was well away from the human encampment did he increase his elevation. This allowed them to better view the terrain below. The trees gave way to sparse vegetation and a rolling terrain that dipped and rose like huge waves in the sea. Boot Plateau rose before them and its sides looked dry and barren, while the top sported vegetation and an abundance of flowers and herbs.

"I don't recognize that plateau," said Sherman.

"It doesn't exist in your time," said Kazin. "It was probably destroyed during the dragon wars."

"It's incredible how much everything has changed since then," remarked Sherman. "It must have been quite the war."

"It won't be long before it happens," continued Kazin. "We need to catch our quarry before it's too late."

"Speaking of which," interrupted Amelia, "the orb is vibrating. It wants us to go northwest."

Kazin changed his course and Amelia gave directions. In about ten minutes Amelia pointed to a narrow gully below. "There's the spot! We have to land there."

Kazin dove downward and soon spotted the carnage below. Bodies were strewn about the area and some ravens were disturbed from their feast.

While Sherman and Amelia disembarked and ran to examine the corpses, Kazin transformed himself back into a human mage. Then he hurried to join them. "Well? What have you discovered?"

Sherman rose from the body of the human soldier he had been checking out. "They're all dead. By the looks of it, the entire human patrol was wiped out. The orcs must have won this battle. That's why the bodies weren't buried." He turned to Kazin. "I guess that's it for our quarry."

Kazin looked around at the bodies. "It doesn't look like anyone was strangled this time. I wonder why."

"These humans did not die by the orcs' weapons," said Amelia slowly. She prodded one of the human corpses with revulsion. She appeared like she was going to be sick.

"What do you mean?" asked Sherman. He looked at the body she was investigating. "The torso is torn open and one arm was hacked off."

Amelia shook her head. "This person was dead before he was stabbed and mutilated. See the area of the wound? There is no sign of significant blood loss or blood-letting. This body was dead before it was hacked up."

A careful examination of the other human bodies turned up the same evidence.

"Amelia's right," said Kazin.

"Damned orcs!" growled Sherman. "I can understand them eating their enemies, but this?"

"The bodies are also in a state of decomposition that would indicate they had been dead for some time," continued Amelia. "The orc corpses are fresher."

"How can that be?" asked Sherman. "They obviously fought each other here."

Kazin turned to Amelia. "Have you been able to identify our quarry yet?"

Amelia shrugged. "I'll try again. We are closer now than we've been to them considering this is where they were attacked." She looked into her orb and concentrated.

A moment later she looked up in confusion. "We haven't caught up to them, Kazin! We're very close, but we haven't caught them yet!"

Sherman straightened from examining a dead horse. "What?! Are you saying this isn't the group we've been chasing? How is that possible?" He looked at Kazin in bewilderment.

Kazin was staring off into the distance. An idea was forming in his head. "I think I know what might be going on." He turned to Amelia. "Did you see what our quarry looks like?"

Amelia concentrated on her orb again. After a time her straining ceased and she looked up a Kazin, perplexed. "I don't get it."

"What did you see?" asked the young mage.

"I - I saw a group of orcs," said Amelia quietly. She sighed and lowered her orb. "It's no use, Kazin. I keep getting different images."

"What you saw is correct," said Kazin gently. "We are chasing a group of orcs."

"What?!" exclaimed Sherman. He looked at Kazin as if he had lost his mind. "There's no way we've been chasing orcs through the human's land! People we've questioned along the way would have reported that to us. I'm sure of it!" He pointed back to the army's encampment. "They certainly would never have wandered through the human army without being cut to pieces!"

"You're quite right," said Kazin. "Until recently, our quarry was in human form."

"Magic?" asked Amelia.

"Perhaps - in a manner of speaking," said Kazin. "I believe the group we are chasing has been jumping from body to body as they go. Once the bodies they possess decay too much, they have to find a new host body to possess." The mage pointed to the bodies around him. "If these humans died before this fight, I'd wager they were strangled to death."

"Strangled?" said Sherman, looking around at the corpses.

"Of course!" exclaimed Amelia. "They deliberately strangled their victims so their new host bodies were intact and viable for a period of time!"

"Precisely," said Kazin, nodding. "What we are dealing with is a group of spirits that jump from body to body."

"That's a lethal combination," said Sherman. "No wonder they got away again, even though they were facing a more numerous enemy." He looked at Kazin. "How do we kill them? If we kill their host bodies, which are already dead, they'll just jump into another one and keep fighting."

"Quite right," said Kazin. "I think the only way to kill them is to dispel the evil souls so they are sent back into the afterlife."

"And how do we do that?" asked Sherman. "With magic?"

Kazin nodded. "Yes. Your sword might be the key here, Sherman. It is a spirit blade, so it has the inherent ability to dispel evil spirits."

"Can't you dispel the spirits with magic?" asked Sherman.

Kazin sighed. "I'm not sure. That magic is typically available to clerics, and we don't have one among us."

Amelia was about to say something but decided against it. Instead, she said, "'Dispel' magic, huh?"

Kazin turned to the red-haired spell caster. "Yes. Do you know 'dispel' magic?"

Amelia shook her head. "No." 'Not yet,' she said to herself.

"Too bad," said Sherman. "Well, we've finished with this investigation. We'd better get moving if we don't want to lose our quarry."

Kazin looked at Amelia. "Which way do we go?"

Amelia consulted her orb and pointed west. "We go that - no, wait." Then she pointed northwest. "We go - no. Just a minute." She scratched her head. "For some reason it's showing two directions. I can't narrow it down."

"They must have split up," said Sherman.

"Yes, that's it," said Amelia. "I've got it. The orcs went west and the human went northwest on horseback."

"Human?" exclaimed Kazin and Sherman in unison.

"There was a survivor?" asked Sherman.

"What did he look like?" asked Kazin, interested.

Amelia reddened. "I'm surprised I haven't seen him before. He has dark hair and a long, dark mustache."

Sherman and Kazin exchanged glances.

"That's the same description we had early in our pursuit!" exclaimed Sherman.

Kazin nodded. "I agree. He has been with the group we have been chasing since the start. He is the key to this all. If we can find him, we will have found our quarry. It is he who is threatening to destroy our history!" Kazin embraced Amelia. "Well done, Amelia! Now we have something to go on. We are now closer than ever to stopping the real threat to history."

Amelia blushed. "Sorry I didn't see him earlier. I guess all the faces I've been seeing are the different people who have had their bodies used to host the evil spirits."

"You couldn't have known that," said Kazin. "But we know now."

"So which way do we go?" interrupted Sherman. "We're not getting anywhere standing around here."

"True enough," agreed Kazin. "I think we'll go after our true quarry. Even if he's on horseback, we should be able to catch up with him."

"I'll cast the haste spell on us again," offered Amelia.

Before long, the trio was underway again. Kazin flew northwest, and before long the trail led back around to the southwest.

"He's heading back to his group of evil spirits," said Amelia. "He led us on a wild goose chase in order to confuse any followers."

"Clever," commented Kazin, his voice rumbling beneath them. "But I don't think he counted on a magical orb tracking him either."

Kazin flew low to the ground at the spot where Amelia claimed their quarry had rendezvoused with his crew. Orc tracks were seen in the mud coupled with the hoof prints of a horse.

The forest here was thicker again, but the vegetation was somewhat different than what they had experienced in the human lands.

"They went straight west," said Amelia. "According to my orb, a very large encampment of creatures lies ahead."

"We'd better be vigilant," said Kazin. "If we -," his sentence remained unfinished as his body suddenly stiffened up. With a great deal of effort Kazin tried to gain altitude, but his efforts were in vain. He rapidly lost altitude and soared to a small clearing below.

"Kazin!" cried Amelia. "What's wrong?"

"I - I can't maintain my dragon form!" gasped Kazin. The ground was rushing up toward them at an alarming rate. "I - I have to land! The magic is too powerful!"

Too late, Amelia realized what she needed to do. Nevertheless, she cast a 'magical shield' spell for what it was worth. The interference to the spells below was enough for Kazin to concentrate and land at a full run. No sooner had he come to a stop when he began to transform back into his human form. Sherman and Amelia immediately jumped to safety just in time before the dragon was replaced by a young mage who lay on the ground, quivering like a leaf.

Amelia ran up to the mage and knelt by his semiconscious form. "Kazin!" she wailed.

Sherman drew his sword and stood guard, poised to do battle with whatever or whoever showed themselves. If anyone wanted to harm his friends, they would have to go through him first.

"Kazin!" cried Amelia again. She chanted a quick spell of healing but there was no physical injury she could direct her spell at. The mage was now unconscious.

A few moments later, noises could be heard and some lizardmages appeared from among the trees. They hissed upon seeing the intruders.

"Stand back!" warned Sherman, holding up his sword menacingly. The lizardmages hissed again.

"Where is the dragon?" hissed one. "It should be here."

"This is the spot," said another one. "I'd swear it."

They didn't appear to be concerned about Sherman and his sword.

It was obvious why when more lizardmages appeared. There were a good thirty of them in the group.

Sherman eyed them warily while Amelia frantically tried every spell she could think of to revive Kazin. The big warrior suddenly wished he had help in this situation.

"Not good," hissed a lizardmage. "We need the dragon." He turned to one of the others, a female judging by the smaller stature and lighter skin colour. "Get the patrol that was assigned to protect us. They can hold onto these spies until we finish searching the area. I'm sure the warlock will be interested in interrogating them. In the meantime, we'll keep searching for the dragon. It has to be around here somewhere. Its mind should be cleared so it won't know to fly away."

"Very good," hissed the female. "It will give the orcs something useful to do instead of grumbling of boredom." She turned to get the orc patrol.

A few lizardmages remained to guard the prisoners until the patrol arrived. The rest resumed their search for the dragon.

Sherman remained alert and considered attacking while the enemies were minimal, but one look at Kazin told him it wasn't worth the risk. Until the mage woke up, it wasn't worth doing anything. Kazin was their only ticket out of that place. He had to be revived, and soon.

Chapter 29

rch Mage Gresham pondered his decisions of the last few days. The most recent was sending Arch Mage Sasha to assist the northern cause with twelve other dragon riders, something that was necessary with the impending ogre battle. Fighting on two fronts was not something he wanted to be doing, but it could not be helped. The reports from aerial familiars in the north could not be ignored. But if their reports could be believed, such large numbers of ogres would be almost impossible to stop. A dozen or so dragons would only help to a point. Once the two sides became embroiled in battle, it would be difficult, if not impossible to intervene with the dragons because there was too great a risk of affecting friendly units with the enemy. Dragon flames were not that precise. If only the dwarves would help - then they stood a chance.

Gresham climbed onto his dragon's back and gave the order to lift off. Horath didn't argue. He simply sprang into the air. His wing had been healed almost to perfection by the high cleric herself. The dragon was now more than capable of going into battle again.

Now Gresham was going to do an investigation into the disappearance of the patrol in the west. Two other dragons and their mounts joined him. Belham and Fillith flanked his right; while an arch mage named Norma flying a green dragon by the name of Vanhar flanked his left. They flew in formation and kept at a height that permitted good oversight of the ground below, while being close enough to see if there was any sign of anything unusual.

"Let me know when you spot the security patrols," he called to his aides. As he spoke, he caught sight of what he thought was a dragon ahead, but it was gone so fast he wasn't sure he had actually seen anything at all. He shook his head irritably. He should get some sleep. Hallucinations were not helpful at this point.

They flew for only about ten minutes when Belham shouted and pointed ahead to their right. "My dragon spotted the security patrols! They're not far ahead!"

The dragons reached the patrols and overtook their position. A few of the patrol members spotted the dragons above them and when they saw the dragon riders, they waved.

Gresham waved back but maintained his course. He held onto his hat as the wind whistled past. "We can alert the patrols to danger if we see a threat!" called Gresham.

"That should give them confidence, seeing us patrolling above them," said Norma.

"It wouldn't hurt to assign a dragon to assist each ground patrol with a dragon rider," said Belham.

"I've thought of that," said Gresham. "At first there were too few of us to risk it, but now that we have a good sized air force we can chance it, particularly in light of the fact that a patrol has gone missing. We need to be vigilant."

"We have been using dragons to patrol along the Jackal River," pointed out Arch Mage Norma, "but going farther afield would be a good idea."

"Initially we didn't want the enemy to know we had control of dragons," said Gresham, "but once word gets out that we sent dragons to the north against the ogres, it won't matter that we're seen with them here."

"It doesn't matter," said Belham. "Let them know. Maybe they'll give up and go home."

"Or they'll devise a way to harm our dragons and make us withdraw where we will be ineffective," said Gresham.

"My biggest concern," said Norma, "is how the other dragons will react when they are drawn into the battle. I think our attention will be on defending ourselves from them."

"You could be right," said Gresham. "We can only hope some of them will be convinced to join us."

Suddenly Belham laughed.

"What is it?" asked Gresham.

"Fillith just told me she has relatives who won't harm her if they see her. She thinks they might side with her if she can persuade them we are friends."

"That's great news!" exclaimed Gresham. "When we get back, I'll get all of the dragon riders to talk to their dragons to see if they can obtain allies!"

The trio flew for a considerable distance. At one point Gresham shook his head. "We'll have to turn back. We haven't seen any sign of the missing patrol, or anything else for that matter. It's doubtful the patrol has gone this far afield."

"We're also getting close to enemy territory," added Belham.

"We can go back on a different trajectory," suggested Norma. "We might spot something we may have missed the first time around."

"Good idea," said Gresham. He signaled his dragon to start a turn.

"I think I've spotted something!" called out Belham. He squinted through the overcast sky to his right.

As the trio neared the spot, they could see signs of a battle below. Ravens and vultures circled the area.

"Something happened here, all right," said Norma. "I'll wager our patrol was ambushed here."

The group prepared for landing and Gresham did a spell check for magic. "Hmm," he said. "There was some magic present here recently, but I can't determine what it was or where it originated."

"Are there any threats now?" asked Belham.

Gresham shook his head. "No. It's safe to proceed."

The three dragons landed and the mages hopped to the ground. As they went to investigate the bodies, Norma called to them. "A dragon was here recently. These marks on the ground are definitely from a dragon."

Gresham and Belham examined the area Norma had pointed out. "There are footprints here too," said Gresham, pointing. "One larger set of boot prints and a medium and smaller set as well. Those last two aren't from a soldier's boot. They may have been from either civilians or mages."

"I doubt human civilians are this far away from human territory," said Belham.

"If it were mages or clerics," said Norma, "it would explain the traces of magic you detected."

Gresham nodded. "Perhaps." He looked at the others. "It looks like they weren't in any danger, since their prints are evenly spaced. They must have come upon this scene and investigated like we are doing right now."

"Who were they?" wondered Norma, "and how did they get here?"

Gresham recalled his earlier encounter with a dragon and its riders. "I have a feeling we're not alone out here."

"What do you mean?" asked Belham. He looked around. "Is someone watching us?"

Gresham shook his head. "No. I suspect they're long gone." He sighed. "But I suspect we'll run into them eventually."

"Are they enemies?" asked Norma.

Gresham shrugged. "I don't know. I'm thinking - and hoping - they're allies." He turned and led them to the place where the bodies lay. A head count confirmed the entire patrol had been wiped out, but they seemed to have done well, taking the lives of three times as many orcs.

"We'll report this back to the search patrol and call off their search," said Gresham. "There's nothing they can do for them anyway."

"Are we just going to leave them here?" asked Norma.

Gresham clenched his jaw. "As a rule, we don't leave our soldiers unburied, but we're too close to enemy territory here. It's too dangerous to spend any length of time here, even for burying bodies. It's better if we didn't. If the enemy returns, they'll assume we don't know about this skirmish yet. They could potentially return and set up another ambush, waiting for our search patrol to arrive. It would be wise to make them wait for nothing."

"That's too bad," said Norma, looking around at the bodies. "They deserve better."

"They took a great risk coming out so far," said Gresham. "I'm sure their orders to stay within a reasonable distance of the encampment were ignored. They knew the risks of venturing so far afield."

"But still," said Norma.

Gresham put a hand on her shoulder. "I know. I feel the loss as well. It's obvious they fought well, given the odds. They must have fought while they were dying, judging by their badly beat up bodies. They will be remembered. We have lost some valuable soldiers."

Satisfied that there was no more left to learn, Gresham and the others mounted their dragons and returned to alert the rescue patrol.

Chapter 30

arran used his cavalry as effectively as he could. After blowing the dragon conch shell, he sent them in to strafe the front lines of the ogres as they marched south into human territory. Although doing considerable damage, the mounted dwarves were cut down a few at a time, reducing their effectiveness with each successive attack. He then decided to change tactics, or his forces would be decimated before the infantry arrived. He signaled his forces into two fronts. Each front would then charge the sides of the multitudes of ogres. But instead of from the front, they attacked from the rear. This forced the forward-moving ogres to stop and turn to meet the oncoming tide of cavalry. Failure to do so would leave them vulnerable and unable to retaliate. This had the desired effect. The sides of the ogre army were forced to stop and fight while the center of the army still forged ahead. Instead of one big mass of bodies, the ogre army became long and strung out. This lack of depth was important when the infantry finally arrived.

As if on cue, the first ranks of the dwarven army crested the hill to the northwest. Cheers could be heard by the thinning ranks of cavalry at the sight of the reinforcements.

Olag came riding up to Harran to report the news. He had been riding his horse hard. Unable to use a weapon himself in his dwarven form, he chose to use his horse to run down ogres in his path. Even if he didn't kill very many of them, he did succeed in upsetting their balance, allowing the dwarves they fought to gain the upper hand and finish the job. "The infantry is approaching."

Harran nodded. "I saw them."

"The lizardmages are still hiding in the middle of the group," reported Olag. "We can't get near them."

Harran clenched his jaw. The lizardmages were his biggest problem. Their magic was the thorn in his side in this battle. They continued to down his cavalry with magic unmolested, despite the extra resistance offered by the dragon conch. They did nearly as much killing as the ogres, but without suffering any casualties. "We'll have to break through with the infantry."

"It's funny," mused Olag. "There are no lizardmages wielding bows. They are all capable of using magic. A few generations before my time, many lizardmen no longer had the ability to cast spells. My race was created due to this inequality."

"Kazin said that magic in these days was stronger," said Harran. "I suspect it was no different with your race. As their magical power waned, some of them must have lost the ability entirely."

"That's probably the case," said Olag. "Things have certainly changed since then."

A female lieutenant rode up to Harran. She was the one who was present when Harran had come out of the mountain. "The infantry has arrived, Sir."

Harran nodded. "Have them form a wedge pattern. We need to penetrate through to their lizardmages." He handed her the dragon conch. "Here. Use this after you've passed on the orders."

The lieutenant saluted. "Yes, Sir!" She took the conch and rode to meet up with the infantry leaders.

As she rode off with her instructions, Olag pointed. "A dragon!"

Harran looked up into the sky to see a dragon approaching the scene. Soon others followed. There were only seven or eight of them, but Harran knew it was only the beginning. Ahead to the south, oblivious to the approaching dwarven army, he saw the advance forces of ogres as they met up with the meager defense of the town of Shara. Even with the handful of mages, the humans there had no chance to defend themselves. Even as he watched, the tide of monsters did not stop as they crashed through the barricades and overwhelmed the villagers. Black smoke rose to the sky as the village went up in flames. The sight was not unlike the burning and plundering at the Velden Iron Mine, which had fallen before Harran's forced had arrived.

Now the dwarven infantry made their debut. Exhaustion from the forced march was put to the back of their minds as they saw their severely depleted cavalry battling an army much too large for them to handle alone. There was no honour in allowing their brothers at arms to do all the work alone. The dragon conch was blown and they surged forward with renewed energy and cries of battle. They charged into the throng of ogres with a vengeance that belied their stature.

Harran was happy to see the influx of dwarves and moved to join the remaining cavalry. From what he saw, the ogres were still far more numerous than they. There were undoubtedly more dwarves assembling for the war, but no one knew when they would arrive. Navigating through the collapsing tunnels in the mountains was undoubtedly a severe hindrance to the remaining reinforcements.

Now the dragons swooped down to attack. Not surprisingly, they concentrated their fire on the lizardmages who were steadfastly using their magic. Finally the lizardmages experienced casualties. This took some of the heat off the dwarves and they were able to concentrate on the ogres before them. Cries and shouts could be heard all across the battlefield.

In the distance, ogres could be seen heading south toward the human town of Velden. The village of Shara was now nothing more than a smoking ruin.

More dragons appeared in the west and flew to meet the front lines of the ogres. As a unit, they seared the ogres in their tracks. This uniform attack caught Harran's eye. He didn't expect dragons to attack in unison. All of the dragons flying around in his area were attacking randomly and chaotically. The dragons in the new group fired a few more fireballs into the oncoming ogres and worked their way closer to Harran and his dwarves. Half expecting an attack from above, Harran shouted to his troops to prepare for the devastating attack he had seen upon this group's arrival. But as the dragons neared, he saw riders on their backs. The lead dragon was a large black one. The rider on his back sought out the dwarven leader and flew toward Harran. When he was spotted, the rider waved down to him. These dragons were friends!

Harran hailed the dragon and beckoned the female lieutenant to come to him.

She rode up to him, her horse's nostrils flaring from exertion. "Sir?"

"Change tactics to encircle the ogres!" he commanded. "These new dragons won't be effective if we are mixed together with the enemy!"

"But the lizardmages -," began the lieutenant.

Harran waved his arm. "Don't worry about them! We need to allow the dragons to do their work!"

The lieutenant nodded. She liked this new king. He was no stranger to battle tactics. She rode off to give the orders.

A new battle was suddenly underway, causing Harran to wonder whether his decision was the right one. Above, in a crescendo of shrieks and cries, the first dragons clashed with the ones who had just arrived. Some of the original dragons sided with the newcomers, while the rest turned to fight them. Fire lit the sky as though the sun burned brightly. Fire rained down on those below them, randomly burning friend and foe alike. Screams rent the air.

As if things couldn't get any worse, a new force of creatures joined the fray. Coming from the northeast were the most fearsome creatures yet. With bellows loud enough to be heard across the entire battlefield, the minotaurs announced their presence.

The ogres, who were content to continue fighting their way south despite the pesky dwarves, had no choice but to turn back to meet this new threat. Now they had to deal with someone their own size.

The arrival of minotaurs was not regarded as good news by the dwarves, who were sworn enemies of the minotaurs. The only good thing was the fact that the ogres didn't like them either.

Now true chaos began. Each race fought the other. There were no alliances except that of the dwarves and humans, and the few dragon riders above them. The humans in the town of Velden had to fight for themselves because the dwarves had their hands full. The smoke rising from the town was evidence of their lack of success. The dragon riders above them tried to break away from their battle above to do what damage they could to the ground units, but had to take back to the air as soon as more wild dragons appeared on the horizon. At least they were able to drive the wild dragons away successfully for the most part.

One dragon, burning with flames, plunged into the ground with a thunderous crash, crushing creatures and dwarves and sending many others flying with the impact.

Harran was too busy to notice, leading a cavalry charge into an area filled with ogres and minotaurs. He ordered a nearby lieutenant to recall the cavalry on the far flank to bring them away from the bulk of the minotaurs. He reasoned that using the ogres as a buffer would keep more dwarves alive. As his group hacked their way through the chaos, he heard a voice he knew well.

"Having fun yet?"

Harran turned and saw Zylor, grinning from ear to ear. "Zylor!" exclaimed Harran. He rode up to the minotaur. "No, I'm not having fun. I'd like to get out of here. Things are getting too chaotic for my liking."

Zylor's grin widened. "Isn't it glorious?"

Despite himself the dwarf laughed. "You would say that, wouldn't you?"

"You could have used the ring anytime," said Zylor.

"The only reason I'm still here is I was waiting for the real king to show up. I can't leave until -," he broke off as his lieutenant rode up to him.

"Sir!" she cried above the commotion. She eyed Zylor warily while pointing to a group of dwarves on the horizon bearing a flag.

"At last!" said Harran. He turned to his lieutenant. "That's your new king, lieutenant."

The lieutenant looked bewildered and started to object.

Harran saluted the lieutenant. "Lieutenant, you have done well. I have to go now. You should report to the king at once. I was only here as a substitute. My duty is finished."

The lieutenant started to shake her head. "But Sir, you are -."

"That's not important," said Harran. "Go! Your king awaits!"

Meanwhile, Zylor was busy with some ogres who had gotten too close, so he didn't see as the lieutenant looked back at Harran as she rode away. She rode slowly, looking forlornly at Harran several times. Finally she stopped, saluted Harran, and turned to report to the real king. Her horse increased its speed and she rode proudly, not looking back at the dwarf who she admired and would never see again.

"Goodbye," said Harran sadly. "In another life, in another time -," he shook his head. "In another time, indeed!" He turned to Zylor, who had dispatched the ogres. "Let's get Olag."

They didn't have long to search. At some point Olag had been knocked from his horse and he was forced to find an outcropping of rock behind which to hide. It was only a matter of time, however, before he was spotted and attacked. Hunkered down low, in his original form, he fired arrows one after another into any enemy that approached.

Zylor was astounded at the accumulation of bodies the skink warrior had piled up with arrows protruding from their necks. He simply gaped at the pile in astonishment. "He must have shot fifty ogres here!" he exclaimed.

Olag recognized the minotaur's voice and lowered the arrow he was about to shoot. "Zylor? Is that you?"

Zylor grinned. "It is I." His arm waved over the mound of ogres, with a few lizardmages thrown in. "Did you do this?"

Olag hissed. "What do you think?" He spotted Harran with the minotaur. "Do we get to go now?"

Harran nodded. "Yes. Let's get out of here." He glanced over to where the new king stood, watching the battle before him. The lieutenant was almost there. The king would have one mystery he would never solve, thought Harran. He pulled out his ring and Olag and Zylor followed suit.

"What if someone sees us?" asked Olag suddenly.

"I don't care," said Harran. "Kazin may need our help and we're not much use to him here."

As one, the three companions rubbed their rings, and vanished, with the sound of the dragon conch ringing in their ears. As they disappeared, the earth trembled and chaos resumed on the battlefield.

Chapter 31

ll familiars are unanimous in their reports," said Arch Mage Sallow. He twisted the tips of his long mustache nervously. "The war against the entire ogre army has commenced."

"Here we go," said Gresham.

Sallow continued. "The Velden Mine has been decimated, and the village of Shara has been overrun. The town of Velden itself is holding with the help of the mages from the Tower of Sorcery, but it doesn't look good. Fortunately, it seems the dwarves have finally arrived to help, and they are striking at the northwest flank of the ogre army."

"I wouldn't write off Velden yet," said Gresham. "Arch Mage Toele has gone there with a contingent of high ranking mages. He may be a grumpy character, but he's no slouch either. He has his share of battle experience under his belt. If anyone can hold off the ogres, he can."

"I hope so," said Sallow.

"And what of the dragons?" asked Arch Mage Penna. She didn't have a dragon of her own, but didn't want one either since she wasn't fond of heights. Content to stay on the ground, she organized the spell casters in the army. This was not an easy task and demanded most of her attention.

"There are untamed dragons present," said Sallow, "but our dragon riders have been doing a good job of chasing them away. The dragons seem to be more reluctant to fight against others of their own kind. In fact, some of the untamed dragons have joined our side, but that doesn't compare to the new arrivals who are drawn to the magic of the numerous spell casters. Sasha and her group are finding little time to do damage to selected ground troops."

"That's what I was afraid of," mumbled Gresham. "At best we will be keeping the untamed dragons too busy to involve themselves in the battle. Whether that's a good thing, remains to be seen."

A young mage appeared and ran up to Arch Mage Sallow. He whispered into his ear for a few moments and then ran off. Sallow's expression darkened.

"What is it?" asked Gresham.

"The latest familiars have returned from the north. It appears the minotaurs have gotten involved. A sizeable contingent of the creatures has joined the fray."

Gresham swore.

General Holden, who was also present, shook his head. "Then all is lost. We cannot fight two large armies on two fronts." Holden had become the new general since the original one had succumbed to his injuries from the previous battle.

"This is bad, indeed," said Penna. She looked at Gresham and could see his thoughtful expression. "Gresham?"

"You know," said Gresham slowly, "that may not be such a bad thing under the circumstances."

"How so?" asked Penna.

Gresham lifted his hat and scratched his head. "Minotaurs and ogres have been mortal enemies for a long time, long before humans arrived in these lands."

"What difference does that make?" asked Holden. "They're everyone's enemies."

"True," said Gresham, "but their appearance may benefit us in that their attention will be on the ogres, at least initially."

"Maybe," said Sallow. "And they do have to go through the ogres to get to our forces."

"Let's hope the dwarves are smart enough to use the ogres as a buffer as well," added Penna.

"It's too bad we can't get that message across to the dwarves," said Holden.

"Yes," said Gresham. "All of our dragons will be busy very soon and we can't spare any messengers. It would have been a perfect task for a mage with a young dragon under his control, one not big enough to become involved in battle. But we don't have one, so we'll have to do without." He turned to Sallow. "And our region? You said earlier things were in motion?"

Sallow nodded. "The bulk of the warlock's army has moved a day's travel east and they've set up for the night. They are now a day and a half from here. However, it's unknown when they will rise and attack, but it certainly looks imminent. I suspect he's waiting for a small contingent of creatures to circle south of us, but what he hopes to accomplish with such a small force is unknown."

"Maybe he wants us to think we are surrounded as a ploy to make us assume his army is bigger than we thought," suggested Penna. "The psychological aspect of a war can be devastating if fear is used to your advantage."

"Perhaps," conceded Gresham, "but I think the warlock has something else up his sleeve."

"One other unconfirmed report from our familiars," continued Sallow, "is the possible presence of dragons in the warlock's army. I say unconfirmed because the army has archers as well as magic defending their perimeter. Our aerial familiars can't break through without being shot down with arrows or magic. Even the eagle familiars are unable to do anything with their keen eyesight and high altitude. The lizardmages have put up some sort of shield that prevents visual contact with certain parts of the army compound."

"Then how do you know they might have dragons?" asked Penna.

"There were two reports that lead us to suspect the presence of enemy dragons," said Sallow. "First of all, one familiar - a mouse - has reportedly made it through the enemy lines and caught sight of the beasts. Any sizeable familiar would undoubtedly have been killed for food within minutes in the enemy camp, but being small and scrawny, the mouse was likely not considered worth hunting down for a snack by the orcs or goblins. The only problem is the familiar in question has a habit of embellishing its stories from time to time in order to be taken seriously."

"Nevertheless," said Gresham, "if the information is accurate, it could have dire consequences for us if we ignored it. What is the other report?"

"The other one was a report from a raven who spotted a dragon appear out of nowhere just west of our encampment. It told its master the dragon suddenly appeared and two individuals climbed upon its back. Then it flew out of sight to the west at an amazing speed and was gone. It could have been spying on our activities. The fact that it was invisible is a little unnerving, wouldn't you say?"

Gresham nodded. "An invisible dragon, you say? Interesting. That may explain some things. We have done experiments with invisibility on our dragons and the magic won't work. Someone may have found a way around that problem." He straightened. "With what we now know, I recommend we prepare for the eventuality that the enemy has dragons under their control just as we do. We need to forewarn the other dragon riders and formulate a battle strategy to cope with this."

"I agree," said Penna. "After our last few confrontations with this warlock, I wouldn't ever underestimate his capabilities."

"We all know what must be done," said Gresham. "I suggest we get to work at once."

The others agreed.

Chapter 32

alado observed his surroundings carefully as he wandered through the warlock's camp with his entourage of orcs. It was quickly becoming dark and the cool night air was setting in earlier than usual. Tents were set up in clusters and the various races bunched together in groups of their own kind. Bonfires were set up here and there with wood from the surrounding forest. Some of the bonfires had spits set up with unknown carcasses being roasted for the benefit of those nearby. Orcs and their smaller cousins the goblins milled about in small groups. The goblins with their pointed ears and pointy chins hovered near some of the spits in the hopes of snatching pieces of meat from unwary creatures, who weren't always watching the progress of their supper. One goblin was caught in the act of stealing some meat and ran full tilt from the scene as an angry orc shambled after it, threatening all sorts of nasty things once he got his hands on the thief.

Galado even passed a section of the camp where some human mercenaries were camped. They were settling down for supper as well and were passing around a flask of dwarven ale they had somehow acquired. When they saw Galado, they gave a curt nod, which he returned. These were men and women who had no compunction about fighting their own kind. Their reasons varied, from revenge to financial gain.

The entrance into the camp had gone fairly smoothly. One stepped forward to report to a lizardmage who was accompanied by several orcs. He informed them the patrol had been ambushed, but had prevailed, and some new information had come to light that had to be reported to the warlock at once.

The lizardmage hissed in a manner that could have indicated fear. "You'll have to report it yourself." Obviously no one wanted to face the warlock's wrath. Even if good news was reported, the warlock was known to become angry if he was interrupted at a bad time.

The lizardmage then inquired about Galado's presence, and One told him Galado was a defector. He had been instrumental in defeating the ambushers as a sign of his allegiance.

Satisfied, the lizardmage opened the gate and allowed them to enter. He pointed to the large tent in the distance. "The warlock's tent is over there."

One grunted like an orc and led them into the camp.

Now they continued toward the warlock's tent. Galado stepped close to One so he could hear. "We need to take out - or should I say replace - the sentries outside of the warlock's tent. We need to do so quietly while no one is watching."

One nodded. "Right, Boss."

"Once you're in position as a sentry, I'll need you to watch closely for any threats. Anything unusual must be reported immediately. If you don't have time to report, kill first and we'll deal with them later."

"Right, Boss."

"When I'm ready, I'll give you a signal and I want you to ensure no one enters the warlock's tent - and I mean no one," commanded Galado.

"You got it, Boss," said One.

Galado stopped and turned to his crew. "We can't all go to the tent or it will look suspicious. I'll take One, Two, Eight and Ten. The rest of you should go and mingle. Maybe you can find some creatures who are alone and take control of their bodies. It isn't uncommon that these creatures kill one another from time to time, even if they are on the same side in this war. But it wouldn't hurt to have a good mix. I'll need leaders among all the groups. Be particularly careful of the lizardmages. If one of you succeeds in taking the body of one of them, remember that you won't be able to cast magic. I know that without magic those creatures are pretty useless, but I would like to know what they are up to, and to do that you have to be one of them."

"Understood," said several orcs.

Galado nodded. "Good. You can report back to me when you have been successful."

The orcs turned and left, except the ones Galado had selected.

"You four come with me," instructed Galado.

They followed him to a spot overlooking the warlock's tent from the side. Light from the torches filtered out through the entrance highlighting a pair of human guards who looked bored. Galado and his team ducked behind a cart laden with supplies meant strictly for the warlock and his guests. There Galado and his team waited, hidden from view of the sentries, as well as anyone else in the camp.

Nearly an hour passed. Galado yawned and forced himself to stay awake. It had now been several days since Galado had slept. Fatigue was setting in and was much more noticeable when he was at rest. He fervently wished he could get this over with. Fortunately, voices could be heard and the tent's doorway was pulled aside. The light from within brightened the area as a number of commanders exited. The orc and goblin commanders left first, shambling quickly from the scene to the encampment beyond, where they eventually split up to go to their own command posts. A single human mercenary commander exited next. He was tall but well built. He strode confidently down the path and disappeared.

"It wouldn't hurt to take control of him," whispered Galado, "but there's no real hurry. I'm sure he will do fine for the time being."

One grunted is response. Orcs didn't know how to whisper.

Then four lizardmen exited the tent. They were quiet until they were out of earshot of the sentries. Then one of them spoke. "It's your turn to deal with the cyclops, Friss. They are not a pleasant race to deal with."

Friss hissed. "I was hoping you'd forget to pass them off to me, Galar."

Galar hissed in laughter. "Not on your life! One day is enough to last me a lifetime!"

The other lizardmages hissed.

Soon their banter was lost as they moved away. As the tent doors were pulled shut by the goblin-orc, the sentries relaxed again, prepared for another long night of boredom once again.

"This is it," whispered Galado. "You guys circle around back. I'll create a diversion and you guys can do your thing. Silence is absolutely imperative!"

The four orcs faded off into the shadows as Galado gave them a head start. Then he rose and approached the sentries.

"Hey guys!" said Galado in a loud whisper, "did you hear?"

The sentries stiffened and peered into the darkness ahead of them. When they saw another human approaching, they relaxed.

"Hear what?" asked one sentry in a partially quiet voice. He did not want to arouse the warlock needlessly. He was acutely aware of the warlock's wrath as was everyone in the camp.

He got no answer. A powerful green arm suddenly materialized and wrapped itself around his neck, squeezing tightly. The second sentry was not able to help, as his neck was being throttled by a similar arm. Within moments, both sentries were dead, their weapons removed by a third orc as a precaution.

Galado nodded and One and Two exited their bodies to take the new human ones. Then they stood up and resumed their positions in front of the tent. Eight gave them their weapons back.

"Take the bodies away," Galado instructed Eight and Ten.

Ten suddenly left his body and took over One's former body. When he rose, he grinned at Galado. "This body is bigger. It will be easier to drag the other body away."

"Go ahead," said Galado. Eight and Ten each took a dead orc body, slung it over their bulky shoulders, and left. "Don't forget to find some other bodies before you come back," whispered Galado after them. Then he turned to One and Two. "It's time. Don't let anyone in. Understand?"

"Yes, Boss," whispered One and Two together.

Galado nodded in satisfaction. Then he took a deep breath and entered the tent. The conference room was still lit up with torches and a battle map was on the table with markings all over it. There was no one around and it was very quiet. The thick tent walls hid any sounds from outside.

Suddenly, there was a slight noise in the adjacent chamber and Galado remembered the goblin-orc. He stood to the side of the entrance to the antechamber and waited. Murmuring to himself, the goblin-orc came into the conference room to begin cleaning up the mess the commanders had made. With a swift motion, Galado brought the haft of his sword down on Gorc's head. Gorc went down without a sound. Galado dragged Gorc's body back into the antechamber and concealed the body behind a cabinet. Then he listened to be sure no one had heard. After several moments of listening to only his own heartbeat, Galado glided into the next chamber. Sitting on a chair facing away from the entrance was the warlock. He appeared to be studying a book by the light of several candles and didn't notice the intruder.

Galado studied the sparse furnishings in the room and recalled the layout of the rest of the tent. There was nowhere to hide, and anyone entering the tent without permission would be detected by the sentries. The time was near at hand. He was not too late. There his body sat, oblivious to the fact that he would meet an early demise any moment now. But this was going to be different. This was his opportunity to rectify the situation. He would wait until the time had passed. Once that happened, he would not die. Then he could pursue his plans to wipe out the humans from these lands and rule the entire continent with all the creatures serving one ruler - him!

Galado drifted quietly back into the antechamber. He sat his fatigued body down on a chair and prepared to wait. A gap in the curtains allowed him an unobstructed view of the warlock. Any ambitious lizardmages who tried to enter the chamber with magic would be dealt with swiftly and mercilessly. But Galado knew that wouldn't be possible. The warlock had cast a spell to prevent such an intrusion. He was too clever for that. He never trusted other spell casters and did what he could to protect himself from them.

Anyone who managed to get past Galado's sentries would have to go through him if they wanted to get to the warlock. The commotion alone if this happened would alert the warlock and he would intervene with his powerful magic. The plan was foolproof. He would save himself from an untimely demise and rule the land after winning the war!

So the wait began. There was no way he could be stopped now. Galado figured once the threat was over, his spirit should automatically go back into his original body. It was only a matter of time. As he waited, his body relaxed. He yawned. His eyelids became heavy. His mind was filled with plans for the upcoming battle, and plans for the future.

He did not notice as his body stood up. Then it took a step forward. Then another, each step bringing him closer to the warlock, who still did not see or hear him. Finally he was right behind the warlock. His sword arm began to rise, imperceptibly at first, then more deliberately. The Sword of Dead glinted as it righted itself for the kill. With a sudden thrust, it slammed home, piercing the heart of its intended victim.

The warlock half rose in surprise. Then he looked down at the end of the sword protruding from his chest. With nothing more than a gasp, he sagged back into his chair. He was dead.

Right then Galado awoke. Instinctively, he withdrew the sword and staggered backward, falling to the floor in shock. He stared uncomprehendingly at the corpse before him. His corpse. What had he done?

Suddenly laughter filled his head. It was the laughter of the body's original owner, Sir Wilfred Galado. "Foiled!" cried Wilfred in glee. "You have been foiled! You thought you could prevent your demise, but you failed! You will never be free to accomplish what you have started!"

Galado stared stupidly at his corpse. Why couldn't he jump right into his body like his crew? What prevented him from doing it? Why was he stuck in this body while his own sat there lifeless?

A vibrating sensation suddenly manifested itself in the sword. It began to shimmer, the light and darkness fighting for supremacy more fiercely than ever before. Then the darkness surged from the sword, causing it to momentarily become so bright Galado had to shield his eyes. Then the dark cloud streaked across the room into the warlock's body. At that instant, a deep rumble could be felt from deep within the earth. It shuddered vehemently, causing some tents in the encampment to collapse. Dragons waiting for their masters stirred restlessly, and some creatures lost their balance and fell to the ground. The tremor lasted about a minute before subsiding.

323

Suddenly, impossibly, the warlock rose to his feet. Slowly, he turned to look at Galado. His eyes burned like tiny suns. His mouth became a crooked grin and he laughed. The laugh was deep and booming, and felt like it came from deep under the ground.

"At last!" he roared, his deep voice booming like a drum. "At last I'm free!" He looked down at Galado and pointed an accusing finger at him. Then he lifted his finger and lifted Galado up off the floor without touching him. "You will serve me or die!"

Galado was in no position to argue, hovering helplessly above the floor. "I'll serve you!"

"Good!" said the warlock. He dropped Galado unceremoniously to the floor. "We have work to do."

"Oh, no!" wailed the voice in Galado's head. "What have I done?"

Gorc appeared in the chamber, rubbing his head. "Sir? I heard -."

"Gorc!" boomed the warlock, "inform the commanders to move out!"

"Now?" asked Gorc.

"Now!" commanded the warlock.

Gorc cast a brief glance at Galado and then hastily departed, not wanting to know how Galado had appeared, or why.

Part IV

No Time Left To Lose

Chapter 33

The orcs drew warily nearer, surrounding Sherman and his companions.

A brief tremor shook the ground for several seconds and slowed their advance.

"Stand back, I say," said Sherman for the fifth time. He waved his sword menacingly.

"Put your weapon down and you will not get hurt," said one orc. "We won't kill you because the warlock may have some questions for you."

"We'll die first," snarled Sherman. He was stalling for time. Kazin had not regained consciousness yet and Amelia was still bending over his inert form.

"Just do as you're told," said the orc. "You're outnumbered. You stand no chance against us."

"I beg to differ," said a familiar voice.

The orcs turned as one to see who had spoken. Standing alone, wielding an ice axe, was a minotaur. He grinned at his audience.

"Whoever moves first gets an arrow in their skull," said another familiar voice from a spot several feet away. The speaker was concealed in the bushes.

"You're surrounded," said a third gruff voice from a different location. It was a dwarf with an ice axe.

"You guys are a sight for sore eyes!" cried Sherman in relief.

"You're never -," began the orc who had first spoken. He didn't finish his sentence as an arrow embedded itself in his skull. He fell to the ground with a thud.

"I warned you," said Olag.

After that an earthquake struck and a battle ensued. Several orcs at a time were frozen in place as Harran's ice axe waved past them.

They stood no chance on his back swing as the axe shattered them into thousands of tiny fragments.

Zylor was content with ignoring the freezing effect of his axe and slicing his enemies like kindling. He mowed them down with ease. Sherman's sword cut through the creatures like a hot knife through butter, felling everything in sight. Even Olag's arrows kept pace, downing one orc after the next.

Some lizardmages appeared and were preparing to cast spells but Olag's arrows made short work of them. One lizardmage succeeded in casting a fireball, but it went wide, landing on the ground beside Amelia.

"Oh, for crying out loud!" snapped the red-haired mage irritably. She stood up and faced the enemy. Raising her hands, she cast a spell and the trees around them reached out, grabbing the nearest orc or lizardmage with their branches and tangling them up. The more the enemy struggled, the tighter the branches and roots became. Within a few minutes there was not one enemy left standing. Those who were caught by the trees were crushed to death and then dropped to the ground.

Amelia wordlessly went back to tending to the mage.

Then the earthquake stopped.

Sherman heartily shook hands with the rest of the companions, embracing the dwarf and welcoming him back to their midst.

"It was quite the adventure," said Harran.

"We'll talk about it later," said Sherman. He went over to where Kazin lay and gently pulled Amelia aside. "We have to get out of here, Amelia. You can work on Kazin as we travel." Then he deftly picked up the much smaller mage and swung him over his shoulder. He nodded at Amelia. "Lead the way."

Amelia withdrew her orb and led the companions from the area.

"If you get tired, let me know," said Zylor to the big warrior.

Sherman looked over at the minotaur and smiled. "Not a chance."

The companions made good headway and did not encounter any more enemies. They traveled without incident, following Amelia's orb. As they went, Amelia healed a small cut Harran had sustained after the last fight and a gash that Zylor had received on his left arm. "You guys should tell me when you get hurt so I can heal you!" she warned.

"It might have happened before we joined up with you," said Harran.

"I didn't even notice my wound," said Zylor.

The mage just shook her head in exasperation.

Kazin was still unconscious and murmured from time to time. One word that came up often was 'Filbar'. They stopped once, at Amelia's urging, to consume some food, and then were on their way again.

"I guess it's only fair that we carry Kazin for a while," said Sherman. "He's carried us more than his fair share of the time."

"Speaking of which," said Zylor. He came over to take the mage from Sherman's shoulder. Sherman was relieved to have a break but said nothing, knowing that any indication of weakness on his part would make Zylor insist upon carrying Kazin the rest of the way himself.

Soon evening was approaching so they stopped for another break. The clouds were departing and the sky was beginning to clear. Zylor put Kazin down and Amelia immediately hovered over him. Sherman took the opportunity to fill the others in on their progress. He included the theory that their quarry was jumping from body to body because they were some sort of evil spirits.

Harran whistled. "They're going to be difficult to stop."

Sherman nodded. He talked about Kazin's theories and concluded with their journey and subsequent crash landing.

Harran was surprised they were so close to the enemy encampment. "Out of the frying pan into the fire."

Zylor chuckled. "Suits me fine! The more we do battle the more I feel like I'm useful. Besides, now that we're out of human territory, I can be myself again."

A moan could be heard as Kazin started to come to. Everyone hurried over to see how the mage was doing.

Kazin moaned again and opened his eyes. He blinked several times. "Either I'm dreaming or Harran has been found."

Sherman chuckled. "You're not dreaming. Harran's back, along with the others. They just saved your hide." He looked across at Amelia. "Your red-haired girlfriend did most of the work, though."

Kazin sat up groggily. "Well done, all of you."

"But you were dreaming about something too," said Amelia. "You were mumbling about 'Filbar'."

Kazin sighed. "I guess I ought to tell you about that."

"About what?" asked Amelia.

"Remember when we were camped prior to entering the human encampment and you and Sherman woke to an earthquake and I was gone?" asked Kazin.

"Yes," said Amelia.

"Well, I may have caused an unwanted change in history," said Kazin. "I heard a dragon's cry and went to investigate. I discovered a mage who had captured a dragon - a very young one. Well, it didn't bode well for the mage. He was killed by the dragon and the dragon stole the orb that contained its life force. Around that time, I was discovered, so the dragon became bold and attacked me."

"Oh, no," said Amelia. "Were you hurt?"

Kazin shook his head. "Not badly. It's just that when the dragon and I made contact, there was a loud explosion. There was no reason for it until I had a few seconds to think about it, thanks to the earthquake that happened then. Anyway, I acted on a hunch and asked the dragon if its name was Filbar. It was. The dragon was surprised by the fact that I knew its name and it flew away."

"I don't get it," said Amelia.

Kazin smiled wanly. "Filbar is the name of the dragon I defeated and obtained the orb from. That's how I became a dragon mage."

Amelia's eyes widened. "You mean - you encountered yourself?"

Kazin nodded. "The dragon part of myself, anyway. I was fearful that encounter may have altered history. But then I thought that if it had, I wouldn't have succeeded in taking the orb and becoming a dragon mage, and wouldn't be back here on this quest in the first place."

"I see," said Amelia. "I think."

"If that's true," argued Sherman, "the dragon that you became must have been many generations old. Even dragons couldn't live that long, could they?"

"I thought about that," said Kazin. "I thought about that for a long time. The only conclusion I could come to is that the dragon was able to live for so long because it had its life force contained within the orb. There is a great deal of magic contained within the orb. If the dragon was able to draw the power from the orb, it could potentially sustain itself for several lifetimes. You already know I will live a much longer life span because of the orb and its power. This would be no different."

"Then I guess you're a lot older than you look," said Olag.

Kazin laughed. "Trust me, I sometimes feel like that's true."

"You said the earthquake struck when you made contact with the dragon," said Harran. "Do you think the two are related?"

"I'm not sure," said Kazin. "Why do you ask?"

"Well," said Harran slowly, "when I got close to Ironfaust before he took command of the throne, I felt a tremor. I couldn't help thinking at the time that it was more than a coincidence. After all, my testimony before the king shouldn't have happened. My testimony may have been the catalyst that motivated Ironfaust to act when he did."

Kazin's eyes widened. "You spoke to King Hammarschist?"

Harran nodded. "Yes. Not by choice, mind you."

"What else did you do?" asked the mage.

Harran related the highlights of his adventure, ending with the war in the north and the earthquake that made fighting difficult for everyone.

"Well," said Kazin after Harran had finished. "I guess we're all interfering with history whether we like it or not. That could very well explain the earthquakes. Obviously, when any one of us does something significant, earthquakes are prevalent. It stands to reason. The earthquakes we experienced earlier on for no apparent reason may have been caused by our quarry as he interfered in history."

"That makes sense," said Sherman.

Kazin rubbed his head. "My head hurts".

"I know what you mean," said Sherman. "It's from all the thinking."

"Will you be alright?" asked Amelia. She gave the warrior a look.

"What?" said Sherman innocently.

"I think so," said Kazin. "I've never been hit with so much magic before." He looked around. "Where are we?"

"We're not far from the enemy encampment," said Amelia. "The orb is directing us there since that's where our quarry has gone."

"Good," said Kazin. He shakily got to his feet. "We'd better keep moving. I'll formulate a plan to get us into the encampment as we go."

"I can carry you," offered Sherman.

Kazin shook his head. "That will be unnecessary. My strength is returning rapidly. It feels like someone has used excessive healing magic on me." He looked at Amelia, who blushed.

"I didn't know if you were injured, so I applied healing magic on you just to be sure," she explained.

Kazin smiled. "Thanks." He slapped Zylor on the shoulder and shook hands with Harran and Olag. "It's good to have you back, my friends."

The companions continued their journey and came within sight of the enemy encampment within the hour. Darkness had set in and fires were lit with the scent of roasting meat in the air. The companions hunched down and Kazin briefed them on his plan. Zylor and Olag were to enter the camp as new recruits and were instructed to investigate the southern half of the encampment for any information or unusual activity. The rest of them were going to become orcs for the time being so they could spy on the northern portion of the camp while tracking their quarry using the orb. Zylor and Olag were to rendezvous with the rest of the group in a half hour using the rings Kazin had given them to bring them to the master ring he wore. They were given a head start so the whole group wouldn't arrive all at once.

The minotaur and skink warrior entered the encampment without any trouble despite the fact that Olag was an unusual creature they had never seen before. Offering to sign up, they were readily ushered in with directions to a recruiting tent.

They had no trouble finding the recruiting tent but did not stop there. They moved on and went past a number of orc tents. Some orcs looked up at them momentarily, but did not show any interest in the newcomers. A bit farther on they encountered a small group of minotaurs mixed in with the ogres. Being so far away from home, it wasn't a surprise there were so few of them in this army. Zylor guessed they were probably minotaurs who had been banished from the minotaur realm in disgrace for one reason or another.

One of the minotaurs was sitting on a log and looked up to see Zylor and Olag. He rose to his feet upon seeing a kinsman of his own race. Then he peered at Olag and exclaimed, "What is that?!"

"I am a skink warrior," said Olag, puffing out his chest. "I come from a land many days travel, west of here."

"I have been there," corroborated Zylor. "It is a savage race capable of inflicting considerable damage in a short time. I recommend you do not upset him. I know his kind. They do not take kindly to insults."

The minotaur laughed. "Surely you jest? Why, I could tear it apart with one hand behind my back!"

Zylor laughed. "You would have ten arrows in your body before you moved two steps if you tried that!"

The other minotaurs around the fire laughed, but the minotaur who was speaking was not impressed. "I think not!" he growled. "You toy with me!" He made a motion to come toward Olag and suddenly found an arrow embedded in his knee. Lurching wildly, he fell down with a yelp.

The other minotaurs stood up in alarm.

Zylor laughed as the first minotaur sat up, pulling the arrow from his knee. "I warned you but you didn't listen. This creature has proven his honour in battle. Otherwise, I would not be accompanying him. You obviously have much to learn, my brother in arms." He nodded at Olag and the two of them moved away. The minotaurs in the group glared at the strange newcomers with a combination of malevolence and respect. None of them wanted to challenge a minotaur who was larger than they, fearless in their presence, and more confident than their leader, who was nursing an injured knee.

"This isn't over!" called the injured minotaur.

Zylor didn't respond. His message had gotten across. Don't mess with him or his companion.

The two companions continued to watch and listen to happenings around them but learned nothing useful. The only thing that seemed a little strange was when a cyclops came trudging toward them. The creature moved as if in a hurry, panting as it went. It ambled right past them without acknowledging them. There was a distant look in its eye and both Zylor and Olag were thankful it didn't look them in the eye. They weren't prepared for its gaze and would surely have been paralyzed if it had.

"That's strange," commented Olag.

"Very," said Zylor. "Maybe we should follow it."

Olag agreed and they turned to pursue it at a safe distance. Before long, it met up with a creature that limped toward it out of the darkness.

"Is it you?" asked the cyclops.

"Yes," responded the limping creature. As it came into the torchlight, Zylor and Olag were shocked. It was the minotaur that Olag had shot!

"Couldn't you find a better host?" asked the cyclops.

"I didn't know until it was too late," said the minotaur. "But it doesn't matter. I can get another one soon enough." He turned and looked over to where Zylor and Olag stood watching. It was too late to duck out of sight, so the companions were shocked again when the minotaur gave no sign of recognition at seeing them.

As the cyclops and minotaur wandered out of sight, Olag muttered, "OK. If that doesn't qualify as something unusual, I don't know what does."

"That doesn't make sense!" exclaimed Zylor. "There's no way that minotaur could have ignored us like that! We weren't that far away that he couldn't recognize us - not after what you did to him! His damaged honour would be foremost on his mind!"

"You heard what the cyclops said about finding a host," said Olag. "Maybe one of the ones we're chasing stole the minotaur's body."

"That must be it," growled Zylor. "Let's see if we can catch up to them. They might lead us to the rest of their group."

Olag agreed. "But let's make sure we're not spotted this time."

"Agreed," said Zylor.

✘   ✘   ✘   ✘   ✘

Meanwhile, Harran was given the amulet so he could be turned into his orc form without Kazin having to maintain the spell. Then Kazin turned Sherman, Amelia and himself into orcs and they entered the encampment. No one at the entrance even looked at them twice, and the lizardmage in charge didn't think it was worthwhile to question a small group of orcs who had somehow found their way outside the perimeter.

No one paid any heed to the four orcs who wandered through the encampment.

"No one is paying any attention to us," observed Amelia.

"That's not surprising," said Kazin. "You've got to be one of the ugliest creatures I've ever seen."

Amelia glared at the orc next to her.

Sherman guffawed, spittle dripping from the place where his bottom orc teeth protruded. "Oh, I don't know. She looks like just your type!"

Kazin laughed, drool dripping from his own mouth. "You don't say!"

Finally, Amelia had to laugh as well. They all looked disgusting. "I guess I know how Zylor must have felt going around like a human all the time."

Harran shook his head, spittle splattering left and right. He growled. "Here we are, going into a hornet's nest of enemies, and you guys are busy admiring each other's appearance. No wonder no one is taking us seriously!"

Everyone laughed, drooling as they did. Looking at each other's ridiculous faces only made them laugh harder. They didn't stop until they noticed a few nearby lizardmen staring at them suspiciously. With some difficulty, their laughter subsided and they shambled their way deeper into the encampment.

"This army is much larger than the human one," commented Sherman. "I don't see how the humans can win this."

"I don't know," said Kazin. "History doesn't tell us who won. I don't think either side won, because the world somehow fell apart before the battle ended. There was a major disaster around the time of the war. The earthquakes we've been experiencing are only a foreshadow of things to come."

Before long, the companions discovered the yard where the dragons were being held. Numerous lizardmages surrounded the yard and no one was given admittance. Kazin sensed the magical warding and steered the others away so they would not set off any kind of magical alarm.

"That's not good," said Sherman. "If this army has dragons under their control, the human army won't have a chance."

"Those dragons looked kind of dazed," remarked Harran. "Do you suppose they're hypnotized or something?"

"They could very well be," said Kazin. "That's what it felt like when they brought me down. My mind was becoming very sleepy."

"They don't have very many dragons," said Amelia. "I only counted about ten or twelve."

"That's good," said Sherman. "The human army had about three times as many. Hopefully that can make up for the smaller army."

"Don't forget about the random factor," said Harran.

"Random factor?" asked the big warrior.

"The wild dragons," said Harran. "The wild dragons are drawn to magic. They were a problem for the dragons in the north who were battling the ogres. I suspect there will be many more of them involved in this battle with so many spell casters on either side. Don't expect the dragon riders to be as effective as you think. They'll have their hands full dealing with the aerial threat."

"This is going to be one heck of a battle," commented Sherman. "From what there was left of the history books, you'd never guess the size and scale of the dragon wars. It was obviously a lot bigger, and more devastating than I would have guessed."

"And we'll be right in the middle of it," said Kazin.

At that moment, an earthquake could be felt deep within the earth. Creatures everywhere scrambled to keep their balance. Tents collapsed. Occasional cries could be heard as minor injuries were sustained. Even the dragons shifted about nervously.

Kazin and his group moved out of the light to a shaded area away from any torches.

"What does your orb show?" asked Kazin, looking at Amelia.

Amelia opened a pouch at her side similar to what orcs often used. The orb was a bright red and it vibrated in her hands. She examined it quickly before replacing it back in the pouch and closing it up so as not to attract attention. She looked at Kazin with fear in her eyes. "That's it! History has been changed! Whatever we were supposed to stop has occurred! There is no way to change it! Whatever happens from here on has the capacity to affect the future!"

Kazin swore and looked around. They had been so close!

A horn sounded, followed by others. Creatures everywhere sprang into action. The order to move out was issued. Groups and battalions formed as they prepared to march. Commanders ran past and entered the dragon pen. They selected their dragons and mounted in preparation for take-off.

Creatures ran helter-skelter, going about their tasks and finding their battle groups. A weapons cart rolled by, with orcs handing out weapons to those who had none. Another horn sounded. A large figure appeared, wearing a shimmering metallic blue cape. He ran toward the dragon pens. As he got there, he barged through the lizardmages who guarded it. He flung them aside like toys if they got in his way.

Another rumble was felt. This time the ground seemed to shift. Very few of the creatures standing on the ground, including Kazin and his group, kept their balance this time. The stars above seemed to fly past with dizzying speed, while a sudden, deafening wind roared out of the east. A loud crack was heard, followed by a crunching noise that deafened the ear drums. Then the stars stopped moving very suddenly, as did the ground, throwing everyone to the ground again. The wind also disappeared.

As everyone regained their footing a second time, they were astounded by what they saw. Directly east of their location was the human army encampment! The entire terrain that had divided them had been swallowed up, and now they were face to face with their enemies! Only a band of loose gravel and mud separated them!

From his vantage point, Kazin could see that the human encampment was in a shambles, not being immune to the changes in the earth. The whole human army was struggling to get organized, especially in light of the fact that the enemy was suddenly right on their doorstep.

The warlock had finally mounted his dragon and rose into the air with a few of his fellow dragon riders in tow. They turned east to combat the human dragon riders who had already launched themselves into the air a few moments earlier.

Battalions of orcs and other creatures formed and began to march out toward the human encampment, while the human forces who had recovered first formed into tight ranks to meet this assault.

"Kazin, what do we do?" asked Amelia anxiously. The tide of creatures grew as they got organized and followed their comrades into battle. "According to the orb, the monsters will win this war and drive the humans from this land! The balance has been upset!"

By now the dragons in the pen and the lizardmages who guarded them had dispersed. Everyone was concentrating on the battle before them.

"Follow me," said Kazin. He led them into a nearby unoccupied tent that had withstood the earthquakes and wind. Once inside, he negated the spells on them and they resumed their normal appearance.

At that moment Zylor and Olag appeared among them.

"What did you find out?" asked Kazin.

"We found a couple of the evil spirits you told us about," said Zylor. He quickly related the mysterious actions of the minotaur and cyclops. They had followed them to a spot where a group of assorted creatures huddled around a human with a long black mustache. "He looked kind of familiar," said Zylor. "He was apparently giving them orders. We tried to get closer to see if we could listen in on their conversation. That's when the big earthquakes hit. After the earthquakes ended, we decided to check on the rest of you to make sure no one was in trouble."

"Can you lead us to them?" asked Kazin.

Zylor nodded. "I think so. They were headed in this direction when we left."

"Ok," said Kazin. "Our priority is to destroy them before they alter things any more than they already have. But first there is something I have to do." He led them to the entrance of the tent. Just inside, he stopped. Then he told them to stay back while he prepared to do a spell.

"What are you doing?" asked Amelia.

"You said history has been altered and the balance has been upset," said Kazin. "It that's true, then my actions won't make a difference, so I'm going to attempt to restore the balance so history can be restored. The time to intervene is now. We haven't got anything to lose." He braced his feet and jabbed the end of his staff into the ground. The orb atop the staff glowed with a brilliant white.

Unlike the other spells Kazin had been casting, this spell was far more complicated. He cleared his mind of everything around him. Then he drew from deep within himself and chanted the ancient words to the spell. His voice was low and almost inaudible, and rose in pitch and loudness as he chanted. As he finished the spell, he was almost yelling. At the conclusion, he let out his breath as though he had just lifted a very heavy object. The orb brightened and turned a bright yellow in colour. Rising from the orb was a wisp of white smoke. It gained intensity and became larger and flame orange in colour. It gradually coalesced into the shape of a face with eyes that were blinding to behold. A mouth formed and emitted a moan that sent chills through everyone's spine.

"Who summons me from my slumber?" it moaned.

"I do," said Kazin. "I am Arch Mage Kazin."

The face moaned again. "I do not know you. How did you learn the spell to summon me?"

"You gave it to me," said Kazin.

"Impossible!" moaned the voice. "I do not remember giving you that information."

"That's because you have given it to me in the future," said Kazin. "It was in exchange for our collaborated efforts. I am now in the past, so you won't know this yet."

The face shimmered for a while. Then it responded. "It is possible. You do not belong in this time. But you must prove your statement. You would have known my name."

"Your name in the future was Tyris," said Kazin. "I do not know what you call yourself now."

"You speak the truth," said the face. "That is one of my names. Tell me, why are you in this time in history?"

"I am here because history has been altered," said Kazin. "Someone has altered it and I need to correct things or history will be rewritten or possibly erased."

"That is a grievous crime!" exclaimed the face. "I will help you in this!" There was another pause. "It is not too late to correct things, Arch Mage Kazin, but we must act quickly." Suddenly the face grew into an entire body. It was the body of a woman, engulfed in flames. Her hair was long and flowing, and was extremely graceful in form.

Kazin was startled. He had expected a male, not a female.

Sherman gave a low whistle. "Not bad!" he whispered.

Tyris actually smiled at this comment. "A beautiful woman is often most dangerous, warrior." She turned to Kazin. "What must I do?"

Kazin pointed through the tent opening to where the first ranks of soldiers were already battling creatures. "For one, I need to even the odds. The creatures are too numerous for the humans to hold off for long."

Tyris nodded. "I can do this."

"I also have to find a way to fend off the threat of dragon flame," said Kazin, pointing to the dragons in the air. Already dragons had appeared and were engaged with dragon riders from both sides.

Tyris looked up. "Ah! Magnificent creatures! They are my favourite among those who roam the world!" She looked at Kazin. "These I will not destroy."

"Can you protect the humans on the ground from their flames?" asked Kazin.

Tyris nodded. "This I can do."

"Many thanks, Tyris," said Kazin, bowing.

Tyris moved a hand close to Kazin's cheek. The hand felt warm to the touch, and didn't burn as expected. "You are a handsome creature. You are new to this land. What do you call your race?"

"We are humans," said Kazin.

"Humans," repeated Tyris slowly. "I welcome our interaction in the centuries ahead."

"If history doesn't alter that," said Kazin.

Tyris withdrew her hand and her face darkened. "Not if I can help it." She examined Kazin's group. "Interesting companions you have," she commented. "Different races working together to a common goal. You humans have much to offer."

"We still have a long way to go," said Kazin.

"Then we should begin," said Tyris. She turned to face the battlefield. Then she changed form into a river of fire and rolled out of the tent in the direction of battle. As she caught up to the back of the monsters' army, she ejected hundreds of tiny fire elementals into their ranks, burning and causing chaos wherever they went.

"That's our Tyris!" said Kazin happily. "We may yet have a chance!"

"I don't like her," said Amelia. Kazin looked at her. "She seems - evil," said the red-haired mage.

Kazin realized Amelia was jealous so he touched her arm. "She's not nearly as pretty as you, Amelia. There's no replacement for real flesh and bones."

Amelia blushed.

"Enough of this mushiness!" growled Zylor. "We should go after those evil spirits."

"Good point," said Kazin. He transformed Harran into an orc and then did the same for Sherman, Amelia and himself. "Let's go!"

The companions exited the tent and watched a few straggling groups of orcs and cyclops wander past in the direction of the battle.

Zylor pointed. "There they are!"

Ahead of them was Galado and his entourage. They brought up the rear of the enemy forces. Galado strode confidently, leading his crew at a brisk pace.

As the companions neared, Sherman and Kazin stopped and looked at one another in astonishment.

"Galado?" they said simultaneously.

Chapter 34

"ow- how can that be?" asked Sherman. "How did Sir Galado get into the past? And why?"

"I don't know," said Kazin, "but obviously it was he who has changed history."

The companions confronted Galado's group and they stopped and faced one another. Some nearby torches flickered on the ominous faces of both parties.

"Get out there and attack!" commanded Galado to the approaching orcs, pointing to the battlefield.

"You won't get a chance to cause any more interference," said Kazin, slobbering down the side of his orc face.

Galado's eyes narrowed. "What do you mean?" he intoned. "Who gave you the authority to give orders?"

"What's wrong with you, Wilfred?" asked Sherman.

Galado looked at the orc who had just spoken. "What did you call me?"

"He's not in his right mind," said another orc. It was Amelia.

"Let's just kill them and be done with it," said an orc next to Galado.

"Well said!" exclaimed Zylor, fingering his axe. "The odds are in our favour!"

"Eleven against six?" asked Harran.

Zylor looked at the dwarf turned orc with a frown. "I know. That means one of us will only get to kill one of them."

"I'd say the odds are a little more substantial than that," said Olag. He pointed beyond them. A group of orcs a short distance away had witnessed the stand-off, and were watching the encounter with interest.

"That's more like it!" said Zylor, grinning.

"Enough of this!" snarled Galado. He pointed to the companions. "Get them!"

"Let's rumble!" growled Harran. He withdrew his ice axe and appeared as himself.

Kazin removed the spell on himself and the others and shot the nearest enemy orc with an ice bolt. The orc fell down, and then rose to its feet again, with a smoking hole through its chest.

At the same time, the two groups clashed as one.

Sherman tried to attack Galado, but one of his orcs intervened, so he had to battle the drooling creature first. He parried twice and then went on the offensive. The orc was no match for the seasoned warrior. One good thrust into the orc's chest was sufficient. Unable to escape the Sword of Dead, the evil spirit screamed as it was sent back to the place it had come from. Galado watched in fascination as his defender fell, never to rise again. His sword tingled in his hand and he looked down at it. He had come across someone with a spirit blade who was able to kill his followers.

Harran swung his ice axe and froze two enemies on the spot. Then he sliced the arm off another. Without stopping, the one-armed orc stepped forward and brought its remaining arm around the dwarf's neck. Harran struggled for a bit and almost lost his grip on his weapon when a lightning bolt from Kazin flew into the orc's shoulder, severing the arm from its body. Completely armless, the orc staggered back. Harran dislodged the arm from around his neck. Then, in a single smooth motion, he spun around and swung his axe clean through its neck. As the orc body fell to the ground, its head tumbling through the air, a wisp of white smoke emerged from the neck. It spiraled around, looking for a new body to inhabit. It didn't find one in time. A strange, ancient chant could be heard nearby. Hearing this, the evil spirit shrieked in agony and dispersed, sizzling as it was torn apart.

Kazin looked at Amelia in amazement. She had cast an 'eradication' spell and had succeeded in eradicating the evil spirit!

Meanwhile, Olag had fired arrows into the limping minotaur who opposed him, but the great beast wasn't even slowed down. The minotaur raised its axe to end the skink warrior's existence and brought it down with all its might. The axe would have succeeded if it wasn't for the intervention of another similarly sized axe coming out of nowhere to stop it. The axes clanged together loudly, loudly enough to be heard above the din of battle in the distance.

"You should pick on someone your own size," snarled Zylor. He gave a great shove to the opposing minotaur and sent him tumbling to the ground.

In the meantime, Olag was already in motion, his ears still ringing. The orcs who had been watching the exchange were now within striking distance and he was felling them rapidly with arrows. His job was made easier with the 'slow' spell Amelia had cast on them. They looked like they were trying to push against a heavy resistance, not unlike what Olag and Zylor had experienced when they had first encountered Amelia themselves.

Kazin was firing ice bolts into Galado's men but could only slow their advance, as they could not be killed.

Sherman pulled his sword free of the orc and turned to meet his next adversary. He didn't get far because he made the mistake of looking into its eye. Olag paused from his assault of the orcs behind them to fire an arrow into the cyclops' eye. The eye exploded in a spray of gore. With a howl, the cyclops staggered backwards, holding the place where its eye had been.

Harran used his axe to freeze a few more orcs who had come up from behind and then turned to attack the cyclops. He hacked through one of its arms and deep into its chest. The evil spirit within emerged, but was no match for Amelia's spell. It sizzled like the previous one and vanished. The cyclops fell to the ground, completely lifeless.

Kazin used a spell to remove the paralysis on Sherman, and the big warrior turned to look for Galado, who was retreating from the fight. He charged forward, slashing the two orcs Harran had frozen moments earlier. Two more evil spirits screamed into oblivion.

Zylor was having a tough time with the other minotaur. He had chopped a lizardmage in half on his way to finishing off the minotaur. He didn't notice the evil spirit depart the dead body of the lizardmage and fly into one of the orcs Olag had shot down earlier. The orc rose up and crept up to Zylor, who was concentrating on his other enemy.

Olag shot more arrows into the orcs but they had no effect. "Zylor, behind you!" cried the skink warrior.

Zylor turned just in time to give the orc a kick, sending it flying. Olag pounced on it and used his dagger to slit its throat. But the orc refused to give up. It tried to put its arm around Olag's neck. Olag managed to squirm free and kicked himself free of the green creature. At that instant, a spell from Kazin incinerated the orc's body. As the spirit rose from the charred corpse, Amelia did her magic and eradicated it like the others.

Zylor's opponent was by now so severely hacked up it was impossible for it to move around any longer. The evil spirit rose from the mangled minotaur body and surged toward the cyclops body, entering it instead. The cyclops clumsily staggered back to its feet. Harran swung his axe past the cyclops' body and froze it in place.

Kazin nodded at Amelia and she nodded back. Kazin cast a lightning bolt through the cyclops' body and Amelia waited for the spirit to emerge. As soon as it did, she cast her spell and eradicated it. The cyclops fell to the ground a second time and lay still.

By now the remaining orcs formerly under the 'slow' spell had come up behind the spell casters. With Amelia casting her 'eradication' spell, her 'slow' spell had been negated. Harran barged through their ranks, freezing them where they stood while Olag sat on the ground pelting them with arrows. Kazin and Amelia cast a 'shield' spell to surround themselves with an invisible barrier and used the reprieve to determine if there were any more evil spirits to eradicate.

Zylor assisted Harran with the remaining orcs, and that's when Kazin spotted the existence of another evil spirit. It was elusive, jumping from one orc body to the next. No sooner did it feel it was in danger before jumping into another body.

The orcs near the spell casters were dispatched, so Kazin and Amelia dropped the magical barrier. Then Kazin anticipated which body the spirit was going to take over next. Amelia nodded that she was ready for her spell.

"Cast your spell at the body over there," said Kazin, pointing to an orc killed by arrows. "I'm going to blast the body the spirit's using now so it will have to jump into that one. We have to catch it just right, before it enters that body."

"Got it," said Amelia.

As the orc moved closer to the orc body Kazin had indicated, Kazin blasted it with a bolt of lightning. Just before it struck, the evil spirit left its host and moved through the air toward the one Kazin had pointed out. At the same time, Amelia cast her spell. The timing was just right. With a scream and a sizzle, the spirit vanished.

Kazin looked over to where Sherman was battling with more of the evil spirits. He told Amelia to check the orb but it hadn't changed. It was still vibrating and glowing with a bright red light. She could not determine the outcome of Sherman's battle.

"Let's go and help him," said Kazin.

By now the last of the orcs were dispatched and the others were ready to follow.

Meanwhile, Sherman was very busy. He had caught up to Galado but had his last two guards to face. One was an ogre, and the other was a female human mercenary. Sweat trickled down the warrior's face as he battled the two opponents at once. The ogre was strong, and drove the big warrior back step by step with his giant club. The mercenary was agile, darting around the two combatants and jabbing her sword at Sherman with every opportunity. Already Sherman was bleeding from several places.

Finally Sherman seized an opening. He feinted toward the ogre, making it move to protect itself from Sherman's deadly sword. Then the warrior swiveled around the ogre, who was in the process of swinging his club. Ignoring the ogre, Sherman made a thrust at the mercenary. Instinctively, she jumped back out of the way, only to be hit with the ogre's club. This prevented her from dodging as Sherman's sword repeated the thrust, jamming deep into her chest. She let out a blood curdling scream as her spirit was removed from this plane of existence. Her body sagged slowly to the ground as Sherman felt the momentary pain of taking a woman's life.

By now, the ogre had recovered from this trick and swung at Sherman's exposed side. The sharp spikes from the ogre's club bit into the warrior's flesh and he went down with a grunt. Then the ogre raised its club to finish the job, but Sherman had the presence of mind to raise his sword. At the last possible second, he rolled out of the way just as the ogre's club crashed down. The lack of an object to strike caused the ogre to overextend itself, and it fell headlong onto Sherman's upturned sword. It convulsed as the evil spirit within was removed from existence. Then it lay still.

Sherman rolled back to retrieve his sword and gingerly rose to his feet. His side was sore and soaked in blood but he ignored it. There was one more battle to fight.

Standing there facing him was Galado.

"You have done well," snarled Galado, "but you will now die. You are in no condition to defeat me." He twirled his sword deftly, showing his expertise with a sword was no joke. Sherman noted that the sword he held was identical to his own. The swords in both men's hands vibrated with magic.

"Why are you doing this?" asked Sherman.

Galado laughed. "You cannot understand, mortal."

"How did you obtain Galado's body?" asked Sherman.

"Are you referring to this body?" asked Galado, indicating himself.

"Yes," said Sherman.

"He was in a place where he did not belong," said Galado. "I simply used his body to prevent my own untimely demise." Galado's face darkened. "It didn't work out as planned." Then his face brightened. "But things are generally happening as I had hoped. The human race will be wiped off the face of this continent!"

"I think you'll be disappointed," said Sherman. "There are things happening that you hadn't counted on."

Galado laughed. "Even you and your friends will not stop what is happening right now!"

Sherman looked to see his companions running up to where they were. Amelia stood out with her glowing orb in her hand.

That momentary glimpse gave Galado the opening that he needed. He brought his sword down on Sherman, who parried at the last instant.

The clang of the two swords pierced the entire region. The magic of the two swords, which shouldn't have been in the same place at the same time, collided. The magical connection of the spirit blades was so powerful it was felt far and wide. Spell casters everywhere lost their concentration. The spells they were casting malfunctioned, with erroneous effects. All low level magic was momentarily disrupted. Only stronger magic was still working.

The colliding of the swords caused the dragons to go into a frenzy. More dragons appeared, drawn to this mysterious event.

An earthquake occurred, creating mountains where there were previously none, and valleys and lakes were formed in places where they previously weren't. The wasteland east of the human realm suddenly rose up out of the ground. It rose to majestic heights, killing a vast army of approaching minotaurs in the process. Those minotaurs would not have the opportunity to reach the battlefield. Other areas of the world changed as well. Some entire continents sank beneath the sea, while other tracts of land broke to the surface. Massive tidal waves were created, their force building up to wash over other continents. This force of water would wreak its havoc on the world for days to come.

For long seconds, the two swords were fused together by their magic. The two combatants glowed with the aura of two brilliant suns. Then they were thrown apart and the clash of the magic was severed.

At the same time, the orb Amelia had used so faithfully suddenly reached its climax. It engulfed the mage's body with a brilliant red hue and flooded the entire battlefield in the distance with red light. When it receded, the mage was lying on the ground, motionless.

"Amelia!" cried Kazin, who had lowered his arm after shielding his eyes from the bright light. He ran to the dormant mage and shook her wildly. "Amelia! Wake up!" There was no response. Tears welled up in his eyes as he looked at the beautiful mage who had helped them so much on this quest. He had always feared he would lose one of his companions, but he knew they knew the risks. Amelia was different. She was a new member of their group and probably didn't have a full understanding of the danger they were in. In addition, he had grown attached to her more closely than he had expected. "I didn't know!" he wailed. "If I had known this was going to happen, I would have done it differently! I - I wouldn't have even attempted it! History be damned!" Still crying, he bent to kiss her on the lips. He felt a hand rest on his shoulder to pull him away from the red-haired mage.

"She was a good person," said Harran gently. "She was an honourable soul."

As another tear fell from Kazin's cheek, it landed on Amelia's lips. There was an imperceptible twitch that Kazin missed. He was about to stand up, when the blue-cloaked mage opened her eyes. But instead of blue, the eyes were bright fluorescent orbs of red. The red hue slowly faded, however, to give way to the blue pearls Kazin had been so fond of.

Amelia smiled. "What's wrong? You look as if you've seen a ghost!"

Kazin cried out jubilantly and held Amelia close to hide his tears of joy. "You're alive!"

Amelia returned the embrace and waited for Kazin to regain his composure.

Meanwhile, Sherman was slow getting to his feet. Galado was no quicker, having been stunned as well. The swords both lay on the ground nearby. As they both stood up, Galado charged the big warrior, knocking him over. A fist fight ensued, as both big men fought to incapacitate the other in order to get to the swords first. Sherman was the stronger of the two, but his wound was giving him trouble, so Galado pummeled him in the side. Sherman collapsed in pain and Galado made a break for his sword. He didn't reach it as an arrow from Olag pierced his leg. He went flying and landed with his hand just out of reach of the swords. Crawling forward, he just about managed to get a grip on one of them when Sherman pounced on him. The two men grunted as they rolled on the ground.

"Can't you do something?" asked Olag. He was unable to get a shot away with the men so close together.

"That would be dishonourable," said Zylor. "This is Sherman's fight. I will not take that from him."

"What about our guests?" said Harran as he came up to them.

Zylor looked where the dwarf pointed. He readied his weapon. "That is where I come in," he said. The commotion that Sherman and the orb had created had drawn the interest of a group of orcs. They were approaching in the hopes of a fight.

Olag had already started firing arrows into them. "I'm sure glad I have unlimited arrows. But my arms are beginning to ache."

Galado laughed as he was on top of Sherman. "I'm free at last! I am no longer bound to this body. It was that damned sword all along!"

The combatants rolled a few more times and Sherman managed to get a foot in between them. Then he shoved Galado aside with a kick that made his side scream in agony. Oblivious to the pain, Sherman took his sword from the ground and lunged at Galado as he was getting up. Seeing the warrior lunging toward him, Galado's evil spirit exited the body just in time. The sword pierced Galado's chest, and he grabbed hold of Sherman's shoulders. The fierce expression softened as Sir Galado once again got hold of his original body. With the evil spirit gone, he had full control of himself again.

"Sherman!" he rasped. "Forgive me!"

Sherman saw the recognition in Galado's face and held onto him. "It's not your fault, Wilfred. You were possessed!"

Galado shook his head. "I stopped him, Sherman. But in so doing, a spirit far more powerful has taken the warlock's body! You must stop it. It will destroy us all!" Sir Galado gurgled and blood appeared at the corners of his mouth. "I - I have caused all this trouble just to give you the sword. You forgot -," his voice faded and Sherman gently laid the soldier down.

"You did what you thought was right, my friend. It was I who forgot the sword. It was me who caused all this to happen."

Sir Galado raised a hand to touch Sherman's face. "Stop the warlock. Then all will not be in vain." He coughed once and his hand fell to his side. His eyes glazed over and he breathed his last.

Sherman closed Sir Galado's eyes and then closed his own to hide the pain. "I will stop the warlock, my friend. You can count in it."

No one noticed as the evil spirit who once controlled Sir Galado moved over to the ogre on the ground nearby. With unusual stealth for such a large creature, the ogre rose and drifted off into the night. The rest of the companions had been too busy fighting the orcs who had come upon them. They were just finished dealing with that threat when Amelia spotted Sherman's wound.

"Sherman!" she cried, running over to him. She only spared Galado a brief glance before tending to his wound. She immediately applied a salve and chanted healing spells. Then she wrapped the wound in some cloth from the clothing of the sword-woman Sherman had killed earlier.

"Now what?" asked Harran as he wiped the gore from the orcs off his axe with more cloth from the sword-woman.

"We should give Galado a decent burial," said Sherman. "He was a good man."

"With all the problems he caused?" asked Olag.

Sherman glared at him. "You mean the evil spirit who controlled him."

"Is the evil spirit dead?" asked Harran.

"I'm not sure," said Sherman. "It might have left Sir Galado's body before I killed him. The sword didn't react like it did with the others."

"The ogre is gone," said Harran, looking around.

"Then the quest is not finished," said Zylor. "That spirit must be slain."

"The spirit is still out there," confirmed Amelia.

"How do you know this?" asked Olag. "You didn't consult your orb."

"The orb is gone," said Kazin.

Amelia nodded. "In a manner of speaking. When the two spirit blades clashed, the orb exploded. Now it seems the orb lives within me. I can see what it shows me. I can see bits and pieces of the future. It seems we can correct the future if we act quickly. There is still time."

"Then we will continue until the threats to history are eliminated," said Kazin. "But first I'll see to it Galado's body is not disturbed." He chanted a spell and Tyris appeared within his orb. "Tyris, I need you to guard Galado's body. Can you do that?"

"Of course," said Tyris. "I will send some of my fiery minions to do the job. They will be there momentarily."

"Thanks," said Kazin. He looked at the others. "We'll begin our search for the evil spirit once Tyris' friends get here."

"No," said Sherman. "The evil spirit can wait. We must stop the warlock."

"Is that part of the mission?" asked Olag.

"It is," answered Sherman. "Sir Galado told me before he died that an even bigger evil spirit controls the warlock."

"Sherman's right," said Amelia. "The warlock should be dead now. Every minute he lives he has the power to change history even more."

Zylor regarded the transformed red-haired mage suspiciously. "Then we will have to destroy the warlock."

Amelia smiled at the minotaur. "Zylor, in order to make things right in the future, we will need to split up once again. Because Sherman is in no condition to travel on foot right now, he can ride on Kazin with me. After Tyris sends her flame creatures here to guard Galado, you will need to lead a group to track Galado's former evil spirit into the battlefield. Because you are a minotaur, you will not be hindered by the orcs. But be aware - the evil spirit will not hesitate to control numerous different bodies as it goes."

"How will we find it?" asked the minotaur. "We no longer have your orb as a guide."

Amelia pointed to Galado's sword. "The spirit blade the evil spirit has been using will sense its presence. The spirit was bound to it since it came from the time travel place. That same blade will seek to send the evil spirit back to where it came from."

"Why couldn't my spirit blade do that?" asked Sherman. "It's the same blade."

"Your blade was newly created," said Amelia. "It hasn't encountered the evil spirit yet. It won't for generations to come."

Zylor picked up Galado's spirit blade and held it aloft. Sure enough, it had a slight blue shimmer to it. The glow deepened when Zylor pointed it a certain way. "It's brighter in this direction," he said.

"That's where to begin your search," said Amelia.

"How did you know that?" asked Harran.

"I see how things are going to happen," said the mage. "Some things, anyway."

"This should definitely make the job easier," said Zylor.

"I'll go with you," offered Harran.

"It might be easier if you used the invisibility ring," suggested Kazin. "You'll find it easier to pass through the enemy ranks if they don't see a dwarf wandering around."

Zylor passed the ring to Harran.

"I get to play with this for once!" said the dwarf happily. He slipped the ring onto his finger and disappeared. "Interesting!"

Zylor turned to Olag. "Coming?"

Olag was taken aback. "You want me along?"

Zylor grinned. "Sure! I could use a good back up on this job."

"Uh, OK," said Olag. He looked a bit embarrassed.

Tyris' flame creatures were seen running in their direction, burning some orcs in the process.

"That settles it!" said Kazin. He transformed himself into a dragon and Sherman and Amelia climbed onto his back. "Good luck!" called the dragon as he lifted off.

Chapter 35

he warlock took delight in the wind as it whistled past his ears. Below, the battle had commenced in full force. Though it was still dark, he could see torches and fireballs on both sides and could tell that his forces were more numerous and in a good position to win the war.

In the air, he could see dragon fire and other magical exchanges as the human dragon riders battled his own forces, and the wild dragons attacked any dragons with riders, regardless of which side they belonged to. Without their own dragon riders, these wild dragons were driven back by the dragon riders who used magic in conjunction with the flames of their dragons. As wild dragons spewed fire on the forces battling below, the warlock noticed how the little fire creatures worked. As the dragon flames reached the ground, the fire creatures absorbed the dragon flames and grew in size. As they did this, the humans who were nearby did not feel the effects of the dragon flames. All of the energy was simply being absorbed by the fire creatures. Every dragon attack made the fire creatures bigger and stronger and capable of protecting more people each time. But even this was not likely to stem the tide of monsters that threatened the meager human forces.

Curious to see other facets of the battle, the warlock used the darkness to steer his mount south to see how things were faring on that side. He flew over and noticed a small, scattered guard of humans on that side of the encampment. Most of them had obviously been called to the main battle to engage the enemy there. Some of the sentries were pointing south and the warlock peered ahead to see the torchlight of an approaching army. As he neared, he could see it was his diversion army in conjunction with a sizeable army of trolls. Saliss had come through! He had roused the trolls and was marching on the human army as instructed. The size of his army would easily overrun the southern sentries in the human encampment. This was too good to be true! The warlock laughed in glee. The war was his! There was no way the humans could counter that, even with superior dragon power. He glided low to his reinforcements and saluted Saliss. The lizardmage commander spotted him and waved back, not knowing that his boss had changed - not in body but in spirit. But the spirit who now controlled the warlock was far more powerful than an ordinary spirit. It knew the warlock's thoughts; it knew his desires and plans; and it could cast magic that was for more powerful than the puny humans he now fought.

Suddenly a wild dragon came shrieking out of the sky above him. Too late to dodge out of the way, the warlock created a magical shield and waited for the wild dragon to spew its fire. As expected, the dragon tried to roast the dragon with its flame. Only it failed to do any damage to the rider or his mount. Veering away, it shrieked in dismay.

Now it was the warlock's turn. He steered his mount to pursue the wild dragon. He commanded the dragon to increase its speed to maximum. The dragon complied and gained on the wild dragon. When he was close enough, the warlock commanded his dragon to fire its flame. But the wild dragon veered to the side and easily avoided the blast of flames.

Still pursuing, the warlock gained on the wild dragon again and commanded his dragon to fire again. As he anticipated, the wild dragon veered to one side to escape the flames. That's when the warlock cast his own fireball - which was almost as powerful as his dragon's fiery breath. Not expecting this tactic, the wild dragon did not move out of the way in time. The warlock's fire engulfed the back of its body.

Shrieking in agony, the wild dragon plummeted to the ground. The warlock howled in delight.

But his joy soon turned to dismay as the burning dragon crashed headlong into the middle of the warlock's army of reinforcements. The burning dragon obliterated a large swath of trolls, as well as some orcs and lizardmages. "No!" shrieked the warlock. He swore and pounded his fist into his dragon's neck hard enough for it to notice and look back at him in fear.

As he flew, the warlock spotted some smaller aerial creatures in the south who approached in a wide formation. As he neared, he could see they were too small to be dragons. What they lacked in size, they made up for in numbers. Before long, he saw that these creatures were pegasi, and they were being ridden by elves.

The warlock frowned. Where had they come from? How many were there? Without coming up with an answer, the time came to engage them in combat. Bracing himself and shielding all but the front of his dragon, the warlock commanded it to fry everything in sight. The dragon flames were devastating. A dozen pegasus elf riders went down in the first blast. Laughing again, the warlock lowered his shield so he could blast the enemy with lightning bolts. Elves and pegasi went down in droves.

The elves could not get close enough or go fast enough to get a shot in at this combination of destruction.

The warlock was so engrossed in his destruction of the pegasus elf riders he wasn't ready as an ice bolt struck his dragon's tail. With a shriek, his dragon rolled sideways to evade this new attacker. The warlock turned to see a white ice dragon on his tail ridden by a female human mage.

Reacting quickly, the warlock urged his mount to do a sharp turn while setting up his shield once more. Then he maneuvered so that he had a good view of his adversary. He waited for the white dragon to blast at him with another ice bolt. This time the icy breath was deflected aside. The warlock canceled his shield long enough to blast the white dragon with a lightning bolt. But his bolt was deflected aside by a magical shield that the human spell caster had in place. She had used the same tactic he had.

The two dragons passed one another and the human spell caster looked like she was about to cast a spell of her own, but she held off as a swarm of wild dragons flew into the fray. Both combatants were drawn apart as they contended with this new threat. The warlock contended frantically with three dragons; one red dragon and two green ones, while the white one had to deal with two black ones.

The warlock used a combination of magic and dragon flame to ward off his opponents and then looked around for the white dragon, but it was lost in the darkness. With that threat momentarily neutralized, the warlock prepared to go after the pegasus elf riders again. But a sudden blast of lightning struck his dragon's belly and the warlock noticed too late a new foe appearing from below him. Manifesting itself out of the gloom was a large bronze dragon ridden by a mage with a pointed hat kinked near the top. Another lightning bolt was unleashed by the mage, but the warlock raised a shield just in time. The bolt was deflected aside.

At the same instant the warlock's shield had been canceled by a 'silence' spell cast by the human mage. The reason for this became clear when the mage and his dragon did not slow down and charged right into him. Both riders were jolted as the dragons struck. The dragons began tangling face to face and clawed and bit at one another viciously. Both spell casters could not cast any spells in this position and the warlock suddenly realized that this was the human mage's tactic all along. With magic neutralized, it was up to the dragons to determine the winner of this fight. The bronze dragon was bigger and stronger, but the warlock's dragon held its own. The only problem now was since neither dragon was flying, they both began to fall while embraced in this epic struggle.

Finally instinct told the dragons to part and both of them frantically flapped their wings to gain altitude. Had they fought only a few seconds longer, they would have both crashed into the ground.

The warlock tried to get his mount to pursue the human mage, but his dragon was too intent on gaining altitude first. As it happened, one of the warlock's lizardmage commanders had seen his predicament and had moved in to tangle with the clever human mage and his dragon. How the human mage didn't lose his hat during the entire altercation was a mystery.

With that threat being dealt with, the warlock looked up to see a large number of wild dragons coming in his direction. They were drawn to his magic, which was more powerful than anyone on the battlefield. In hindsight, the warlock realized he had brought this on himself. His magic had done this. Well, he thought, it couldn't be helped now. He needed his magic to drive the dragons away. Now that he was far enough away from the human mage with the pointed hat, his magic should work again.

He didn't notice the battalions of sword wielding elves and centaurs who marched into the fray below him. They had been successful in their southern battle against the trolls more quickly than anticipated because the trolls had split up on two fronts to fight both the elves and humans. This was thanks to the warlock's desire to have the trolls involved in his war with the humans. This evidently resulted in the trolls' ranks being thinned sufficiently to allow the elven forces an easy victory. Now the brunt of the elven forces headed north to eliminate the other half of the troll army. Because the earthquakes were somewhat less noticeable in the south, they had made good time. But soon they would see more battle than they expected when they saw the massive army of monsters.

✗   ✗   ✗   ✗   ✗

Kazin moved to a comfortable altitude and glanced back at Amelia. "Which way do we go?"

"Just keep going straight ahead, Kazin. You'll probably spot him before I do."

Kazin was suddenly jarred sharply from below. "Ooof!" He felt a shock at the contact.

"What happened?" asked Amelia in concern.

Kazin was jarred again and he twisted to see what had hit him. He only caught a glimpse of a tail. "A dragon is attacking me but I can't see him!"

Then something collided with Kazin's right wing. Another spark lit up the area of contact. "Hey!" he cried. A small dragon was seen retreating out of range.

This time Kazin braced himself and waited, all of his senses on alert. Then he saw it swooping in on his tail. Kazin twisted to get a claw in front of him and he successfully scratched at the wild dragon as it tried to snap at his tail.

"Ow!" cried Kazin as the dragon made contact. He felt a piercing pain in his skull but shook it off. Then the wild dragon swerved and zoomed in with its claw extended. With incredible speed, it raked the claw across Kazin's wing. The electric jolt caused both dragons to twitch away in pain.

"What's going on?" shouted Sherman. "I can barely see the dragon!"

"It's tiny!" yelled Amelia. "Should I put up a shield?"

Kazin tried to increase his speed, but the little dragon outran him. It tried to claw Kazin's tail, but the moment it got close there was another electrical shock bigger than the last time.

"Ouch!" cried Kazin. The small dragon also shrieked and backed off a bit.

"What's going on?" asked Amelia.

Kazin suddenly groaned as he realized what was happening. "Oh, no! Not again!"

"What is it?" asked Sherman.

"It's Filbar," said Kazin. "This isn't good."

"Filbar?" asked Amelia. "You mean -," she looked behind her but couldn't see anything in the darkness. "Oh, no," she repeated.

"What do we do?" asked Sherman.

"I'm not sure," said Kazin. Out of the corner of his eye he saw the dragon approaching from the left. He turned so his back was to the beast. "Use magic to slow him down!"

Amelia rattled off a spell and completed it slightly before the little dragon was about to collide with them. Sherman raised his sword because he had an opening in which to strike. He was about to drive his sword into the dragon's knee when he recalled Kazin's limp. As far as Kazin was concerned, he had always had a limp. But Sherman knew Kazin had never had a limp until this quest had started. He knew whatever had altered the past had caused his limp. Was it his sword? Was it the Sword of Dead that caused Filbar to have a permanent limp, only to be transferred to Kazin later on? Most injuries could be healed, but damage done by his sword would probably never heal. To strike now would have repercussions in the future.

The hesitation Sherman experienced proved to have unexpected results. Filbar, although slowed by magic, still had enough momentum to collide with Kazin. Another electric spark emanated from the contact point of the two dragons and the ground below shuddered with the impact. With Kazin sideways, Sherman lost his hold and fell off. He plunged downward with Amelia's screams in his ears.

"Get lost, Filbar!" shouted Kazin angrily, batting the little dragon away with his wing. The spark from that motion made Filbar pause in his assault. Kazin took the opportunity to dive downward to try to catch his friend before he hit the ground.

"What?!" cried Filbar. "I know that voice!" He tried to follow Kazin down but his body was still affected by Amelia's 'slow' spell.

"Just take your orb and get lost!" yelled Kazin. "If you don't leave us alone, I'll steal that orb from you right now!"

Filbar shrieked. "No! You can't have my orb! I'll hide it! I'll never let you have it!" He turned and fled, but only as fast as an ordinary dragon, because he was still under a 'slow' spell.

Meanwhile, Kazin gained on his friend and caught him out of the air with his right claw. He curved his claw around Sherman's body as gently as he could, considering the warrior's wound, but even then Sherman cried out in pain.

"Sorry!" cried Kazin. He flew to a spot away from the battle and put the warrior down as gently as he could.

Amelia hopped off and immediately used magic to take away Sherman's pain while redressing the wound. The repair was done quickly, and the companions climbed back on Kazin's back. Kazin made a mental note to keep Sherman from fighting too much while they were up in the air.

"Let's try again," said Kazin. He leapt into the air.

They had hardly gone very far when a handful of wild dragons surrounded them. Kazin shielded himself and left an opening for Amelia to cast some spells at one of the dragons. Her slow spell sent one of their opponents spiraling away to safety. A second dragon attacked Kazin with its claws extended but struck the invisible shield and bounced away. It was a large black dragon, larger than Kazin, and it shrieked in anger as it was foiled in its attempt to do damage close up. A third dragon, a green one, bounced off Kazin's other side and flapped its wings to pursue him further. The black dragon belched flames at Kazin but the flames merely bounced harmlessly off the shield. The black dragon shrieked again and swerved away to rethink its attack. Meanwhile, Kazin made a swift move to give Amelia an opening to cast another spell. She waited until the right moment and cast some sort of distortion spell at the green dragon. It reeled and flew off in a daze.

"What kind of spell was that?" asked Kazin.

"I learned it from the ancient spell book," said Amelia. "It's a spell that makes the recipient feel woozy, like they're experiencing many different emotions all at once. It has the effect of distorting their thoughts."

"Impressive!"

"Um, Kazin," said Sherman suddenly.

A jolt brought Kazin back to his senses. The black dragon was trying to attack at close range again.

Kazin swerved, dove, rose, zigzagged, and did all sorts of maneuvers to try to give Amelia an opening, but the black dragon was onto him. It stayed in a position that made it difficult for Kazin to gain an upper hand. At one point Kazin was able to raise the shield enough for Sherman to slash at it with his sword. The sword struck the creature's front leg and sliced it open. The black dragon shrieked and veered away, but now it was very angry. It turned back to its nemesis and fought more ferociously than ever, blasting Kazin with flames and clawing at his shield mercilessly. It even used a ramming technique to try to dislodge Kazin's riders. Remembering what had happened to Sherman earlier, Kazin was becoming angry himself. Whenever he had a chance to belch his flames at the opposing dragon, he was risking the same thing in return. The black dragon knew this and made sure it was facing Kazin during these moments. It obviously had experience in this sort of conflict.

Neither dragon could get the upper hand. This giant black dragon was getting on Kazin's nerves. It was wounded and enraged, and would not let him be. Kazin could not proceed with their mission with the dragon pestering him like this. The last pass when the black dragon clawed at his side was the last straw. Until now, when Kazin had been a dragon, he had always been in control of his emotions. But this time the bloodlust these creatures often experienced seeped into his veins. Without knowing the full consequences of his emotions, Kazin opened his mind to the experience. He immediately understood what Zylor went through whenever he allowed his bloodlust to take over.

"Hold on tight!" commanded Kazin to his passengers. His voice was felt rumbling within his body more than heard above the noise of battle around them. Sherman and Amelia did as instructed, sensing that Kazin was about to do something different.

The black dragon had maneuvered behind them again and was about to let loose with another blast of flame. As it spewed its fire, Kazin dove to the side so swiftly his passengers had to hold on for dear life. The flames missed them by mere inches. Kazin continued to do several more tight maneuvers and succeeded in throwing off the pursuit of the black dragon.

It took a few moments for the black dragon to relocate them, and once it spotted them, it swerved to resume its attack as Kazin had predicted. Amelia half rose to cast a spell but Kazin rumbled, "Stay down!" His voice was firm and uncompromising, so Amelia hunkered down again.

The two dragons circled to head straight for each other. By now the blood lust was surging through every pore in Kazin's body. There would be no backing down this time. Closer and closer the dragons got, neither willing to give way. Kazin's body tensed the nearer they got. Knowing Kazin had an opening in his shield directly in front of him, the black dragon let loose with a blast of fire that was sure to burn his enemy. But Kazin did not veer away. At the last possible second, just before the flame was about to engulf him, he let loose with what could only be described as a lightning bolt of epic proportions. The bolt was a bluish white in colour and was so hot it burned through the other dragon's flames. Sherman and Amelia had to squeeze their eyes shut so as not to be blinded. The lightning bolt burned up the black dragon's flames so they were consumed before they hit Kazin and his riders. The bolt did not stop, however. It continued straight into the open maw of the black dragon, sizzling right through its mouth, neck, body, and then out through its tail, leaving a gaping hole. Kazin did not stop spewing the bolt. It still emitted from his mouth like a sword that grew and grew. He would have collided with the black dragon, but the bolt that tore through its body was now so hot that it blew the black dragon into thousands of tiny fragments just before impact.

The explosion of the big black dragon was so deafening and blinding that all combatants on the battlefield and in the air took note of the incident. Even the dragons were startled by this incredible sight.

Kazin emerged from the glowing dragon fragments and swerved around. A green dragon ridden by a lizardmage turned to engage Kazin, the lizardmage thinking his energy had been expended. Unfortunately, the green dragon didn't have time to let loose with a flame. Kazin blasted another lightning bolt at it. The bolt tore right through the green dragon's neck, severing its head from its body. The lizardmage grabbed uselessly at the dragon's body as it plunged downward like a rock. Cries of pain and fear were drowned out by the sound of the impacts as the great beast crashed down into a large contingent of orcs, its head doing as much damage as its body.

Kazin didn't stop. He turned to engage a nearby red dragon, but it had seen enough. It veered off and did some swift maneuvers to get away from this fearsome dragon.

Seeing dragons veering away from him in fear, Kazin started to cool down, purging the blood lust from his veins and letting the night air cool his body. He now concentrated on finding the warlock and his dragon, knowing most of the other dragons would leave him alone for now.

Chapter 36

"He's right there," said Amelia, pointing. "Straight ahead."

"I see him," said Kazin. The warlock was casting his magic at some nearby wild dragons. His spells varied each time, and sent the wild dragons screaming away in pain. Some dragons were set aflame, others were damaged by ice bolts, and others were magically disabled so they fell to the ground like stones. Without the magical protection of a dragon rider, they were no match for the warlock.

Kazin growled as another wild dragon crashed into the ground below. This warlock was deliberately targeting wild dragons in order to destroy them. Many of them tried to retreat from him, but he pursued them mercilessly until they were injured or destroyed.

If the big black dragon hadn't been such a threat to Kazin or his riders, he would have been content with just scaring it off. Most wild dragons were smart enough to preserve themselves if they encountered a more powerful foe. The black dragon Kazin had faced must have been a dominant one that didn't deal well with defeat.

A sudden blast of flame struck Kazin's left side, but his magical shield held firm and deflected the flames away. A lizardmage had seen him aiming for his leader and was attempting to draw him away.

Kazin swerved to intercept, but the lizardmage turned to flee instead of facing this fearsome dragon. But as Kazin turned back toward the warlock, the lizardmage turned back as well, sending more flames their way.

"He's playing games," commented Sherman, looking back when the flames had dispersed.

"We'll have to take him out," said Kazin. He turned to pursue the lizardmage again.

Then out of nowhere a wide shower of ice bolts fell from the sky. A white dragon zoomed into sight with a female mage on its back. She waved at them while pursuing the lizardmage along with Kazin.

"Hello!" she called over to Amelia and Sherman.

"Hi!" said Sherman. He was taken by the girl's beauty. "You're awfully young for a mage!"

"What's so awful about it?" asked the mage.

"Not a thing," called Sherman.

The white dragon suddenly surged ahead to blast at the retreating lizardmage. "You go after the warlock!" called the mage before she was out of earshot. "I've got this one!" Her dragon belched more of its ice breath at the lizardmage.

The lizardmage was not to be caught, and veered to the side to avoid the blast of ice bolts. Without warning, a sizeable fireball came from below and struck the lizardmage's dragon squarely in the abdomen. With a shriek, the dragon plummeted downward. The white dragon pursued, joined by another dragon ridden by a young mage who smiled at the female on the white dragon.

"It looks like you're too late for that one," said Amelia to Sherman. "She's already taken."

"A few centuries too late," said Sherman. He shook his head sadly. "I could have had fun in this century."

Suddenly Amelia laughed.

"What?" asked Sherman.

"Oh, it's nothing," said Amelia. "I just got a glimpse of the future of those two young dragon riders. Apparently they're Kazin's ancestors."

Kazin looked back at Amelia in surprise.

"They must have survived the dragon wars then," said Sherman happily.

Kazin didn't say anything. Instead, he resumed his pursuit of the warlock, who was now tangling with a group of much smaller opponents. Pegasi were fleeing the warlock's wrath in every direction, with their riders hanging on for dear life.

"That's not fair!" cried Amelia.

"Let's teach him to pick on someone his own size!" snarled Kazin. His bloodlust was beginning to take hold again.

The warlock spotted Kazin well before the companions were within range. He turned his dragon to meet this new adversary.

"Be careful!" admonished Amelia. "He's got strong magic!"

"Get ready to cast your 'nullify magic' spell," said Kazin. "That should even the odds."

"But we'll be exposed to dragon flame!" objected Amelia.

"You're right," said Kazin with a rumble. "I don't want you two to get hurt. Very well. Amelia, you cast whatever defensive spells you need to, and I'll try to get us close enough for Sherman to slash at the warlock or his dragon with his sword."

"He'll likely have a magical shield," said Amelia.

"We'll have to find a way to breach it," said Kazin.

There was no more chance to communicate as the warlock had his dragon fire its flames while he simultaneously cast a lightning bolt at Amelia. Both attacks did no damage as Amelia's shield protected them effectively. Then Kazin blasted his lightning breath at the warlock and his mount. The warlock's magic was more powerful and his shield held.

As the dragons flew past one another, the warlock quickly shot an ice bolt at Amelia. As it bounced off her shield, she grunted with the impact.

"That's a powerful spell!" she exclaimed. "I could hardly maintain my shield against it!"

"I'll bet he sensed that," rumbled Kazin. "He's sure to try it again next time, only with more magical force."

"I hope not," said Amelia.

"He was only testing us on this round," said Kazin. "He's clever."

Kazin circled around and saw the warlock do the same. "I'll cast a shield at the last moment if this trick fails."

"What trick?" asked Sherman.

"Just duck down until I give the word," said Kazin. "Then make an attack with your sword and slash at anything you can. Most likely you'll hit the dragon, but that can't be helped."

"Ok," said Sherman. He held on with one hand while holding his sword ready. His side still hurt, but he used the pain to remain alert.

"Amelia, if I maintain your shield, can you give Sherman magical support? Strength or speed would be helpful."

"Sure," said Amelia.

"Ok," said Kazin. "Hold on." They were still a short way from the warlock but Kazin began his lightning breath anyway.

The warlock didn't veer off, his magical shield easily deflecting Kazin's attack. He waited patiently for Kazin's breath to fade out before making his own attack. But Kazin's lightning breath didn't fade. It grew stronger and hotter the closer he got. The lightning bolt got so hot and bright the warlock had to shield his eyes as the bolt was deflected away to all sides. The heat intensified and his shield wavered. Did this dragon have no end to its lightning breath? He didn't see it until it was too late. The lightning breathing dragon crashed through the weakened shield and cried, "Now!"

An angry warrior with a glowing sword appeared like an apparition and made a blind slash at the warlock's dragon. The warlock cast an ice bolt in the warrior's direction, but his dragon lurched to the side in agony when the spirit blade bit into its neck. The ice bolt went astray and the warlock was forced to hang on while his dragon plummeted toward the ground. No amount of coaxing could get the dragon to return to the fight. Its lifeblood gushed from its wound and its strength was fading fast. In order to save himself from being smashed into the ground with the dragon, the warlock cast a spell on his dragon to give it the strength to land safely. To his surprise, the spell worked reasonably well. The dragon had just enough strength to glide horizontally along the ground before crashing. It slid like a ship on rough seas, leaving a rough swath of earth in its wake. The dragon finally came to rest against a large boulder, sending its rider flying head over heels. The warlock rolled for some time before coming to a stop in a cloud of dust.

Hidden behind some trees, Paul, the artist, had watched the spectacle with interest. He had seen the dragon crash to the ground and was about to draw what he had witnessed, but decided to wait instead. He had no idea the things he would see next would be even more incredible. Those things would leave a permanent impression in his mind, and he would have his work cut out for him in the days and months ahead.

In a daze, the warlock rose to his feet and brushed the dust off his cape. He looked back at his dragon and knew it was dead. He now had to evaluate his options. The battle raged on in the distance while dragons and pegasi with their elf riders battled in the air. Spell casters cast wide varieties of magic and lit up the battlefield along with the flame creatures. Cries of death and agony permeated the air. The ground shook with an endless quake as though the world itself was taking part in the war.

"I think the time has come for you to leave," said a voice behind him.

The warlock turned to face the speaker. It was the warrior who had been riding the dragon who penetrated his shield.

"You have one impressive dragon," said the warlock. He eyed Sherman's sword warily, knowing the damage that blade had inflicted on his own dragon.

"He's the best," said Sherman.

"Maybe," said the warlock, "but now we're on the ground and he can't help you." He cast a fireball at the warrior, but it was deflected by an invisible shield.

A blue robed, red-haired female mage stepped forward. "You'll have to do better than that."

The warlock smiled. "Of course! I almost forgot. You're the one with the magic. But you have no idea how powerful my magic is!" With that he raised his arm and made a flicking motion with his hand. A powerful wind materialized and blasted into the two individuals before him. Everything around them was sent backward in a cloud of dust, but they stood unharmed. Not even their clothing was affected. The warlock looked surprised. "But - how?"

"Your magic isn't as powerful as you think," said another voice. A young, blond-haired mage holding a staff with an orb appeared a short distance away. "You might want to try facing an opponent who has a little bit of magic at his disposal."

"But you're just a young, inexperienced mage!" said the warlock with a wicked smile. "You just need to be put into your place!" He cast an ice bolt in the mage's direction while casting a spell to nullify any magical shields the mage may have been counting on. The ice bolt passed through the spot where the mage had been, but Kazin stood a few feet left of the spot.

"You missed," said Kazin. He smiled.

The warlock growled. "You're clever, I'll give you that." He cast another ice bolt as well as a fireball just to its left in case Kazin tried to do the same trick. He also negated any shields Kazin may have intended to use.

Kazin responded by deflecting the ice bolt and fireball with individual lightning bolts while sending an ice bolt back at the warlock at the same time.

The warlock instinctively batted Kazin's ice bolt aside and regarded Kazin curiously. "You have a good grasp of magic for a boy. Only arch mages have the ability to cast three spells simultaneously." He didn't wait for an answer as he sent an ice bolt at Kazin, along with a fireball that was wide enough to encompass the area he was standing in should he teleport out of the way again. He also negated any shield spell again.

Kazin responded by knocking the ice bolt out of the way with a lightning bolt while teleporting far enough away to avoid the fireball. At the same time, he cast an ice bolt and a fireball at the warlock.

The warlock barely got his shield up in time to avoid Kazin's projectiles. "That's enough!" he growled. He held his arms in the air and a dark, foreboding cloud emerged from his eyes and mouth. The cloud had eerie red eyes high up in its form. The cloud grew to an amazing size and didn't stop growing for about thirty seconds. When it stopped, the warlock's body crumpled to the ground.

"You shall die by giving your body to me!" said a voice from within the cloud. With a sudden surge, it moved toward Kazin.

Amelia screamed, but before it got too close, Kazin gave a single command and his staff lit up. Tyris appeared above the orb and flared with an intense orange light.

"Aieee!" screamed the cloud. It swerved away from Kazin and hovered in the air nearby.

Tyris materialized in her full body and moved to stand beside Kazin. "You will not steal his body! Begone, wraith!"

"You cannot destroy me!" moaned the wraith. "I'll simply find another body to control, and if that one fails, I'll take another one!"

Amelia cast her 'dispel undead' spell but nothing happened.

"Mere mortal magic cannot hurt me!" cried the wraith. "I am not just a wraith. I am a dark wraith!"

Amelia gasped. Dark wraiths were far more powerful than ordinary ones. No wonder her spell didn't work. Only the strongest magic could defeat them.

"What about this?" snarled a voice nearby. Sherman leapt out of the darkness and slashed at the wraith with his sword, but it rose quickly beyond his reach.

"You are right," laughed the wraith. "That spirit blade has the power to reduce me to a weaker state, but it will not completely destroy me."

"Then there is only one solution," said Kazin. He removed his ring of youth, the master ring he had used to bring the other companions back to him previously, and his magical pouch. Handing them to Amelia, he resumed his original form as an old mage. With no metallic objects in his possession, his magic could have maximum effect. The mage looked at Amelia with his wrinkled face, long white beard, and bright blue eyes. "I can't have these on me for this spell to work." Then he began to chant a spell.

After the first few syllables, Tyris turned to him in surprise. "You know this spell?"

Kazin didn't respond as he continued the spell.

"This spell will invoke all of the elementals!" warned Tyris. "Do you know what will happen when all of the elementals walk this plane of existence at the same time?"

Kazin nodded as he neared completion of the spell. The orb atop his staff glowed with a myriad of colours as the spell began to take shape.

"What is the spell he is casting?" asked Amelia.

Tyris turned to her with a serious expression. "It is the spell known as 'lifeforce'."

"What does it do?"

"It has the power to kill, or raise the dead," said Tyris. "It uses magic from all of the elementals. I don't know how he got that spell, but he must have convinced each of the elementals including myself to lend him access to our power at some point in time." She beckoned to Amelia. "We'd better stand back." Around Kazin appeared ghostly humanlike apparitions of the other three elementals - earth, water, and air.

Until now, the dark wraith watched in disbelief, not believing that Kazin could cast such a spell. It thought he was just bluffing. But now it became nervous. "What - what is going on? You can't seriously believe a mortal can cast the 'lifeforce' spell, can you?"

Kazin braced his feet and raised his staff, pointing it at the wraith. His expression became grim as he concentrated on this complex spell.

Too late, the dark wraith realized this was no joke. It tried to flee, but Kazin's spell prevented it from escaping. A bolt not unlike a lightning bolt erupted from the staff and surged into the wraith. At first nothing happened, but then the wraith screamed. "No! You can't destroy -!"

The bolt intensified in brightness and the wraith wailed in agony. Every dark corner of the wraith's cloud was lit up with the 'lifeforce' spell. Soon the dark wraith began to undulate as its parts became disassembled. With a final horrific scream, the dark wraith was no more.

Kazin collapsed to the ground, his magic expended. Many others joined him as the earth shuddered with thunderous force. All of the elementals now had their energy at work in this plane of existence. The forces of fire, water, air, and earth collided and reformed many parts of the world.

While all this was happening and attention was on Kazin and the wraith, a goblin snuck up to the warlock's dead body. Then the goblin collapsed as a spirit left its body and entered that of the warlock. Slowly, the warlock rose to his feet and looked at his hands. He smiled a wicked grin and withdrew the sword from the sheath at his back.

At last! At last he had his real body back! Now he could complete his objective! With his body back, he could rule the world! The warlock frowned as he looked at Sherman, who stood with his back toward him. He should kill that annoying barbarian once and for all.

Slowly, silently, he crept toward the big warrior.

371

Chapter 37

"**L**ooking for someone?" asked a voice behind him.

The warlock turned to the speaker. Facing him was a fierce looking minotaur wielding a spirit blade which glowed. Beside him stood an unknown creature with a bow.

"Don't interfere!" snarled the warlock.

"It's time for you to die!" snarled Zylor in return. He stepped forward, brandishing his sword.

The warlock raised a hand and chanted a spell. Nothing happened. He chanted again with the same result. Then he shrugged. "Oh, well, I'll do this the hard way. I can't be killed anyway." He brandished his sword and took a wary step toward the minotaur, ready to vacate his body the moment the minotaur tried to stab him with the spirit blade. The goblin body was close by and could be used to escape if necessary. As long as he jumped from body to body, he couldn't be caught.

As he approached the minotaur, he was surprised by the creature's next move. The minotaur calmly lowered his sword.

"Huh?" said the warlock. Too late, he noticed the presence of someone behind him. A sword suddenly pierced his chest from behind. He looked down in surprise at the spirit blade within his body. The warlock was oddly amused by the irony. Twice in the same night he was slain by a sword in the back.

The magic from the spirit blade radiated outward, engulfing his senses and entire being. Slowly, painfully, his spirit began to melt away. Screaming, he half turned to see who his attacker was even though he already knew the answer. His spirit vanished in a puff.

"Why don't you just stay dead?" growled Sherman as he kicked the warlock's body down. "The Sword of Dead is not to be trifled with!" He pulled his sword free and sliced the warlock's head from his body as an extra precaution.

"I second that," said an invisible dwarf beside him.

In the darkness, unseen by the heroes, Paul made a hasty sketch of the spirit blade that Sherman wielded. He made a note to himself to follow these mysterious people to see what transpired next.

Everyone turned back to Kazin, who was slowly getting back to his feet. Amelia was all over him but he didn't appear to have any noticeable injuries.

A dragon landed nearby and a mage with a pointed hat disembarked with a white-robed cleric.

The mage with the pointed hat took two long strides before he noticed he was in the presence of a minotaur and a strange creature like a lizardmage. He stopped in his tracks and was prepared to cast a spell.

"Don't shoot!" said Sherman, realizing the danger. "They're allies!"

The mage relaxed a bit and walked over to them uncertainly. He gave Tyris an appraising glance before addressing Kazin. "I'm Arch Mage Gresham. Who are you? What just happened here?"

Kazin smiled. "It's probably better if I don't tell you the answer to that. All I can say is that I'm from a different time and place. What happened here is an event that had the potential to change the future; possibly even erase it. I'm here to correct something that could have upset the balance."

"I see," said Gresham. He looked unconvinced. "Well, all the same, I'd like to thank you for what you did. That warlock was almost invincible."

"That's because he was possessed by a dark wraith," said Amelia. "We destroyed it before it could cause any more trouble."

The arch mage looked at Amelia and his eyes narrowed. "I know you. Aren't you one of the ones I encountered after that dragon fight a few days ago?"

Amelia smiled. "Yes."

Arch Mage Gresham nodded. "I should have known." He nodded at Sherman and noticed his wrapped wound. "Let us attend to your wound! It's the least we can do." He nudged the cleric with him and she immediately set about un-wrapping the injury.

The arch mage looked around. "Where's your dragon?"

Amelia giggled and handed the ring of youth back to Kazin. "Right here."

Kazin shrugged and put on the ring. It didn't matter now, anyway. He immediately appeared as his younger self.

Gresham looked perplexed. "You're that young mage who fell off his horse, so you told me."

"It's a long story," said Kazin, smiling. "You'll find out some things about dragons eventually."

Sherman watched in amazement as the cleric healed his wound. Not only did the wound close up, it healed up almost completely. He swiveled his body. There was no pain, only a little stiffness. Wide eyed, he thanked the cleric. "I've never seen healing that effective before!"

The cleric shrugged. "It was nothing. We do it all the time."

"Kazin did say magic was stronger in this time in history," said Harran. He had removed his invisibility ring and was visible again.

"We'd better get going," said Kazin. He quickly walked over to a spot well away from the others in preparation for his transformation into a dragon.

"Kazin!" exclaimed Amelia. "Your limp! It's gone!"

"What limp?" asked Kazin. "I never had a limp."

"But -," she looked at Sherman helplessly. He had a curious grin on his face. "Sherman, he had a limp, didn't he?"

Sherman looked at the red-haired mage. "Not that I know of. But I remember when we were kids and he stubbed his toe badly. He hopped around on one foot for hours!"

Kazin laughed. "I still remember that! It was no fun, let me tell you."

"But, Sherman!" pleaded Amelia, "he limped ever since I met him!"

"You must be mistaken," said Sherman with a twinkle in his eye.

Harran was grinning too. He realized what Sherman was doing. "I never saw him limp either."

Amelia glared at him. "That's not funny!" Then she looked to Zylor for support.

The minotaur simply shrugged. "It appears our quest was successful."

Amelia was red faced now. "But -." She just shook her head in confusion.

Harran put a reassuring hand on her shoulder. "Just let it be, my dear. All is well."

At that point, Kazin's orb flared and he transformed into a dragon.

Arch Mage Gresham whistled. "Well, I'll be! That explains a few things. I thought that was a dragon orb atop his staff. Funny I never noticed it earlier."

A sudden shriek from a nearby dragon coincided with another major earthquake, drawing Gresham's attention. "All this powerful magic has sent the dragons into a serious frenzy. We need to get airborne again. With all of the lizardmage dragon riders defeated here, we should check on Belham's progress on the northern edge of this battle." He turned to Kazin. "Thanks again for your help, all of you. After this war is over, we'll have to get together to talk." Without waiting for a response, he led the high cleric back to their dragon. They climbed onto its back and it leapt into the air. Within moments they flew out of sight.

"We'd better get going too," said Kazin, lowering his wing to the ground. The companions climbed on, including Tyris.

"I'll protect us from the wild dragons," said the fire elemental. "They will not bother us with me along."

Kazin carried his group back to the spot where Sir Galado's body lay. Miniature elemental creatures stood guard around the fallen soldier.

Everyone disembarked and Kazin returned to his human form.

"If I hadn't used the 'lifeforce' spell to destroy the wraith, I could have used it to revive Sir Galado," said Kazin sadly. "That spell can only be used once per year for reviving, and once per month for killing. I can only revive Galado within three days of his death, but now I have to wait a month before I can use the spell again." As he finished speaking, Kazin realized with a shock that he could have used up the 'lifeforce' spell earlier when he thought that Amelia had died. It was fortunate that he didn't think of it at the time. Had he used that spell, he wouldn't have been able to defeat the wraith, and his mission would have ended as a failure!

A gentle hand rested on Kazin's shoulder and interrupted his thoughts. "Don't let it bother you," said Sherman. "You had to do what was necessary." He lowered his hand. "We will have to find a place to bury him, though." The warrior wobbled as the ground shook beneath his feet.

"I can incinerate his body," offered Tyris.

"Burial is more proper for an honourable warrior," said Zylor. "Cremation is for enemies."

"No offence was intended," said Tyris. "I can send my minions to take him to a safe place within the earth."

"That would be acceptable," said Sherman. "It beats digging a grave."

"What about his sword?" asked Zylor, holding up the second spirit blade.

"Those two spirit blades should be separated," said Kazin. "They shouldn't be in two places at once."

"I can see to it the sword will be put to rest with your friend," offered Tyris.

Zylor was about to lay it down beside the body of Galado when Sherman stopped him. "Wait! Shouldn't my sword be the one that should have to stay behind?" He looked at Kazin. "The sword Galado used was the one that should have stayed in the future."

"Very perceptive, Sherman," said Amelia. "It's good to make that point. It's also important for when you retrieve the sword in the future. The new sword is magically connected to you and will be drawn to you when you come across it many years in the future. Your original sword is also connected to you, but it is much older. It is possible it will not retain the magic for you to use when you find it."

"Then let's keep history accurate," said Sherman firmly. He laid his new sword by Galado's body and took his old sword from Zylor. "This one will do me just fine."

"Will you require any more favours?" asked Tyris. She looked beautiful in her fiery orange flames.

Kazin shook his head. "No. You have done well, Tyris. It was good to see you again."

Tyris nodded. "Then I will return to my plane of existence after depositing the soldier's body." She looked over her shoulder. "I sense there will be guardians for your friend."

In the distance, the companions saw some vague figures shambling toward them.

Harran drew his axe. "Undead!"

"Do not fear them," said Tyris. "They mean you no harm. They are the ones your friend - or should I say your friend's evil spirit - has slain before their time. They are linked to him. They will guard his body until they are no longer needed. Then they will be set free of their attachment." The fire elemental opened her arms to encompass everyone. "Farewell to all of you." Then she lifted off the ground. Her minions followed, carrying Sir Galado's body and sword with them. Slowly, they floated to the west. The group of undead turned to follow the elemental's trail.

"Where will they take him?" wondered Amelia.

"The Plains of Grief," said Sherman solemnly.

Watching from a distance again was Paul. He had been running toward the spot where the companions had gathered, and was out of breath. As he dove for cover behind an outcrop of rock, he had overheard the last part of the conversation despite the noise of battle in the distance. He watched intently as Tyris flew off with Sir Galado and the Sword of Dead. Later, he would spread the first rumours of a powerful spirit blade that was hidden in a secret location to the west. He didn't know what the Plains of Grief were, but remembered the name.

"So can we go home now?" asked Harran.

Kazin smiled at him. "Yes, my friend." He looked at Amelia. "Is the future restored?"

Amelia stared as she looked within herself. Then she smiled. "Yes. Some damage has been done, but history has corrected itself. A few of the things that have disappeared early on are gone, but the anomalies are too few and minor to have an impact."

"Good," said Kazin. "Then we are done here." He regarded his companions with a sad expression. "It's time to go home."

"Do we have to cross that bridge again?" asked Olag.

Kazin shook his head. "No. You're in luck, Olag. The magic I used to go back in time to get you is how I'll be returning you to the future. I can use that magic to go to places I have already been, in times when I've been there. That's why we had to cross that bridge to get here. I've never been to this place or time in history before."

"Good," sighed Olag in relief. He looked at Amelia. "Are you sure history will be correct when I get back? I'd hate to go back only to see my race never existed or something like that."

Amelia smiled. "Your race will be there, Olag. They will be building ties with the humans and the mermaids."

Olag wrinkled his nose. "Oh, I forgot about those pesky little -," he paused. "How do you know about the mermaids? You sound almost like the oracle I once knew. She had that ability to see into the -." His voice broke off and his eyes widened momentarily. Then his eyes narrowed. "Of course. I never considered the possibility before."

A giant hand suddenly clasped the skink warrior's shoulder. "I hope you come and visit me when you get a chance."

Olag looked up at Zylor in surprise. "Really?" Then he looked crestfallen. "I'd be killed on sight if I even showed my face in your realm."

Zylor frowned. "I hadn't thought of that."

Kazin laughed. "I can help you with that." He took a ring from Amelia that he had given her earlier and handed it to Zylor. "Here. This is the master ring I wore that is magically connected to the other rings I gave you earlier to come to me after you found Harran. Olag, if you rub your ring, you will be transported to a spot near Zylor, because he now has the master ring. That way you won't even have to physically travel anywhere to see him. When your visit is over, simply rub your ring again and you will go back to the place you started from."

"That's settled then!" said Zylor happily. He slapped the skink warrior on the back. "I expect to hear from you on a regular basis. I rarely get accurate reports on things going on near North Lake. It's good to know what is happening there, despite our race being so far away."

Olag winced at the minotaur's enthusiastic slap. "You know, it might actually be fun. I'd like to watch the election battles someday."

"You will be invited," said Zylor proudly. "You can sit with me in the upper stands."

"Won't the minotaurs object?" asked Sherman. "They know how you hate lizardmen. You wouldn't want them to think you are under a spell."

"He's not a lizardman," said Zylor sternly. "He's a skink warrior - an honourable one." He looked a t Olag. "Perhaps he can show his skill at archery in the events leading up to the election battles. Archery is one of the contests. It would be interesting to see if anyone could out-shoot Olag."

If Olag could blush he would have.

"Are you ready to return?" asked Kazin.

Olag nodded. "Yes." He shook hands with everyone. When he got to Amelia, he said, "Until we meet again."

"Probably not," said Amelia, "but all the best to you."

Olag gave a sly grin. "Oh, we'll meet again, alright. For once I can see something that even the oracle can't see."

Amelia looked confused.

Olag turned back to Kazin and suddenly remembered something. He removed his quiver of many arrows and held it out to the mage.

Kazin shook his head. "No. You keep it. You've earned it." Then he chanted a spell and pointed it at Olag. Within a few seconds, the skink warrior faded from sight. The mage turned to the others. "Who's next?"

Zylor stepped forward. He grinned his toothy smile. "This was an exciting quest. If you have any more adventures, let me know. I can always squeeze in some vacation time." He shook hands with Sherman. "You can visit anytime too, Sherman."

"I won't be able to get through the mountain that separates us," said the big warrior.

"You still have one of Kazin's rings, do you not?" said Zylor.

Sherman looked down at his hand. "Oh, yeah! I guess I do!"

"The same goes for you," said Zylor, turning to the dwarf. "We will have business issues to discuss between our races. The rings will come in handy for that."

Harran nodded. "Right you are, Zylor. I look forward to our visits." Then he added, "I guess you'll have to go back to a boring lifestyle again, huh?"

"On the contrary!" exclaimed Zylor. "We're currently preparing to dispatch a force of warriors to intercept a threat to the north. Apparently there have been an increasing number of clashes with gargoyles. While this isn't unusual – there are often roving bands of gargoyles up there – they seem to have been getting more organized. My scouts report they have been uniting under the banner of a single gargoyle leader. There are even rumours this leader can cast magical spells! If so, we must deal with this threat sooner, rather than later."

Harran whistled. "A gargoyle who casts magic, eh? Interesting!"

Zylor turned to Amelia and took her dainty hand in his giant one. "It was a pleasure to have known you, Amelia. Until we meet again."

Amelia was about to respond but thought better of it. Why did everyone think they would see her again?

Then the minotaur turned back to Kazin. He withdrew the ice axe he had acquired and held it out. "I should leave this in the time it was created."

Kazin looked at Amelia. "Will this item be missed?"

Amelia studied the axe for a moment. Then she shook her head. "It disappeared from the world around the time of the dragon wars. It hasn't resurfaced since."

Kazin nodded. "I thought so." He looked at Zylor. "Keep it as a memento of your quest. It should keep your guards guessing as to how you acquired it."

Zylor chuckled. "Indeed." He sheathed the axe and straightened. "You may begin."

Kazin cast a spell and the minotaur vanished.

"I guess it's my turn," said Harran. He handed the amulet and the ring of invisibility to Kazin. "I won't need these."

"Thanks," said Kazin. He put the items into his miniature pouch. He saluted the dwarf with the dwarven salute. "You take care of yourself, my friend."

Harran saluted him back. "Any time you need someone on a quest, don't hesitate to call on me." He shook hands with Sherman. "It was fun. Hopefully we see one another again soon." Then he embraced Amelia. "It was good to get to know you, Amelia. So long for now." The dwarf turned to Kazin. "Ok."

Kazin chanted and the dwarf was gone back to his own time.

Kazin turned to Sherman. Tears came unbidden to his eyes. Even Sherman's eyes were moist. He picked up the mage in a bear hug.

"Careful," admonished Kazin. "I'm not as young as I look."

"Oh, yeah," said Sherman, hastily putting down the young looking old mage.

"You take care of yourself," said Kazin. Then he snapped his fingers. "I almost forgot!" He leaned over and whispered into Sherman's ear for a full minute.

"What?" said Sherman in surprise. "You don't say?"

Kazin moved back. "Will you remember all that?"

Sherman nodded. "You can count on it!" He turned to Amelia. "It's been fun." Then his face darkened. "You take good care of my friend here or I'll come after you!" Then he laughed and embraced her. "I'm kidding. I know you'll take care of him. He knows who he can count on!" Then he turned to Kazin. "I'm ready."

"Don't forget your sword."

Sherman withdrew the spirit blade. "It's right here." Then his face registered shock. "Oh, no! It's the wrong one!"

Both Kazin and Amelia looked surprised.

Then Sherman laughed. "Gotcha! I'm only teasing. It's the right one this time. I don't make the same mistake twice - usually."

Everyone laughed.

Then Kazin chanted and pointed his staff. With a deep sense of loss he watched his best friend fade away.

Then he turned to Amelia. "Well, I can't send you back to where you came from since I haven't been there yet."

"That's ok," said Amelia. "We can go where you've been and you can show me around. There might be an adventure in it for us somewhere."

Kazin laughed. "Maybe there will be. With you around, I'm sure trouble will come our way."

Amelia punched him in the arm. Then her expression became curious. "Kazin, what do you suppose your companions meant about seeing me again?"

Kazin laughed again. "Just let it be, Amelia. Olag was right. It's not often that anyone can predict something that the oracle cannot."

"Who is the oracle?"

Kazin laughed again. "You'll see in time. Don't worry." Then he put his arm around Amelia and chanted. In a few moments they vanished.

Not far away, in his concealed location, Paul finally relaxed. He was already thinking about the painting he would make of the strange mage and his battle with the dark wraith. It was an image, firmly imbedded in his mind, that he would never forget, and he wanted to make sure others would see it too. It would become his masterpiece.

Chapter 38

fter Kazin and Amelia disappeared, the world underwent a period of upheaval. Throughout the entire world changes took place. A massive tidal wave washed across the face of the land from east to west via the Bay of Barlin. Many races and people were displaced by this wave as it swept across the land. The human cities near the shore needed considerable rebuilding. Mermaids and fish that lived in the ocean were carried in the wave across the land to end up in a newly created crater. This crater was instantly filled with the water from the ocean and became a lake. It was henceforth called North Lake. The mermaids in this lake were forever separated from their sisters in the ocean.

On the northern front, the ogres had suffered the most casualties. The spell casting lizardmages had attracted the wrath of both the wild dragons and the ones controlled by the human mages. They were soon destroyed, and the ogres no longer had the benefit of magic. They were nearly decimated by the ferocious dwarves on one side and the smaller contingent of minotaurs on the other. The remaining survivors punched a path through their enemies on the northern front and fled to the relative safety of the mountains.

This left the dwarves facing the much smaller group of minotaurs. Without missing a beat, the dwarves drove the minotaurs to the base of the new mountains to the east. There were no records of whether the remaining minotaurs succeeded in climbing the mountains to reach their lands on the other side, but it was a possibility, since the dwarves gave up the pursuit in favour of a new challenge. As they arrived at the foot of the new mountains, they discovered a couple of cave entrances that were worth exploring. Scouts were sent in and quickly returned with reports of numerous caverns filled with minerals and gems. It didn't take long to realize they had found a new home. With their old homes in the Old Dwarven Mountains mined out, these new mountains were a bonanza to be investigated. They found that tunneling into the new mountains was easy and would make a far better home than their old one, which had suffered greatly from the earthquakes. Thus, they undertook a major move, bringing all their gold and treasures from their old home to the new one. Even the golden palace was disassembled and transported to the new capital city. The move took a couple of generations, but the dwarves were motivated and meticulous. When they finally abandoned their old homes, there was little of value left behind.

On the eastern side of the new mountains, the greater forces of the minotaurs didn't even have a chance to get involved in the war. The tidal wave that had washed across some of the human lands also washed directly into the minotaur realm. It slammed through their land and washed right up against the newly formed dwarven mountains. The entire landscape looked different from what had been there previously. It would take the minotaurs years to rebuild.

On the western front of the war, the tidal waves killed over half of the fighters on both sides. Any surviving orcs, goblins, and lizardmen, among others, were driven north into the mountains, and over a period of decades, made their homes in the abandoned areas of the Old Dwarven Mountains that had survived the earthquakes and upheaval.

On the southwestern front, the trolls did not fare well. Most drowned in the tidal waves, and the rest were annihilated by the elves. The trolls who had fought the elves south of the elven territory fared slightly better. Having lost the war, they were driven south into the dessert where they remained from that time on.

The elves fared reasonably well, considering the devastation of the tidal wave. They were able to airlift most of their surviving troops with the aid of the pegasi. Unfortunately, many of the ones riding the centaurs were washed away. The elves returned home to report to the king about the humans' ability to control dragons using magic. When the king heard this, he was astonished by the resourcefulness of the humans. But when he heard that black magic drove dragons into a frenzy and they attacked everything and everyone in sight, he was deeply saddened. Despite the occasional dragon attack on elven villages, elves considered the great reptilian beasts sacred. So he passed a law to ban the use of black magic among his people. Not only would it no longer draw dragons in to attack villages, it would save them from harming one another.

As for the dragons, they dispersed for a time to regions unknown. Their numbers were greatly reduced, and dragon attacks on settlements waned. The human mages who controlled dragons still did so, but new ones became increasingly difficult to find.

Another thing that changed was the fact that human settlers no longer arrived from the old lands. Some ships were dispatched to find out why, but those that came back reported that the old lands were no longer there. All that could be seen was water as far as the eye could see. Some vessels ventured farther out to sea in the hopes that they could find something, but even they failed to find any land. All they reported were rough seas and giant kraken who did not take kindly to ships in their waters. So eventually the humans gave up hope of newcomers coming from the old lands. They were now on their own in a land full of strange people, creatures, and magic.

Epilogue

A gentle breeze caused a slight stir in the pine boughs, allowing the sun to sparkle down through the needles in a shimmering of golden light. The shadows on the tree's branches danced across the face of the headstone underlining the words and dates displayed thereon. Off to the side leaning against a tree sat a figure cowled in black, the garments of a black mage. The mage, who was much older than he appeared, sat half dozing in the warm spring air. His quiet solitude was suddenly interrupted by a whinnying noise off to his left. Through the trees he saw a white unicorn approaching, the sunlight glinting off his silvery horn in a blinding flash of light. As his eyes adjusted to the glare, the mage noticed the unicorn's rider, a black-cloaked mage like himself. The visitor's face was hidden within the hood, but the mage thought he recognized the new arrival when he saw the long, flowing white beard. He shivered despite the warm day.

The unicorn came to a halt as the mage rose to greet them, and snorted as he eyed the man standing there as though he were the intruder. At this point the rider dismounted, slowly and stiffly, his movements betraying great age and fragility. The mage realized the visitor was not just old, he was ancient.

The visitor turned to regard the younger mage, who could only stare at the glowing orbs within the hood. Although the body had aged, the intensity of the eyes were still sharp and alert. Then the old mage sighed and his eyes dimmed slightly.

The younger mage had a shiver run up his spine as he sensed something was wrong.

Then the old mage spoke, his voice quivering but no less authoritative than if he had been young and full of energy. "I'd like a few moments alone with my wife, if you don't mind," he said as he gestured toward the headstone.

The young mage nodded respectfully and stepped aside to allow the older mage to pass.

The older mage took two steps before suddenly turning to regard his counterpart. "When I am finished, please bury me next to my wife. You may use magic as necessary."

The younger mage swallowed hard and nodded. Now he knew what was going to happen. The older mage continued to the grave site and kneeled before the headstone, his head bowed.

The younger mage turned toward the unicorn. "Is he going to -?" he began.

Frosty nodded. "Yes, his time has come. Mine as well."

At this, the young mage looked sharply at the great white beast, fear reflected in his eyes.

Frosty snorted. "Don't worry. It's not quite like that."

The mage looked confused but didn't press the point. He turned back to observe the old mage. "How old is he?"

Frosty snorted again. "Very, very old. Do not worry. Our lives were not in vain. Kazin and I have had many adventures throughout the years and in other times."

The younger mage nodded in understanding. Not many could comprehend the unicorn's statement, but he could.

A good twenty minutes passed in silence before the end came. The old mage took a last breath and sagged onto his side.

The younger mage hesitated, but a gentle prodding by the unicorn behind him forced him into action.

"Do as you were ordered," said the unicorn, his voice sounding strangely like a breath of wind.

Without looking back, the younger mage went up to the body and held his staff high. With a few chants, the ground next to the existing grave of Della the elf was torn open, leaving a man-sized hole. Another chant brought a coffin into being. Using teleport magic, the dead mage was moved into the coffin, his hands crossed over his chest in the traditional burial pose. The young mage then placed the old mage's staff beside him in the coffin. It was then that the mage noticed the orb atop the staff. It was not the orb that surprised him; it was the fact that it gave off no light. The power within had expired. He nodded. It was appropriate.

After saying a silent prayer, the coffin lid was closed, and using teleport magic, the coffin was lowered into the ground. Another spell covered the coffin with dirt while a final one erected a ready-made headstone.

The younger mage regarded his handiwork with satisfaction. It looked as if the grave of the old mage had always been there. He turned back to where the unicorn should have been but he was gone.

Before he could think on this, he heard the snap of twigs off to his right. Suddenly appearing from behind some thickets was the unicorn. He trotted up to the mage and nuzzled him affectionately. "Sorry I'm late. Did I miss anything?"

The mage laughed, more to relieve the tension than to respond to the unicorn's actions. Now everything was falling into place. "Let's go find ourselves an adventure, Frosty." He swung up onto the unicorn's back and rode him to a nearby clearing.

The unicorn sprouted wings and soared into the air. He turned to his rider with a gleam in his eye. "I have just the adventure for us. You'll love it!"

The mage laughed. "I can't wait!" he cried.

As they circled away to the east, the mage couldn't resist one last look down at the spot where the graves were.

The unicorn increased his speed. "Hang on, Kazin!"

Don't miss the other books in
The Dragon Mage Trilogy,

BOOK I:
KAZIN'S QUEST

BOOK II:
CLOAK & DAGGER

Check out www.dragonmagetrilogy.com

Åbout the Åuthor

Carey Scheppner is a first generation Canadian who grew up in a remote Ontario community. He was an avid reader of novels since he could read, and his favourite of these was fantasy novels. As an Electronics Engineering Technician graduate, he excelled in the art of electronics. He tutored English and mathematics in college. Carey also went on to become a director of a board at a credit union and the treasurer of a church. Despite this, he still held a strong interest in fantasy novels and games. After reading a number of predictable novels, he decided to embark on writing his own fantasy novels. He wanted to ensure plenty of action and interesting characters to leave the reader thrilled with the unlimited possibilities of a fantasy world.

Carey enjoys the country lifestyle and enjoys fishing and hunting. It is a means of leaving the civilized world behind to breathe in the freshness of the country air. This leads to an unleashing of the imagination and the creation of strange new worlds...